When the darkness shifts once more, heavier now—crushing me beneath its weight—the others sense my mounting hysteria. Their voices turn less amicable, less prim, less mischievous. *We are sorry, Louise le Blanc. It is too late for you. For all of us.*

NO. I lash against the darkness with all my might, repeating the word over and over again like a talisman. I search for a golden pattern. For *anything.* There is only darkness. *No no no no no—*

Only Nicholina's chilling laughter answers.

Also by Shelby Mahurin

Serpent & Dove
Blood & Honey

The Scarlet Veil

GODS
& MONSTERS

SHELBY MAHURIN

An Imprint of HarperCollinsPublishers

HarperTeen is an imprint of HarperCollins Publishers.

Gods & Monsters
Copyright © 2021 by Shelby Mahurin
Map art by Leo Hartas © 2021 by HarperCollins Publishers
www.epicreads.com
Library of Congress Control Number: 2021937258
ISBN 978-0-06-303894-3
Typography by Sarah Nichole Kaufman
24 25 26 27 28 LBC 12 11 10 9 8

First paperback edition, 2022

To Jordan, *who is less a friend and more a sister*

PART I

Quand le chat n'est pas là, les souris dansent.
When the cat is away, the mice will play.
—French proverb

A NEST OF MICE

Nicholina

Bayberry, eyebright, belladonna
Fang of an adder, eye of an owl
Sprinkle of flora, spray of fauna
For purpose fair or possession foul.

Ichor of friend and ichor of foe
A soul stained black as starless night
For in the dark dost spirits flow
One to another in seamless flight.

The spell is familiar, oh yes, familiar indeed. Our favorite. She lets us read it often. The grimoire. The page. The spell. Our fingers trace each pen stroke, each faded letter, and they tingle with promise. They promise we'll never be alone, and we believe them. We believe *her.* Because we aren't alone—we're never alone—and mice live in nests with dozens of other mice, with *scores* of them. They burrow together to raise their pups, their children, and they find warm, dry nooks with plenty of food and magic. They find crannies without sickness, without death.

Our fingers curl on the parchment, gouging fresh tracks.

Death. Death, death, *death*, our friend and foe, as sure as breath, comes for us all.

But not me.

The dead should not remember. Beware the night they dream.

We tear at the paper now, shredding it to pieces. To angry bits. It scatters like ash in the snow. Like memory.

Mice burrow together, yes—they keep each other safe and warm—but when a pup in the litter sickens, the mice will eat it. Oh yes. They gobble it down, down, down to nourish the mother, the nest. The newest born is always sick. Always small. We shall devour the sick little mouse, and she shall nourish us.

She shall nourish us.

We shall prey on her friends, her *friends*—a snarl tears from my throat at the word, at the empty promise—and we shall feed them until they are fat with grief and guilt, with frustration and fear. Where we go, they will follow. Then we shall devour them too. And when we deliver the sick little mouse to her mother at Chateau le Blanc—when her body withers, when it *bleeds*—her soul shall stay with us forever.

She shall nourish us.

We will never be alone.

L'ENCHANTERESSE

Reid

Mist crept over the cemetery. The headstones—ancient, crumbling, their names long lost to the elements—pierced the sky from where we stood atop the cliff's edge. Even the sea below fell silent. In this eerie light before dawn, I finally understood the expression *silent as the grave.*

Coco brushed a hand across tired eyes before gesturing to the church beyond the mist. Small. Wooden. Part of the roof had caved in. No light flickered through the rectory windows. "It looks abandoned."

"What if it isn't?" Beau snorted, shaking his head, but stopped short with a yawn. He spoke around it. "It's a *church*, and our faces are plastered all over Belterra. Even a country priest will recognize us."

"Fine." Her tired voice held less bite than she probably intended. "Sleep outside with the dog."

As one, we turned to look at the spectral white dog that followed us. He'd shown up outside Cesarine, just before we'd agreed to travel the coast instead of the road. We'd all seen enough of La Fôret des Yeux to last a lifetime. For days, he'd trailed behind us, never coming near enough to touch. Wary, confused, the matagots had vanished shortly after his appearance. They hadn't returned. Perhaps the dog was a restless spirit himself—a new type of matagot. Perhaps he was merely an ill omen. Perhaps that was why Lou hadn't yet named him.

The creature watched us now, his eyes a phantom touch on my face. I gripped Lou's hand tighter. "We've been walking all night. No one will look for us inside a church. It's as good a place as any to hide. If it *isn't* abandoned"—I spoke over Beau, who started to interrupt—"we'll leave before anyone sees us. Agreed?"

Lou grinned at Beau, her mouth wide. So wide I could nearly count all her teeth. "Are you *afraid*?"

He shot her a dubious look. "After the tunnels, you should be too."

Her grin vanished, and Coco visibly stiffened, looking away. Tension straightened my own spine. Lou said nothing more, however, instead dropping my hand to stalk toward the door. She twisted the handle. "Unlocked."

Without a word, Coco and I followed her over the threshold. Beau joined us in the vestibule a moment later, eyeing the darkened room with unconcealed suspicion. A thick layer of dust coated the candelabra. Wax had dripped to the wooden floor, hardening among the dead leaves and debris. A draft swept through from the sanctuary beyond. It tasted of brine. Of decay.

"This place is haunted as shit," Beau whispered.

"Language." Scowling at him, I stepped into the sanctuary. My chest tightened at the dilapidated pews. At the loose hymnal pages collecting in the corner to rot. "This was once a holy place."

"It isn't haunted." Lou's voice echoed in the silence. She stilled behind me to stare up at a stained-glass window. The smooth face of Saint Magdaleine gazed back at her. The youngest saint in Belterra, Magdaleine had been venerated by the Church for gifting a man a blessed ring. With it, his negligent wife had fallen back in love with him, refusing to leave his side—even after he'd embarked on a perilous journey at sea. She'd followed him into the waves and drowned. Only Magdaleine's tears had revived her. "Spirits can't inhabit consecrated ground."

Beau's brows dipped. "How do you know that?"

"How do you *not?*" Lou countered.

"We should rest." I wrapped an arm around Lou's shoulders, leading her to a nearby pew. She looked paler than usual with dark shadows beneath her eyes, her hair wild and windswept from days of hard travel. More than once—when she didn't think I was looking—I'd seen her entire body convulse as if fighting sickness. It wouldn't surprise me. She'd been through a lot. We all had. "The villagers will wake soon. They'll investigate any noise."

Coco settled on a pew, closed her eyes, and pulled up the hood of her cloak. Shielding herself from us. "Someone should keep watch."

Though I opened my mouth to volunteer, Lou interrupted. "I'll do it."

"No." I shook my head, unable to recall the last time Lou had slept. Her skin felt cold, clammy, against mine. If she *was* fighting sickness, she needed the rest. "You sleep. I'll watch."

A sound reverberated from deep in her throat as she placed a hand on my cheek. Her thumb brushed my lips, lingering there. As did her eyes. "I'd much prefer to watch you. What will I see in your dreams, Chass? What will I hear in your—"

"I'll check the scullery for food," Beau muttered, shoving past us. He cast Lou a disgusted glance over his shoulder. My stomach rumbled as I watched him go. Swallowing hard, I ignored the ache of hunger. The sudden, unwelcome pressure in my chest. Gently, I removed her hand from my cheek and shrugged out of my coat. I handed it to her.

"Go to sleep, Lou. I'll wake you at sunset, and we can"—the words burned up my throat—"we can continue."

To the Chateau.

To Morgane.

To certain death.

I didn't voice my concerns again.

Lou had made it clear she'd journey to Chateau le Blanc whether or not we joined her. Despite my protests—despite reminding her *why* we'd sought allies in the first place, why we *needed* them—Lou maintained she could handle Morgane alone. *You heard Claud.* Maintained she wouldn't hesitate this time. *She can no longer touch me.* Maintained she would burn her ancestral home to the ground, along with all of her kin. *We'll build new.*

New what? I'd asked warily.

New everything.

I'd never seen her act with such single-minded intensity. No. Obsession. Most days, a ferocious glint lit her eyes—a feral sort of hunger—and others, no light touched them at all. Those days were infinitely worse. She'd watch the world with a deadened expression, refusing to acknowledge me or my weak attempts to comfort her.

Only one person could do that.

And he was gone.

She pulled me down beside her now, stroking my throat almost absently. At her cold touch, a shiver skittered down my spine, and a sudden desire to shift away seized me. I ignored it. Silence blanketed the room, thick and heavy, except for the growls of my stomach. Hunger was a constant companion now. I couldn't remember the last time I'd eaten my fill. With Troupe de Fortune? In the Hollow? The Tower? Across the aisle, Coco's breathing gradually evened. I focused on the sound, on the beams of the ceiling, rather than Lou's frigid skin or the ache in my chest.

A moment later, however, shouts exploded from the scullery, and the sanctuary door burst open. Beau shot forward, hotfooting it past the pulpit. "Bumfuzzle!" He gestured wildly toward the exit as I vaulted to my feet. "Time to go! Right now, right *now,* let's *go*—"

"Stop!" A gnarled man in the vestments of a priest charged into the sanctuary, wielding a wooden spoon. Yellowish stew dripped from it. As if Beau had interrupted his morning meal. The flecks of vegetable in his beard—grizzled, unkempt, concealing most of his face—confirmed my suspicions. "I said get *back* here—"

He stopped abruptly, skidding to a halt when he saw the rest of us. Instinctively, I turned to hide my face in the shadows. Lou flung her hood over her white hair, and Coco stood, tensing to run. But it was too late. Recognition sparked in his dark eyes.

"Reid Diggory." His dark gaze swept from my head to my toes before shifting behind me. "Louise le Blanc." Unable to help himself, Beau cleared his throat from the foyer, and the priest considered him briefly before scoffing and shaking his head. "Yes, I know who you are too, boy. *And* you," he added to Coco, whose hood still cloaked her face in darkness. True to his word, Jean Luc had added her wanted poster beside ours. The priest's eyes narrowed on the blade she'd drawn. "Put that away before you hurt yourself."

"We're sorry for trespassing." I lifted my hands in supplication, glaring at Coco in warning. Slowly, I slid into the aisle, inched toward the exit. At my back, Lou matched my steps. "We didn't mean any harm."

The priest snorted but lowered his spoon. "You broke into my home."

"It's a church." Apathy dulled Coco's voice, and her hand dropped as if it suddenly couldn't bear the dagger's weight. "Not a private residence. And the door was unlocked."

"Perhaps to lure us in," Lou suggested with unexpected relish. Head tilted, she stared at the priest in fascination. "Like a spider to its web."

The priest's brows dipped at the abrupt shift in conversation, as did mine. Beau's voice reflected our confusion. "What?"

"In the darkest parts of the forest," she explained, arching a brow, "there lives a spider who hunts other spiders. L'Enchanteresse, we call her. The Enchantress. Isn't that right, Coco?" When Coco didn't respond, she continued undeterred. "L'Enchanteresse creeps into her enemies' webs, plucking their silk strands, tricking them into believing they've ensnared their prey. When the spiders arrive to feast, she attacks, poisoning them slowly with her unique venom. She savors them for days. Indeed, she's one of the few creatures in the animal kingdom who enjoy inflicting pain."

We all stared at her. Even Coco. "That's disturbing," Beau finally said.

"It's *clever*."

"No." He grimaced, face twisting. "It's *cannibalism*."

"We needed shelter," I interjected a touch too loudly. Too desperately. The priest, who'd been watching them bicker with a disconcerted frown, returned his attention to me. "We didn't realize the church was occupied. We'll leave now."

He continued to assess us in silence, his lip curling slightly. Gold swelled before me in response. Seeking. Probing. Protecting. I ignored its silent question. I wouldn't need magic here. The priest wielded only a spoon. Even if he'd brandished a sword, the lines on his face marked him elderly. Wizened. Despite his tall frame, time seemed to have withered his musculature, leaving a spindly old man in its wake. We could outrun him. I seized Lou's hand in preparation, cutting a glance to Coco and Beau. They both nodded once in understanding.

Scowling, the priest lifted his spoon as if to stop us, but at that moment, a fresh wave of hunger wracked my stomach. Its growl rumbled through the room like an earthquake. Impossible to ignore. Eyes tightening, the priest tore his gaze from me to glare at Saint Magdaleine in the silence that followed. After another beat, he grudgingly muttered, "When did you last eat?"

I didn't answer. Heat pricked my cheeks. "We'll leave now," I repeated.

His eyes met mine. "That's not what I asked."

"It's been . . . a few days."

"How many days?"

Beau answered for me. "Four."

Another rumble of my stomach rocked the silence. The priest shook his head. Looking as though he'd rather swallow the spoon whole, he asked, "And . . . when did you last sleep?"

Again, Beau couldn't seem to stop himself. "We dozed in some fishermen's boats two nights ago, but one of them caught us before sunrise. He tried to snare us in his net, the half-wit."

The priest's eyes flicked to the sanctuary doors. "Could he have followed you here?"

"I just said he was a half-wit. Reid snared him in the net instead."

Those eyes found mine again. "You didn't hurt him." It wasn't a question. I didn't answer it. Instead I tightened my grip on Lou's hand and prepared to run. This man—this *holy* man—would soon sound the alarm. We needed to put miles between us before Jean Luc arrived.

Lou didn't seem to share my concern.

"What's your name, cleric?" she asked curiously.

"Achille." His scowl returned. "Achille Altier."

Though the name sounded familiar, I couldn't place it. Perhaps he'd once journeyed to Cathédral Saint-Cécile d'Cesarine. Perhaps I'd met him while under oath as a Chasseur. I eyed him with suspicion. "Why haven't you summoned the huntsmen, Father Achille?"

He looked deeply uncomfortable. Shoulders radiating tension, he stared down at his spoon. "You should eat," he said gruffly. "There's stew in the back. Should be enough for everyone."

Beau didn't hesitate. "What kind?" When I shot a glare over my shoulder, he shrugged. "He could've woken the town the moment he recognized us—"

"He still could," I reminded him, voice hard.

"—and my stomach is about to eat itself," he finished. "Yours too, by the sound of it. We need food." He sniffed and asked Father Achille, "Are there potatoes in your stew? I'm not partial to them. It's a textural thing."

The priest's eyes narrowed, and he jabbed the spoon toward the scullery. "Get out of my sight, boy, before I change my mind."

Beau inclined his head in defeat before scooting past us. Lou, Coco, and I didn't move, however. We exchanged wary looks. After a long moment, Father Achille heaved a sigh. "You can sleep here too. Just for the day," he added irritably, "so long as you don't bother me."

"It's Sunday morning." At last, Coco lowered her hood. Her lips were cracked, her face wan. "Shouldn't villagers be attending service soon?"

He scoffed. "I haven't held a service in years."

A reclusive priest. Of course. The disrepair of the chapel made sense now. Once, I would've scorned this man for his failure as a religious leader. For his failure as a man. I would've reprimanded him for turning his back on his vocation. On God.

How times had changed.

Beau reappeared with an earthen bowl and leaned casually against the doorway. Steam from the stew curled around his face. When my stomach rumbled again, he smirked. I spoke through gritted teeth. "Why would you help us, Father?"

Reluctantly, the priest's gaze trailed over my pale face, Lou's grisly scar, Coco's numb expression. The deep hollows beneath our eyes and the gaunt cut of our cheeks. Then he looked away, staring hard at the empty air above my shoulder. "What does it matter? You need food. I have food. You need a place to sleep. I have empty pews."

"Most in the Church wouldn't welcome us."

"Most in the Church wouldn't welcome their own mother if she was a sinner."

"No. But they'd burn her if she was a witch."

He arched a sardonic brow. "Is that what you're after, boy? The stake? You want me to mete out your divine punishment?"

"I believe," Beau drawled from the doorway, "he's simply pointing out that *you* are among the Church—unless you're actually the sinner of this story? Are you unwelcome amongst your peers, Father Achille?" He glanced pointedly at our dilapidated surroundings. "Though I abhor jumping to conclusions, our beloved patriarchs surely would've sent someone to repair this hovel otherwise."

Achille's eyes darkened. "Watch your tone."

I interrupted before Beau could provoke him further, spreading my arms wide. In disbelief. In frustration. In . . . everything. Pressure built in my throat at this man's unexpected kindness. It didn't make sense. It couldn't be real. As horrible a picture as Lou painted, a cannibal spider luring us into its web seemed likelier than a priest offering us sanctuary. "You know who we are. You know what we've done. You know what will happen if you're caught sheltering us."

He studied me for a long moment, expression inscrutable. "Let's not get caught, then." With a mighty *harrumph*, he stomped toward the scullery door. At the threshold, however, he paused, eyeing Beau's bowl. He seized it in the next second, ignoring Beau's protests and thrusting it at me. "You're just kids," he muttered, not meeting my eyes. When my fingers wrapped around the bowl—my stomach contracting painfully—he let go. Straightened his robes. Rubbed his neck. Nodded to the stew. "Won't be worth eating cold."

Then he turned and stormed from the room.

DARKNESS MINE

Lou

Darkness.

It shrouds everything. It envelops me, constricts me, pressing against my chest, my throat, my tongue until it *is* me. Trapped within its eye, drowning in its depths, I fold in on myself until I no longer exist at all. I am the darkness. This darkness, mine.

It *hurts*.

I should not feel pain. I should not feel anything. I am unformed and unmade, a speck in all of Creation. Without shape. Without life or lung or limb to control. I cannot see, cannot breathe, yet the darkness—it blinds. The pressure chokes, smothers, building with each passing second until it rends me apart. But I cannot scream. I cannot think. I can only listen—no, *sense*—a voice unfurling within the shadows. A beautiful, terrible voice. It snakes around me, *through* me, and whispers sweetly, promising oblivion. Promising respite.

Surrender, it croons, *and forget. Feel no pain.*

For a moment or a thousand moments, I hesitate, considering.

To surrender and forget appeals more than to resist and remember. I am weak, and I do not like pain. The voice is so beautiful, so tempting, so strong, that I nearly let it consume me. And yet . . . I cannot. If I let go, I will lose something important. *Someone* important. I cannot remember who it is.

I cannot remember who *I* am.

You are the darkness. The shadows press closer, and I fold myself tighter. A grain of sand below infinite black waves. *This darkness is yours.*

Still I hold on.

COCO'S FLAME

Reid

Coco leaned against the headstone beside me. A weatherworn statue of Saint Magdaleine towered over us, her bronze face shadowed in the gray twilight. Though she had long closed her eyes, Coco didn't sleep. She didn't speak either. She merely rubbed a scar on her palm with her opposite thumb, over and over until the skin chafed. I doubted she noticed it. I doubted she noticed anything.

She'd followed me into the cemetery after Lou had ransacked the scullery for red meat, unsatisfied with the fish Father Achille had prepared for supper. There'd been nothing inherently wrong with the way Lou had attacked the beef, even if the cut hadn't been fully cooked. We'd been famished for days. Our breakfast of stew and lunch of hard bread and cheese hadn't assuaged our hunger. And yet . . .

My stomach contracted without explanation.

"Is she pregnant?" Coco asked after a long moment. Her eyes flicked open, and she rolled her head to face me. Voice flat. "Tell me you've been careful. Tell me we don't have another problem."

"She bled two weeks ago, and since then, we haven't—" I cleared my throat.

Coco nodded and tipped her chin skyward once more, closing her eyes on a heavy exhale. "Good."

I stared at her. Though she hadn't cried since La Mascarade des Crânes, her lids remained swollen. Traces of kohl still flecked her cheeks. Tear tracks. "Are you . . ." The words caught in my throat. Coughing to clear it, I tried again. "I saw a tub inside if you need to bathe."

Her fingers clamped around her thumb in response, as if she could still feel Ansel's blood on her hands. She'd scrubbed them raw in the Doleur that night. Burned her garments in Léviathan, the inn where so much had gone wrong. "I'm too tired," she finally murmured.

The familiar ache of grief burned up my throat. Too familiar. "If you need to talk about it . . ."

She didn't open her eyes. "We aren't friends."

"Yes, we are."

When she didn't answer, I turned away, fighting a scowl. Fine. She didn't want to have this conversation. I wanted to have it even less. Crossing my arms against the chill, I'd just settled in for a long night of silence when Ansel's fierce expression rose behind my lids. His fierce conviction. *Lou is my friend*, he'd once told me. He'd been willing to follow her to Chateau le Blanc before I had. He'd kept her secrets. Shouldered her burdens.

Guilt tore through me. Jagged and sharp.

Like it or not, Coco and I *were* friends.

Feeling stupid, I forced myself to speak. "All I'm saying is that after the Archbishop passed, it helped me to talk about it. About *him*. So . . ." I shrugged stiffly, neck hot. Eyes burning. "If you need to . . . to talk about it . . . you can talk to me."

Now she did open her eyes. "The Archbishop was a sick fuck, Reid. Comparing him to Ansel is despicable."

"Yeah, well"—I stared at her pointedly—"you can't help who you love."

She dropped her gaze swiftly. To my shame, her lip quivered. "I know that."

"Do you?"

"Of course I do," she said with a hint of her old bite. Fire lit her features. "I know it's not my fault. Ansel loved me, and—and just because I didn't love him the same *way* doesn't mean I loved him any less. I certainly loved him more than *you*." Despite her heated assurance, her voice cracked on the last. "So you can take your advice and your condescension and your *pity*, and you can shove them up your ass." I kept my face impassive, refusing to rise. She could lash out. I could take it. Lurching to her feet, she pointed a finger at me. "And I won't sit here and let you *judge* me for— for—" Her chest heaved on a ragged breath, and a single tear tracked down her cheek. When it fell between us, sizzling against the snow, her entire body slumped. "For something I couldn't help," she finished, so soft I almost didn't hear.

Slowly, awkwardly, I rose to stand beside her. "I'm not judging you, Coco. I don't pity you either." When she scoffed, I shook my head. "I don't. Ansel was my friend too. His death wasn't your fault."

"Ansel isn't the only one who died that night."

Together, we looked to the thin plume rising from her teardrop.

Then we looked to the sky.

Smoke obscured the setting sun, dark and ominous above us. Heavy. It should've been impossible. We'd been traveling for days. The skies here, miles and miles from Cesarine—where smoke still billowed from tunnel entrances, from the cathedral, the catacombs, the castle, from cemeteries and inns and alleyways—should've been clear. But the flame beneath the capital wasn't simple fire. It was black fire, unnatural and unending, as if birthed from the bowels of Hell itself.

It was Coco's fire.

A fire with smoke to envelop an entire kingdom.

It burned hotter than regular flame, ravaging both the tunnels and the poor souls trapped within them. Worse, according to the fisherman who'd accosted us—a fisherman whose *brother* happened to be an initiate of the Chasseurs—no one could extinguish the blaze. King Auguste contained it only by posting a huntsman at each entrance. Their Balisardas prevented the blight from spreading.

It seemed La Voisin had spoken truth. When I'd pulled her aside in Léviathan, before she'd fled to the forest with her surviving Dames Rouges, her warning had been clear: *The fire rages with her grief. It will not stop until she does.*

Toulouse, Thierry, Liana, and Terrance were trapped in those tunnels.

"It still isn't your fault, Coco."

Her face twisted as she stared at the statue of Saint Magdaleine. "My tears started the fire." Sitting heavily, she folded her knees to her chest. Wrapped her arms around her shins. "They're all dead because of me."

"They aren't all dead." Immediately, my mind snapped to Madame Labelle. To her hemlock chains, her damp prison cell. To the king's hard fingers on her chin. Her lips. Rage kindled my blood. Though it made me despicable, relief flickered as well. Because of Coco's fire, King Auguste—my *father*—had more important things to deal with than my mother.

As if reading my thoughts, Coco said, "For now."

Fuck.

"We have to go back," I said gravely, the wind picking up around us. I imagined the scent of charred bodies in the smoke, of Ansel's blood on the earth. Even armed with the Dames Rouges and loup garou—even armed with the *Woodwose*—we'd still lost. Once again, I was struck by the utter foolishness of our plan. Morgane would slaughter us if we marched alone on the Chateau. "Lou won't listen to me, but maybe she'll listen to *you*. Deveraux and Blaise stayed behind to search for the others. We can help them, and afterward, we can—"

"They aren't going to find them, Reid. I told you. Anyone left in those tunnels is dead."

"The tunnels shifted before," I repeated for the dozenth time, wracking my thoughts for something—anything—I could've missed in our previous arguments. If I persuaded Coco, she could persuade Lou. I was sure of it. "Maybe they shifted again. Maybe Toulouse and Thierry are trapped in a secure passage, safe and whole."

"And maybe Liana and Terrance turn into house cats on the full moon." She didn't bother lifting her head, her voice dangerously apathetic once more. "Forget it, Reid. Lou is right. This has to end. Her way is as good as any—better, even. At least we're moving forward."

"What was the *point* of gathering allies, then?" I fought to keep the frustration from my voice. "We can't kill Morgane on our own."

"We clearly can't kill her with allies either."

"So we find new ones! We return to Cesarine, and we strategize with Deveraux—"

"What *exactly* are you expecting him to do? Who are these mysterious allies you hope to find? Shall Claud just . . . grow them on trees?" Her eyes hardened. "He couldn't save Ansel in La Mascarade des Crânes. He couldn't even save his *own* family, which means he can't help us either. He can't kill Morgane. Face it, Reid. This is our path forward. We can't search Cesarine for ghosts."

I unclenched my jaw. Heat worked up my throat. I didn't know what to do. "My mother isn't a ghost."

"Your mother can take care of herself."

"Her *life*—"

"—depends entirely on how adeptly she can lie." Beau strolled toward us casually from the church's kitchen, pointing a lazy finger at the smoke-filled sky. "Our father will be desperate to end this fire, even if he must enlist a witch to do it. As long as the clouds quite literally hang above our heads, your mother is safe. Apologies for eavesdropping, by the way," he added. "I wanted to know if either of you had noticed my new beard." He paused. "Also, Lou hasn't blinked in half an hour."

I frowned. "What?"

"She hasn't blinked," he repeated, dropping to the ground beside Coco and lifting a hand to her nape. His fingers kneaded gently. "Not once. She's spent the last thirty minutes staring at the stained glass in silence. It's unsavory. She even managed to frighten the priest away."

Unease pricked my stomach. "You timed her blinks?"

"You haven't?" Beau arched a brow in disbelief. "She's *your* wife—or lady friend, paramour, whatever label you've settled on. Something is clearly wrong with her, brother."

The wind built around us. At the edge of the church, the white dog reappeared. Pale and spectral. Silent. Watching. I forced myself to ignore it, to focus on my brother and his asinine observations. "And you don't have a beard," I said irritably, gesturing to his bare chin, "if we're voicing the obvious." I glanced at Coco, who still hid her face on her knees. "Everyone grieves differently."

"I'm telling you this goes beyond *different.*"

"Do you have a point?" I glared at him. "We all know she's undergone recent . . . changes. But she's still Lou." Unbidden, I glanced back to the dog. He stared at me with preternatural stillness. Even the wind didn't ripple his fur. Standing, I lifted my

hand and whistled low. "Here, boy." I stepped closer. Closer still.
He didn't move. To Beau and Coco, I muttered, "Has she named
him yet?"

"No," Beau said pointedly. "Or acknowledged him at all, for
that matter."

"You're fixating."

"You're deflecting."

"You still don't have a beard."

His hand shot to his whisker-less chin. "And *you* still don't
have—"

But he stopped short when several things happened at once.
The wind picked up suddenly as the dog turned and disappeared into the trees. An alarmed *"Look out!"* rent the air—the
voice familiar, *too* familiar, and sickeningly out of place amidst
the smoke and shadows—followed by the earsplitting screech of
metal tearing. As one, we looked up in horror. Too late.

The statue of Saint Magdaleine splintered at the waist, bust
careening in the wind toward Beau and Coco. She seized him
with a shriek, attempting to drag him out of the way, but their
legs—

I launched forward, tackling the fallen statue midair, landing
hard as Coco and Beau snatched their feet away. Time stood still
for a brief second. Beau checked Coco for injury, and she closed
her eyes, shuddered on a sob. Wincing at the pain in my side, I
struggled to catch my breath, to sit up—to—

No.

Pain forgotten, I whirled, scrambling to my feet to face the
newcomer.

"Hello, Reid," Célie whispered.

White-faced and trembling, she clutched a leather bag to her chest. Shallow cuts and scrapes marred her porcelain skin, and the hem of her gown hung in tatters around her feet. Black silk. I recognized it from Filippa's funeral.

"Célie." I stared at her for a beat, unable to believe my eyes. She couldn't be here. She couldn't have traversed the wilderness alone in only silk and slippers. But how else could I explain her presence? She hadn't just *happened* upon this exact spot at this exact moment. She'd . . . she must've followed us. *Célie.* The reality of the situation crashed over my head, and I gripped her shoulders, resisting the urge to shake her, hug her, scold her. My pulse pounded in my ears. "What the *hell* are you doing here?" When she drew back, nose wrinkling, I dropped my hands and staggered backward. "I'm sorry. I didn't mean to—"

"You didn't hurt me." Her eyes—wide, panicked—dropped to my shirt. Belatedly, I noticed the dark liquid there. Metallic. Viscous. The fabric beneath clung to my skin. I frowned. "It's just that you—well, you're covered in blood."

Bewildered, I half turned, lifting my shirt to examine my ribs. The dull ache in my side felt more like a bruise than a wound.

"Reid," Beau said sharply.

Something in his voice halted my movements. Slowly, I followed his finger to where Saint Magdaleine lay in the snow.

To where tears of blood dripped down her cheeks.

LA PETITE LARME

Reid

After a moment of harried, whispered conversation—as if the statue could hear us—we retreated to the safety of the sanctuary. "It was that wretched dog," Beau said, throwing himself into the pew beside Coco. Near the pulpit, Lou rose. Candlelight illuminated half of her face, bathing the rest in shadow. A chill swept down my spine at the chthonic image, as if she were cut in two. Part Lou and part . . . something else. Something dark.

She frowned, eyes flicking between Célie and me. "What is this?"

"*This*," I said, rougher than intended, turning to scowl at Célie, "is nothing. She's going home in the morning."

Célie lifted her chin. Tightened her hands on the strap of her leather bag. They trembled slightly. "I am not."

"Célie." Exasperated, I led her to the pew beside Lou, who made no move to greet her. Odd. I'd thought the two had formed a tentative bond after what they'd endured in La Mascarade des Crânes. "You just saw how dangerous it is here. Everyone in the kingdom wants us dead."

"*I* don't want us dead." Beau crossed his ankles on the pew in front of him, slinging an arm over Coco's shoulders. When his gaze flicked to Célie, she flushed crimson. "Thank you for the warning, by the way, Mademoiselle Tremblay. It seems everyone else has forgotten their manners. Appalling, really. That statue would have crushed us if not for you."

"Statue?" Lou asked.

"The statue in the cemetery . . . fell," I murmured. I didn't mention the tears.

Ignoring both of us, cheeks still pink under Beau's perusal, Célie sank into a deep curtsy. "Y-Your Highness. They alone have not forgotten their manners. Please forgive me."

He arched a brow, smirking at me over her bowed head. "I like her."

Coco lifted her hood to hide her face. Though she didn't settle into Beau's arm, she didn't lean away, either. "She shouldn't be here."

"It's that dog," Beau repeated emphatically. "Wherever he goes, catastrophe follows. He was there when the fisherman tried to drown us too."

Célie frowned. "But the fisherman didn't—" At our stares, she stopped abruptly, blush deepening. She lifted a delicate shoulder. "The boat capsized on a swell. Do you not remember?"

"Have you been *following* us?" Lou asked.

Célie refused to look at anyone.

I sat heavily, resting my forearms on my knees. "What are you doing here, Célie?"

"I—" Her expression open, painfully vulnerable, she glanced between Lou, Beau, and Coco before settling on me. "I would like to help."

"Help," Lou echoed. Mocking.

Célie's brows furrowed at her tone. "I believe I—I believe I have resources that could benefit the group in its pursuit of M-M—" She broke off again, hoisting her leather bag higher and squaring her shoulders. "In its pursuit of La Dame des Sorcières."

"You can't even say her name," I muttered, rubbing my temples.

"I do not need to say her name to kill her."

Kill her.

Good Lord.

An unexpected cackle sounded from Lou, who grinned wide and lifted her hands to clap once. Twice. Three times. The odd glint had returned to her eyes. "Well, well, it seems the kitten has finally found her claws. I'm impressed." Her laughter burrowed under my skin, clawed at my stomach. "But my mother is not a mouse. How do you plan to kill her? Will you curtsy? Invite her to tea?"

Yes, I'd clearly misinterpreted their relationship.

By the flex of Beau's jaw, he'd done the same. "Leave her alone, Lou."

Célie flashed him an appreciative look. Bolstered, she continued in a stronger voice, "I don't know *how* to kill her—not precisely, not *yet*—but I do have information in my possession. You were correct before, Your Highness." From her leather bag, she withdrew a crisp linen envelope. I recognized Jean Luc's handwriting on the front. "King Auguste has postponed your mother's execution indefinitely. He plans to utilize her magic to eradicate the fire."

Beau nodded to me. "I told you so."

When she extended the envelope, I skimmed its contents before handing it back. "Thank you for this, Célie. Truly. But I can't let you stay. What if something happened to you? I wouldn't be able to live with myself." I paused, frowning anew. Come to think of it— "What did your parents say about this?"

She sniffed reprovingly. "Nothing at all."

My frown deepened.

"They don't know you're here, do they?" Beau smirked, arching a brow. "Clever little minx. I suppose it's better to ask forgiveness than permission."

Groaning at the implication, I buried my face in my hands. "*Célie.*"

"*What?*" Her tenuous composure snapped in an instant, and I straightened. Startled. In all the years I'd known her, Célie didn't *snap*. "You needn't worry about them sending the kingdom after me, Reid. When I last disappeared, it took *quite* some time before help arrived, if you care to remember. Heaven forbid anyone know my father cannot control his own household."

I blinked to hide my shock. Though I'd known Monsieur Tremblay had failed as a father, apparently, I'd underestimated how much. "Jean Luc will come after you. He'll bring the whole of the Chasseurs with him."

She shook the envelope in my face. "Jean Luc knows I am here. He *watched* me steal my father's carriage, for God's sake, and scolded me through the whole ordeal." I stared at her. I'd never known her to thieve, either. Or take the Lord's name in vain. She exhaled hard through her nose, stuffing the envelope into her cloak. "Regardless, I'd have thought *you* would appreciate my intervention. If I travel with your band of notorious witches and fugitives—pardon, Your Highness—Jean cannot arrest any of you without also arresting me. That will not happen. He will pursue you no further."

"Oh, to have seen the look on his face." Beau's own face twisted as if pained. "Further proof that there is a God, and He hates me."

"It doesn't matter." I shoved myself to my feet, eager to end this argument. To find Father Achille and alert him of the situation, to request an additional blanket for the night. "You can't come with us."

Seething, she watched me pass in silent fury, her shoulders square and her spine ramrod straight. Her fingers white around her leather bag. "What I *cannot do*," she finally said through clenched teeth, "is look my parents in the eye. They want to pretend nothing happened. They want to return to life as it was before. But they cannot make me." Her voice dipped dangerously low. "*You* cannot make me. The thought of s-sitting at home—curtsying to noblemen, sipping *tea*—while Morgane remains at large physically sickens me." When I didn't pause my stride, she continued desperately, "She trapped me in that coffin with Filippa for weeks, Reid. *Weeks.* She—she t-tortured me, and she mutilated those children. What I *cannot do* is nothing."

I froze at the pulpit. Surely I'd misheard her. Surely this sudden dread in my chest—it was misplaced. I didn't turn. "She what?"

A sniff in response. "Do not make me repeat it," she said.

"Célie—" When I finally moved toward her, nausea churning, she stopped my advance with the swipe of her hand. Tears fell freely down her cheeks. She didn't hide them. Didn't brush them away. That hand swung her leather bag from her shoulder, dumped its contents on the rotten floor: jewelry, *couronnes*, gemstones, even a chalice. The others stared at the small treasure trove, agog, but I couldn't see past Célie's words. Couldn't stop . . . picturing them.

Filippa had been older than us by a few years. Unlike Célie, she'd acted as my sister. A prim, disapproving sort of sister, but a sister nonetheless. The thought of Célie trapped with her corpse—*months* after burial—made my stomach roll violently. I choked down bile.

"I didn't just steal my father's carriage," Célie whispered into the silence. She gestured to the glittering pile. "I robbed his vault as well. I assumed we would need currency for our travels."

Beau rose for a closer look, dragging Coco along with him. "How did you *carry* all of this?" He eyed Célie's arms with unabashed skepticism as Lou shadowed their footsteps.

Coco toed the coins without interest. "And where is your carriage?"

At last, Célie dropped the leather bag. Her fingers flexed. "I left it with the stable boy at the inn."

"And your footman?" Kneeling, Beau prodded the bag cautiously, like it was crafted from human skin. Perhaps it was. Monsieur Tremblay had once dealt in dangerous magical objects. The witches had killed Filippa for it. "Your driver?"

"I drove myself."

"*What?*" Though Beau whirled, it was *my* voice that cut through the room. "Are you out of your mind?"

Lou cackled again, inordinately pleased with the entire situation.

Shooting her a glare, I stormed back to the group, my own temper brewing dangerously close to the surface. I took a deep breath. Another. "That's it. This is over. I'll speak to Father Achille, and he'll arrange an escort to take you back to Cesarine at daybreak." Roughly, I began shoving the jewelry back into her leather bag. Even filled with heavy jewels, it remained weightless in my hand. Perhaps not human skin, but assuredly magic. Fucking Tremblay. Fucking *Célie*. If a witch had happened upon her with this bag, she would've met the same fate as Filippa. Perhaps that was what she wanted. Perhaps after La Mascarade des Crânes, she had a death wish.

I sure as hell wouldn't indulge it.

"*Hold it.*" Coco seized my arm unexpectedly, her voice the sharpest I'd heard in days. Her fingers shook. Pushing back her hood, she snatched a locket from me. When she lifted it to the candlelight, her face—paler now, nearly ashen—reflected back on its golden surface. Filigree twined around the diamond at the oblong pendant's center. The pattern they created resembled . . . waves. Quietly, coldly, she asked, "Where did you get this?"

Lou appeared at her shoulder in an instant. With the diamonds reflected in them, her eyes gleamed almost silver.

Célie had the sense to yield a step. "I—I told you. I stole it from my father's vault." She glanced at me for reassurance, but I could give her none. I'd never before seen this intensity—this *possession*—in either Coco's or Lou's gaze. Their reactions were . . . unsettling. Whatever relic Célie had inadvertently brought us, it must've been important. "It was my favorite piece as a child, but it—it doesn't open. Father couldn't sell it."

Coco shuddered as if insulted before withdrawing a blade from her cloak. I stepped hastily in front of Célie. "Oh, please," Coco snarled, pricking the tip of her finger instead. A single droplet of blood dripped onto the diamond and beaded into a perfect circle. Then—incredibly—it sank beneath the stone's surface, swirling bright crimson. When the color dissipated, the locket clicked open.

We all leaned closer, entranced, to see a crystal-clear surface within.

Lou recoiled.

"*La Petite Larme*," Coco said, her voice softening. Her anger momentarily forgotten.

"The Little Tear," Beau echoed.

"A mirror made from a drop of L'Eau Mélancolique." She gazed at her reflection with an inscrutable expression before refocusing on Célie. Her lip curled in distaste once more. "It wouldn't open because it doesn't belong to you. It belonged to my mother."

A pin could've dropped in the sanctuary, and we would've heard its every echo. Even Father Achille—who'd stormed through the scullery doors in an apron, clutching a soapy dish and growling about noise—seemed to realize he'd interrupted a tense moment. His eyes narrowed on Célie and the gold at her feet. "Célie Tremblay," he acknowledged gruffly. "You're a long way from home."

Though she offered him a polite smile, it was brittle. Fraught. "I beg your pardon, *monsieur*, but I do not believe I've had the pleasure of your acquaintance."

"Achille," he said, lips pursing. "Father Achille Altier."

Coco snapped the locket shut. Without a word, she replaced her hood.

"Nice apron." Beau grinned at the hand-painted roses on Father Achille's apron. Brushstrokes large and uneven, they looked as though they'd been painted by a child. In blue and red and green.

"My nieces made it for me," Father Achille muttered.

"It really brings out your eyes."

Father Achille chucked the dish at him. Though Beau managed to catch the slippery plate against his chest, water still splattered his face on impact. Father Achille nodded in righteous satisfaction. "That's the last dish of yours I'll be washing, boy. You can scrub the rest of them yourself—and the scullery, thanks to her." He jerked his thumb toward Lou in irritation. "There's a bucket and a mop waiting for you."

Beau opened his mouth to protest indignantly, but Célie interrupted. "Father Achille." She swept into another curtsy, though not as low this time. Not as grand. She eyed his flowered apron and disheveled robes—the disrepair of the sanctuary—in thinly veiled disapproval. "I am pleased to meet you."

Father Achille shifted awkwardly before her, as if unaccustomed to such pristine manners. If I hadn't known better, I would've said he looked uncomfortable under her scrutiny. Embarrassed, even. "I knew your mother," he finally said by way of explanation. "When I lived in Cesarine."

"Of course. I will pass along your regards."

He snorted again. "Better not. I said I knew her, not that I particularly liked her." At Célie's scandalized expression, he muttered, "The feeling was mutual, I assure you. Now"—he straightened with as much dignity as he could muster—"it isn't my business to ask what you're doing in Fée Tombe, Mademoiselle Tremblay. It isn't my place to tell you how stupid you are for taking up with this lot. So I won't. Because I don't care. Just make sure you don't cause any trouble before you leave."

I stepped forward as he turned on his heel. "She needs an escort back to Cesarine."

"Reid." Célie actually stamped her foot now. "Stop being so—so—"

"Pigheaded?" Beau suggested.

Father Achille scowled at us over his shoulder. "I am not a babysitter."

"See?" Triumphant, she beamed, pointing a finger in the air. "He will not take me, and the journey is far too hazardous to travel alone. I must remain here. With you."

My jaw clenched. "You had no problem hazarding it before."

"Yes, but—" Something akin to nervousness flitted through her eyes, and her smile vanished. "I—I might've . . . fibbed before. A small, inconsequential thing," she added hastily at my expression. "I told you I'd left my coach at the stable, but really, er, in *actuality*, I might've made a wrong turn—"

"A wrong turn where?" I demanded.

"To the lighthouse."

Father Achille slowly turned.

"I lost sight of you all just before dawn." Célie twisted her hands together at her waist. "When I came to the fork in the road, I—I chose the path leading away from the village. I never dreamed you'd seek shelter in a church. Really, I am extraordinarily lucky to have found you at all—"

"*Darling* Célie," Beau interrupted. "Please get on with it."

She flushed again, dipping her head. "O-of course, Your Highness. Forgive me. When I neared the lighthouse, something moved in the shadows. It—it spooked Cabot, of course, and he nearly drove us off the cliff in his haste to flee. A wheel snapped on the bluff. I managed to free Cabot before the whole carriage tumbled into the sea . . . or at least, it *would've* if the creature hadn't wrenched it free." She shuddered. "I've never seen such a monster. Long, matted hair and skin cloaked in shadow. Sharp white teeth. It smelled of rot too. Decaying flesh. I'm quite certain if I hadn't escaped on Cabot's back, it would've eaten us both." She exhaled heavily, lifting her eyes to mine. "So, you see, I left *Cabot* at the stable, not my carriage. I simply cannot return for it while it remains in the creature's possession, and I cannot risk traveling without it either. I *must* stay with you, Reid, or I'll never make it home at all."

"*Cauchemar*," Lou murmured.

I extended a weary hand to her. "What?"

With a small smile, she laced her fingers through mine. They remained like ice. "I didn't say anything."

"Yes, you—"

"A *cauchemar* has indeed taken up residence in the lighthouse." At our blank looks, Father Achille grudgingly added, "A nightmare. That's what the villagers call it, anyway. It found us here in Fée Tombe three days ago, and they're all terrified." He scowled and shook his head. "The fools are planning to raze the lighthouse in the morning."

Something in his scowl made me pause. "Has this *cauchemar* harmed anyone?"

"Aside from me?" Célie asked. "It nearly frightened Cabot and me to death!"

Coco scoffed beneath her hood. "What a tragedy that would've been."

"Coco," Beau admonished. "That was beneath you. If you're going to be spiteful, at least be clever about it."

"Not spiteful at all," she said sweetly. "I would've mourned the horse."

"I beg your pardon?" Célie wheeled around to face her, mouth slack with disbelief. "I—I am terribly sorry about your m-mother's necklace, Cosette, but I didn't *know*—"

I spoke over her. "Has the *cauchemar* harmed anyone?"

Father Achille shrugged. "It hardly matters."

"It matters to me."

"That mob is coming, boy. You'll get yourself killed."

"You don't care."

"That's right." His nostrils flared. "I don't. *Cauchemars* are notoriously cruel, but this creature hasn't yet attacked. Last night, it broke into the boucherie and stole some scraps, but that's the extent of my knowledge." When I exchanged a glance first with Lou, then with Beau, he gritted his teeth and said, as if the words physically pained him, "You should stay out of it. This isn't your fight."

But a mob burning an innocent creature alive sounded exactly like my fight. They would do the same to Lou, if given the chance. The same to Coco. My mother. Me. Familiar anger, thick and viscous, simmered in my gut. These villagers alone weren't guilty. Though they would slaughter this innocent, Morgane had tortured and maimed my siblings, my brothers and sisters—all collateral damage in this war they hadn't chosen. A war this *cauchemar* hadn't chosen.

No more.

A brief stop at the lighthouse wouldn't hurt anything. We could warn the *cauchemar* before the mob struck—perhaps even free it—and still leave by sunrise. It was the noble thing to do. Lou might've chosen the wrong path for us, but this felt a step in the right direction. Perhaps it would set us on a new course. A better one.

At the very least, it would delay our arrival to Chateau le Blanc. And perhaps . . .

"I vote no." Coco's voice cut sharp from beneath her hood. "*Cauchemars* are dangerous, and we can't afford distractions. We should proceed to the Chateau."

Lou grinned and nodded.

"If we help this *cauchemar*," I murmured, "perhaps it'll help us. *Here* is your mysterious ally, Cosette. No trees required."

Though I couldn't see her face, I could feel her glower.

Shaking my head, I handed Célie my blanket before returning to my pew. Lou didn't let go of my hand. Her thumb traced the veins along my wrist. "We need Célie's carriage," I said. "Whether or not she returns home."

Célie's head snapped up. "A carriage would speed our travel considerably."

"Yes." I considered her for a long moment. Rather, I *reconsidered* her. A muscle twitched in my jaw at her hopeful expression, at the determined set of her shoulders. This was not the Célie I'd always known. "It would."

Throwing his hands in the air, Achille stalked to the scullery to be rid of us. "Fools, all of you," he said over his shoulder, voice grim. "A *cauchemar* is strongest at night. Act at first light before the mob attacks. Whatever you do, don't let them see you. Fear makes people stupid." With one last look between Célie and me, he shook his head. "But courage makes 'em stupid too."

AN INSIDIOUS PRESENCE

Lou

From the darkness, a voice arises.

Not *that* voice. Not the terrible one that croons and beckons. This voice is sharper, biting, cutting. Familiar. It does not tempt me. It—it *scolds* me.

Wake up, it snaps. *You aren't dead yet.*

But I do not know this word. I do not understand death.

No one does. That's not the point—or maybe that's the entire *point. You're fading.*

Fading. The darkness offers oblivion. Sweet relief.

Fuck that. You've worked too hard and too long to give up now. Come on. You want more than oblivion. You want to live.

A ghostly chuckle reverberates through the shadows. Through the unending black. It curls around me, caressing the jagged edges of my consciousness, soothing the broken shards at my center. *Surrender, little mouse. Let me devour you.*

I hurt. With each pulse of the darkness, the pain intensifies until I cannot bear it.

It's your heart. The sharp voice returns, louder now. Louder than even the rhythmic drumming. *Tha-thump. Tha-thump. Tha-thump.* Instinctively, I shy away, but I cannot hide from the sound. From the pain. It echoes everywhere, all around me. *It's still beating.*

I try to process this, try to peer through the darkness to where a heart might indeed beat. But still I see nothing.

Don't hide from it, Lou. Own your pain. Use it.

Lou. The word is familiar, like the exhalation on a laugh. The breath before jumping, the gasp when you fly instead. It's a sigh of relief, of irritation, of disappointment. It's a shout of anger and a cry of passion. It's . . . me. I am not the darkness. I am something else entirely. And this voice—it's mine.

There you are, it says—*I* say—in unabashed relief. *About time too.*

However, on the wings of one realization comes another, and I flex abruptly, pushing against the crushing black. It responds in kind, no longer simple darkness but a sentient presence all its own. An insidious presence. It feels wrong, somehow. Foreign. It shouldn't be here—wherever *here* is—because this place . . . it belongs to me too. Like my heartbeat. Like my name. Though I flex again, testing my strength, spreading myself further, pushing and pushing and *pushing*, I meet only ironclad resistance.

The darkness is unyielding as stone.

A GAME OF QUESTIONS

Reid

Lou's fingertips skimmed my leg in time with the others' rhythmic breathing. With each inhale, she walked them upward. With each exhale, she turned her wrist, trailing downward with the back of her hand. Wind whistled through the cracks in the sanctuary, raising gooseflesh on my arms. I sat rigid beneath her touch, heart pounding in my throat at the subtle friction. Tense. Waiting. Sure enough, those fingers gradually crept up, up, *up* my thigh in slow seduction, but I caught her wrist, slid my hand to cover hers. To pin it in place.

A foreign emotion congealed in my blood as I stared at her hand beneath mine. I should've ached, should've tightened with that familiar hunger, that *heat*, that left me almost fevered when we touched. But this knot in my stomach . . . it wasn't need. It was something else. Something *wrong*. While the others had prepared for bed a half hour ago, a general sense of dread had enveloped me. That dread had only intensified when Beau, the last awake, had finally drifted to sleep, leaving Lou and me alone.

Clearing my throat, I squeezed her fingers. Forced a smile. Brushed a kiss against her palm. "We have an early morning. We'll need to leave Fée Tombe after we free the *cauchemar*. It'll be another long few days on the road."

It sounded like an excuse.

It was one.

A low noise reverberated from her throat. She hadn't worn her ribbon since we left Cesarine. My gaze dropped to her scar, healing yet still puckered, angry. She stroked it with her free hand. "How does one *free* a *cauchemar*?"

"Maybe we can reason with it. Convince it to return to the forest."

"And if we can't?"

I sighed. "We can only warn it about the mob. We can't force it to do anything."

"And if it decides to *eat* the mob? If our warning allows it the chance to do so?"

"It won't," I said firmly.

She considered me with a half smile. "You've developed quite an affinity for us, haven't you?" Her grin spread. "Monsters."

I pressed a kiss to her forehead. Ignored the unfamiliar scent of her skin. "Sleep, Lou."

"I'm not tired," she purred, her eyes too bright in the darkness. Too pale. "We slept all day." When her hand crept up my chest once more, I caught it, lacing my fingers through her own. She misinterpreted the movement. Mistook it for an invitation. Before I could blink, she'd hoisted her knee across my lap to straddle me, lifting our hands awkwardly above our heads. When she arched her lower back, pressing her chest into mine, my stomach dropped like a stone. Shit.

I fought to keep my gaze impassive. Of course she wanted to—to touch me. Why wouldn't she? Less than a month ago, I'd craved her like an addict. The subtle curve of her hip, the thick wave of her hair, the impish gleam in her eyes. I'd been unable to keep from pawing at her every moment of the day—the presence of my own *mother* hadn't stopped me. Even then, however, it'd been so much more than physical.

From the very start, Lou had woken me up. Her presence had been infectious. Even infuriated, exasperated, I'd never stopped wanting to be near her.

Now I glanced at Beau, at Coco, at Célie, praying one of them would stir. Hoping they'd open their eyes and interrupt. But they didn't wake. They slept on, heedless of my inner struggle.

I loved Lou. I knew that. Felt it in my bones.

I also couldn't stand the sight of her.

What was *wrong* with me?

Anger cracked open as she moved her lips against my ear, nibbling the lobe. Too many teeth. Too much *tongue*. Another wave of revulsion swept through me. *Why?* Was it because she was still mourning? Because *I* was? Because she'd attacked her supper like a rabid animal, because she'd only blinked twice in the past hour? I mentally shook myself, irritated with Beau. With *myself*. She'd been stranger than usual, yes, but that didn't justify the way my skin crawled when she touched me.

Worse still, these thoughts—this looming dread, this unsettling aversion—they felt like a betrayal. Lou deserved better than this.

Swallowing hard, I turned to meet her lips. She kissed me back enthusiastically, without hesitation, and my guilt only deepened. She didn't seem to sense my reluctance, however. She pressed closer instead. Rocked her hips against mine. Clumsy. Eager. When she again dropped her mouth to my throat, sucking at my rapid pulse, I shook my head in defeat. It was no good. My hands descended on her shoulders.

"We need to talk."

The words came of their own volition. She blinked in surprise, and what looked like . . . insecurity flickered in her pale eyes. I hated myself for it. I'd seen Lou insecure approximately twice in our entire relationship, and neither instance had boded well for us. It vanished as quickly as it'd come, however, replaced by a wicked gleam. "That involves tongues, yes?"

Gently, firmly, I slid her from my lap. "No. It doesn't."

"Are you sure?" Crooning, she leaned into me seductively. Or at least, that was her intent. But the movement lacked her usual finesse. I leaned back, studying her overbright eyes. Her flushed cheeks.

"Is something wrong?"

Tell me what it is. I'll fix it.

"You tell me." Again, her hands sought my chest. I seized them with tightly leashed frustration, squeezing her icy fingers in warning.

"Talk to me, Lou."

"What would you like to talk about, *darling* husband?"

I took a deep breath, still watching her closely. "Ansel."

His name fell between us like a carcass. Heavy. Dead.

"Ansel." She tugged her hands away with a frown. Her eyes grew distant. Shuttered. She stared at a spot just over my shoulder, her pupils expanding and contracting in tiny, nearly imperceptible movements. "You want to talk about Ansel."

"Yes."

"No," she said flatly. "I want to talk about you."

My own eyes narrowed. "I don't."

She didn't respond right away, still staring intently as if searching for . . . what? The right words? Lou had never cared for the right words before. Indeed, she reveled in saying the wrong ones. If I was honest with myself, I reveled in hearing them. "Let's have another game of questions, then," she said abruptly.

"What?"

"Like in the patisserie." She nodded quickly, almost to herself, before facing me at last. She tilted her head. "You didn't eat your sticky bun."

I blinked at her. "What?"

"Your sticky bun. You didn't eat it."

"Yes, I heard you. I just—" Shaking my head, I tried again, bewildered. "I don't have your sweet tooth."

"Hmm." She licked her lips salaciously. When her arm snaked behind me along the pew, I resisted the urge to lean forward. When her fingers threaded through my hair, however, I couldn't resist. She followed like a plague. "Venison is delicious too. Salty. Tender. At least," she added with a knowing smile, "if you eat it directly." I stared at her in confusion. Then horror. She meant if you ate it *raw.* "Otherwise rigor mortis toughens the meat. You have to hang the animal for a fortnight to break down the connective tissue. Makes it hard to avoid the flies, of course."

"When the hell have you eaten *raw deer?*" I asked incredulously.

Her eyes seemed to glow at the expletive, and she hummed with excitement, leaning toward me. "You should try it. You might like it." Then— "But I suppose a huntsman would have no need to skin a deer in his ivory tower. Tell me, have you ever suffered hunger?"

"Yes."

"*Real* hunger, I mean. Have you ever suffered cold? The kind that freezes your insides and leaves you like ice?"

Despite the hostility of her words, her voice held no contempt. Only curiosity. *Genuine* curiosity. She rocked back and forth, unable to keep still, as she watched me. I glared back at her. "You know I have."

She cocked her head. "Do I?" After pursing her lips, she nodded once more. "I do. Yes, of course. The Hollow. Dreadfully cold, wasn't it?" Her index and middle fingers walked up my leg. "And you're hungry even now, aren't you?"

She giggled when I returned her hand to her lap.

"What"—I cleared my throat—"is your next question?"

I could humor her. I could play this game. If it meant breaking through to her, if it meant unraveling what had . . . *changed* in her, I would sit here all night. I would help her. I *would*. Because if this truly was grief, she needed to talk about it. *We* needed to talk about it. Another stab of guilt shot through me when I glanced down at her hands. She'd clasped them together tightly.

I should've been holding those hands. I couldn't force myself to do it.

"Oooh, questions, questions." She brought her interlaced knuckles to her lips, musing. "If you could be anyone else, who would you be?" Another grin. "Whose skin would you wear?"

"I—" I glanced at Beau without thinking. She didn't miss the movement. "I wouldn't want to be anyone else."

"I don't believe you."

Defensive, I asked, "Who would you be?"

She lowered her hands to her chest. With her fingers still laced together, she could've been praying. Except for the calculated gleam in her eyes, her fiendish smile. "I can be whoever I want to be."

I cleared my throat, fought to ignore the hair lifting on my neck. Lost. "How do you know about *cauchemars*? I've studied the occult my entire life, and I've never heard of such a creature."

"You've *extinguished* the occult. I've lived with it." She cocked her head. The movement sent a fresh shiver down my spine. "I *am* it. We learn more in the shadows than we ever do in the sun." When I didn't answer, she asked abruptly, simply, "How would you choose to die?"

Ah. I eyed her knowingly. *Here we go.* "If I could choose . . . I suppose I'd want to die of old age. Fat and happy. Surrounded by loved ones."

"You wouldn't choose to die in battle?"

A startled breath. A sickening thud. A scarlet halo. I pushed my last memory of Ansel aside, looking her squarely in the eye. "I wouldn't choose that death for anyone. Not even myself. Not anymore."

"*He* chose it."

Though my heart twisted—though even his name brought uncomfortable pressure to my eyes—I inclined my head. "He did. And I'll honor him for it every day of my life—that he chose to help you, to fight with you. That he chose to face Morgane with you. He was the best of us." Her smile finally slipped, and I reached out to grip her hand. Despite its icy temperature, I didn't let go. "But you shouldn't feel guilty. Ansel made the decision for himself—not for you or for me, but for *him*. Now," I said firmly before she could interrupt, "it's your turn. Answer the question."

Her face remained inscrutable. Blank. "I don't want to die."

I rubbed her frigid hand between my own, trying to warm it. "I know. But if you had to choose—"

"I would choose not to die," she said.

"Everyone dies, Lou," I said gently.

She leaned closer at my expression, running her hand up my chest. In my ear, she whispered, "Says who, Reid?" She cupped my cheek, and for just a second, I lost myself in her voice. If I closed my eyes, I could pretend a different Lou held me this way. I could pretend this icy touch belonged to another—to a foul-mouthed thief, a heathen, a witch. I could pretend her breath smelled of cinnamon, and her hair flowed long and brown down her shoulders. Could pretend this was all part of an elaborate joke. An *inappropriate* joke. She would've laughed and flicked my nose at this point. Told me I needed to loosen up. Instead, her lips hovered over mine. "Who says we have to die?"

Swallowing hard, I opened my eyes, and the spell broke.

MY NAME IS LEGION

Lou

There are very few advantages to losing possession of one's body—or rather, losing *awareness* of one's body. With no eyes to see and no ears to hear, no legs to walk and no teeth to *eat*, I pass my time floating in darkness. Except . . . can one even *float* without a body? Or am I merely existing? And this darkness isn't *quite* darkness, is it? Which means—

Oh god. I'm now existing inside Nicholina le Clair.

No. *She* is existing inside *me*, the body-snatching bitch.

Hopefully I'm on my monthly bleed. She'd deserve it.

Though I wait for her response, impatient, no ghostly chuckle answers my provocation, so I try again. Louder this time. Shouting my thoughts—can one have thoughts without a brain?—into the abyss. *I know you can hear me. I hope my uterus is rioting against you.*

The darkness seems to shift in reply, but still she says nothing.

Forcing myself to concentrate, I push against her oppressive presence. It doesn't budge. I try again, harder this time. Nothing. I don't know how long I push. I don't know how much time has passed since I regained consciousness. Time has no meaning here. At this rate, I'll reclaim my body in approximately three hundred years, waking in a grave as more dust than skeleton. At least my mother can't kill a skeleton. At least they don't have uteruses.

I think I'm going mad.

With one last vicious shove, I resist a fit of rage. Emotions seem . . . different in this place. They run wild and unchecked without a body to cage them, and sometimes, in moments like these, I feel myself—whatever form I've now taken—slip into them, unadulterated. As if I *become* the emotion.

Reid would hate it here.

The thought of him lances through my consciousness, and a new emotion threatens to consume me. Melancholy.

Has he noticed I'm not myself? Has anyone? Do they realize what's happened to me?

I refocus on Nicholina, on the darkness, before the melancholy swallows me whole. It does little good to dwell on such things, yet debilitating cold creeps through the mist, my subconscious, at another unwelcome thought: how could they have noticed? Even before La Voisin and Nicholina betrayed us, I wasn't myself. I still feel those splintered edges, those fissures in my spirit I broke willingly.

One bites deeper than the rest. An open wound.

I shy away from it instinctively, though it pulses with whiskey-colored eyes and curling lashes and soft, lyrical laughter. It aches with a lanky arm around my shoulders, a warm hand in my own.

It throbs with empathy, with a feigned accent and a stolen bottle of wine, with shy blushes and not-quite birthdays. It burns with the sort of loyalty that no longer exists in this world.

He didn't make it to seventeen.

Ansel sacrificed everything, cracked me wide open, and I allowed Nicholina to slither into that crack. That's how I repaid him—by losing myself entirely. Self-loathing churns, black and noxious, in the pit of my consciousness. He deserved better. He deserved *more*.

I would give it to him. As God or the Goddess or just the dark of my fucking soul as witness, I would give it to him. I would ensure he didn't die in vain. In response, an unfamiliar voice startles me by murmuring, *Oh, bravo.*

The inky mist contracts with my fright, but I push against it viciously, searching for the new presence. This isn't Nicholina. This certainly isn't *me*. And that means . . . someone else is here.

Who are you? I ask with feigned bravado. Mother's tit, how many people—or spirits, or entities, or *whatever*—can possibly fit within a single body? *What do you want?*

You needn't be frightened. Another voice this time. As unfamiliar as the last. *We cannot hurt you.*

We are *you.*

Or rather, a third adds, *we are her.*

That's not an answer, I snap. *Tell me who you are.*

A brief pause.

Then a fourth voice finally says, *We don't remember.*

A fifth now. *Soon you won't either.*

If I had bones, their words would've chilled them to the marrow. *How . . . how many of you are there?* I ask quietly. *Can none of you remember your name?*

Our name is Legion, the voices reply in unison, not missing a beat. *For we are many.*

Holy hell. Definitely more than five voices. More like fifty. Shit, shit, *shit*. Vaguely, I remember the verse they recited from a passage in the Archbishop's Bible, the one he loaned me in the basement of Chasseur Tower. The man who spoke it had been possessed by demons. But these—these aren't demons, are they? Is Nicholina possessed by *demons*?

Alas, we do not know, the first says amicably. *We have lived here for unknown years. We could be demons, or we could be mice. We see only what our mistress sees, hear only what our mistress hears.*

Mice.

She talks to us sometimes, another adds, and somehow I sense its mischievous intent. I just *know*, as if its stream of consciousness has merged with mine. *We jest, by the way. We aren't called Legion. Stupid name, if you ask us.*

We use it on all the newcomers.

Always gets a rise.

Plucked the verse straight from your memories this time, though. Are you religious?

It is impolite to ask if someone is religious.

She isn't a someone *anymore. She's one of us. We already know the answer, anyway. We're being polite.*

On the contrary, it is quite rude to look through her memories.

Save the sermon for when the memories have gone. Look here. They're still fresh.

An uncomfortable prickling sensation descends as the voices bicker, and again, I instinctively know they're rifling through my consciousness—through *me*. Images of my past flicker in and out of the mist faster than I can track, but the voices only press closer, hungry for more. Dancing around the maypole with Estelle, drowning in the Doleur with the Archbishop, straining at the altar beneath my mother—

Stop it. My own voice cuts sharply through the memories, and the voices draw back, surprised but chastised. As they should be. It's like an infestation of fleas in my own subconscious. *My name is Louise le Blanc, and I am most definitely still a* someone. *I'd tell you to stay the hell out of my head, but since I'm not sure this even* is *my head, I'll assume separation is impossible at this point. Now, who's the last newcomer to this place? Can anyone remember?*

Silence reigns for one blissful second before all the voices start talking at once, arguing over who's been here the longest. Too late, I realize the error in my judgment. These voices are no longer individuals but an eerie sort of collective. A hive. Annoyance quickly churns to anger. Longing for hands with which to throttle them, I try to speak, but a new voice interrupts.

I am the newest.

The other voices cease immediately, radiating curiosity. I'm curious myself. This voice sounds different from the rest, deep and low and masculine. He also called himself *I*, not *we*.

And you are? I ask.

If a voice could frown, this one does. *I . . . I believe I was once called Etienne.*

Etienne, the others echo. Their whispers thrum like insect wings. The sound is disconcerting. Worse—I *feel* the moment they manifest his full name from his memories. From *my* memories. *Etienne Gilly.*

You're Gaby's brother, I say in dawning horror, remembering as they do. *Morgane murdered you.*

The voices practically quiver with anticipation as our memories sync, filling in the gaps to paint the entire portrait: how Nicholina possessed him and walked the forest under pretense of a hunt, how she led him to where Morgane lay in wait. How Morgane abducted him, tortured him within the bowels of a dank, dark cave only a handful of miles from the blood camp. And La Voisin—how she'd known all along. How she'd practically delivered Etienne's and Gabrielle's heads to Morgane on a silver platter.

Part of me still can't believe it, can't process my shock at their betrayal. My humiliation. Josephine and Nicholina have allied with my mother. Though I didn't like them, I never suspected them capable of such evil. They sacrificed members of their own coven to . . . what? Return to the Chateau?

Yes, Etienne whispers.

He knows because he saw it all happen through Nicholina's eyes, even after the real Etienne had perished. He witnessed his own desecrated body propped against my tent. He watched helplessly as Morgane kidnapped Gabrielle for the same fate, as my mother tormented his little sister, as Gaby finally escaped from La Mascarade des Crânes.

Except . . .

I frown. There are noticeable *gaps* in his memory. A small hole here, a gaping one there. My own involvement in the skull masquerade, for example. The color of Gabrielle's hair. Each gap fills as I think of it, however, as my memory supplements his own, until the timeline is mostly complete.

Despite being, well, *dead*, he witnessed it all as if he was there.

How? I ask warily. *Etienne, you . . . you died. Why haven't you passed on?*

When Nicholina possessed me, I joined her consciousness, and I—I don't think I ever left.

Holy shit. My shock spreads wildly into outright horror. *Has Nicholina possessed all of you?*

I can feel them sift through our memories once more, piecing together our collective knowledge of Nicholina, of La Voisin, of blood magic. The darkness seems to vibrate with agitation as they contemplate such a fantastical and *impossible* conclusion. And yet . . . how often did Nicholina speak of mice? Gabrielle claimed she and La Voisin ate hearts to remain eternally young. Others whispered of even blacker arts. Their understanding resolves as mine does.

Somehow, Nicholina has trapped their souls in this darkness with her forever.

Yours too, the prim one sniffs. *You are one of us now.*

No. The darkness seems to press closer as their words ring true, and for a moment, I can't speak. *No, I'm still alive. I'm in a* church, *and Reid—*

Who says we're all dead? the mischievous voice asks. *Perhaps some of us are still alive, somewhere. Perhaps our souls are merely fragmented. Part here, part there. Part everywhere. Yours will shatter soon enough.*

When the darkness shifts once more, heavier now—crushing me beneath its weight—the others sense my mounting hysteria. Their voices turn less amicable, less prim, less mischievous. *We are sorry, Louise le Blanc. It is too late for you. For all of us.*

NO. I lash against the darkness with all my might, repeating the word over and over again like a talisman. I search for a golden pattern. For *anything.* There is only darkness. *No no no no no—*

Only Nicholina's chilling laughter answers.

THE LIGHTHOUSE

Reid

The first light of dawn haloed Father Achille in the sanctuary doors. He waited as I roused the others. No one had slept well. Bags swelled beneath Célie's eyes, though she did her best to pinch color into her pale cheeks. Coco yawned while Beau groaned and cracked his neck. My own ached, despite Lou's fingers kneading the knotted muscle there. I shrugged away from her touch with an apologetic smile, motioning toward the door.

"The villagers won't rouse for another hour or so," Achille said, handing each of us an apple as we filed past. "Remember what I said—don't let them see you. The Chasseurs have an outpost not far from here. You don't want anyone following you to . . . wherever it is you're going."

"Thank you, Father." I tucked the apple into my pocket. It wasn't shiny. It wasn't red. But it was more than he owed us. More than others would've given. "For everything."

He eyed me steadily. "Don't mention it." When I nodded, moving to lead the others through the churchyard, he caught my

arm. "Be careful. *Cauchemars* are heralded as harbingers of doom."
I lifted an incredulous brow, and he added, grudging, "They're
only seen before catastrophic events."

"A mob isn't a catastrophic event."

"Never underestimate the power of a mob." Beau draped his
arm casually across Coco's shoulders as they waited, leaning
against a tree. Mist clung to the edges of their hoods. "People are
capable of unspeakable evil en masse. I've seen it happen."

Father Achille released my arm and stepped away. "As have I.
Take care."

Without another word, he disappeared into the foyer, closing
the door firmly behind him.

A strange sensation twinged my chest as I watched him go. "I
wonder if we'll ever see him again."

"Not likely," Lou said. The thick mist nearly engulfed her
slight frame. Behind her, a white shape slipped through a break
in the haze, and amber eyes flashed. I scowled. The dog had
returned. She hadn't noticed, instead extending her arm down
the hillside. "Shall we?"

The village of Fée Tombe had been named for its sea stacks of
hematite. Black, sparkling, the rocks rose from the sea for miles
on end in the disjointed shapes of faerie wings—some tall and
thin with spiderlike webs of silver, others short and stout with
veins of red. Even the smallest stacks towered over the sea like
great, immortal beings. Waves crashed around the wreckage of
ships below. From our path along the bluff, the broken masts

and booms looked like teeth.

Célie shivered in the icy breeze, wincing as her foot caught and twisted between two rocks. Beau cast her a sympathetic look. "It isn't too late to turn back, you know."

"No." She lifted her chin stubbornly before wrenching her foot free. More rocks skittered from the path and tumbled into the sea below. "We need my carriage."

"Your *father's* carriage," Coco muttered. She kept one hand on the sheer cliff face to her left—the other clenched tightly around *La Petite Larme*—and edged past. Beau followed carefully, picking his way through the uneven terrain as the path narrowed and spiraled upward. At the back of the group, I kept my own hand fisted in the fabric of Lou's cloak.

I needn't have bothered. She moved with the grace of a cat, never slipping, never stumbling. Each step light and nimble.

Color rose high on Célie's cheeks as she tried to maintain our pace. Her breathing grew labored. When she stumbled again, I leaned around Lou and murmured, "Beau was right, Célie. You can wait in the chapel while we deal with the *cauchemar.* We'll return for you before we leave."

"I am *not*," she seethed, skirt and hair whipping wildly in the wind, "waiting in the chapel."

Sweeping past Célie, Lou patted her on the head. "Of course you aren't, kitten." Then she cast a sidelong look down her right shoulder, to where the sea crashed below. "You needn't be worried, anyway. Kittens have nine lives." Her teeth flashed. "Don't they?"

My hand tightened on her cloak, and I tugged her backward, bending low to her ear. "Stop it."

"Stop what, darling?" She craned her neck to look at me. Eyes wide. Innocent. Her lashes fluttered. "I'm *encouraging* her."

"You're terrifying her."

She reached back to trace my lips with her pointer finger. "Perhaps you don't give her enough credit."

With that, she twisted from my grip and strode past Célie without another look. We watched her go with varying degrees of alarm. When she vanished around the bend after Coco and Beau, Célie's shoulders relaxed infinitesimally. She took a deep breath. "She still doesn't like me. I thought she might after . . ."

"Do you like her?"

A second too late, she wrinkled her nose. "Of course not."

I jerked my chin to indicate we should continue. "Then there isn't a problem."

She said nothing for a long moment. "But . . . *why* doesn't she like me?"

"Careful." I moved to steady her when she tripped, but she jerked away, overcompensating and falling hard against the cliff. I fought an eye roll. "She knows we have history. Plus"—I cleared my throat pointedly—"she heard you call her a whore."

Now she whipped around to face me. "She *what*?"

I shrugged and kept walking. "At the Saint Nicolas Day celebrations, she overheard our . . . discussion. I think she took it well, all things considered. She could've murdered us on the spot."

"She . . . she *heard* me . . . ?" Eyes widening with palpable distress, she lifted a hand to her lips. "Oh, no. Oh, no no *no*."

I couldn't resist this time. My eyes rolled to the heavens. "I'm sure she's been called worse."

"She's a *witch*," Célie hissed, hand dropping to clutch her chest. "She could—she could *curse* me, or, or—"

"Or *I* could." The smile that carved my lips felt harder than usual. Like it'd been hewn from granite. Even after Lou had risked life and limb to save her in the catacombs, Célie still considered her an enemy. Of course she did. "Why did you follow us, Célie, if you disdain us so?" At her expression, I shook my head with a self-deprecating laugh. A brittle one. Hers wasn't an unprecedented reaction. If Coco hadn't set the tunnels ablaze, would the denizens of La Mascarade des Crânes have returned for us? Would they have brought fire of their own? Yes, they would've, and I couldn't blame them. I'd have once done the same. "Forget it."

"No, Reid, wait, I—I didn't mean—" Though she didn't touch me, something in her voice made me pause. Made me turn. "Jean Luc told me what happened. He told me . . . about you. I am so sorry."

"I'm not."

Her brows lifted, puckered. "You're not?"

"I'm not."

When I didn't elaborate, her frown deepened. She blinked rapidly. "Oh. Of . . . of course. I—" Blowing air from her cheeks, she planted an abrupt hand on her hip, and her eyes sparked again with that unfamiliar temper. "Well, I'm not either. Sorry, that is.

That you're different. That *I'm* different. I'm not sorry at all."

Though she'd spoken in frankness rather than spite, her words still should've hurt. They didn't. Instead, the nervous energy thrumming just beneath my skin seemed to settle, replaced by peculiar warmth. Perhaps peace. Perhaps . . . closure? She had Jean Luc now, and I had Lou. Everything between us had changed. And that—that was okay. That was *good*.

When I smiled this time, it was genuine. "We're friends, Célie. We'll always be friends."

"Well then." She sniffed, straightening and fighting her own smile. "As your *friend*, it is my duty to inform you that your hair is in dire need of a cut and that your coat is missing two buttons. Also, you have a hickey on your throat." When my hand shot upward to the tender skin near my pulse, she laughed and strode around me, pert nose in the air. "You should cover it for propriety's sake."

There she was.

Chuckling, I fell into step beside her. It felt nice. Familiar. After another moment of comfortable silence, she asked, "What will we do after we warn the *cauchemar*?"

The peace I'd felt fractured, as did my smile. "We journey to the Chateau."

Her hand fluttered to her collar once more. A nervous habit. A telling one. "And—and then what? Just how do we plan to defeat Morgane?"

"Watch where you're going." I nodded to a dip in the path. Sure enough, she stumbled slightly. I didn't reach for her this time, and she caught herself without my help. "Lou wants to burn the castle to the ground." The dead weight returned to my chest. To my voice. "And everyone in it."

"How will she do that?"

I shrugged. "How does a witch do anything?"

"How does it work, then? The . . . magic?" Her expression took on a shyer quality, her chin ducking quickly to her chest. She turned to face forward once more. "I've always been curious."

"You have?"

"Oh, don't play coy, Reid. I know you were curious too." She paused delicately. "Before."

Before. Such a simple word. I kept my gaze impassive. "It's a give and take. For Lou to raze the Chateau, she'll have to destroy something of equal value to herself."

Célie's voice held wonder. "And what might that be?"

I don't know. The admission chafed. Lou had provided no details. No strategy. When we'd pressed her, she'd simply smiled and asked, "Are you afraid?" Beau had responded immediately with a resounding *yes*. I'd privately agreed. The entire plan—or lack thereof—made me uneasy.

Like God had plucked him from my thoughts, my brother's shout rent the air. Célie and I looked up in unison to see part of the cliff give way. Rocks rained down upon us, striking first my shoulders, my arms, then my head. Sharp pain exploded, and stars burst in my vision. Reacting instinctively, I thrust Célie out of harm's way, and Beau—he—

Horror unfurled in my gut like a deadly snake.

As if in slow motion, I watched as he lost his footing, as he flailed wildly through the air, as he tried and failed to find purchase among the falling rocks. There was nothing I could do. No way I could help. Lunging forward anyway, I gauged the distance between us, desperate to catch some part of him before he plunged to the sea—

Coco's hand shot through the rockfall and seized his wrist.

With another shout, Beau swung in her grip like a pendulum. He thrust his free hand upward to grip the edge of the rock, and together, the two struggled to drag him back onto the path. I raced ahead to help, my heart pounding a deafening beat. Adrenaline—complete, unadulterated *fear*—coursed through my system, lengthening my stride and shortening my breath. By the time I reached them, however, they lay sprawled in a tangled heap. Their chests rose and fell haphazardly as they too tried to catch their breath. Above us, Lou stood at the top of the bluff. She gazed down with a hint of a smile. Just the slightest curve of her lips. The white dog growled and disappeared behind her. "You should really be more careful," she said softly before turning away.

Beau glared at her in disbelief but didn't respond. Sitting up, he wiped a shaky hand across his brow and glanced at his arm. His mouth twisted in an ugly slash. "Goddamn it. I tore my *fucking* sleeve."

I shook my head, cursing bitterly under my breath. His *sleeve*. He'd nearly plunged to his death, and all he cared about was his *fucking sleeve*. With a convulsive, full-body shudder, I opened my mouth to tell him just what he could do with said sleeve, but an odd choking noise escaped Coco. I stared at her in alarm—then incredulity.

She wasn't choking at all.

She was *laughing*.

Without a word—her shoulders still shaking—she reached out to tear the fabric of his opposite sleeve. His mouth fell open in outrage as he tried to pull away. "*Excuse* you. My mother bought me this shirt!"

"Now you match." She clutched his arms and laughed harder. "Your mother will approve when she sees you. *If* she ever sees you again, that is. You did almost die." She slapped his chest as if the two had shared a hilarious joke. "You almost *died*."

"Yes." Beau searched her face warily. "You mentioned that."

"I can mend your shirt, if you'd like," Célie offered. "I've a needle and thread in my bag—" But she broke off when Coco continued to laugh wildly. When that laughter deepened into something darker. Crazed. Beau pulled her into his arms without hesitation. Her shoulders shook now for an entirely different reason, and she buried her face in the crook of his neck, sobbing incoherently. One of his arms wrapped around her waist, the other across her back, and he held her tightly, fiercely, murmuring soft words in her ear. Words I couldn't hear. Words I didn't *want* to hear.

I looked away.

This pain wasn't for me. This vulnerability. I felt like an interloper. Watching them together—the way Beau rocked her gently, the way she clutched him for dear life—it brought a lump to my throat. Anyone could see where this was headed. Coco and Beau had danced around each other for months. Just as clear, however, was the inevitable heartbreak. Neither was in a position to start a relationship. They shared too much hurt between them. Too much grief. Jealousy. Spite. Even well-adjusted, the two would've been wrong for each other. Like water and oil.

I glanced up at Lou. We'd been wrong for each other too.

And so, so right.

With a sigh, I started up the path, my footsteps heavy. My thoughts heavier. Célie followed quietly behind. When we reached Lou, I laced her cold fingers through mine, and we turned to face the lighthouse.

Beau and Coco joined us several minutes later. Though her eyes remained swollen and red, she no longer cried. Instead she held her shoulders straight. Proud. Riddled with holes, Beau's shirt still smoked slightly, revealing more skin than prudent in January. They didn't speak of what had transpired, and neither did we.

We studied the lighthouse in silence.

It rose from the earth like a crooked finger beckoning to the sky. A single stone tower. Dirty. Dilapidated. Dark against the dawn. No flames flickered in the basin beneath the slanted roof. "The stable boy said no one lights the torches anymore," Célie said, her voice low. I didn't ask why she whispered. The hair on my neck had lifted inexplicably. The shadows here seemed to collect thicker than natural. "He said they haven't been lit for years."

"The stable boy talks a lot." Beau glanced between us nervously. He kept his arm firm around Coco's waist. "Do we . . . has anyone actually *seen* a *cauchemar*?"

"I told you," Célie said. "It was a great hulking beast of tooth and claw, and it—"

"Darling, no." Beau lifted his free hand with a forced smile. "I meant"—he struggled for the right words for a moment before shrugging—"has anyone *else* seen a *cauchemar*? Preferably someone who didn't run away screaming?"

Coco flashed him a grin. Amused. It seemed out of place on her grim face. With a start, I realized I couldn't remember the last time she'd genuinely smiled. Had she ever? Had I seen it? When she pinched his ribs, he yelped and dropped his arm. "You have a beautiful falsetto yourself," she said. "I'd almost forgotten."

Though she grinned wider at his outrage—his surprise—her bravado felt fragile. Delicate. I didn't want to see it break. Buffeting Beau's shoulder, I said, "Do you remember the witch on Modraniht?"

His mouth flattened. "We do not speak of her."

"*I* remember." Coco shot me an appreciative look. It was there and gone in the blink of an eye. So brief I might've imagined it. "She quite liked your little performance, didn't she?"

"I'm an excellent singer," Beau sniffed.

"You're an excellent *dancer*."

I laughed despite myself. "I remember Beau running away screaming that night."

"What is this?" He looked between us, brows and nose wrinkling in alarm. "What's happening here?"

"She *told* you what a *cauchemar* looks like." Though Coco didn't look at Célie—didn't acknowledge her existence whatsoever—I suspected her admission was the only apology Célie would receive. "Don't be an ass. Listen."

With a long-suffering sigh, Beau inclined his head in Célie's direction. She stood a little straighter. "My apologies, *madame*," he muttered, sounding like a peevish child. "What I *meant* was has anyone ever *fought* a *cauchemar*? Some actual experience might be the difference between surviving this encounter intact and having our heads thrown to sea."

"Is that your fear?" Lou tilted her own head to study him. She'd grown unusually silent since reaching the lighthouse. Unusually still. Until now, her eyes hadn't wavered from the thick shadows at the base of the tower. "Decapitation?"

His frown matched her own. "I—well, it doesn't seem particularly pleasant, no."

"But do you fear it?" she pressed. "Does it haunt your dreams?"

Beau scoffed at the peculiar question, not bothering to hide his exasperation. "Show me someone who doesn't fear decapitation, and I'll show you a liar."

"Why?" Coco's eyes narrowed. "What is it, Lou?"

Lou's gaze returned to the shadows. She stared at them as if trying to decipher something. As if listening to an unspoken language. "A *cauchemar* is a nightmare," she explained in an offhand voice. Still distracted. "It'll appear differently to each of us, assuming the form of our greatest fears."

A beat of horrific silence passed as her words sank in.

Our greatest fears. An uncanny awareness skittered down my spine, as if even now, the creature watched us. Learned us. I didn't even *know* my greatest fear. I'd never given it thought. Never given it voice. It seemed the *cauchemar* would do it for me.

"Have you—have you fought one?" Coco asked Lou. "A *cauchemar*?"

A sly grin crept across Lou's face. Still she studied the shadows. "Once. A long time ago."

"What shape did it take?" Beau demanded.

Her eyes snapped to his. "That's very personal, Beauregard. What shape will it take for *you*?" When she stepped toward him, he took a hasty step back. "Not decapitation. Not drowning either." She cocked her head and stalked closer, circling him now. She didn't grin. Didn't mock. "No, your fear isn't quite so vital, is it? You fear something else. Something peripheral." When she inhaled deeply, her eyes lighting with recognition, I seized her hand and yanked her to my side.

"This isn't the time or place," I said tersely. "We need to focus."

"By all means, Chass"—she waved to the rotten door—"lead the way."

We all stared at it. No one moved.

I peered behind us to the village, to the dozens of pinpricks of light. The sun had risen. The townspeople had gathered. They'd start their trek soon. We had half an hour—maybe a quarter more—before they ascended on us. On the unwitting monster inside.

You should stay out of it, boy. This isn't your fight.

I squared my shoulders.

With a deep breath, I moved to open the door, but Célie—
Célie—beat me to it.

Her hand seemed paler and smaller than usual against the dark wood, but she didn't hesitate. She pushed with all her might—once, twice, three times—until the hinges finally swung open with a shriek. The sound pierced the early morning silence, frightening a pair of seagulls from the rafters. Beau cursed and jumped.

So did Lou.

With one last, deep breath, I stepped inside.

LE CAUCHEMAR

Reid

The lower floors had no windows to let in the early morning sun, so the lighthouse's interior remained dark. The air dank. Stale. Broken glass littered the floor, glinting in the narrow swath of light from the door. A small, frightened creature skittered across it, and the shards tinkled under its tiny paws. I looked closer.

Mirrors. Broken mirrors.

They each reflected different pieces of the circular room—rusted hooks on the walls, coiled ropes atop them, bowed beams overhead. A moldy bed sat in one corner, along with a tarnished iron pot. Remnants of the last keeper who'd lived here. I moved farther into the hodgepodge space, watching as the reflections shifted. Now Célie's wide eye. Now Beau's drawn mouth. Now Coco's tense shoulders. Lou kept a hand on my lower back.

Beyond our footsteps, no other sound penetrated the silence.

Perhaps the creature had already moved on. Perhaps Father Achille had been mistaken.

The door slammed shut behind us.

Both Coco and Célie leapt into Beau with identical shrieks. He somehow missed both of them, however, startling sideways with a vicious curse. The two had no choice but to clutch each other as I stormed past, wrenching the door open once more. "We're fine," I said firmly. "It was the wind."

That same wind caressed my cheeks now, bringing with it a soft bout of laughter.

Was that . . . ?

My heart nearly seized.

Looking around wildly, I pivoted in a full circle. The others imitated my movements with panicked expressions. "What is it?" Coco flicked a knife from her sleeve. "Did you hear something?"

My heartbeat thundered in my ears. "I thought I heard . . ." *The Archbishop*, I almost finished, but the words caught in my throat. I thought I'd heard the *Archbishop*. But that couldn't be. He wasn't here. He never laughed. I didn't *fear* him.

It was La Fôret des Yeux all over again. Instead of trees, the *cauchemar* mocked me, twisting my thoughts into nightmares. It could've hidden in the shadows. Célie had described a hulking beast, but perhaps it could change shape. We knew virtually nothing about this creature or its abilities. Its appetite.

I took a steadying breath.

Cauchemars are notoriously cruel, but this creature hasn't yet attacked.

Cruel or no, it hadn't harmed anyone. That laugh—it was a figment of my imagination. A defense mechanism the *cauchemar* had cultivated to protect itself. To *protect* itself. Not to attack. Not to kill or maim or eat.

Still, its tactics weren't exactly endearing. When the laughter returned a second later, I slipped a blade from my bandolier, whirling toward the source.

It hadn't been the *cauchemar* at all.

It'd been Lou.

I slowly lowered my blade.

Oblivious, she leaned around me to peer into the room, still chuckling softly. "I can smell the fear in this place. It's potent. Alive." When we stared at her, nonplussed, she pointed to the walls. "Can you not scent it? It coats the ropes"—her finger turned to the soft floorboards—"paints the glass. The entire room is slick with it."

"No," I said stiffly, wanting to throttle her. "I don't scent anything."

"Perhaps it's *your* fear I smell, then, not the *cauchemar*." When the wind gusted through once more, her grin faded, and she tilted her head again. Listening. "It does feel different, though. It feels . . ." But she kept the words she would've spoken, trailing into silence instead. Her hand clenched on my back. "I think we should leave."

Surprised by her reaction—yet somehow not—I approached the spiral staircase in the center of the room. The wood had half-rotted. Tentatively, I tested the bottom step with my foot. It dipped beneath my weight. "We will. After we warn the creature. After we ask for its help."

For a short moment, she looked likely to argue. Her lip curled. Her eyes darkened. Just as quickly, however, her expression cleared, and she dipped her chin in a slight nod, brushing past me up the stairs.

We ascended the next two floors in a single-file line. One step at a time. Slow. Cautious. We paused only to inspect the dilapidated rooms beyond, but the *cauchemar*—if here at all—remained hidden.

"What was that?" Beau whipped his head to the door on our right, to the ominous groan behind it. "Did you hear—?" Something creaked overhead, and another gust of wind swept up the staircase. He spun to face Coco. "Was that you?"

Her eyes darted all around us. "Why would I be *moaning*?"

It was a mark of Beau's panic that he didn't respond. Instead, he nearly tripped over Célie as she stooped to collect something from the moldy stair. It gleamed through her fingers in the darkness. A shard of mirror. Straightening, she held it out in front of her like a knife.

A beat of silence passed as we stared at her. "What?" she hissed defensively, face nearly white. "No one gave me a weapon."

To my surprise, Coco responded by bending to retrieve her own shard. She held it poised in her free hand, saying nothing of the knife in her other, and nodded once in Célie's direction. Then she nudged Beau. He looked between them, aghast. "You cannot be serious. We're more likely to wound ourselves than the *cauchemar* with such rubbish."

Rolling my eyes, I pressed a dagger into his palm before picking up my own piece of glass. At Célie's incredulous stare, one corner of my mouth quirked up. "What?" I shrugged and continued upward, not looking back. "It was a good idea."

We crept toward the final floor in silence. When the door below slammed shut again, Beau's whisper quickly followed. "I'm as opposed to airing my dirty laundry as anyone, but perhaps—in light of the circumstances—it might help to . . . discuss our fears?" The step beneath him heaved an ominous groan, and he exhaled sharply. "For example, if one of you could reiterate how you'd never *dream* of ignoring or forgetting me, that would be grand. It's a ridiculous notion, I know, but for the sake of—"

"Quiet," Lou snapped. The staircase ended with a door directly overhead. She tilted her head again, hesitating, before pushing it open and slipping through. I followed, nearly flattening her when I climbed to my feet. She'd stopped abruptly to take in the final floor: an open room without walls to shield us from the elements. Only a handful of beams held the roof in place, and sun spilled in from every direction, banishing the last of the shadows. I breathed a sigh of relief. The *cauchemar* wasn't here. *Nothing* was here save an enormous fire basin. Built into the center of the stone floor, it stood empty. No wood or ashes. Except—

Lou stood perfectly still, the wind whipping her pale hair across her face.

Except it wasn't empty at all.

From the basin, an enormous figure rose.

Cloaked in soiled fabric, it charged toward us with blackened, outstretched hands. I lunged to Lou's side, but she'd already moved, surging forward with lightning quickness. When she lashed out with her blade, clipping the creature's midsection, it

reared backward like a great bear. Though a hood shielded its hair, its face, its *teeth*, it swiped at Lou with one massive paw, and she sailed through the air. I dove after her—catching her wrist before she could slide from the room's edge—as the others attacked, their knives and mirrors glinting in the sunlight. "Stop!" The wind carried away my shout. "Don't hurt it! We're here to *warn* the creature, not—*stop!*"

The *cauchemar* stumbled back a step, hands still raised, but didn't hesitate to knock Coco's glass aside and roar when she slashed its thigh. She danced out of reach before it could wrap its hands around her neck—and then the first terror came.

Though Lou had warned us, nothing could've prepared me for the horrifying jolt of fear. Of *pain*. My vision flashed white, blinding me, and I slipped, crouching down to one knee. From the others' startled cries, they experienced the same.

A black room, blacker chains. Cold against my skin. Wrong. Blood slides from my wrists to the floor in a steady drip. I count each drop. She returns at the top of each hour. Thirty-six hundred seconds. Thirty-six hundred drops. When the door creaks open at drop thirty-five hundred and sixty-two, I choke back a scream. A saw. A handsaw. She lifts it to the candlelight. "Is it in your bones, I wonder? Like theirs?"

I fell to my hands as the faceless woman advanced. Gasping for breath. Shaking my head. Forcing my eyes to see reality instead of the glint of bone: to see Lou, writhing on the floor beside me, to see Coco in the fetal position, Beau flat on his back, Célie wide-eyed and trembling.

I threw my glass shard, and it stuck, point-first, in the

creature's shoulder. Lurching to my feet, I tore another knife from my bandolier. The *cauchemar* stood its ground. A rumbling noise built in its chest, but I ignored the growl and advanced. The others struggled to join me in vain. Another wave of fear crippled us before we could reach the beast.

Alone. I'm alone. Where is he? Where is he where is he where is he—

I gritted my teeth and continued, disoriented, stumbling against the flickering white like a drunkard.

"Speak." A high, imperious voice. Her voice. "Or I shall pluck out your brother's eyes. It is a fitting punishment, yes? He rendered you mute. I shall render him blind." But I cannot speak. Drugged. The drug. It congeals in my system. The manacle at my throat chokes me. Moan. I try to moan, but she only laughs. His screams fill the air. His pleas.

Oh my God.

This wasn't right. I didn't fear torture. I wasn't *mute*—

More images flashed. Broken pieces, fragmented horror. A swollen jaw. Irrepressible hunger. Empty syringes, the burning pain of infection. A chilling laugh and stale bread. And through it all, an acute, unbearable panic.

Where is he where is he where is he where is he

Wolves howling.

Eucalyptus.

Moonbeam hair.

Moonbeam hair.

I blinked rapidly, my vision clearing with Lou's. With a shrill battle cry, she rushed forward, knife raised. I caught her around the waist, spinning her away from the *cauchemar*. It still waved its hands frenetically, as if—as if trying to tell me something. My stomach churned violently. "Hold. I think—I think it's—"

In a clumsy, disjointed movement, the *cauchemar* pulled back its hood.

I stared at it.

Contrary to Célie's description, the *cauchemar* didn't have shadow-cloaked skin or sharp teeth. Its hair was matted, yes, but its swollen eyes inspired more fear than its namesake. Its broken jaw evoked more rage. My vision tunneled to its lacerated thigh, to the angry red streaks of disease on its russet skin. To the blood crusting its tattered pants. This *cauchemar* had been beaten. Badly.

It also wasn't a *cauchemar* at all.

It was Thierry St. Martin.

Lou twisted from my grasp and sprinted toward him once more. Incredulous, I caught her wrist. "Lou, stop. *Stop*. This is—"

"Let me go," she seethed, still struggling viciously. Frantic. *Distraught*. "Let me kill it—"

Anger flared hot and sudden. Tightening my grip, I dragged her back to my side and kept her there. "Stand down. I won't ask again. This is Thierry. Remember? Thierry St. Martin."

At his name, Thierry sagged with relief against the stone basin. I felt his presence in my mind—saw a picture of my own face—before he slurred a single word.

Reeeiddd.

I resisted the urge to go to him, to sling an arm around his shoulders for support. He looked likely to collapse. Lowering my voice, trying to soothe, I murmured, "I'm here. Everything will be all right. Lou recognizes you now. Isn't that right, Lou?"

She finally, *finally* stopped struggling, and I relinquished my hold on her. "Yes." Voice soft, she looked between Thierry and me for a long moment. I stood perfectly still, wary of the odd gleam in her eyes—savage and bright, like that of a cornered animal. "Yes, I recognize him."

Then she turned and fled.

Barreling into the others, knocking them aside, Lou didn't slow as she reached the door. Célie pinwheeled backward on impact, but Coco caught her elbow before she free-fell down the stairs. Swearing viciously in response, Beau hurled insults after Lou, but she didn't stop. The shadows closed around her as she raced out of sight.

Thierry lifted a weak hand. Two of his fingers appeared broken. Voice hitched with urgency, slow with concentration, he said, *Caaatch . . . her.*

I didn't stop to think. To hesitate. To consider the resolve hardening in my chest. This sensation—this fiery sense of justice, of righteousness—it felt familiar. Unsettlingly so.

She darted down the stairs below me with unnatural swiftness, already near the ground floor. In seconds, she'd be out the door. "Lou!" My shout reverberated with unexpected fury. I didn't understand why my hands shook or my teeth clenched. I didn't understand *why* I needed to catch her. But I did. I needed to catch her like I needed to breathe. Beau had been right—something was wrong here. Terribly, terribly wrong. It went beyond her magic. It went beyond Ansel's death. Beyond mourning.

Like fruit left in the sun to rot, Lou had split open, and something foul had grown inside.

Perhaps it'd happened during La Mascarade des Crânes. Perhaps before, perhaps after. It didn't matter. It *had* happened, and though my instincts had tried to warn me, I'd ignored them. Now they propelled my feet forward faster. Faster still. They told me if Lou reached the door—if she disappeared into the cliffs beyond—I'd never see her again. That could not happen. If I could just catch her, *talk* to her, I could make things right. I could make *her* right. It didn't make any sense, but there it was. This chase had suddenly become the most important of my life. And I wouldn't ignore my instincts any longer.

When she cleared the last stair, I took a deep breath.

Then I gripped the spiral railing and vaulted over it.

Dank air roared in my ears as I plunged to the ground. Eyes widening over her shoulder, Lou bolted for the door. "Fu—" Her expletive ended in a shriek as I landed on top of her. Twisting onto her back, she clawed at my face, my eyes, but I seized her wrists and pinned them to the floor. When she continued to buck and thrash, I straddled her waist, broken glass tearing into my knees as we grappled. My weight kept her restrained, however. Immobilized. She smashed her head into my jaw instead. Grinding my teeth, I pushed my forehead against hers. Hard. "Stop it," I snarled, flattening myself against her. The others descended the stairs in a cacophony of shouts. "What is *wrong* with you? Why are you running?"

"The *cauchemar*." She struggled harder, panting feverishly. "It—it transformed into—into Thierry—" But the lie crumbled in her mouth as Thierry limped forward. In the shards of mirrors, his very real hatred refracted from every angle. His very real injuries. Coco followed, dropping to the floor beside us. She thrust her bloody forearm to the air above Lou's mouth, the unspoken threat clear. "Don't make me do it, Lou."

Lou's chest rose and fell rapidly beneath mine. Sensing the battle lost, she bared her teeth in a saccharine smile. "Is this how you treat a friend, Cosette? A sister?"

"Why did you run?" Coco repeated. No warmth lingered in her expression as she gazed at her friend. Her sister. Instead, Coco's eyes glittered with frigid, impenetrable cold. The two could've been perfect strangers. No—enemies. "Why did you attack him?"

Lou sneered. "We all attacked him."

"Not after we'd seen his face."

"He startled me. Look at the state of him—"

At this, Thierry's hands curled into fists. Beau winced at his purple fingers. "Perhaps we should return to the chapel, procure supplies," he suggested. "You need medical attention—"

Herrrr, Thierry interrupted, the word strained, breathless inside our minds.

Célie gasped at the mental intrusion, her eyes flicking wildly between Thierry and me.

"*Her*, who?" I asked. "What happened to you?" My voice echoed too loud in the dilapidated room, my flushed cheeks and corded neck reflecting back at me in the broken mirrors. I looked unbalanced. Out of control. "Where have you been?"

But it seemed he couldn't answer. Pictures flickered wildly again, each more incoherent than the last. When his black gaze fixed pointedly on Lou, my stomach plummeted. My hands turned to ice. Sick with trepidation, with regret, I spoke through gritted teeth. "Tell me, Thierry. Please."

He moaned and slumped against the balustrade. *Her.*

Célie shook her head as if trying to dislodge an irksome fly. She couldn't shake his voice from her mind, however. Couldn't impede his magic. Dazed, she stammered, "But—but what does Louise have to do with"—she gaped at his various injuries before hastily looking away—"w-with your misfortunes?"

"He can't answer you. Not yet." Coco's fierce gaze never wavered from Lou. "He's exhausted and injured, and the magic required for speech is too much."

"Was he—do you think he was tortured?"

"Yes."

"But *why?*" Célie asked, clearly horrified. "By whom?"

Coco's eyes narrowed. "He answered the last for us."

As one, we all looked to Lou, but her attention remained fixed on Coco. They studied each other for what felt like an eternity— neither blinking, neither revealing a flicker of emotion—before a slow, uncanny grin split Lou's face. "Two princesses fair, one gold and one red," she sang, her voice familiar yet not. "They slipped into darkness. Now the gold one is dead."

A chill snaked down my spine at the odd words. At her smile.

And her eyes—something shifted in them as she stared back at us. Something . . . sinister. They flickered almost silver, like—

Like—

My mind viciously rejected the possibility.

Lou cackled.

Recoiling, Coco exhaled a breathless curse. "No." She repeated the word like a mantra, her hand flying to her collar, tearing her mother's necklace from her throat. "No, no, no, no, *no*—" When she slid the locket along her bloody forearm, it glowed briefly scarlet before clicking open. She thrust it toward me. "Lift her up. Lift her up *now*."

I hastened to comply, but Lou struck with the speed of an adder, her teeth sinking deep into the soft flesh of my cheek. I reared backward with a roar. Lifting her knee with alarming force, she connected with my groin. I folded instantly at the spike of white-hot pain. Stars dotted my vision, and waves of nausea wracked my frame. Vaguely, I heard Lou spring to her feet. But I couldn't move. Couldn't *breathe*.

Célie nudged my ribs with her boot. "Get up," she said, voice low and panicked. Glass crunched and bodies thudded somewhere beyond me. She kicked my side again. "She's getting away. Get *up*!"

Groaning, I forced myself to my feet. Though my entire lower half ached, I leapt to join Beau and Thierry near the door, where they struggled to contain Lou. She hissed and spat as Coco tried to force blood to her lips. With one man holding her on each side, I stepped behind, wrapping an arm around her waist and seizing her hair in my fist. I forced her head backward. The movement bared her face to Coco, who acted quickly, smearing blood across Lou's mouth.

Lou screamed and seized instantly. Blisters formed where the blood touched her lips.

"What is it?" I asked wildly. My stomach rioted with fear, with regret, with treacherous, treasonous *resolve*. I did not let go. "What've you done?"

"I thought your blood would just *subdue* her—" Beau's frantic voice echoed my own. He watched in horror as Lou's back bowed, as she finally slumped in our arms.

Coco stepped back, eyes blazing with satisfaction. "The blood of an enemy poisons."

The blood of an enemy poisons.

Nonsensical words. Ludicrous ones. And yet . . .

Realization began to take shape in my gut, even as my mind still protested.

Beau shook Lou with rising hysteria, his breath labored. His face red. "What the *fuck* does that mean?" He shook her harder. "Is she—have we just—?" But Coco only grasped Lou's chin in answer, forcing open one fluttering eyelid. *She isn't dead.* I repeated the words, trying to calm the thunderous beat of my heart. To ignore my mounting apprehension. *She isn't dead. She isn't dead. She isn't dead. She's just—*

"You said something was clearly wrong with her." Coco retrieved her locket from where it'd fallen to the ground. Lou twitched in response. "You said it went beyond grief."

"That doesn't mean we *poison* her," Beau said incredulously. "She's still *Lou*. She's still my *sister.*"

"No." Coco shook her head with vehemence. "She isn't."

Lifting the mirror in the locket to Lou, she revealed the stark truth at last: I held long black hair in my hand, not white. The waist I clasped wasn't right either. Though I couldn't feel her bones beneath my fingers, I could see each rib in her reflection. Her skin appeared sickly. Alabaster pale. Not the smooth and freckled gold I loved. And scarred—so very scarred.

My pulse slowed to a dull, steady rhythm as I took in the truth. A poison all its own. I felt its cold touch in my chest, felt it crystallize around my heart. When it crept down my spine, my legs—debilitating me—my knees gave out, and I crumpled, dragging Lou's body down with me. I stared at her slack face in my lap. Those dark circles beneath her eyes had deepened since yesterday. Her cheeks had grown sharper. She'd been fighting an altogether different poison. A disease.

Nicholina le Clair.

Fire burst through the ice like lava, melting everything in its path. My hands shook. My chest heaved. "Get her out," I snarled.

NO ROSE WITHOUT A THORN

Reid

Coco crossed to the door swiftly in answer, throwing it open, allowing sun to stream into the dilapidated room. But the sun—it did little to banish the shadows now. Instead, it refracted rainbows of light across broken mirrors, and those broken mirrors . . . they didn't work right either. They reflected Lou back to me.

This wasn't Lou.

"Get her out," I repeated, engulfing the would-be Lou in my arms. My shoulders—my back—rounded to shield her from her own reflection. She didn't stir at the contact. Beneath my fingers, her pulse felt thready and weak. Her skin even colder than usual. "Get her out *now*."

"We need to move." Coco hurried back to my side, looping an arm under mine. She tried to hoist me to my feet as angry voices echoed toward us from the cliffs beyond. The villagers. The mob. "They'll be here any moment." To Thierry, she added, "Is there a back entrance?"

He nodded with supreme effort. He still couldn't speak,

however, instead pointing to the bed. Beau rushed to shift it. Below, a heap of ropes and rusted pots hid a trapdoor. Kicking them aside, he struggled to lift the iron handle. "Thank God you have a carriage, Célie."

"I don't—well, actually, I"—she wrung her hands frantically before finishing in a rush—"the wheel shaft snapped on the rocks."

Beau whipped around to stare at her. "It *what?*"

"The whole mechanism is completely busted. We can't use it."

"You said you had a carriage!" Beau heaved at the door with renewed purpose. "That implies a *functional* one."

Célie stamped her foot, her eyes wide on the door. "Yes, well, no one would have let me come along otherwise!"

"Explain." Ignoring them both, I spoke through numb lips. My voice shook as I looked up at Coco. "Please."

She knelt beside us, face softening infinitesimally as she reached out to brush Lou's forehead. "*La Petite Larme* reflects the truth. It cannot lie."

"How?"

"I told you. Its mirror came from a drop of L'Eau Mélancolique. The waters have magical properties. Sometimes they heal, sometimes they harm." She glanced back at the open door, craning her neck to see beyond it. The sun had fully risen now. We'd run out of time. "But they always tell the truth."

I shook my head in a slow, disoriented movement, even as the villagers' voices grew louder. They'd round the bend at any second. "No. I mean how is *she*—how is she inside of—" But I couldn't finish the question. My throat closed up around the words. I dropped my gaze back to Lou. To the blisters on her lips. Self-loathing churned in my stomach. I hadn't noticed. How could I not have *noticed*?

"There's a spell in my aunt's grimoire," Coco explained quickly. Individual voices could be heard now. Individual words. She renewed her efforts to pull me to my feet. "A spell of possession. Old magic." *Possession.* I closed my eyes as Coco's voice darkened. "My aunt betrayed us."

"But *why*? We promised her the Chateau—"

"Perhaps Morgane did too."

"A little help here?" Beau panted. My eyes snapped open as Célie darted to join him.

"But it makes no *sense*," I insisted, voice hardening. "Why would she ally with the witch who's abused your coven at every turn?"

Hinges shrieked as Beau and Célie finally managed to open the trapdoor. The voices outside grew louder in response. Purposeful. Agitated. When neither Coco nor I moved, Beau waved animatedly toward the earthen tunnel. "Shall we?"

Coco hesitated only a second more before nodding. Célie hesitated longer.

"Are we sure this is safe?" She peered into the dark hole with palpable panic. Twin circles of white surrounded her irises. "The last time—"

But Coco caught her elbow as she passed, and the two vanished into the tunnel together. Beau abandoned the trapdoor—it fell open fully with a thunderous *crack* of wood on wood—to help Thierry navigate the room. The latter's entire chest heaved with each breath. Each step. His body was failing. That much was clear. After passing him to Coco, Beau finally turned to me. "Time to go."

"But Lou—"

"Will die if we stay here. The villagers are going to raze this place to the ground." He extended a hand. "Come on, little brother. We can't help her if we're dead."

He had a point. I gathered Lou in my arms and followed.

Beau slipped in behind us, clumsily maneuvering an arm through the gap between door and floor to wrench the bed back in place. He cursed, low and vicious, when the door slammed shut on his fingers. Footsteps thundered overhead not a second later. We didn't linger, racing after the others without another word.

The tunnel let out about a mile down the cliff's face, where a rocky path led to the beach. Black sand glittered in the early morning light, and the rocks of Fée Tombe leered down at us, macabre and unnatural. Like sentient beings. I shuddered and laid Lou's body across the sand, careful to remain in the shadow of the cliffs. If any villager thought to glance below for their *cauchemar*, they wouldn't see us here. Wouldn't descend with their torches and pitchforks.

I whirled to face Coco, who'd extracted a vial of honey from her pack. She fed it to Thierry carefully before lifting her forearm to his lips. He swallowed once, twice, and the contusions on his face immediately began to fade. With a shuddering sigh, he collapsed back against the rocks. Lost consciousness within seconds.

But he would be fine. He would heal.

Lou would too.

"Fix her." My word brooked no argument. "You have to fix her."

Coco glanced at Lou before bending to rifle in her pack, her face a mask of calm. Her eyes remained tight, however. Her jaw taut. "There is no *fixing* her. She's possessed, Reid. Nicholina has—"

"So cast Nicholina out!" I roared, my own mask exploding in a wave of fury. Of helplessness. When Coco jerked upright, glaring at me in silent rebuke, I clenched my head in my hands. Fisted my hair, pulled it, tore it, *anything* to combat the fierce ache in my chest. Shame colored my cheeks. "I'm sorry. I didn't mean it. I'm sorry. Just—please. Cast Nicholina out. Please."

"It isn't that simple."

"Yes, it is." Desperation laced my voice now. I dropped my hands, pivoted sharply on my heel. Paced. Back and forth. One, two, three, four, five, six. One, two, three, four, five, six. Faster and faster, my footsteps carved a jagged path in the sand. "In the book of Mark, Jesus cast demons into a herd of six thousand pigs—"

"This isn't the Bible, Nicholina isn't a demon, and I'm not the son of *fucking* God." She splayed her hands, facade cracking just slightly, and gestured to the sand and waves around us. "Do you see any pigs?"

I spoke through gritted teeth. "I'm *saying* there's a way to remove her. We just have to find it."

"And what happened to the possessed after Jesus cleansed them?"

"Don't be stupid. They were *healed*."

"Were they?" Her eyes flashed, and she tore a vial of blood from her pack. "The human body isn't meant to house more than one soul, Reid."

I spun to face her, my own hands flying upward. "What are you saying?"

"I'm saying this doesn't end the way we want it to end," she snapped. "I'm saying even if we *miraculously* manage to evict Nicholina, Lou won't be the same. To have touched another soul so intimately—not just in a sonnet or some other bullshit symbolic way, but to have actually *touched* another soul, to have shared the same *body*—I don't know if Lou's will survive intact."

"You mean—her soul could be—"

"Fragmented. Yes." She marched forward, dropping to her knees beside Lou with more force than necessary. Black sand sprayed in Lou's pale hair. I mirrored her movements on Lou's other side, sweeping the sand away. "Part of it might go with Nicholina. *All* of it might go with Nicholina. Or"—she uncorked the vial, and the acrid stench of blood magic assaulted my senses— "Lou could already be gone. She was in a bad way. Nicholina wouldn't have been able to possess her otherwise. Her spirit was weak. Broken. If we force Nicholina out, Lou might . . ." She took a ragged breath. "She might be an empty shell."

"You don't know that," I said fiercely.

"You're being willfully ignorant."

"I'm being *hopeful*."

"You think I don't *want* to believe Lou will be okay?" She shook her head in disgust. No—in pity. She pitied me. My teeth clenched until they ached. "That Nicholina will go easily, that Lou will wake up and smirk and ask for fucking sticky buns? You think I don't *want* to pretend the past three months never happened? The past three *years*?" Her voice broke on the last, her facade finally splintering, but she didn't cower. She didn't look away. Even as fresh tears slipped down her cheeks, as every emotion shone clear in her eyes. Every unspoken fear. Her voice flattened as she continued. "You're asking me to hope, Reid, but I can't. I won't. I've hoped too much and too long. Now I'm sick with it. And for what? My mother left, Ansel died, my aunt betrayed me. The person I love most in this world has been *possessed*." She scoffed through her tears, through the smoke that curled from the sand, and lifted the vial to Lou's lips. "Why should I hope?"

I seized her wrist to still the movement. Forced her to meet my eyes. "Because she's the person you love most in this world."

She stared at me over our hands. Her fingers tightened around the vial. "Let me go."

"What are you doing?"

"*Healing* her." She snatched her wrist back, wiping furiously at her tears. "Because apparently, I can't heal myself. I'm sick with hope, but I can't make it go away. It's still here, even now. Poisoning me." When she looked back at Lou, one of her tears dripped from her cheek to Lou's throat. To Lou's scar. Together, we watched—silent and anxious—as the tear sizzled against her skin, transforming the silver gash into something else entirely.

Into a vine of thorns and roses.

Delicate, intricate—still silver and raised on her skin—the scar looked less a disfigurement now. More a masterpiece.

And it was.

Behind us, Célie gasped. A small, wondrous sound. "*Il n'y a pas de roses sans épines.*"

There is no rose without a thorn.

Coco said nothing, staring at the scar with a frightfully blank expression. I hardly dared breathe. One blink. Two. When her eyes opened on the third, resolve had crystallized sharp and bright within them. I nearly wept. "My blood poisoned Lou because Nicholina has assumed control," she said. "I can't use it to heal her." She lifted the vial once more. "We'll use my aunt's blood instead. It won't evict Nicholina, but it'll counteract the effects of mine. It's powerful—more powerful than anything on this earth. It's also rare. I nicked it from her tent at the blood camp." She grinned then. A truly terrifying grin. "I'm sure she won't mind."

Parting Lou's lips, she tipped the entire vial between them. Honey followed.

Color immediately returned to Lou's cheeks, and her breathing deepened. The blisters on her mouth vanished. The transformed scar, however, remained. If I looked too close, it seemed to . . . ripple in the breeze. Unconsciously, I lifted a hand to touch it, but

Beau cleared his throat, startling me. He'd moved closer than I'd realized.

I dropped my hand.

"What happens when she wakes up?" he asked.

Coco's grin faded. "We exorcise Nicholina."

"How?"

Silence reigned in answer. Waves lapped the black sand. A lone gull cried overhead. At last, Célie offered a tentative, "You said . . . you said my father's locket—"

"My *mother's* locket," Coco corrected her.

"Of course." Célie nodded in haste, trying her best not to look horribly, terribly out of her depth. "Y-You said the magic of your mother's locket stems from L'Eau Mélancolique. It showed us Nicholina's true reflection."

"And?"

"You said the waters can heal."

"I also said the waters can harm. They were created from the tears of a madwoman." Coco stood, tucking the empty vials back into her pack. I remained beside Lou, tracking the rise and fall of her chest. Her eyelids began to twitch. "They're volatile. Temperamental. They're just as likely to kill Lou as to restore her. We can't risk it."

Between one breath and another, an idea sparked. My gaze darted to Célie. The empty sheath on my bandolier—right above my heart—weighed heavier than usual. I hadn't felt its absence since Modraniht. "We need a Balisarda, Célie." I scrambled to my feet. Sand flew in every direction as I rushed toward her. "Jean

Luc—you can contact him, right?" She murmured something unintelligible in response, her gaze dropping to her boot with keen interest. "If you ask, he'll bring you his Balisarda, and we can—"

"And we can what?" Beau asked, perplexed. Célie stooped to pick up a whitewashed shell, hiding her face altogether. "*Cut* Nicholina out of her?"

"We'd just need to break her skin with the blade," I said, thinking rapidly. Yes. Yes, this could work. I plucked the seashell from Célie's hand and discarded it. She watched it go with a forlorn expression, still refusing to look at me. "A Balisarda dispels enchantments. It would exorcise Nicholina—"

Beau lifted a casual, mocking hand. "Just how deep would we need to cut, brother? Would it be a simple slice down her arm, or would a spear through her heart suffice?"

I shot him a glare before gripping Célie's freed hands. "Write to him, Célie." Then, in another burst of inspiration, I spun toward Coco. "You could magic him the letter, like you did with your aunt in the Hollow."

"Magic a letter into Chasseur Tower?" Coco rolled her eyes. "They'd lash him to a stake by morning."

Célie pulled her hands from mine. Gentle at first, then firm. She reluctantly met my eyes. "It matters not. He will not come."

"Don't be ridiculous. He's mad about you—"

"No, Reid," she insisted. "The conclave has assembled in Cesarine to elect a new Archbishop. It's why he didn't follow me in the first place. His presence has been requested by the priests, by the *king.* He cannot come here, and I cannot ask him—not for this. Not for Lou. I am sorry."

I stared at her for a beat.

Not for this. Not for Lou. The imperiousness in her voice punctured my hope. My foolish optimism. Had she just . . . dismissed us? As if *this* weren't equally important as the Church's conclave? As if this wouldn't decide the fate of the kingdom in a more tangible way? Lou might not have been the only player on the board, but she was certainly the most critical. Only a fool wouldn't recognize that.

Jean Luc wasn't a fool. Neither was Célie.

When I next spoke, ice coated my voice. My veins. "Lou risked everything for you."

She blinked in surprise at my tone. Her mouth opened and closed like a fish. "I— Reid, of course I am very grateful for that! I would never presume to—to deny her heroism or involvement in my rescue, but she—" Cheeks coloring, she leaned closer, as if speaking a dirty word. "Reid, she is a *witch*. If there were even a *possibility* of Jean abandoning his responsibilities to save her—of forsaking his oath as a Chasseur—of course I would ask, but—"

"But we're a witch," Nicholina cackled gleefully, sitting upright in the sand, "so you will not risk the question. Pity. Such a pretty, pretty pity, you are. Such a pretty, pretty porcelain doll."

I jerked her hands behind her back, holding her wrists captive. Beau joined me, poised to help if she struggled. But she didn't. She merely gazed serenely up at Coco, who crouched in front of her. "*Bonjour, notre princesse rouge.* I must say you look terrible."

"You look better than I've ever seen you."

"Ah, we know." Grinning with Lou's lips and Lou's teeth, she gazed down at herself. "This skin suits us."

Flames erupted in my chest at her words. *This skin.* "She isn't a suit," I snarled, tightening my hold on her wrists until they threatened to snap. I knew I shouldn't. I couldn't help it. I wanted to hurt her, to *force* her out violently if necessary. When she laughed in response—tipping her head back with relish, leaning fully into my chest—I felt my hands twist. Another second, and her bones would shatter. Just one more second. Just *one.*

She moaned in pleasure.

"Yes, Reid. *Yes.*" Tongue flicking out to lick her teeth, she dropped her head to my shoulder. "Hurt me. Hurt this body. This suit. We'll enjoy it, yes. We'll savor each bruise."

I recoiled instantly, hands shaking. Blood roared in my ears. Beau caught her wrists between heartbeats. His mouth firmed when she turned to nuzzle his chest. "Mmm. A *prince.* I tasted your cousin once."

Coco gripped her chin, forcing her to meet her eyes. "Kink is consensual, Nicholina. We're going to remove you one way or another. It won't be kinky. It won't be consensual. But it will hurt."

"Oooh, tell me, with the captain's holy stick? I wonder how he'll help you? Will he prick, prick, prick—"

"There shall be no pricking," Beau interrupted. "Holy sticks or otherwise. No unnecessary force either," he added, glancing pointedly between Coco and me. "Nicholina might be, well, *Nicholina,* but she's hiding behind Lou. Who knows what Lou can see and hear? What she can feel?"

Nicholina laughed again. "I said she's dead, she's dead I said. The gold one is gone. I'm here instead."

I ignored her, nodding with a deep breath. Lou wasn't dead. She *wasn't*. Suppressing a red haze of anger, I took her wrists back from Beau. Though physically repulsed—at her, at *myself*—I rubbed the angry skin there with my thumbs. This was Lou. This was Nicholina. They couldn't be the same person, yet somehow, now, they were.

A golden pattern twined around our hands. Slowly, carefully, I fed it until the red tint in my vision faded. As my anger dissipated, so too did the marks on her wrists. With it, another burst of inspiration struck. I couldn't heal her with a Balisarda, but perhaps I *could* heal her with magic. Closing my eyes, breathless with hope, I cast my net of gold in search of an answer. A cure, a restorative. Anything to purge Nicholina's presence. The patterns coiled and undulated in response, but none connected. They simply drifted outward into nothing. Frustrated, I pulled at each one to examine it, to determine its asking price, but I sensed nothing from them. No gain. No give. These patterns weren't functional. When I plucked one on a whim, snapping my fingers, it fell limp in my hand instead of dispersing.

Concentrating harder, I tried again. Nothing.

Though I hadn't routinely practiced magic, I hadn't expected my patterns to simply . . . wilt. *Could* they wilt? No. No, Nicholina must've been blocking me somehow. As often as I'd tried to dispose of my magic, I knew it *couldn't* go away so easily. Perhaps my intent had been wrong.

I focused anew. *Help me exorcise Lou.*

Nothing.

Help me force Nicholina out of Lou.

The patterns floated aimlessly.

Help me heal Lou. Help me hurt Nicholina. Help me make her like before.

The patterns continued to wander. A vessel nearly burst in my forehead now. I lost track of the others' conversation entirely. *Please.* Please. *Help me save her.*

At the last request, the patterns thrummed, growing brighter and collecting into a single cord. Those familiar voices whispered in my ear—*save her, save her, save her*—as I followed the pattern to a face.

To . . . to Morgane's face.

My entire body recoiled in realization, in horror, and my eyes snapped open. Not that. *Anything* but that. The cost would be too great, no matter the outcome.

Still hovering around Nicholina, the others blinked at me. "Er . . ." Beau's brows dipped. "Are you constipated, brother?"

I cast the pattern from my mind. I couldn't act on it. I *wouldn't*. "My magic won't work."

"If you'd been listening"—he jerked his head to Coco—"she just said the magic of one witch can't undo another. It has to be a different kind. Something old. Something powerful."

"What did she have in mind?"

"What do *I* have in mind, actually." Sniffing, he straightened the lace cuff of his sleeve. A ridiculous display. It still dangled from his shoulder. "You're all quite clearly forgetting we have a god at our disposal."

"Ah, *yes*. King of the forest, the horned god." Nicholina rocked back and forth, still laughing maniacally. "Out of all his names, he chose *Claud*."

Coco ignored her, lips pursing in deep thought. "I *could* magic him a letter, but if he remains in the tunnels, it'll burn before he sees it."

Beau looked at her as if she were stupid. "He is a *god*."

My realization dawned at the same moment hers did. "We pray to him," I breathed.

"No." Beau shook his head in distaste. "*You* pray to him. He likes you better than me."

"Everyone likes me better than you."

"Coco doesn't."

"I don't like either of you," she said irritably. "I also don't pray."

"Why not?" I asked.

"Just do it, Reid."

They all looked to me then: Beau petulant, Coco impatient, Célie apprehensive. Heat crept up my throat at the judgment in her eyes, though she tried to hide it. To her credit, she didn't speak. Didn't express any objection, any disapproval. Nicholina had no problem doing it for her. Her voice floated up on a croon. "Pray, huntsman. Pray to the old gods. Will your god mind, I wonder? Will he open the ground and cast you under?"

I cleared the uncertainty from my throat. "God doesn't deny the existence of other deities. He—He just commands us to worship no other gods before Him." When she tilted her head back, a smile nearly cleaving her face in two, I focused my attention on the waves. The horizon. I had a job to do. Unlike Coco, I *did* know how to pray. I'd done it every day—multiple times per day—for most of my life. Praying to Deveraux would be no different.

Except it was. Deveraux wasn't a nameless, faceless divinity. He was a fiddler, for Christ's sake.

I winced at the apt profanity.

Delicate fingers touched my elbow. Célie's earnest face looked up at me. She swallowed, clearly torn, before whispering, "Perhaps you could . . . start as you would the Lord's Prayer."

I was going to Hell. Still, I nodded, closing my eyes and trying to disassociate. To compartmentalize.

Our Father who art in . . . Cesarine, hallowed be thy name.

I felt the others' stares on my burning cheeks. Felt their fascination. Felt like a complete and total idiot. This wasn't going to work. Deveraux was *a* god, not *the* God, and if I hadn't been damned before, I would be now. No sense in further ceremony. Irritably now, I called, *Deveraux? I don't know if you can hear me. You probably can't. It's me. Reid.* Nothing happened. *Nicholina has possessed Lou, and we need you to exorcise her. Please.* Still nothing. I tried again. *Can you meet us? We're in a small village along the coast of northern Belterra called Fée Tombe. It's about three days from Chateau le Blanc. You probably already know that. You probably already know all of this. Or you don't, and I'm talking to myself like a jackass.*

I cringed again, cracking an eye open.

Beau searched the cliffs for a moment before frowning. "Well, that was underwhelming." He glanced to the sky instead. "He is god of the wilderness, right? I didn't mishear his pretentious little speech?"

Coco squinted down the beach. "King of flora and fauna."

"Frankly, his silence is insulting. He could at least send a bird to shit on our heads or something." Beau harrumphed and turned to me. "Are you sure you're doing it properly?"

I scowled at him. "Would you like to try?"

"Let's not be rash. Perhaps you should give it another go."

I forced my eyes shut. Launched another prayer into the ether with all my concentration. *Please, Claud. Answer us. We need help. We need you.* When he still didn't answer, heat prickled my collar. I opened my eyes. Shook my head. "His silence is answer enough."

Beau's hands fell to his hips. "What are we supposed to do, then? We have an empty bandolier, a negligent god, and"—he gestured to Nicholina in distaste—"an *abysmal* poet. Oh, don't give me that look. Your work is derivative at best and juvenile at worst." His frown deepened as he looked to each of us in turn. "What else is there?"

I'm sick with hope, but I can't make it go away. It's still here, even now. Poisoning me.

Only the sound of the waves answered.

And there it was.

I met Coco's gaze directly. "We don't have a choice."

Shaking her head with regret, she closed her eyes and whispered, "The Wistful Waters."

PART II

La nuit porte conseil.
The night brings advice.
—French proverb

DEATH AT THE WATERS

Nicholina

The huntsman and the princess mean to punish me with their poisoned ropes, but we relish the friction. We rub until our wrists are raw. Until *her* wrists are raw. Because it's the mouse and her huntsman who suffer most—she cannot feel it, no, but *he* can. He knows she's trapped. She knows it too. She doesn't see the gold as we do. Though she summons it, though she pleads, it cannot listen. We will not let it. And if voices not our own murmur a warning, if they hiss—if they know we do not belong—the patterns cannot fix it. They can only obey.

We can only obey.

Even if something *is* wrong. Even if below the gold magic, a newfound presence lingers. A newfound presence waits. I do not like it. I cannot use it. Unknown to the mouse, it coils like a snake preparing to strike, to protect. It is a gift, and it frightens us.

We cannot be frightened.

They were never meant to know, to suspect. Now they gather their packs to find L'Eau Mélancolique. Nasty waters. Cursed waters. They hide secrets but reveal them too, oh yes. But they cannot reveal this one. Not mine. They cannot spill its truth.

The princeling watches me while the others pack, but he watches his princess more. It matters not. We do not want to escape. They seek L'Eau Mélancolique, but Chateau le Blanc is its sister. Its neighbor. We will not struggle. We will not fight. Though our right hand is numb, they do not know our left has sensation. Has pain. We can move through pain. And the gold cannot respond to the mouse, no, but it must respond to us. Though I fear it—though it does not trust me—we will send a message. It is necessary.

The gold bursts in a delicate spray as the letters carve themselves into our flesh. Into our back. THEY KNOW. And then—DEATH AT THE WATERS.

Our mistress will not be pleased with us.

I am disappointed, Nicholina, she will say. *I told you to kill them all.*

We glance at our wrists. At the red smear of blood there. *Her* blood. La Princesse Rouge. *Kill them all,* she will say. *Except the princesses.*

Except the princesses.

More potent than pain—more potent than magic—our fury simmers and bubbles, a poison all its own. Noxious. We must not kill her. Though she has forsaken her family, forsaken my mistress, we must obey.

We must make our mistress proud. We must show her. Then she will realize our worth, yes, she will realize our love. She will never speak of her treacherous niece again. But the others . . .

I will drown them in L'Eau Mélancolique.

They think they've trapped me with their ropes, with their threats, with their bane, but their threats ring empty. They know nothing of pain. No, no, no, *true* pain lies outside the sensation of blood and skin. It lies beyond blisters.

It lies deep within.

The mice continue squeaking as the huntsman pulls me forward. Rocks line the path at the edge of the forest. Above us, thick smoke still darkens the afternoon sky. Below, waves crash tumultuously, oh yes. They warn of a storm. Of calamity. *Do not fret, little mouse,* we tell the princess, inhaling deep. Reveling. *The dead should not remember.*

I am not dead.

Soon, we promise. *Very soon, your mother shall devour your body, and we in turn shall devour the rest. Like a mouse in a trap.*

One might say you're the mouse now, Nicholina.

Oh?

My mice press closer, ever curious, and we smile as the huntsman scowls over his shoulder. "Is something funny?" he snaps. Though we smile all the wider, we will not answer. He cannot stand our silence. It aggrieves him, and he expels a sharp breath through his nose, muttering a promise of violence. We welcome it. *Relish* it.

The mouse continues without hearing his words. We laugh because he cannot hear hers either.

It's true, she insists. *The others were never meant to know about La Voisin's betrayal. They were never meant to know about* you. *But you failed at the lighthouse, and Morgane won't forget it. I know my mother. You've broken her trust. She'll kill you at the first opportunity—like a mouse in a trap.*

We scoff through her nose, smile vanishing. *Our mistress will protect us.*

Your mistress will sacrifice you for the greater good. Just like my mother will sacrifice me. As if sensing something within us—she senses *nothing*—she pushes brazenly against our consciousness. We feel each kick, each elbow, though she has no feet or arms. It matters not. She cannot touch us, and soon she will fade into the others. Soon she will be ours. *You've chosen the wrong side, Nicholina. You've lost. Reid and Coco will never allow us near the Chateau now.*

My mice hiss and whisper their uncertainty. *She knows nothing,* I croon to them. *Hush now, mouses.* "The dead should not remember, beware the night they dream. For in their chest is memory—"

The huntsman jerks us forward viciously, and we stumble. A crow startles from a nearby fir.

It has three eyes.

You know what's coming, Nicholina. It isn't too late to stop it. You can still relinquish my body, ally with us before Morgane and Josephine betray you. Because they will *betray you. It's only a matter of time. Me, Reid, Coco, Beau—we could protect—*

Bitterness pulses through us at the promise. Promises, promises, empty promises. They taste black, acrimonious, and we shall choke her with them. We shall fill her throat with eyes, eyes, *eyes* until she cannot breathe beneath their weight. Her consciousness does not flinch under our pressure. We push harder. We restrict and contract and compress until at last she recoils, hardening into a small, hopeless blemish. A blight in our nest. *You think you are clever*, we hiss, *but we are cleverer. Oh yes. We shall kill them all—your precious* family—*and you shall forget each one.*

NO—

But her panic means nothing. It tastes empty, like her promise. She is already dead.

Her friends will join her soon.

A MURDER OF CROWS

Reid

Nicholina stopped walking abruptly. Her face twitched and spasmed as she muttered what sounded like *nasty* over and over again. Her mouth twisted around the word. "What's nasty?" I asked suspiciously, tugging her forward. She yielded a single step. Her eyes fixed on a distant tree at the edge of the forest. A fir. "What are you looking at?"

"Ignore her." Coco glanced at us over her shoulder, huddling deeper in her cloak. Along the coast, the wind blustered stronger than in La Fôret des Yeux. Colder. "The sooner we reach a village, the sooner we'll find black pearls for Le Cœur Brisé."

"Pearls." Beau scoffed and kicked a rock into the sea. "What a ridiculous payment."

"Le Cœur guards L'Eau Mélancolique." Coco shrugged. "The waters are dangerous. They're *powerful*. Without payment, no one broaches their shores."

Beside Thierry, Célie wrinkled her nose as I forced Nicholina another step. Two. "And you think we'll find these ... black pearls in the next village?"

"Perhaps not the *next* one." Coco marched back to prod Nicholina along. She'd seemed to grow roots. She still stared at the fir tree, tilting her head in contemplation. I looked closer, the hair on my neck rising. A solitary crow perched there. "But there are a handful of fishing villages between here and L'Eau Mélancolique."

Worse still—the white dog had reappeared, stalking us with those eerie, silent eyes. With a panicked curse, Beau kicked another rock at him, and he disappeared in a plume of white smoke.

"Aren't black pearls . . . rare?" Célie asked delicately.

Yes. Thierry noticed the crow as well. His brow furrowed. Though he hadn't spoken his plans aloud, I suspected he'd travel with us as long as we continued north. Toward L'Eau Mélancolique. Toward Chateau le Blanc. Morgane had tortured him and his brother—that much had been clear in his memories—yet Thierry was here. Toulouse wasn't. *But anything can be bought for the right price*, he said softly.

"*Move*, Nicholina," Coco snapped, joining me at the rope. Nicholina jolted at the words, and we realized our mistake too late. With a vindictive smile, she curled her pointer finger toward her palm.

A single feather fell from the crow's wing.

"Oh, *shit*—" Hastily, Coco tried to recoat the ropes, but the sharp scent of magic already punctured the air. The feather touched the forest floor. Alarmed now, I pulled sharply on Nicholina's wrists, but she smashed her head into my nose, flinging herself backward on top of me. We both crashed to the ground as the feather began to—to *change*.

"A mouse in a trap," she hissed. "Who are the mice now?"

The delicate black filaments multiplied, slowly at first, gaining momentum. Melting together into a misshapen lump of clay. From that clay, another bird formed, identical to the one perched in the tree. The latter cawed again, and from the former, a second feather fell. Another bird rose. Three now. All identical. Nicholina cackled.

But the birds hadn't finished yet. Within the span of five heartbeats, five more had formed. They multiplied faster. Ten now. Twenty. Fifty.

"Stop it." I crushed her hands in mine—those hands that should've been rendered numb, useless—but she twisted away as the birds rose above us in a horrifying black mass. Scores now. Perhaps hundreds. "Reverse the pattern. Do it *now*."

"Too late." Laughing in delight, she bounced on her toes. "Look, huntsman. It's a murder of crows. They shall peck, peck, peck all your flesh, flesh, flesh." The plague above us built like a tidal wave preparing to break. "Did you hear me, huntsman? Crows. Murderous ones. Tell me, which shall they eat first: Your eyes or your tongue?"

Then the wave broke.

The birds swooped as one, arrowing toward us with alarming speed. Though I threw up my hands against the onslaught, frantically searching for a pattern, they attacked with single-minded focus. Talons slashed my face, my fingers. Beaks tore into my knuckle. Others drew blood from my ear. Coco tackled

Nicholina to the ground, and the two scrabbled in the snow as the crows descended on the others, pecking skin, pulling hair.

Angry caws muffled Célie's panicked shrieks, Beau's vicious curses, Nicholina's outraged cries. I craned my neck to see her writhe as Coco recoated her ropes with blood. The crows didn't stop, however. My own blood streaked down my forearms, my neck, but I kept my head bowed, searching. Gold rose in a tangled web.

There.

I yanked the pattern with all my might, and a powerful gust of wind blasted the birds backward. I braced as it blasted me too. A necessary sacrifice. I needed space to breathe. To *think.*

I secured neither. More birds darted to replace the others, shrieking indignantly.

It was no good. There were too many of them. Too many *patterns.* Seizing Nicholina, I charged toward the cliffs with talons on my neck. Coco sprinted behind with Beau, and Thierry swooped Célie up in his arms to follow.

"Reid!" I didn't slow at my brother's incredulous shout. "What are we *doing?*"

No. I maintained my focus, searched blindly for the right cord. If we hoped to survive with our eyes and tongues, we'd have to jump. My vision pitched at the thought. Madame Labelle had once said a witch could fly with the right pattern. Deveraux had said a cardinal couldn't if it didn't believe.

Well. We were about to test their theories.

If you're listening, Deveraux, please, please, *help us—*

I didn't get the chance to finish the prayer.

A deafening roar shook the cliffside, the trees, and an amethyst wing parted the clouds of smoke overhead. An *enormous* amethyst wing. Membranous. Razor-tipped. Fire sprayed in a wide arch, silhouetting the great, hulking shape of a serpentine body. A scaled leg appeared. A barbed tail.

An entire dragon followed.

THE DRAGON AND HER MAIDEN

Reid

I could only stare as it dove toward us.

It roared again, and from its great mouth, more fire spilled forth. The heat of it nearly blistered my skin. Finally regaining my senses, I dropped to the ground, covering Lou's body as the crows overhead shrieked in agony. Their burning corpses fell around us like macabre rain—those that fell at all. The dragon incinerated most midair. It snapped vicious jaws around others, devouring them whole.

The others had tumbled with me, covering their heads as if their arms might shield them from the dragon's flames. Except Thierry. He too had fallen, but he didn't cower, instead gazing at the dragon with an unfathomable expression. I could've sworn it looked like—like *relief*. But that couldn't be right. We'd leapt from the pot into the fire. Literally.

Even with magic, with knives—even if I'd still wielded my Balisarda—we couldn't hope to defend ourselves against a *dragon*. We had to flee. Now. While we still had a chance. We just needed a diversion. Quickly, I pulled at the golden web of patterns. Something loud. Something big. Something to slow the beast as we sprinted for the cliff. Could I fell a tree? A *forest* of trees? Yes. A cage of wood for—

For a fire-breathing dragon.

I closed my eyes. *Fuck.*

But I was out of time. It'd have to do. Bracing myself for the consequences, I gathered the golden cords in my hand. Before I could pull, however, the dragon snorted, and fresh smoke engulfed us. I glanced up. Spotted a miniature flame through the haze. My eyes narrowed as I looked closer, harder. It wasn't flame at all, but hair. Red hair. A person.

Seraphine smiled down at me from the dragon's back.

The earth shook as it landed with another roar, tossing its great head. Between one blink and the next, its horns unraveled into lavender curls, and its tail rippled into black satin. Reptilian eyes blinked to brown. Amethyst scales smoothed to skin.

"*Thierry.*" Voice low and hoarse, Zenna caught Seraphine in her arms, transformation complete, before placing her swiftly on her feet. They both hurried toward their fellow troupe member. I gaped at them. We all did. Even Nicholina.

Zenna. Seraphine. He reached them just as Seraphine extended her arms, and he lifted her from the ground to spin her in a circle. *You're here.*

"So are you." Zenna didn't look pleased. "Imagine our surprise when Claud sensed you at last—in northern Belterra, of all places. Not the tunnels we'd been searching for weeks." She seized one of his hands. "We've been worried sick, Thierry. Care to tell us where you've been? Where is Toulouse?"

Thierry's face fell.

I pushed myself to my feet, pulling Nicholina up with me. "You—you're—"

"A dragon, yes." Zenna heaved a long-suffering sigh, and smoke curled from her nostrils. After inspecting Thierry one last time, she casually wiped the blood from her lips. She'd painted them gold today. They matched the blooms embroidered on her gown. "*Bonjour, Mort Rouge.* Shall we all digest together? Go ahead. Take a moment."

"It's going to take a hell of a lot longer than a *moment.*" Beau staggered upright and dusted off his trousers in vain. "This is—I can't believe—we shared the same bed, and you never *told* me? I slept with a dragon!" He whirled to face me as if I hadn't heard him, arms splayed wide. "An actual dragon!"

Coco stood faster than humanly possible. "You *what?*"

He lifted his hands just as quickly. "It was entirely platonic." When her eyes narrowed to dangerous slits, he retreated a step in my direction. I ignored him. Nicholina had wormed away from me. I pulled her back with a scowl. "I was cold," Beau continued defensively, "so Seraphine offered her spot."

Seraphine rested her head on Thierry's shoulder. Refused to release his arm. He squeezed her hand with equal fondness, like a brother might a sister. "Some nights I can't sleep," she said.

"Yes, exactly." Beau nodded to Coco. "She's unusually kind, this one, even read to me until I—"

"She *did*?" Coco clapped her hands together with a terrifying smile. "Do tell me more. Tell me *all about* your cold night between Zenna and Seraphine."

"Well, it wasn't cold after that," Beau said, either woefully ignorant or determined to prove his innocence. "I woke up sweltering. It was terrible. Almost died of heatstroke."

"My temperature does run hotter than a human's," Zenna said.

"You see?" Beau nodded again—as if this settled the matter for good—while I tightened Nicholina's binds. "Tell her, Zenna. Tell her it was platonic."

Zenna arched that brow again. "Does it matter?"

Coco mirrored her expression. "Yes, Beauregard. Does it?"

He stared between them in horror.

"Don't make me tie your ankles too, Nicholina." I planted her in front of me when she tried to wriggle away again. "I'll do it. I'll carry you all the way to L'Eau Mélancolique if necessary."

She leaned back, rubbing her cheek against my chest like a cat. "I think I'd like that, huntsman. Oh, yes. I think I'd like it very much."

Mirroring my own frown, Zenna inhaled deeply. If she detected a new scent from Lou, she said nothing, instead shaking her head and returning her attention to Thierry. "Where is your brother, Thierry? Where is Toulouse?"

Though Thierry stiffened, he exhaled a resigned breath. *Toulouse remains at the Chateau. I . . . escaped.*

"Chateau le Blanc?" Zenna's eyes flashed gold. Her pupils narrowed to slits. "Why? What happened?"

Thierry shook his head reluctantly. *Morgane captured us in the tunnels. Or rather,* she *did.* He jerked his chin toward Nicholina, who giggled and leaned forward, smacking her lips as if blowing him a kiss. Zenna growled. Thierry, however, continued unde-terred. *When the lights went out, she attacked. She'd cut my arm before I knew what had happened. She drank my blood. When she commanded Toulouse and me to lock ourselves away from La Mascarade des Crânes— to wait for her return—we had no choice. We had to obey.* He looked to me apologetically. *We heard your screams, but we couldn't intervene. I am sorry.*

I returned his gaze with as much solemnity as I could manage while Nicholina attempted to twirl in my arms. Like we were dancing. "I don't blame you for what happened."

He nodded. *She collected us eventually. She and her mistress. La Voisin. They handed us and the wolves over to La Dame des Sorcières without hesitation. Morgane was . . . interested in us. In our magic. She incapacitated us with her injections and led us to the Chateau.*

Smoke unfurled from between Zenna's clenched teeth.

I cannot relive the horrors she inflicted upon us there. I will not. She wanted to—to discover the source of our magic. To test its limits. To study its differences from hers. I believe she did the same with the wolves. He watched silently as Beau, Coco, and I bore Nicholina to the ground like we'd done in the lighthouse. Coco forced her mouth open. Nicholina smashed her forehead into Coco's face. *Or perhaps now she simply likes to inflict pain. Either way, she experimented on us.*

"Thierry," said Seraphine.

"I will rend her head from her shoulders," said Zenna. "And I will eat it."

Célie waited with bated breath. "How did you escape?"

In the end, my voice saved me. Thierry gave a sardonic laugh. *The witches on duty that night were younger. They'd never tended me before. Some sort of celebration raged above, and they arrived late, tipsy, to administer my injection. I could just feel my hands. My feet. I doused the lantern, waited for them to unlock the door. When they did, I projected my voice down the corridor. It disoriented them. When they turned toward the projection, I—I—* He closed his eyes then. As if he couldn't bear the memory. *I overpowered them.*

"They deserved it," Zenna snapped.

Perhaps. Their last cries alerted others to my escape, however. I couldn't find Toulouse. They'd separated us, used each to torture the other— He broke off abruptly, chest heaving. At last, he whispered, *I had no choice but to leave him.*

Seraphine touched his shoulder. "You could never have saved him without first saving yourself."

I lost my way in the forest. I intended to go back. I need to go back. Unshed tears sparkled in his dark eyes when he finally opened them. *I can't leave him alone.*

Zenna bent to meet his gaze directly. "And we won't. We will return to Chateau le Blanc for Toulouse. For the wolves. Then we will raze that wretched castle to the ground with Morgane le Blanc and her Dames Blanches inside. This I promise you."

"Promises, promises," Nicholina muttered beneath her breath. "*Empty* promises. My mistress will be safe, yes, my mistress will be waiting."

"Your mistress will *keep* waiting." I readjusted my grip to enunciate the point. The crows couldn't happen again. We'd need to be more vigilant. From here until L'Eau Mélancolique, I'd release her only for Coco to recoat her ropes. If she still planned to take Lou to Josephine—to Morgane—she'd have to drag my corpse behind. Exhaling slow, heavy, I asked Zenna, "How are you here? You said Claud *sensed* Thierry?"

She turned those golden eyes toward me. "Claud is not like you. He is not even like me."

"Yes, but—why didn't he sense Thierry before? Why couldn't he have found Thierry in the tunnels? Before Morgane—" I stopped myself from asking the next question. Nicholina asked it for me.

"Before she *tortured* him?"

Fresh smoke erupted from Zenna's nose. "Claud has never claimed to be the supreme deity, huntsman. Only divine. He is not omniscient, and he is not omnipotent. He *did* sense Thierry in the tunnels. When the Hellfire sparked, however"—she cast a baleful look in Coco's direction—"he lost the connection. We believed the fire's magic had cloaked Thierry's presence. We didn't realize it was Chateau le Blanc. When Thierry escaped its enchantment three days ago, Claud felt him once more. I flew north to find him immediately." After blinking with secondary, vertical eyelids, her eyes flicked back to brown. "Seraphine and I have scoured these mountains for days. We couldn't fly low enough to properly search without risking exposure, forcing us to *walk*." Her lip curled at the word.

Seraphine patted her arm. "When we reached Fée Tombe this morning, Zenna finally caught Thierry's scent. Still fresh. We followed it to the lighthouse, where we met with an angry mob."

"They'd already chased you away," Zenna growled, "but we followed." A cruel smile curved her painted lips. "The crows were a tasty coincidence. You are welcome."

"Wait a moment." Lifting a finger, Beau frowned between them, incredulous. Perhaps indignant. "Does this mean Claud didn't send you for *us*? Did he not hear our prayer?"

Zenna arched a brow. "Your arrogance astounds."

"It's hardly *arrogant* to expect the help of a friend—"

"He is not your friend. He is a *god*. If you speak to him, he will listen. He will *not*, however," she added firmly, eyes narrowing, "always answer. You do not have a god at your beck and call, any of you. He is of the Old World, and as such, he is bound by the Old Laws. He cannot directly intervene."

Beau's frown deepened to a scowl. I spoke before he could argue. "Can you help us, then? Nicholina has possessed Lou. We have to exorcise her."

"Do not insult my intelligence." Nostrils flaring once more, Zenna leaned forward to stare into Lou's eyes. "Yes, I recognize the blight you call Nicholina. Long ago, I knew her by a different name. *Nicola*."

Nicholina jerked, snarling, "We do not speak that name. We do not speak it!"

Zenna tilted her head. "But I am only a dragon. I cannot exorcise anyone."

"The Wistful Waters can," I said swiftly. "We're journeying there now. Perhaps you could . . . join us." I held my breath as

I waited, hardly daring to hope. With a dragon on our side, we would reach L'Eau Mélancolique within the day. She could fly us there. She could protect us. Nicholina—even Morgane—wouldn't dare threaten a *dragon*.

Zenna didn't answer right away. Instead she stepped backward, away from us. She straightened her shoulders. Stretched her neck. "Witches are gathering at Chateau le Blanc. We have spied them in the mountains, through the forest. More than we have ever seen. If we are to rescue Toulouse, we must act swiftly. I am sorry."

"But we can help you! No one knows Chateau le Blanc like Lou does. After we find the pearls for Le Cœur, after we exorcise her—"

"After Toulouse *dies*, you mean." Her teeth continued lengthening. Her eyes gleamed gold. "Let me be clear, huntsman—Louise le Blanc may be the center of your universe, but she is not the center of mine. I have made my decision. Every moment I spend arguing with you is a moment Toulouse could lose his life."

"But—"

"Every moment I spend arguing with you is a moment I might eat you instead."

"He understands," Coco said smoothly, stepping in front of Nicholina and me. She raised a hand to motion me backward. Nicholina lunged forward to snap at it. "Go." Coco jerked her head. "Save Toulouse and the wolves. Raze the Chateau. Just—kill Morgane while you're at it." She gestured to the crow carcasses all around us. "Two birds, you know."

Zenna nodded as Thierry moved to clasp my shoulder, considered Nicholina's teeth, and thought better of it. *We shall see each other soon,* mon ami.

I managed a small smile. Zenna was right, of course. Lou *was* my priority. Toulouse was theirs. "Good luck, *frère*. Be careful."

The two of them backed toward the cliff without another word. Seraphine lingered beside us, however, as if searching for words and finding none. At last, she whispered, "I wish we could help more."

Coco kicked aside a burning crow. "You've helped enough."

"We will kill Morgane if we can," Seraphine promised.

Zenna didn't change as the werewolves did. Her bones didn't crack or break. Instead, she shifted with the grace and showmanship of a performer, lifting an elegant arm in the air. The other clutched her train. With a flourish of satin, she whirled, and at the center of her turn, her entire body exploded upward. Outward. Like a flame sparked into existence.

"Beautiful," Célie breathed as Zenna extended a jeweled claw to Thierry. He climbed atop it, and she lifted him to the smooth amethyst scales between her wings.

Seraphine smiled. "She is, isn't she?"

Then the dragon collected her maiden, and they launched into the sky.

LITANY

Lou

Reid, Coco, Beau, Ansel, Madame Labelle. Reid, Coco, Beau, Ansel, Madame Labelle.

I repeat the names like a litany in the darkness. I envision each face. The copper of Reid's hair, the cut of Coco's cheekbones, the arch of Beau's brows, the color of Ansel's eyes. Even the fabric of Madame Labelle's gown when I first saw her: emerald silk.

A pretty color, Legion muses, remembering the gold leaf walls and marble floors of the Bellerose, the grand staircase and the naked ladies. *A pretty . . . brothel?*

Yes. Those are tits.

They press closer, listening to each name in fascination, examining each memory. Except Etienne. His presence lingers apart from the rest, but weaker now. Faded. He's forgotten his own name again, so I remind him. I will *keep* reminding him. *Reid, Coco, Beau, Ansel, Madame Labelle. It's Etienne. You are Etienne.*

I am Etienne, he whispers faintly.

We hoped once too. Legion coils around him, not to bolster but to soothe. They see only one outcome to our situation, but I refuse to accept it. I *refuse*. Instead, I remember the scent of Pan's patisserie, the sweet cream of sticky buns. The wind in my hair as I leap rooftop to rooftop. The sensation of flying. The first light of dawn on my cheeks. *Hope matters not.*

Hope matters most, I say fiercely. *Hope isn't the sickness. It's the cure.*

As they consider my words, the darkness saturates with their confusion, their skepticism. I don't allow it to taint my own thoughts. *Reid, Coco, Beau, Ansel, Madame Labelle. Reid, Coco, Beau, Ansel, Madame Labelle.*

The darkness has thinned in places, however, and within it, I can see glimpses of . . . Nicholina. Her memories. They slip across the surface of the shadows, as slick and bright as oil in water, mingling with my own. Snippets of a lullaby here. Ginger hair and warm hands there, a clandestine smile and an echo of laughter— genuine laughter, not the eerie, artificial kind she uses now. Warmth envelops that particular memory, and I realize it isn't her laughter at all. It comes from another, someone she once held dear. A sister? A mother? Pale skin, freckled flesh. Ah . . . a lover.

Reid, Coco, Beau, Ansel . . .

Panic seizes me at the last. There's someone else, isn't there? I've forgotten—*who* have I forgotten?

Legion croons mournfully. *Hope matters not.*

I am Etienne, he breathes.

The darkness drifts apart in answer, revealing the temple of Chateau le Blanc. But this place . . . I've never known it. Blood runs as a river from the temple down the mountainside, soaking the hair and hems of the fallen witches in its path. I recognize none of them. Except one.

Nicholina stands in the center of the clearing, her hands and mouth dripping blood.

Oh my god.

Never before have I seen such carnage. Never before have I seen such *death*. It pervades everything, coating each blade of grass and permeating each beam of moonlight. It hovers like a disease, thick and foul in my nose. And Nicholina revels in it, her eyes bright and silver as she turns to face La Voisin, who steps down from the red-slicked temple. Behind her, she drags a bound woman. I can't see her face. I can't tell if she's alive or dead.

When I look closer, horrified, the scene returns to darkness, and a familiar voice slithers down my spine.

Do you fear death, little mouse?

I do not recoil, reciting their names. *Reid, Coco, Beau, Ansel.* Then— *Everyone fears death. Even you, Nicholina.*

Her ghostly chuckle reverberates. *If you cannot master this one simple fear, you will not survive L'Eau Mélancolique. Oh, no. Our husband plans to baptize us, but he doesn't realize. He doesn't understand. Our mistress will stop him.* The image of a dragon flashes—there and gone before I can properly see. *Even if not, the waters go down, down, down, down, and there they drown, drown, drown, drown.*

My own surprise and bewilderment stretch between us now. L'Eau Mélancolique? Though I wrack my memory to place the name, the darkness only seems to condense around it. I know those words. I *know* them. I just can't—I can't seem to *remember* them. Fresh panic swells at the realization, but—no. I won't give in. I push against the darkness angrily.

Reid, Coco, Beau, Ansel. If Reid plans to baptize me in these waters, he must have a reason. I have to trust him. *I can swim.*

It has nothing to do with swimming. Another image arises through the inky mist. A woman. She walks with purpose toward an unnaturally smooth sea—a sea so smooth it resembles the face of a mirror. Endless. Gleaming. She doesn't break stride as she crosses into its depths, and the water . . . it seems to absorb her movements. Not a single ripple breaks its surface. She keeps walking, submerging her knees. Her hips. Her chest. When her head slips beneath the water, she does not reemerge. *You aren't the first to seek the waters' embrace. Many have come before you, and many will come behind. She cherishes her lovers. She kisses each to sleep, tucking them in bed and healing them with brine.*

A thought strikes like lightning. *What happens to you if I die?*

You've seen an Ascension, she says. I feel rather than see her turn her attention to Etienne, who trembles beneath her observation. He's forgotten his name again. *The soul can live for an indefinite amount of time without a body.*

Indefinite isn't forever.

No.

So . . . you could die if I do.

It will not come to that.

Why not?

Another chuckle. *My mistress resides at the Chateau. She will have brought my body. If you succumb to the waters' lure, I will return to it. You will die, and I will live.*

How do you know your body is there? I ask her, pushing again. Repeating the names. *You've failed, Nicholina. My mother attacked you, and you openly challenged her. Your mistress needs her more than she needs you. Perhaps your body won't be there at all. Perhaps you* will *die.*

I have not *failed.* The darkness writhes in agitation at the words, and Legion hisses and spits. The emotion only partly belongs to them, however. No, they also feel . . . curious, and there—deep within their essence—a sense of longing pervades. A sense of hope. *My mistress tasked me with bringing you to Morgane le Blanc—* Nicholina spits the name—*and I will do so, regardless of your foul family. We will see who dances and who drowns.*

Reid, Coco, Beau.

Laughing again, Nicholina withdraws.

Reid Coco Beau Reid Coco Reid Coco Reid Coco

Hold on, Etienne says.

Then he slips into Legion once more.

Wake up, little mouse.

I rouse as if waking from deep sleep, and immediately, I sense something has changed. Though darkness still shrouds everything, it dissipates into eerie wisps at Nicholina's words, drifting in the wind. Clinging to trees and rocks and—

And people.

I study the man beside me. Copper hair tousled, he stalks along a mountain path with rope in his hand, bickering with the young woman beside him. *Look at them, Louise. Look one last time. Your family.* A hateful pause. *Have you forgotten them?*

Though their names rise slowly, as if through tar, I hold on to each for dear life. Reid and Coco. *No.*

Coco's dark eyes—so dark they're almost black—lift to the sky before landing on me. No. Not on me. On Nicholina. "Even with the pearls, you know we're walking into a trap, right?"

Nicholina giggles.

Shaking his head, Reid pulls us along faster. My vision pitches with each step. "Not necessarily."

They will die, Nicholina croons. *All of them. My mistress will come. She will cut out their hearts.*

They will not. She will not.

"We don't have a choice." Reid's words brook no argument. "The Wistful Waters are our only hope."

"And after? What then, Reid?" They both stare at me for a long moment. "Chateau le Blanc is near. With Lou as herself again—if Zenna doesn't raze the castle to the ground—maybe we *could* slip inside and . . . finish this."

The two walking in front slow their footsteps at the last. Both black-haired. Both unfamiliar.

"It was *Nicholina* who wanted to storm the Chateau," Reid says adamantly, "not Lou. Which means it's the last thing we should do. Morgane and Josephine might be expecting . . ."

But his voice begins to fade as the scene shifts around me.

Say goodbye, Louise. The shadows thicken and solidify into darkness once more. It crushes me beneath its weight, and I'm swept away—away from Reid, away from Coco, away from light. *You will not see them again.*

Yes, I will.

The words are quiet and small, so insignificant that Nicho-lina doesn't hear them. But others do. Though Etienne is gone, Legion wraps their presence around me, folding me into their depths. Their intent is not to harm, however, not to claim. Instead they hold me apart. They keep me together. *Hope isn't the sickness.* They hum their own litany now. Their own prayer. *It's the cure.*

ANOTHER GRAVE

Reid

Célie emerged from the trees clad in fitted pants and knee-high leather boots. She'd tucked a billowing shirt into them. Jean Luc's shirt. I recognized the stitching on the collar, the sleeves. Deep blue—Chasseur blue—and gold. On her head, she wore a feathered cavalier hat. On her face, she wore a neatly trimmed beard.

Beau burst into laughter.

"What?" Hastily, she looked down at herself, smoothing her shirt. Checking her hair, tucking an errant strand into her hat. "Is it not convincing?"

"Oh, it's convincing," he assured her. "You look like an idiot."

Beside me, Nicholina giggled from her spot on the ground. We'd bound her wrists again, coating her entire hands in Coco's blood. Now she couldn't move a finger if she tried.

Startled, perhaps even scandalized by Beau's bald honesty, Célie's brows shot up. "Cosette often wears trousers—"

"But not a *beard*," Beau said. "You don't need a disguise, Célie. Your face isn't on those wanted posters."

"Well, I—I just thought I might—" Her face flamed. "Perhaps I'm not wanted by the Crown, but my father will eventually search for me. Jean Luc has spies throughout the kingdom. Should I not take precautions?" At our impassive stares, she lifted her chin defiantly and repeated, "Cosette and Louise wear trousers."

Beau spread his hands with a smirk. "And there it is."

Her eyes narrowed. "Your Majesty, please take no offense, but you are a good deal less pleasant than I would have liked to believe."

Still chuckling, he slung an arm over Coco's shoulder. "None taken, I assure you."

Coco pushed him away. "He gets that a lot."

Crooking his finger at Célie, Beau led her into the first village.

We'd decided the two of them would search for black pearls. Though not ideal, Coco and I needed to remain with Nicholina. We couldn't easily drag her through the streets with bound and bloody hands. I shuddered to think of her actually *speaking* if we did find someone who sold them.

By the third village, I'd heard enough of her to last a lifetime.

She reclined atop a rock on the edge of the forest now, moaning and tugging against her rope. Her hands hung limp and useless from her wrists. Like bloody carcasses. "We're *hungry*. Shall we venture into just one hamlet? Just one? Just one, just one, to have some fun?" She cast me a wicked glance. "Just one to find a sticky bun?"

I looked away from her blistered hands. Couldn't bear the

sight of them. "Shut your mouth, Nicholina."

Coco lazed within the roots of a knotted tree while we waited. She picked at the fresh cut on her palm. "She won't stop until you do."

"Oooh, clever mouse." Nicholina sat up abruptly, leering at me. "We don't just live beneath *her* skin, no no no. We live beneath *yours*. It's warm and it's wet and filled with *short— angry—breaths—*"

"I swear to God, if you don't stop talking—"

"You'll do *what*?" With a cackle, she pulled at her ropes again. I pulled back. She nearly toppled from the rock. "Will you harm this pretty skin? Will you strike this freckled flesh? Will you punish us, oh husband, with a good, hard *thrash*?"

"Ignore her," Coco said.

Heat suffused my face. My neck. My hands clenched the rope. I could ignore her. I could do it. She wanted a reaction. I would give her none.

Another handful of minutes passed in silence. Then—

"We need to relieve ourselves," Nicholina pronounced.

I scowled and shook my head. "No."

"Perhaps in the trees?" She continued as if I hadn't spoken. "Perhaps they deserve it. Naughty, naughty trees. Perhaps they'll *observe* it." Rising to her feet, she cackled at her own perverse joke. I tugged her rope irritably.

"I said no."

"No?" Disbelief—still feigned, still disingenuous, as if she'd somehow expected my response—laced her voice. *Lou's* voice.

The sound of it made me ache and rage in equal measure. "You'd have us piss down our leg? Your own wife?"

"You aren't my wife."

A sick wave of regret washed through me at the familiar words. At the memory. The ring I'd once given Lou, golden band and mother-of-pearl stone, weighed heavy in my pocket. Like a brick. I'd kept it with me since Léviathan, anxious to return it to her. To slide it back on her finger where it belonged. I would do just that at L'Eau Mélancolique. I would marry her right there on the beach. Just like last time, except proper now. Real.

Nicholina gave a feline grin. "No, we aren't your wife, are we? Which makes us your . . . what, exactly?" A pause. She leaned closer, brushing her nose against mine. I jerked back. "She fought, you know," she breathed, still grinning. My entire body went still. My entire being. "She screamed your name. You should have heard her in those last moments. Absolutely terrified. Absolutely *delicious*. We savored her death."

It wasn't true. Lou was still in there. We would free her.

"She can't hear you, pet." Nicholina pursed her lips in a sugar-sweet display of sympathy, and I realized I'd spoken the words aloud. "The dead don't have ears. She won't hear your cries, and she won't see your tears."

"That's enough," Coco said sharply. Though I could see her trying to tug the rope from me, I couldn't feel the movement. My fist remained locked. Blood roared in my ears. "Shut the hell up, Nicholina."

She fought, you know.

Nicholina giggled like a little girl. Shrugged. "All right."

She screamed your name.

I took a deep breath. In through my nose. Out through my mouth. One after another. Again and again.

You should've heard her in those last moments. Absolutely terrified.

I should've been there.

It's your fault it's your fault it's your fault

Beau and Célie arrived at that moment, and Coco succeeded in tugging the rope from me. Glowering at their empty hands, she snapped, "Nothing? Again?"

Célie shrugged helplessly while Beau lifted said hands in a lackadaisical gesture. "What would you like us to do, Cosette? Shit the pearls into existence? We aren't *oysters*."

Her nostrils flared. "Oysters don't shit out *pearls*, you idiotic piece of—"

"Shit?" Nicholina supplied helpfully.

Coco closed her eyes then, forcing a deep breath, before looking up at the sky. Though smoke still obscured the sun, it must've been late afternoon. "The next village is about two hours up the road. It's the last one before L'Eau Mélancolique." Her expression hardened, and she met my gaze. Jaw still clenched, I nodded once. "Reid and I will search it too."

"What?" Beau looked between the two of us incredulously. "Célie and I are *perfectly* capable—"

"I am *sure* that's true," she snapped, "but this isn't the time for a pissing contest. We need to find those pearls. This is our last chance."

"But"—Célie leaned forward, blinking rapidly—"but *Nicholina* . . ."

Coco lifted her fist. She'd wrapped the rope around it. The movement forced Nicholina closer, and Coco stared directly into her eyes. Every word promised violence. "Nicholina will behave herself. Nicholina doesn't want to die, and she's wearing the face of the most notorious witch in Belterra." She tugged her closer. Nicholina had stopped grinning. "If she causes a scene—if she steps one *toe* out of line—they'll lash her to a stake right there in Anchois. Nicholina understands that, doesn't she?"

Nicholina sneered. "You won't let us burn."

"We might not be able to save you."

Nicholina glowered now but said nothing. Though I reached for her rope once more, Coco shook her head and started forward. "She stays with me," she said over her shoulder. "You can't bring yourself to kick her ass, but I can. It's what Lou would want."

Anchois boasted three dirt-packed streets. One of these led to the dock, where dozens of fishing boats bobbed along black water. One housed the villagers' ramshackle dwellings. Carts and fish stands littered the market of the third. Though the sun had fully set, firelight danced on merchants' faces as they hawked wares. Shoppers slipped arm in arm between them, calling to friends. To family. Some clutched brown paper packages. Others wore seashell necklaces. Bits of agate sparkled in the hair of impish children. Gnarled fishermen gathered at the beach to sip ale in groups of twos and threes. Grousing about their wives. Their grandchildren. Their knees.

Coco peered down the market street, trying to see through the gaps in the crowd. She'd tied one of Nicholina's hands to hers. The sleeves of their cloaks hid all blisters. All blood. "We should split up. We'll cover more ground that way."

I tugged Célie away from a cart of scrying stones. "Fine. You two go to the dock, ask if anyone has heard of black pearls in the area. We'll search the market."

A gleam of wonder entered Célie's eyes as she watched a young man pull a roughly hewn flute from his pocket to serenade another. Some maidens nearby giggled. One even stepped apart from the rest, brave enough to dance. Célie nodded eagerly. "Yes. Let us do that."

Coco eyed us, skeptical. "Is this what you've been doing, Célie?"

Beau scoffed and shook his head. Mutinous.

I gripped Célie's elbow with pointed assurance. "If they're here, we'll find them."

Though Coco still seemed doubtful, she relented with a nod, fidgeting with the locket at her throat. Readjusting her hood. "Fine. But you'd better search the market, not stroll down memory lane." She jabbed a finger at my nose. "And be in plain sight when we get back. I want to see hands." Jerking her chin toward Beau and Nicholina, she left Célie and me standing alone in humiliated silence.

Heat pricked my ears. Her cheeks burned tomato red.

"Thanks, Cosette," I muttered bitterly. Forcing my jaw to unclench, I took a deep breath, adjusted my own cavalier, and guided Célie into the street. When the merchant rattled his scrying stones in our direction—he'd carved them from fish bones—I kept walking. "Don't listen to her. She's . . . going through a lot."

Célie refused to meet my gaze. "I don't think she likes me."

"She doesn't like anyone but Lou."

"Ah." For a split second, resentment flashed across her doll-like features. But then she smoothed her face into a polite smile, squaring her shoulders. Straightening her spine. Always the lady. "Perhaps you're right." Her smile turned genuine as she spotted a shabby confiserie. "Reid, look!" She pointed to the tins of almond candy in the window. Calisson. "It's your favorite! We simply must purchase some." With a pat to her leather satchel—I'd slung it over my shoulder, where it jostled against my own—she tried to steer me toward the confiserie's pink door.

I didn't move. "We're here for black pearls. Not candy."

Still she tugged on my wrists. "It'll take two minutes—"

"No, Célie."

As if Coco's reprimand had struck the ground between us like a bolt of lightning, she dropped my hands. Pink returned to her cheeks. "Very well. Lead the way."

We made it all of two minutes before she stopped again. Anger forgotten, she peered ahead at a group of men huddled around a barrel. Eyes wide and childlike, curious, she asked, "What are they doing?"

I glanced over their shoulders as we passed. A handful of dirty bronze *couronnes* littered the top of the barrel. A pair of wooden dice. "Gambling."

"Oh." She craned her neck to see too. When one of the men

winked at her, motioning her closer, I rolled my eyes. Some disguise. She tapped her satchel again, oblivious. "I should like to try gambling, I think. Please hand over my bag."

I snorted and kept walking. "Absolutely not."

She made an indignant noise at the back of her throat. "I beg your pardon?"

Though I'd barely met Violette and Victoire, I imagined this was how an elder brother felt. Exasperated. Impatient. Fond.

"Reid."

I ignored her.

"*Reid.*" She actually stamped her foot now. When I still didn't turn, didn't acknowledge her inane request, she seemed to snap, tearing after me and latching on to the bag with both hands. Hissing like a cat. Her nails even scored the leather. "You will release my bag this *instant.* This is—you—this is *my* bag. You cannot control it, and you cannot control *me.* If I wish to gamble, I shall gamble, and *you* shall—" Finally, I swung around, and she swung with me. My hand shot out to steady her when she stumbled backward. She swiped it away with an unladylike snarl. "*Give me my bag.*"

"Fine. Here." I tossed the satchel to her, but it slipped from her fingers. Coins and jewelry alike spilled across the snow. Cursing, I knelt to block the gamblers' view with my shoulders. "But you promised to help us. We need your *couronnes* to buy the pearls."

"Oh, I am well aware you need my help." Angry tears sparkled in her eyes as she too knelt, returning fistfuls of treasure to her bag. "Perhaps *you* are the one in need of a reminder." I glared pointedly at interested passersby. My hands swiftly joined hers, and though she tried to swat me away—

I straightened abruptly, my fingers curling around familiar glass. Cylindrical glass. Cold glass. Her nails cut into my knuckles as I moved to withdraw it. "Wait!" she cried.

Too late.

I stared at the syringe in my palm. "What is this?"

But I knew what it was. We both did. She stood perfectly still now, her hands knotted together at her waist. She didn't blink, didn't breathe. I didn't blame her. If she moved, her tearful facade might shatter, and the truth might spill forth. "Where did you get it?" I asked, voice hard.

"Jean gave it to me," she whispered, hesitating briefly, "when I told him I was leaving."

"When you told him you were coming to find us."

She didn't contradict me. "Yes."

My gaze snapped to her face. "Were you going to use it?"

"What?" Her voice cracked on the word, and she clutched my forearm, oblivious to Coco's and Beau's heads bobbing through the crowd. They hadn't yet spotted us. "Reid, I would never—"

"You're still crying."

She wiped her face hastily. "You know I cry when I'm upset—"

"Why are you upset, Célie? Did you think you'd lost it?" My fingers closed around the glass. The hemlock injection didn't warm, however. Devil's Flower, the priests had called it. It'd grown on the hillside of Jesus's crucifixion. When his blood had touched the petals, they'd turned poisonous. "It shouldn't matter if you had. You weren't going to use it."

"Reid." Her hand on my arm crept downward. Even now, she ached to have it in her possession. "It was just a precaution. I never planned to use it on you or—or anyone else. You must believe me."

"I do believe you." And I did. I believed she'd never *planned* to use it. If our reunion had gone wrong, however, she wouldn't have hesitated. The fact that she'd brought it here, that she'd *hidden* it, meant she'd been prepared to hurt us. I tucked the syringe in my pocket. "You know this is poison, right? Standard issue. Witch or no, it'd incapacitate you much faster than it would me. It'd take down Jean Luc. King Auguste. All of them." She blinked in confusion, confirming my suspicions. She'd thought it a weapon unique against witches. I shook my head. "Fuck, Célie. Are you really that afraid of us? Of me?"

She flinched at the profanity, color rising high on her cheeks. But not in embarrassment. In *anger*. When she lifted her chin, her voice didn't waver. "Is that even a question? Of *course* I fear you. A witch murdered Filippa. A witch locked me in a coffin with her remains. When I close my eyes, I can still feel her flesh on my skin, Reid. I can still *smell* her. My *sister*. Now I'm terrified of the dark, of sleep, of dreams, and even awake, I can hardly breathe. I'm trapped in a nightmare without end."

My own anger withered to something small. Something shameful.

"So, yes," she continued fiercely, fresh tears spilling down her cheeks, "I packed a weapon against witches. I hid it from you.

How could I do otherwise? Whether or not I like it, you're a witch now. You're one of them. I'm trying—truly, I am—but you cannot ask me not to protect myself." She took a deep, steadying breath then, and met my gaze. "Truthfully, you cannot ask me anything. I won't live in another grave, Reid. You've moved on. It is time for me to do the same."

Though a hundred words of comfort rose to my lips, I didn't utter one. They weren't enough for what she'd suffered. No words would ever be enough. I handed her the syringe instead. She seized it instantly, lifting it to her eyes with a truly terrifying expression. Not like Lou. Not like Coco. Not like Gabrielle or Violette or Victoire. Like Célie.

"When I next see Morgane, I will stab this needle in her heart," she promised.

And I believed her.

A SIMPLE FAVOR

Reid

Beau, Coco, and Nicholina found us shortly after. I drew them into the shadow of an abandoned stall, away from the whispers of the villagers. "Well?" Coco looked between the two of us expectantly. "Anything?"

Nicholina snickered while Célie stuffed the injection into her pocket. "We, ah—my apologies, but Reid and I got . . . well, *distracted.*"

Coco frowned. "Distracted?"

"We haven't found them yet," I said shortly, hoisting her satchel back over my shoulder. "We need to keep looking."

"The waters go down, down, down," Nicholina sang, her face hidden within the hood of her cloak. "And there you'll drown, drown, drown."

Coco lifted a hand to rub her temple. "This is such a shit show. No one at the dock knew anything, either. One of them threw a *hook* at us when we asked about black pearls. He must've heard rumors about L'Eau Mélancolique." She sighed. "Fishermen. They're superstitious on the best of days, but they fear melusines most of all. I wouldn't be surprised if he calls the Chasseurs. They'll be swarming these streets by morning."

Beau held up a stack of rumpled wanted posters in his hands. "At least he didn't recognize us."

"And we won't be here by morning." I flicked a finger, and the last of my anger leapt onto the papers. Beau yelped when they caught flame, dropping them into the cart. Our faces burned to ash within seconds. "The stalls will be closing soon. Let's turn this market upside down."

An hour later, we regrouped at the end of the street. Bad-tempered. Empty-handed.

Nicholina swayed in the wind. A tendril of white hair swept free of her hood. "Drown, drown, drown."

Scowling, Coco peered through the crowd again. But one could hardly call it a crowd now. Most of the villagers had retired for the night. Only a handful still danced in the street. They stumbled from wine, clutching each other and giggling. By the water, only the staunchest of fishermen remained. And the drunkest. "We should go. There's nothing here. Tomorrow we can circle back—"

Beau slashed a curt hand. "I *told* you. We looked everywhere. There were no pearls in any of those villages."

I too scoured the carts nearest us. Whitewashed coral. Drift-wood chimes. Baskets of woven seaweed, cups of crystallized sea salt, jars of preserved anchovies. Jars and *jars* of anchovies. Beau knocked one to the ground in frustration, and the glass shattered. Célie leapt backward with a startled cry. When the oil soaked her boots, he snorted, and she retaliated by kicking an anchovy at his face.

Children. I was surrounded by children.

"Enough." Voice sharp, I pivoted in one last circle to ensure I hadn't missed anything. But my desperation yielded nothing new. Anchois boasted no pearls, black or otherwise.

"My apologies." Célie sniffed in a dignified way. "It shan't happen again."

"You're going to smell like fish for at *least* a fortnight," Beau said.

Exhaling hard through my nose, I wheeled to face him. "Could you at least *try* to stop provoking everyo—"

A wooden sign behind him caught my attention. A familiar name.

LA CURIEUSE MADAME SAUVAGE
PRICES AVAILABLE UPON REQUEST

I frowned and nudged him aside. Madame Sauvage. I knew that name. How did I know that name? The sign itself— half-hidden and half-rotted—stood between a stall of spindly combs and a barrel of fish oil. I pointed to it. "That wasn't there before, was it?"

Coco's eyes narrowed as she followed my finger. "I don't see anything."

"Well, look. It's right—" I blinked, and the words died on my tongue. I was pointing at the fish oil, not the sign. Because there *was* no sign. Dropping my finger hastily, I shook my head.

Blinked again. "I—never mind."

"Nothing there," Nicholina said, her voice unexpectedly harsh. She tugged on Coco's hand. "Nothing, nothing."

Coco huffed impatiently before drawing her cloak more tightly around her. "If you're *quite* done—" But her eyes widened when she glanced back. "That—that wasn't there before."

Slowly, as if cornering a frightened animal, my gaze returned to the stall and barrel. Sure enough, the wooden sign had rematerialized between them. Emerald and aubergine silk fluttered from the cart behind it. As if it'd been there all along.

"Magic," Célie whispered.

Coco and I shared a wary glance before creeping forward.

Though I clutched a knife in my bandolier, the cart itself didn't *seem* dangerous. Jewelry of all shapes and colors gleamed from the cluttered shelves. Real jewelry. With gemstones and precious metals, not fish bones and octopi tentacles. An assortment of dusty bottles joined them. Dried flowers. Leather-bound books. On a ledge at the back, a crimson-and-gold snake slumbered in a glass cage. Célie approached it in fascination.

I took a deep breath, trying and failing to suppress my unease.

No, it didn't seem dangerous, but there—displayed proudly on the middle shelf—three black pearls nestled in a bed of velvet. It couldn't have been coincidence. When Beau moved toward them, eager, I stilled him with the shake of my head, glancing around for the owner. This mysterious Madame Sauvage. Though nowhere to be seen, she'd tacked a scrap of parchment to the sign:

Coco caught the tail of the emerald silk between two fingers. "Perfect. Makes this easy."

"Too easy," I said before grasping her meaning. Then— "Wait. You want to *steal* them?"

"I'm a thief, Reid." Gaze suddenly alert, she glanced from the cart to the street, assessing the landscape. Tracking the couple closest us. They strolled past hand in hand, oblivious to our presence. When I stepped in front of her, blocking her view, she smirked. "Lou is a thief too, you know. And as soon as we've saved her, you can soak in your virtue until your fingers wrinkle with it. Until then . . ." She slipped past me, lifting a casual shoulder. "We need these pearls. It's better if no one sees our faces." Her eyes lit on something behind me, and she laughed, tossing them my way. "Perfect. A reward for your silence."

I caught the leather pants against my chest. "This isn't funny."

"*Au contraire.* Lou is going to need a laugh after all of this." Her smirk faded then. "You told me to hope, Reid, but hope means nothing without action. I will do whatever it takes to save her. *Whatever* it takes. Are you willing to do the same? Or shall Lou fall on the sword of your principles?"

I glared at her.

"Fabulous. Now. Don't move. You make an excellent shield."

Jaw clenched, I crushed the leather in my fist, watching as she sauntered toward the pearls. When Nicholina moved to knock them aside with her elbow, I caught the rope, untying it from Coco with deft fingers. I wrapped it around my own wrist instead. When Coco glanced back at me, I nodded. This wasn't right, but Lou wasn't right, either. The *world* wasn't right. After L'Eau Mélancolique, I would pay Madame Sauvage back with interest. I would find a dozen black pearls to replace these three, and—

Wait.

Only three?

"There are five of us," I said.

"That shouldn't be a problem." Heart leaping to my throat, I whirled toward the new voice. Coco's hand froze above the pearls. An elderly woman stepped around the cart, her shoulders stooped and her face deeply lined. She wore an olive scarf around her silver hair. Innumerable rings on her ears, her fingers, her toes. Her *bare* toes. An emerald cloak dragged on the ground behind. She grinned, revealing crooked teeth. "Humans can't enter L'Eau Mélancolique. The waters drive them mad."

Nicholina hissed beneath her hood, drawing into me.

I studied the woman. "Have we . . . met before, *madame?*"

"Perhaps? Then again, perhaps not. I have one of those faces, I fear. *Le visage de beaucoup, le visage d'aucun.* The face always seen—"

"—the face never remembered," I finished the old adage by rote. But . . .

Her smile turned knowing. "Hello, dearies. Welcome to my cabinet of curiosities. How may I serve you today?"

Recognition finally dawned at her words, and different shelves rose in rapid succession, each a knife wound in my memory: dancing rats and glass beetles, pointed teeth and butterfly wings. An ugly marionette, a mother-of-pearl ring, and . . . an old woman.

An old woman who'd known more than she should.

Might I interest you in calla lilies? They're said to symbolize humility and devotion. The perfect blooms to end any lovers' quarrel.

Half-healed punctures, all. Still bleeding at the edges.

"Madame Sauvage," I said, lip curling.

She smiled kindly. "*Bonjour*, Reid. What a pleasure it is to see you again." Her smile faded as she took in Nicholina, whose face remained hidden. "Oh, dear." The woman tittered. "I would greet our fair Louise, but it seems another has taken residence—" She stopped abruptly, tilting her head. "Well, well, well . . . more than one someone, I think, and a powerful one at that." Her smile returned full measure, and she clapped her hands in delight. "Louise le Blanc, both cursed *and* blessed. How *riveting*."

More than one someone? I frowned. She meant Nicholina, of course, but—*blessed*?

"You would know," Nicholina snarled with something like fear. "Oh, yes, you would recognize—"

"Ah, ah, ah." With a shake of Madame Sauvage's finger, Nicholina's voice ceased. Her body seemed to grow roots. "That is *quite* enough from you, Nicola. There shall be no blood or secrets spilled in my cart. Please, be still and observe."

"How do you—?" I asked.

"You three know each other?" Célie interrupted, nonplussed.

Madame Sauvage winked. The gesture didn't suit her withered

face. "I suppose one could say that. Last we met, their quarreling nearly shattered my windows." Though she adopted an air of careful indifference, curiosity sparkled in her dark eyes. "I trust our lovebirds have reconciled?"

Still incredulous, confused, I threw the leather pants on a nearby shelf. "It's none of your business."

She *hmph*ed at my tone, but her impish smile didn't waver. Her gaze flicked from me to Célie, lingering on where Beau and Coco hovered near the snake. "Just so, and yet . . . it seems you are once again in need of assistance."

"How much for the pearls?" Coco asked.

"The pearls," Madame Sauvage repeated softly. She looked positively spry. "Well, my dear, the pearls are nearly priceless. What are you willing to give for them?"

Anything.

Nicholina still hadn't moved.

"We have coin," I said automatically. "Lots of coin."

"Oh dear." Madame Sauvage tittered again and shook her head. "Oh dear, oh dear, oh dear. That won't do, will it? I don't sully my hands with money."

A flash of surprise crossed Coco's face. "What *do* you want, then?"

"Whatever it is," Beau muttered, "it can't be good."

Madame Sauvage's entire face split into a grin. "Oh, *no*, Your Highness, you have entirely the wrong idea! Never fear, 'tis nothing nefarious. You see, I deal only in simple favors. Just tokens, really. Trifles."

I scowled. "Nothing simple about a favor."

"What favor?" Coco asked, part apprehensive and part impatient. "Just tell us, so we can do it."

"Of course, of course." If possible, Madame Sauvage's smile widened. "As I said, it's quite simple: one favor for one pearl. My apologies," she added to Beau and Célie, inclining her head, "but truly, L'Eau Mélancolique is no place for humans. 'Tis dark and dangerous, dears. More than monsters lurk within its depths."

Beau scoffed in disbelief. "What are we supposed to do, then? Twiddle our thumbs on the shore?"

"How do you know so much about L'Eau Mélancolique?" Coco asked at the same time.

"Tell us the favors." I raised my voice over theirs. Yes, this strange little cart had appeared from thin air. This stranger little woman seemed to know all our plans, to know Nicholina. Truthfully, she seemed more . . . inquisitive than nefarious, and what choice did we have? We needed the pearls. *Her* pearls. We could deal with the consequences after we'd procured them.

The woman in question rubbed her gnarled hands together. "We'll start with the easy one, yes? Just a kiss."

Just a kiss.

Silence descended like a knife dropped point-first. Instead of lodging at our feet, however, it hovered over our heads. Deadly and sharp. No one dared look at another. I didn't glance at Célie or Nicholina. Neither peeked at me. Beau and Coco stared resolutely at the floor. Finally, I asked, "Between . . . who?"

Cackling, Madame Sauvage lifted a crooked finger to Beau and Coco.

The knife hit its mark.

Beau stiffened. Coco gaped. The tension knotting my own spine, however, left in a rush, and I tried not to sigh with relief. Célie had no qualms. She sagged against a basket of beetles with a shaky laugh.

"The liars, of course." Madame Sauvage nodded with what might've been encouragement. Or glee. "They shall kiss, and the truth shall out. There is truth in a kiss," she added to Célie and me conspiratorially. Célie nodded, though I suspected not because she agreed. No. Because she'd do anything to avoid Madame Sauvage's ire now.

I nodded right along with her.

Coco barely moved her lips as she mumbled, "I'm not lying about anything."

Beau snorted at that.

Though sympathetic to Coco's plight—truly—I reached over to squeeze her shoulder. "Whatever it takes, right?"

She scowled at me.

I smothered a grin. I wasn't enjoying this. I wasn't.

Pushing my hand aside with a muttered curse, she stepped forward. Stopped. Closed her eyes and inhaled deeply. When she opened them again, stony resolve had hardened in their depths. She nodded once to Beau, who looked strangely reluctant. He didn't shrink from her gaze, however. Didn't ease the tension with a joke. He simply stared at her, unmoving. "Just do it," she said. "Hurry up."

He grimaced at the words but took a small step forward, lowering his voice. "If I remember correctly, Cosette, you don't like it hurried." Another step. Coco's fingers still trembled. She fisted them in her skirt. "Not with me."

"I don't like anything with you."

One side of his mouth quirked as he looked down at her, but my own humor faded at his expression. I didn't want to see the emotions in his eyes. I didn't want to see the tenderness. The ache. Even so, his reluctance shone just as clear. He didn't want to kiss her. Not here. Not now. Not like this. "Liar," he whispered.

Then he lowered his lips to hers.

A heartbeat passed as they stood there, bodies rigid and separate. Lips barely touching. Two heartbeats. Three. With a sigh of resignation, Beau moved to pull away, but Coco—

I rolled my eyes.

She wouldn't let him. Her hands crept up his neck, into his hair, holding him there. No. Bringing him closer. Deepening the kiss. When her lips parted on a sigh, he didn't hesitate, his arm snaking out around the small of her back and hauling her flush against him. But it wasn't close enough. Not for Coco. She pressed harder, clutched him tighter, until he chuckled and walked her backward. When her back hit the nearest shelf, he lifted her atop it, spread her knees to push between them. Slow and measured. Unhurried. Until she bit his lip. Something seemed to snap in him then.

Beside me, Célie watched their hands grow frantic—their breaths louder—with round, startled eyes. Her cheeks flamed scarlet. "Oh my," she said.

I averted my gaze. "This has been a long time coming."

"Or *not* coming," Madame Sauvage said, arching a wry brow.

I cringed at the innuendo. "How old *are* you?"

"Young enough, boy. I'm young enough."

Right. With *that* imagery in my head, I cleared my throat. Beau had just slid a hand up Coco's calf, hooking it around her knee to pull her closer. His fingers caressed her skin there. I repeated the sound, louder this time, and grinned despite myself. "Hello! Yes, pardon!" My grin deepened when he pulled back abruptly, as if surfacing from deep water. Blinking slow. Breathing heavy. "As it seems to have escaped your notice, *there are other people here.*"

He still didn't acknowledge us, however. He stared at Coco instead. She stared at him. Neither spoke for several seconds. At last, with infinite gentleness, he brushed his lips against her forehead and stepped away, tugging her skirt back into place. "We'll finish this later."

Her awareness seemed to return then. Her sense. She leapt from the shelf hastily, knocking aside a bin of glass eyes. They scattered across the floor of the cart. When she tripped on one, pinwheeling into Nicholina, Beau caught her arm. She tried to tug it away. "Don't *touch* me. I'm fine." She slipped on another eye, kicking it viciously in response. "I said I'm *fine.*"

His face fell at her outburst, and he scowled, releasing her. "Say it one more time." When she stumbled away, nearly upsetting another basket, he shook his head. "Maybe I'll believe you."

She watched him stalk from the cart with overbright eyes, her arms wrapped tight around her middle. Her shoulders hunched. As if their kiss had inflicted a physical wound. I looked away quickly when her gaze caught mine. "Don't say a word," she snapped, storming past me into the street. She didn't follow Beau.

"Ah, *l'amour.*" Madame Sauvage stared after them with a wistful expression. "I told you the truth would out." When she clapped her hands together once more, turning the full force of her gaze onto me, I recoiled. "Now. It is your turn, young man. Hold out your hand, please."

"I would . . . rather not," I said dubiously.

"Nonsense. You want your pearl, don't you?"

I glanced after Beau and Coco. "That depends."

But it didn't, not really, and we both knew it. Swallowing hard, I extended a hand toward her. To my surprise, she withdrew a small pouch from her sleeve and upended its contents in my palm. Célie inched closer, tilting her head. "Seeds?" she asked in confusion.

And so they were.

Madame Sauvage closed my fingers around them with a pleasant smile. "Just so. Your task is simple, dear boy: plant them."

I frowned down at the mundane things. "Plant them?"

Madame Sauvage turned to bustle around her cart, returning items to their proper places. "What else does one do with seeds?"

"I—" Shaking my head, I stuffed them back in their pouch. "What are they?" *Stupid question.* I tried again. "Where—where do you want me to plant them? When?"

"Those decisions are up to you."

When I cast Célie an incredulous glance, she shrugged, gesturing first to the pearls, then to the street. I swept the black gems into the pouch with the seeds. Madame Sauvage didn't stop me, instead plucking a live mouse from her sleeve and dropping it into the snake's reservoir. She cooed at the snake as it uncoiled. Like a mother with her babe. Célie gestured to the street again. Wilder this time. Emphatic.

But it didn't feel right to just *leave*. And Nicholina—she still stood silent and rooted. Clearly Madame Sauvage wasn't a simple peddler. "Why are you here, Madame Sauvage? How did you— how did you find us?"

The woman looked up as if surprised to find us still standing there. "Why are *you* here, young man? You've collected your pearls. Now be on your way."

She waved her hand once more, and Nicholina gasped. Stumbled. Next second, she lunged at Madame Sauvage with a snarl, but I pulled my wrist sharply, forcing her to a halt. The hood slipped from her face, and she glared between the two of us in silent fury.

"It doesn't feel very nice, does it? To lose bodily autonomy?" Madame Sauvage shooed us from the cart without further ceremony. "A lesson well remembered, Nicola. Now, go. You all have rather more pressing matters of which to attend, don't you?"

Célie clutched my arm when I didn't move, pulling me down the steps.

Yes. Yes, we should go, but—

My gaze caught on a glass display of pastries near the snake. They *definitely* hadn't been there before. Torn between trepidation and interest, between fear and inexplicable ease, I nodded to them. "How . . . how much for the sticky bun?"

"Ah." Madame Sauvage brightened abruptly, plucking the pastry from its case and wrapping it in brown paper. She followed us down the steps before extending it to me. "For you? Free of charge."

I regarded her warily.

"Never fear." She tugged her sign from the mud. An oddly mundane gesture amidst the uncanny circumstances. "We shall meet again soon, Reid Labelle. Plant those seeds."

With a cheery wink, she vanished before our eyes, taking her sign and her strange little cart with her.

LE CŒUR BRISÉ

Reid

"We're here," Coco said softly.

A quarter hour ago, she'd forced us to stop, to bear Nicholina to the ground and tip a sleeping tincture down her throat. It hadn't been pretty. It hadn't been fun. I still had bite marks on my hand to prove it.

We stood beneath the shadow of a lone cypress tree—at least, I thought it was a cypress. Below the smoke and clouds, true darkness had fallen once more. The forest at our backs stood eerily still. Even the wind had ceased here, yet a hint of brine still tinged the air. No waves, however. I heard no waves. No gulls, either. No signs of life at all. Shifting my feet uneasily, I took in the path ahead. Narrow and rocky, it disappeared into fog so thick I could've cut it with a knife. A chill skittered down my spine at what could be lurking within it. Despite no signs of Morgane and Josephine, the hair at my neck lifted. "What now?"

Coco came to stand beside me. "We keep going. Straight down."

"Into *that*?" Beau too stepped forward, halting at my other side. He eyed the fog skeptically. "Can we not?"

"L'Eau Mélancolique lies past it."

"Yes, but surely we can find less overtly ominous access."

"Le Cœur Brisé is everywhere. One doesn't *access* the Wistful Waters without him."

Célie swallowed hard. "But—we only have three pearls. Madame Sauvage said humans aren't allowed near the waters. She said they could drive us mad."

"The waters can drive anyone mad. Human or witch." Coco straightened her shoulders, still staring into the mist. "But you're right. We just have three, so we'll—we'll walk the path as far as Le Cœur allows, but only Reid, Nicholina, and I will continue to shore." Her eyes flashed to mine. "If we can pass his test."

"What *test?*" I asked with mounting unease. "No one said anything about a test."

She waved a curt hand. "You'll pass." Glancing at Nicholina, however, she added, "I'm not so sure about her, but he only tested us the once. Maybe he won't this time either—"

Beau pounced on this new information, whirling to point a finger at Coco. Triumphant. Furious. "I *knew* you were hiding something."

"Lou and I played at L'Eau Mélancolique as children," Coco snapped. "It's hardly a secret. Of course we ran into Le Cœur a time or two. He liked us, so he didn't ask for pearls. We brought him tricks instead."

Célie blinked in confusion. "But you said we needed black pearls."

Huffing impatiently, Coco crossed her arms and looked away.

"We do. We *did*—just not all the time. Lou once magicked them into spiders when he touched them. He's terrified of spiders."

A beat of silence.

"And he *liked* you?" Beau asked, perplexed.

"He liked me better than Lou."

"Enough." I hoisted Nicholina higher in my arms, starting toward the path. Tendrils of fog stretched out to meet me, curling around my boots. My ankles. I kicked them away. We were so close. *Too* close. "We didn't come all this way to leave now."

BUT LEAVE YOU SHALL. An abrupt, unfamiliar voice thundered around me, *through* me, and I stumbled, nearly sending Nicholina face-first into the mist. By the others' reactions—Célie actually screamed—they'd heard it too. The mist at my feet visibly thickened, swirling up my legs now. I felt its pressure like a vise. Panicked, I leapt backward, and the mist released me. It didn't stop thickening, however. It didn't stop speaking. *IF YOU CANNOT DRINK OF THE WATERS AND SPILL THEIR TRUTH.*

I nearly stepped on Célie in my haste to retreat.

"What is it?" She clutched my arm, clutched Nicholina's arm, clutched anything to ground herself in reality. But this *was* our reality—possessions, harbinger dogs, shape-shifting dragons, talking *mist*. It would never end. "Is it Le Cœur?"

In answer, the mist slowly darkened, drawing in on itself as a spider might spin its web. Growing limbs. A head. A pair of chilling coal-black eyes. Despite the ominous voice, those eyes softened on Coco as their owner stepped forth. Powerfully built—taller even than me—the man heaved a booming laugh and opened his arms to her. She hesitated for only a second before rushing forward. Voice hitching with laughter—perhaps tears—she buried her face in his chest and she said, "I've missed you, Constantin."

Beau stared at them, dumbstruck, as they embraced. I might've found his expression comical if I too hadn't felt this revelation like a blow to the head.

Constantin. *Constantin.* I knew the name, of course. How could I ever forget? Madame Labelle had held me captive with it in the Bellerose all those months ago, weaving magic with her tale of star-crossed lovers. Of magic rings and seas of tears and witches and holy men. Of Angelica and *Constantin.* The saint who'd gifted the Church his blessed sword, the original Balisarda. I'd carried a part of him with me for years, unaware his sword hadn't been blessed at all, but enchanted by his lover. She'd wanted to protect him. He'd wanted her magic. When he hadn't been able to take it from her, he'd eventually taken his life instead.

This couldn't be the same man. Of course it couldn't. The story said he'd died, and even if he hadn't, he would be thousands of years old now. Long dead. And Coco—she hadn't spoken a word about knowing Constantin during Madame Labelle's tale. She would have told us. Surely. Lou's life had been tangentially tied with him and Angelica, whose ill-fated love had first sparked the war between the Church and Dames Blanches. She would've told us. She *would've.*

"Constantin." Beau said the name slowly, tasting it. Remembering. "I know that name. Aren't you supposed to be dead?"

Coco stiffened at his brash words, but Constantin merely

chuckled. Ruffling her hair, he gently disentangled himself from her arms. "My reputation precedes me."

"You're Le Cœur Brisé?" I asked in disbelief. "The Broken Heart?"

His dark eyes glinted. "The irony is not lost on me, I assure you."

"But you aren't . . . you aren't *the* Constantin. You're not him." When he simply stared at me, I exhaled a harsh breath and looked at Coco, unable to articulate the sudden, painful flare of emotion in my chest. She hadn't told us. She'd . . . withheld information. She hadn't lied—not exactly—but she hadn't told the truth either. It felt like a betrayal.

"Right." Shaking my head, I tried to refocus. "How?"

"Who cares?" Beau muttered, near indiscernible.

Constantin extended his arms. "I am cursed eternal, huntsman, because I yearned for more."

Coco cast him a slanted look. "I think you went a bit further than that."

"You're right, of course, Cosette. I broke a woman's heart in the process—my one true regret in life."

Rolling her eyes, Coco said, "Constantin leapt from these cliffs. When Angelica wept her sea of tears, the waters . . . revived him." She gestured to the mist around us. The very mist from which he'd formed. "Their magic gives him life. Now he serves as a warning."

We all stared at her. "What does that mean?" Beau finally asked.

"It means Isla poked her nose in like a prying busybody,"

Constantin said, surprisingly pleasant given the circumstances. He swept a hand down his arm, his bare chest. He wore nothing save the cloth around his waist, his lower half obscured by mist. Condensation collected on his skin, curled in his hair. "She watched everything between Angelica and me, and when the waters intervened, she swept in and cursed me to guard the women of these waters—and their magic—forever."

Célie's gaze darted. "The women of these waters?"

"The melusines." Constantin's face contorted with distaste. "Fish women. *Fickle* women."

"Temptresses," Coco added. "The ones who dwell here are also truth tellers. Some are seers. The waters have given them strange abilities."

My arms began to burn, and I readjusted my grip on Nicholina. "Who is Isla?"

Constantin snorted in response. "The queen of the melusines."

"Claud's sister," Coco said at the same time.

"Is she a goddess, then?" Célie asked.

Constantin bowed slightly, inclining his head. "Some would call her such. Others would not. Either way, she is very old and powerful. If you seek an audience, however, I must warn you: she cannot interfere in the affairs of humans. Not without repercussion."

Coco touched his arm. "We aren't here for her, Constantin. Not yet, at least." She looked to Nicholina, to Lou in my arms, and her entire body seemed to wilt once more. Constantin followed her gaze, his sharp eyes tracking over Lou's sallow skin, her gaunt cheeks. He hummed a low note of understanding.

"Louise is ill."

"And possessed," I added a touch desperately.

His eyebrows shot up. "You believe the waters will heal her."

"They healed you," Beau pointed out, "and you were dead."

Constantin parted the mist with his hands, the tendrils curling between his fingers. It struck me as an idle gesture. An apathetic one. "It's true. If anything can heal her, these waters can. Though they started as mere tears, they've become as sentient as the pulse within a Dame Rouge, as connected as a Dame Blanche to this land. Angelica was a seer, and her magic shaped them. The waters see things we cannot see, know things we cannot know. I am part of them now, yet even I do not grasp the future as they. I have lived a hundred human lives, yet even I cannot comprehend their knowledge."

I struggled to extract the pearls from my pack while maintaining my hold on Nicholina. Beau extended his arms instead. Reluctantly, I handed her over before thrusting the pearls at Constantin. To my surprise, his hands felt solid. Warm. He truly was alive. "Our payment," I said.

His fingers curled around the pearls. His eyes flicked to Coco. "Are you sure?"

She nodded resolutely. "She's my best friend."

He shrugged then, and the pearls dissolved into mist. "Very well. On her head be it." To the rest of us, he asked, "Who accompanies the fair maidens?"

I stepped forward. "Me."

"Of course." His gaze swept from my head to my toes. He *hmph*ed as if displeased. As if the mud on my boots, perhaps the bandolier on my chest, offended him. "I've heard of your exploits,

Reid Diggory. I've heard of your glory in my legacy. I've heard all about the death and blood on yours and your brethren's hands." He paused for me to respond, but I didn't give him the satisfaction. I didn't give him any reaction at all. "To be honest, you remind me of a much younger version of myself."

"I am nothing like you."

He tilted his head. "Time changes us all, does it not?"

"La-di-da, mysterious bullshit, ominous warnings." Beau repositioned Nicholina with stiff, awkward movements, exhaling an aggrieved breath. "Should we keep standing around, or—?"

"Point taken." Constantin grinned, and with the wave of his hand, Beau and Célie vanished. Both just . . . vanished. Nicholina's weight landed solidly back in my arms.

"Where did you send them?" Coco asked, voice rising in panic. "I mean—are they safe?"

Constantine's eyes glittered knowingly. "No one is safe here, Cosette. Not even you. I protected you and your friend as children. This time, however, you seek the waters as an adult of your own volition. I can no longer bend the rules. You too must drink and speak truth. Now"—he stepped aside, gesturing to the path before us, the path still concealed by semisolid mist—"shall we?"

She swallowed visibly.

When I strode forward, however, she slipped her arm through mine, hurrying to keep up. "Have you never drunk before?" I asked her quietly. Though I couldn't hear Constantin following, I sensed his presence behind us as we trekked down the path. It sloped gently, evenly, despite the rocks. Silence still coated everything. "In all the times you visited?"

"Just once," she whispered back, "when I tried to see my—" But she stopped abruptly, squeezing my arm tight. "When Lou and I tried to swim in the waters. Constantin never made us drink of them otherwise. We usually just played along the shore."

"And that one time?" I asked.

She shuddered. "It was awful."

"What did you see?"

"What I wanted most in the world."

"Which was?"

She scoffed but didn't withdraw her arm. "Like I'd tell you. I already spoke it once. I'm not speaking it again."

"You aren't serious." An ache started to build in my right temple. "How can I know what to expect if you won't—"

"You can't," Constantin interrupted, materializing directly in front of us. We both skidded to a halt. "None know what the water will show them. Desires, fears, strengths, weaknesses, memories—it sees truth and demands truth in turn. All you must do is acknowledge it."

At his words, the mist behind him began to clear. It moved slowly, deliberately, each tendril creeping apart to reveal a vast, impossibly smooth body of water. It stretched between two mountains, extended as far as the eye could see. To the horizon. Beyond. The moon—silver as a freshly minted coin—shone clear and bright across its glassy surface. No smoke here. No waves either.

Not a single sound.

Constantin flicked his wrist, and from the fog, three chalices formed, solidifying into simple iron. They waited in the sand at the edge of the water. Almost touching it. Not quite. Gently, I lowered Nicholina to the ground. She didn't stir when I lifted her eyelid, checked her pulse. "What did you *do* to her? She's barely conscious."

"It's a simple sleeping solution—lavender, chamomile, valerian root, and blood." Coco shrugged nervously. "It's *possible* that I overdid it."

"She will drink," Constantin said, his form beginning to fade, "or she will die."

I couldn't suppress a snarl of frustration. "You're a real son of a bitch, you know that?"

When he lifted his hands, they dissolved into mist. Another arrogant smile. "I am a simple guardian. Drink of the waters, and spill their truth. If you succeed, you may enter their healing depths. If you fail, you will leave this place, and you will never return."

"I'm not going anywhere—" But even as the words left my mouth, I felt the mist constrict around me like iron manacles, knew staying upon failure wouldn't be an option. The mist—or Le Cœur, or the waters, or the magic itself—wouldn't allow it. Only when I muttered a terse agreement did the manacles dissipate. I still felt their presence, however, hovering over my skin. Their warning.

"Drink of the waters," Constantin repeated, near immaterial now, "and spill their truth." Only his eyes remained. When they found Coco, they softened, and a tendril of fog reached out to caress her face. "Good luck."

He left us standing alone in the moonlight, staring down at our chalices.

THE WATERS' TRUTH

Reid

I still remembered the exact moment I received my Balisarda. After each tournament, a banquet was held to honor the champions, to welcome them into the ranks of brotherhood. Few attended outside of the Chasseurs and Church, and the celebrations never lasted long—a quick address, a quicker meal. No toasts. No music. No revelry. A modest affair. The next morning, however, the real exhibition would begin. The entire kingdom would come to Cathédral Saint-Cécile d'Cesarine to watch the induction ceremony. Aristocrats and paupers alike would dress in their finest. Initiates would line the aisle. At the altar, the Archbishop would stand with the inductees' Balisardas. They would adorn the communion table, polished and resplendent in their velvet boxes.

I'd been the only inductee at my ceremony. Mine had been the only Balisarda.

Jean Luc had stood at the end of the aisle, hands clasped behind his back. His face tight. His body rigid. Célie had sat in the third row with her parents and sister. She'd tried to catch my eye as I'd marched down the aisle, but I hadn't been able to look at her. I hadn't been able to look at anything but my Balisarda. It'd called to me as a siren's song, the sapphire glittering in the filtered sunlight.

I'd repeated my vows by rote. Shoulders straight and proud. After, the Archbishop had broken tradition to embrace me, but his public display hadn't embarrassed me. I'd been pleased with it. Pleased with myself. So, so pleased. And why not? I'd trained religiously for years—I'd bled and sweat and sacrificed—all for this moment.

When I'd reached out to finally accept my Balisarda, however, I'd hesitated. Just for a second.

Part of me had known, even then, this sword—this life—would bring pain. Part of me had known I would suffer.

I'd chosen it anyway.

Just as I chose it now.

My fingers wrapped around the cold metal of my chalice, and I knelt to fill it. No ripples emanated when I broke the waters' still surface. Instead, it seemed to absorb the movement. Frowning, I tried to slip my hand beneath as well, to splash, to create movement, but I met with an invisible wall. I pushed harder. My hand stopped a hair's breadth over the surface—so close I could feel the wintry cold emanating from the waters. I still couldn't touch them. Expelling a harsh breath, I abandoned the attempt. Constantin had said as much.

I eyed the iron chalice warily. This wouldn't be pleasant.

"Wait." Coco clasped my forearm when I moved the cup to my mouth. "Lou first. I don't know what'll happen when we drink, but I doubt we'll be able to help her."

"I don't think we *can* help her." Still, I lowered my hand. "We don't know what the waters will show her. How can we fight an invisible foe?"

"I'm not saying she's incapable of fighting her own battle." Coco rolled her eyes and bent to fill the other chalices. "I'm saying she's unconscious. She'll need help with the actual drinking."

"Oh." Despite the seriousness of our circumstances, heat crept up my throat. I hurried to help her lift Lou, gently pulling her onto my lap. "Right."

"Tilt her head back."

I obliged, fighting the instinct to knock the chalice aside as Coco brought it to Lou's lips. Because Coco was right—if anyone could do this, Lou could. I held her secure, and slowly, carefully, Coco opened her mouth and tipped the water in. "Easy," I warned her. "Easy."

Coco didn't take her eyes from the task at hand. "Shut up, Reid."

Nothing happened when the cold water touched Lou's tongue. Coco poured a little more. It trickled from one corner of her mouth. Still nothing. "She isn't swallowing," I said.

"Yes, *thank* you—" But Coco stopped abruptly when Lou's eyes snapped open. We both stared down at her. Coco placed a tentative hand on her cheek. "Lou? How do you feel?"

Her eyes rolled to the back of her head in response, and her mouth opened on a violent scream—except no sound came out. Silence still reigned. The waters, however, rippled in an eerie sort of acknowledgment. Gripping her shoulders, I watched helplessly as she scratched at her face, her hair. Like she would tear Nicholina out by force. Her head thrashed. "*Shit.*" I struggled to hold her, but Coco pushed me backward, downing her chalice in a single swallow.

"Hurry!" She tossed her cup aside, bracing her hands against the shore. "Drink now. The sooner we spill our truths, the sooner we can dip Lou in the—" But her eyes too rolled backward, and though her body didn't seize as Lou's had, she fell sideways, comatose, her cheek hitting the sand. Eyes still rolling.

She'd looked like this once before. Seeing nothing. Seeing everything.

A man close to your heart will die.

Cursing bitterly—casting one last look at Lou, who'd gone limp on my lap—I tossed back the contents of my own chalice. If possible, the water tasted even colder than it'd felt. Unnaturally cold. Cruelly cold. It burned my throat all the way down, solidifying to ice in my stomach. In my limbs. In my veins. Within seconds, movement became difficult. Coughing, gagging, I slid Lou from my lap as the first tremor rocked my frame. When I collapsed forward on hands and knees, the edges of my vision paled to white. Strange. It should've gone dark, not light, and—

The burn in my lungs vanished abruptly, and my vision cleared. I blinked in surprise. Blinked again. This couldn't be right. Had I not drunk enough? Straightening, I glanced first to my empty cup, then to Lou and Coco. Surprise withered to confusion. To fear. They'd disappeared in the mist as completely as the others. I shot to my feet. "Lou? Coco?"

"I'm here!" Lou called from down the shoreline. Surprised, relieved, I hurried after her voice, peering through the mist and darkness. Though the moon still suffused the scene in soft silver light, it illuminated little now. Shafts of it shone through the mist intermittently. Blinding me one moment. Disorienting me the next.

"Where are you? I can't—"

Her hand caught mine, and she stepped into sight, grinning and whole. I stared at her in disbelief. Where her skin had been wan and sickly, it now shone gold, dusted with freckles. Where her hair had been shorn and white, it now spilled long and lustrous down her back, chestnut and sable once more. I caught a strand of it between my fingers. Even her scars had healed. Except . . . except one.

I traced a finger over the thorns and roses at her throat. At my touch, her eyes fluttered shut. Mist undulated around her face, casting her in an ethereal haze. "Do you like it? Coco could make a killing doing this—transforming the macabre into the macabrely beautiful."

"You're always beautiful." Throat tight, I could barely speak the words. She wrapped her arms around my waist, resting her ear against my heart. "Are you . . . better?" I asked.

"Almost." Grinning anew at my wary expression, she stood on her tiptoes to kiss me. "Come on. I want to show you something."

I followed blindly, my heart in my throat. A voice at the back of my mind warned it couldn't be this easy—warned I shouldn't trust it—but when Lou laced her fingers through mine, pulling me farther into the mist, I let her. Her hand felt warmer than it'd been in ages. And that scent in the air—like magic and vanilla and cinnamon—I inhaled it deeply. An innate sense of peace spread outward from my chest. Of course I didn't hesitate. This was Lou. She wasn't a Balisarda, and I wasn't walking down the aisle. I wasn't pledging my fate. I'd already done that.

"How did you exorcise Nicholina?" I asked dreamily. "What did the waters show you?"

She smiled at me over her shoulder, lit from within. "I don't remember you being so chatty, husband."

Husband. The rightness of the word felt warm. Heady. I grinned and draped my free arm across her shoulders, tucking her firmly against my side. Craving her warmth. Her smile. "And I don't remember *you*—"

—*spilling her truth*, my mind chastised. *You haven't either. This isn't real.*

My smile slipped. Of course it was real. I could feel her against me. Slowing to a stop, I gripped her tighter, spun her around. When she looked up, arching a familiar brow, my breath caught in my throat. Truly, she seemed to be glowing with happiness. I felt like I could fly. "Tell me," I said softly, brushing a strand of hair behind her ear. "Tell me what you saw."

"Let me show you instead."

I frowned now. Was her skin—was it actually glowing? She

waved her hands, and the mist around us thinned, revealing a stone altar behind her. On it, a young woman lay prone, bound, and gagged. She struggled to support her head, which protruded past the altar. Her hair—white as the snow and the moon, white as her gown—had been braided. The plait fell from her nape to the stone bowl beneath her throat. I stepped closer in alarm. The girl looked . . . no, *felt* . . . familiar. With her turquoise eyes, she could've been a sixteen-year-old Lou, but that wasn't right. She was too tall. Too strong. Her skin pale and unfreckled.

"Look at her, darling," Lou crooned with a dagger in her hand. I stared at it, unable to understand where it'd come from. Unable to grasp why she had it. "Isn't she lovely?"

"What are you doing?"

She tossed the dagger into the air, watching it rotate up, down, catching it by the handle. "I have to kill her."

"What? No." I tried to stand between them, but my feet wouldn't move. The mist had crept forward while I'd studied the girl, solidifying around us. My breathing quickened. "Why? Why would you do that?"

She cast me a pitiful look. "It's for the greater good, of course."

"No. That—no, Lou." I shook my head vehemently. "Killing that child won't solve anything—"

"Not just *any* child." She sauntered toward the altar, still tossing her knife and catching it. The girl watched with wide eyes, struggling harder, as the scene around us continued to evolve. The waters disappeared, and true mountains formed. A temple in a meadow. Scores of women all around, dancing wildly in the moonlight. Black-haired triplets and a witch with a holly crown. But the girl on the altar couldn't escape. The mist held her trapped in place like a pig for slaughter while Lou pointed the knife at her throat. "*This* child. I alone am willing to do what must be done, darling. I alone am willing to sacrifice. Why can't you see that? I will save *everyone*."

Bile rose in my throat. "You can't do this. Not—not her. Please."

She stared at me sadly, knife still poised above the girl. "I am my mother's daughter, Reid. I will do anything to protect those I love. Would you not kill"—she kissed the girl's throat with the blade—"for me?"

Incredulous, angry, I nearly broke my legs trying to wrench free. "I wouldn't ki—"

The lie blackened and cracked before I could finish it. Like ashes on my tongue. My ashes.

I *had* killed for Lou. The Archbishop hadn't been innocent, no, but the others—the ones before him? I'd killed them for less than love. I'd killed them out of obligation, out of loyalty. I'd killed them for glory. But . . . that wasn't quite right either. *Drink of the waters, and spill their truth.*

I could see the cracks in their magic now. Their Lou had been so convincing. So perfect. Like the Lou I'd preserved in my memory. But reality wasn't perfection, and neither was she—not then and not now. She'd once told me it hurt to remember the dead as they were, rather than who we wanted them to be. Memory was a dangerous thing.

Time changes us all, does it not?

I was no longer the boy who'd pined after his Balisarda, who'd first held it with reverence, with pride, yet part of me remembered him. Part of me still felt his longing. Now, perhaps for the first time, I saw the truth clearly. I'd killed the Archbishop because I loved Lou. I'd killed innocents because I loved the Archbishop. Because I'd loved my brethren, my family. Every time I'd found a home, I'd fought tooth and nail to keep it.

Just like Morgane.

A thin line of scarlet wet Lou's blade. It colored the girl's neck like a ribbon. "You once said I'm like my mother." Lou stared at the blood on her knife, transfixed. "You were right." Quicker than I could react, she slashed the girl's neck, turning to face me as the latter choked and gurgled. Her movements slowed within seconds. Scarlet stained the white stone irrevocably. "You were right."

Drink of the waters, and spill their truth.

"Yes." The mist around my feet vanished with the word, and I strode forward purposefully, swallowing bile. I didn't look at the girl. Didn't memorize her face. My chest cleaved in two with the effort. This wasn't real. Not yet. Not *ever*—not if I could help it. "Yes, Lou, you are like your mother." I took her chin in my hand, forcing her to look at me. "But so am I."

The second the words left my lips, a wide grin broke across her face. "Well done, you." And then the ground began to crumble, the altar and temple falling away to white sand and still water. A rushing sound filled my ears, and Lou's chin vanished between my fingers. I clutched only empty air. Sand abraded my knees, and I glanced down to my discarded iron chalice. I touched it gingerly. Still cold.

"You've returned." Constantin's amused voice punctured the silence as I sat backward, stunned. "After Coco, I might add." He winked at her where she sat frozen beside me, clutching her knees.

At my anxious look, she muttered, "I'm fine."

"Did you speak your truth?"

"Every word."

"You aren't going to repeat it, are you?"

"Never."

Constantin chuckled before snapping his gaze to Lou, who started to stir. He rubbed his hands together in anticipation. "Ah, excellent. Right on time."

I moved to her side just as she opened her eyes. Her gaze darted from me to Coco, to the endless sand beyond us, and she bolted upright, craning her neck to look behind. "Lou?" I asked in confusion, lifting a hand to touch her forehead. Her bite hadn't healed—I hadn't expected it to, not yet—and her color looked paler than usual. As white as her hair. She scrabbled backward on her hands, still searching the beach wildly.

"Where are they?" Her voice pitched high, girlish, and my heart dropped. Not Lou at all, then. "Where are they hiding? Where are they waiting? They're near, they're near. They must be here."

I stared at her in disgust. In pity. "No one else is here, Nicholina. Just you."

"No, no, no." She rocked back and forth as Coco had done, shaking her head frenetically. Wincing as she did. "It's a trap. They're here, oh yes, and they're waiting, hiding, creeping through the mist—"

Coco knelt in front of her, grasping her chin in her fingers. "They aren't coming. Accept it. Move on. Better yet—switch sides. Nicholina, my aunt isn't the person you want her to be. Morgane is even worse. They don't value you. They don't accept you. You're a tool to them—a means to an end—just like the rest of us."

"*No.*" The word tore from Nicholina in a guttural snarl, and she clawed at her own face, scoring the skin there. When I leapt to intervene, those nails raked down my chest instead. "*You.* I shall deliver you with the mouse, yes, yes, yes, and we shall cut your heart into thirds—"

Constantin tsked in disapproval and waved his hand. The mist answered by swirling around her in a violent tornado, trapping her in place. Nicholina howled in rage. "They will kill us both, stupid mouse. Stupid, *stupid* mouse. We cannot dance, no, but we *can* drown. Down, down, down, we can drown. There is no hope. Only *sickness.*"

Then she spoke again.

Warmth suffused my entire body.

"I thought you weren't"—her voice pitched lower than before, and she gritted her teeth in concentration—"worried about dying? Or have you—finally—accepted the truth?"

Lou.

I couldn't breathe. Couldn't calm the racing of my heart. It was her. It was *Lou.*

The waters must've weakened Nicholina enough for her to break through, or—or perhaps they demanded truth, even now. They knew Nicholina didn't belong. They knew whose body she inhabited.

Constantin sighed. "The bickering was diverting at first. Now it isn't. Spill your truths, all of you, or leave this place in peace. I don't have all night."

"Really?" Lou fought to smile, still panting. "What else—do you have to do? This is—your sole purpose—isn't it?"

He glowered at her. "Charming as always, Louise."

She bowed, failing to hide her grimace as Nicholina threw them against the cage. "I—try."

"Your truth," he insisted, voice hard.

Her face spasmed, and when she opened her mouth once more, I wasn't sure who spoke: Lou or Nicholina. Either way, their truth spilled from them unapologetically. Strong and without strain. "I am capable of great evil." The words hung in the air between us, as sentient as the mist. They waited, coiled, for my response. For my clarification. For my own truth.

I looked directly in her eyes. "We all are."

As if exhaling on a sigh, the words dissipated. The mist went with it, leaving Lou sprawled unceremoniously in the sand. Constantin nodded. "Very good, each of you. One of life's greatest trials is to acknowledge our own reflections. Tonight, you have seen yourselves. You have drunk of the waters, and you have spilled their truth." He extended his hand to the shore. An emotion I couldn't place shone deep in his eyes. Perhaps sadness.

Wistfulness. "Go now. Let their wisdom flow through your veins and restore you." To Coco, he murmured, "I hope you live your truth, Cosette."

She gazed out at the waters with an identical expression. "I hope so too."

In the stillness of the moment, Nicholina lunged toward the path with a feral cry. A desperate cry. I caught her before she could escape, hauling her over my shoulder. Her fists pounded my back, weaker than they should've been. Her hands still tender and raw. When she moved to kick my groin, I caught her shin, holding it away from me. My own hope swelled in my chest. Bright and savage. "You're going to injure yourself."

"Let me go!" She bit my shoulder like a rabid animal, but the thick wool of my coat prevented much damage. "You'll kill us! Do you hear me? We'll drown! We cannot dance beneath these waters. We are too heavy, too *many*—"

"Enough." I marched her toward the water with steely determination. This time, my feet broke its surface without resistance. We'd been granted permission to enter. To heal. Behind us, Constantin vanished, leaving Coco to stand alone. She gave a curt nod. "We finish this now, Nicholina. Get. The. Hell. Out. Of. My. Wife."

She shrieked as I threw her headfirst into the waters.

MATHIEU

Lou

The water was freezing—shockingly and cripplingly so. My muscles seized on impact, and my breath left in a painful, startled rush. My lungs immediately shrieked in protest.

Fucking fabulous. Fucking *Reid*.

He'd meant well, of course, but couldn't the heroic brute have checked the waters' temperature first? Perhaps taken a dip himself? I certainly couldn't dance as a block of ice. And my eyes—I couldn't see *anything*. Whatever moonlight had shone above hadn't managed to penetrate below, plunging us into pitch blackness. A fitting end for Nicholina, that. A true taste of her own medicine. If possible, she seemed to like the dark even less than me, and in her utter hysteria, she thrashed wildly, vying for control. Sinking us like a brick.

Stop it. Clenching my aching teeth, I struggled to move my arms and legs in unison. She floundered in the opposite direction, and our skirt tangled in our feet, thick and heavy and dangerous. We sank another inch, and another and another, each of our panic feeding the other, heightening to a collective sort of frenzy. *Nicholina*, I said sharply, ignoring the roaring of my heart. It nearly exploded in my chest. *Stop struggling. We need to work together, or we're both going to die. I'm a strong swimmer. Let me lead—*

Never.

The voices echoed her. *Never, never, never.* They swarmed around us, panicked and hysterical, and we sank faster still, weighed down by our heavy cloak and gown. I pulled at the former while Nicholina tried to loosen the latter. Swearing viciously, I joined her instead, and together—miraculously in unison—we unknotted the laces with stiff, clumsy fingers. She kicked at the skirt as I clawed at our cloak. Within seconds, both floated away from us through the black water, ominous and slow, before disappearing altogether.

Still we sank.

Shit. It was like swimming through oil, through tar. My lungs burned as I strained upward, and Nicholina finally, desperately mimicked my movements. *That's it. Keep going. Left foot, right foot, left foot, right foot.*

We dance, we dance, we dance.

But we weren't dancing at all. Already, white stars popped in my vision, and my head pounded from lack of oxygen. Sharp pain pierced my ears. And . . . and something else. Something worse. Too late, I realized that Nicholina's veil—the darkness that had shielded her subconscious—had vanished altogether. The waters had stripped it. At last, her every thought, every feeling, every fear flooded our shared consciousness with startling clarity. Faces flashed. Pieces of memories, bits of sentiment tied to each one. Fervor and affection and hatred and shame. It was too much.

Too many. I didn't want them. Her emotions didn't stop coming, however—so intense, so *painful*—and the full force of her being crashed into me like a tidal wave.

And so did my magic.

Gold and white exploded with blinding intensity, everywhere at once. Though I tried to catch a pattern—a pattern to swim, a pattern to shield, a pattern to *anything*—Nicholina's emotions overwhelmed everything. They buffeted me.

What are you doing? What are you doing? She urged me onward, voice frantic, realizing too late what had happened. She hadn't known her veil had lifted. Though she tried to summon it once more, the waters had shredded it beyond repair. *Dance, little mouse! You must dance! Right, left, right, left, right!*

But the waters didn't drown us now. She did. Unadulterated emotion robbed what little of our breath remained, pulling us both beneath the onslaught. We sank and sank and sank with each fresh wave. No. We sank *into* each fresh wave. The darkness around us pricked with light.

And suddenly, we weren't in the Wistful Waters at all.

Lavender brushed my fingertips. Its scent perfumed the summer air, sweet and sharp and heady, and overhead, a single fat cloud drifted past. I glanced around warily. I knew this place. I knew the mountains all around us, the creek trickling at the edge of the field. As a child, I'd played here often, but it hadn't been filled with lavender then, only grass and the gnarled stumps of pear trees. Manon said a grove had once grown in this valley, but Morgane had torched it in an inexplicable fit of rage before we were born. Had the lavender preceded the trees? Or had it come after?

Something shifted beside me, and I tensed instinctively, whipping around to face it.

My heart leapt to my throat.

"You're . . . *you*," I said in disbelief.

Nicholina stared back at me, her silver eyes wider than I'd ever seen them. Her skin paler. The scars on her chest shone stark and gruesome in the bright sunlight, and her black dress—tattered and dirty—seemed incongruous with this happy place. Glancing down at my own body, I lifted my hands experimentally, and they responded without hesitation. I flexed my fingers. At the sight of them straightening, curling back into my palms, a bubble of laughter rose in my throat—*my* throat. Not ours.

Unable to help myself, I lifted my face to the sun, savoring its warmth. Just for a moment. I didn't know where we were, I didn't know *how* we were, and I didn't care. Instead, I felt . . . whole. Curious sensation flowed through my limbs, as if the waters had not only restored me but strengthened me too. Empowered me. Or perhaps I'd finally died and entered the Summerland. Or was this Heaven? Neither would explain Nicholina's presence, yet what else could it be?

Panic sliced through my reverie, sharp and unexpected, and my smile vanished as quickly as it'd come. Because it hadn't been *my* panic. No, the emotion had come from someone else. I groaned loudly in realization: Nicholina recognized this place too. Though her thoughts came too quickly to untangle, a sense of longing permeated them. A sense of despair.

Fuck.

I shook my head.

Though our bodies had separated, it seemed our consciousness had not, and no god would ever be cruel enough to saddle me with Nicholina for eternity, which meant—which meant this wasn't Heaven at all. I glared up at the crystal-blue skies. The single cloud there seemed to mock me, and I couldn't stop a harsh chuckle. It took the shape of a burning cross.

Worse—now I couldn't feel my magic at all. Cautious, curious, I tried to summon the golden patterns in my mind, but they didn't rise. Though the veil between Nicholina and me hadn't re-formed, they'd simply . . . vanished. Whatever magic fed this place, it clearly wasn't like mine. It wasn't like hers either. It was more powerful than both, and it'd stripped us equally bare.

When a familiar voice crooned a lullaby behind us, we turned simultaneously. Nicholina's panic deepened to dread, interlaced with my own morbid curiosity. "Who is that?" I asked, watching two figures approach. A slender, dark-haired woman—perhaps my age—bounded hand in hand with a sallow-faced little boy. Deep shadows drained the life from his eyes, yet still he laughed, breathless, and tried to keep up. Sensing his struggle, the woman swept him up in her arms. They fell to the ground together, still laughing, rolling amidst the lavender. Neither of them noticed us. "Sing for me, *maman*," he begged her, sprawling across her chest. He wrapped frail arms around her neck. "Sing me a song. *S'il vous plaît.*"

She squeezed him gently. In her pale eyes, adoration and anxiousness shone in equal measure. My heart twisted in response.

Beside me, Nicholina had stilled, her attention rapt on the little boy's face. "And what song shall I sing, *mon bébé?*" the woman asked.

"You know the one!"

Her nose wrinkled in distaste, and she smoothed the hair from his forehead. Black like hers. "I don't like that one. It's too . . . grim."

"Please, *maman.*" His pale eyes sought hers earnestly. Indeed, he could've been the woman's miniature. "It's my favorite."

She scoffed in fond exasperation. "*Why?*"

"It's scary!" He grinned, revealing a chipped front tooth and dimples. "It has monsters!"

Rolling her eyes, the woman sighed. "Very well. But just the once. And don't—don't sing it with me this time, all right? Please?" I would've frowned at the odd request if I hadn't felt her unease echoing through Nicholina. If I hadn't known what would happen three weeks hence. This little boy . . . he wouldn't get better. He'd die a slow, painful death in the days to come, and this—this wasn't my hell, after all.

It was Nicholina's.

But she hadn't always been Nicholina. Once, she'd been Nicola.

I couldn't look away.

Closing her eyes, the woman leaned back into the lavender, and the boy nestled his face in the crook of her neck. I knew the words of the song before she sang them. They resounded in my very bones. "*Beneath the moon of harvest, a ripple stirs the leaves.*" With a high, clear soprano, she sang the eerie lullaby slowly, still stroking the boy's hair. "*The veil is thin, the ghouls a'grin, rattling the eaves.*"

He giggled as she continued.

"*A bridegroom hears them calling, wakes from eternal sleep, to seek his love, his Geneviève, who married her Louis. Beyond her glowing window, fair Geneviève doth sing*"—despite his mother's request, the boy began humming along—"*to the babe upon her breast. The bridegroom starts to weep.*" She hesitated now, her hand stilling on the boy's hair as he continued the song without her.

"*The dead should not remember. Beware the night they dream. For in their chest is memory*—"

"Of a heart that cannot beat," the woman said softly, no longer singing. The boy grinned, and together, they finished the disturbing lullaby. "*Beneath the moon of harvest, a ripple stirs the leaves. The veil is thin, the babe a'grins, and even ghouls shalt grieve.*"

The boy let out a loud, delighted cackle. "He was a *zombie*. Right, *maman*? The bridegroom was a zombie?"

"I think a ghoul," she offered, her eyes unfocused. She still clutched the boy's head to her chest, tighter than necessary. "Or maybe a different sort of spirit. A wraith."

"Will I become a wraith too, *maman*?"

She closed her eyes as if pained. "Never."

The conversation drifted from there. Nausea churning in my stomach, I watched as they eventually stood, walking hand in hand back the way they'd come. Nicholina did not blink. She stared at the boy's back with naked longing, unwilling to spare even a glance at the woman. At the boy's mother. Nicola. "What was his name?" I asked quietly.

She answered with equal softness. "Mathieu."

"Mathieu le Claire?"

The boy grew smaller and smaller in the distance. "I was only seventeen," she whispered instead, lost in her memories. I saw the events in her mind as clearly as the field of lavender: how she'd loved a man—a fair-skinned, ginger-haired man from their mountain village—and how they'd conceived a child who they in turn loved without question, completely and unconditionally. How the man had died unexpectedly from the cold, how their son had fallen ill shortly after, how she'd tried everything from magic to medicine to heal him. She'd even taken him to a priest—or the closest approximation to one—in a distant land, but he'd explained Mathieu's sickness as "divine retribution" and turned them away.

Nicholina had killed him. His had been the first life she'd ever taken.

She hadn't known La Voisin then. If she had, maybe Mathieu would've—

"Out of my thoughts, little mouse," she snarled, jerking her head back and forth as if to dislodge an irksome fly. "We don't want to see it, no, we don't want to see—"

"You were seventeen." I repeated her words slowly, pivoting to look around us again, studying the silhouette of the mountains. When I'd played here as a child, one crag had resembled a crone's crooked nose. The rock that had formed its wart, however, wasn't visible now, and that couldn't be right. Mountains didn't simply *move.* "How old *are* you, Nicholina?"

She hissed through stained, too-sharp teeth, anger sparking

like kindling. And I pitied her. Those teeth had once been beautiful. *She* had been beautiful. Not just of face and form, but also of spirit—the sort of spirit that drove a mother to the ends of the earth to save her child, the sort who loved with everything in her being. The sort who held nothing back. Yes, Nicola had been beautiful in all the ways that counted—and all the ways that didn't too—but beauty faded with time.

And Nicholina had lived too long.

How did you become like this? I'd asked her the question once, sitting in the dark and dirt of Léviathan. She hadn't given a proper answer then. She didn't need to give one now. I knew without her opening her cracked lips, without her lifting her girlish, uncanny voice. She'd lived too long, and time had ravaged her to a withered husk of the woman she'd once been.

Rage washed through her at my pity, or perhaps at the memory of her dead son. Like a wild animal, savage and trapped, she spat, "You wish to be in Hell, Louise le Blanc? We shall oblige you. Oh, yes, we shall drag you down, down, down—"

When she lunged, wrapping skeletal fingers around my throat, black waves crashed upon us once more. They flattened the lavender, enveloped the sun, swept us up into their treacherous current. My lungs screamed in agony as our situation resolved with knife-sharp clarity.

We weren't in Hell, and we weren't in Heaven either.

Ears bursting, vision pitching, I scrabbled at Nicholina's hold, but those fingers pressed into more than flesh now. They dug into consciousness, ripped through memory. The two of us foundered, tossed mercilessly through the waves, until Nicholina regained purchase, nearly crushing my windpipe. I felt that pressure everywhere. In my head, in my chest, in my heart. White exploded all around us as I tore free, and we pitched headlong into another memory.

Through a curtain.

A hush fell over the audience as we crashed onto the stage, and insidious fear bloomed at the sight before us: Reid caging me against his chest, my body deathly still in his arms. My hair long and brown, my face bloody and bruised. My dress torn. I glanced, panicked, to the right, where the Archbishop would step out in mere moments. And the crowd—who lay in wait, watching me? Would they recognize me? Would they find me at last?

Nicholina took advantage of my terror, seizing my hair and wrenching my face upward. "Look at yourself, mouse. Smell your fear even now, so thick and delicious. So lovely." She inhaled deeply against the scars on my throat. "And you fear so much, don't you? You fear your own mother, your own father. You fear your own *husband*." When she licked down the column of my neck, I twisted from her grip, smashing my crown into her face and staggering forward. She wiped a hand across her bloody nose before bringing it to her lips. Her tongue flicked out like a snake's. "But you should feel *lucky* you tricked him, oh yes, because if you hadn't tricked him—such a tricky little mouse— he never would've loved you. If he had known what you are, he never would've *held* you beneath the *stars*."

I glanced over my shoulder to where Reid and I still stared at each other, frozen. From the wings of the theater, Estelle moved to help me. Nicholina laughed. "You burned her, Louise. Your fear *burned* her."

When Reid flung me away, I winced, watching as my battered body hit the stage once more.

But there—in his gaze—

He was frightened too.

He was frightened, yet he rose with the stagehands when they came. Though his hands shook, he didn't fight them, didn't cower or plead or flee. And I wouldn't either. Fear was inevitable. We all made our choices, and we all suffered our consequences. We all felt fear. The *trick* was learning to live with that fear, to continue forward in spite of it. "I didn't mean for any of this to happen," I murmured, longing to reach out and touch his face. To smooth the furrow between his brows. To tell him everything would be all right. "But I'm glad it did."

Squaring my shoulders as Reid had done, I turned back to face Nicholina. Her eyes burned with silver light, and her chest rose and fell rapidly. Like me, she struggled to catch her breath, yet this strength in my limbs was hers as well. The waters had healed us both. And suddenly, I understood.

The Wistful Waters *healed*.

They didn't exorcise malevolent presences.

I'd have to do that myself.

Gritting my teeth, I launched myself at her.

WHAT IT IS TO DROWN

Lou

As soon as I touched her skin, she rolled, and the waters swept us up again. Nicholina snapped at my throat. Prying her mouth open—*keeping* it open—I swam with the current this time instead of against. But so many currents swirled around us now, some warm and some cold, some familiar and some foreign. Hundreds upon thousands of them. And I still couldn't breathe, couldn't *think*, as images rushed past in the water: fragments of faces, bits of skyline, sights and scents and sensations. Each beckoned and threatened simultaneously, like crooked fingers in the dark. They pulled me in every direction, clawing at my hair and tearing at my chemise. My panic became a living thing as I struggled to swim, to fend off Nicholina's gnashing teeth. How could I exorcise her without drowning myself in the process?

On the heels of that thought came another, swift and sudden and sure.

I could drown *her* instead—if not in water, then in emotion. Perhaps both.

Instinctively, I kicked down an unfamiliar current, and we spiraled into the temple by Chateau le Blanc.

Blood still coated the mountainside, and there, in the center, Nicholina stood with her maw dripping like a wild animal's—*Nicholina*, not Nicola, because in her hand, she held a human heart.

Triumph flared through us both, hot and heady. Triumph and hideous shame.

I encouraged the latter, fanning it higher as we grappled. Hotter. It became a weapon in my hands, and I wielded it like a knife, cutting through the quick of her. Piercing her very heart. This shame—it might kill her, if I let it.

"What did you do, Nicholina?"

"What was *necessary*." Her teeth finally sank into my fingers, and I cried out, tearing skin as I pulled them away. She spat blood. "We killed our sisters, yes, and we feel no shame," she lied, continuing on a single breath. "We would've killed her too. We would've killed for our mistress."

"Who—?"

But Nicholina attacked me with new fervor as we watched La Voisin drag an unconscious woman from the temple steps. I sidestepped, craning my neck with a powerful, inexplicable urge to see the woman's face. La Voisin obliged by tossing her to the ground, but past-Nicholina sprang toward them, obstructing my view. The present one wheeled and charged at me once more. I thanked any god listening—the very waters themselves—for rescinding our powers in this place. When she lashed out, I caught her wrist and twisted. I had skill enough without magic, but it would've been impossible to fight a wraith.

Will I become a wraith too, maman?

The thought made me hesitate, made me *sick*, and Nicholina spun, her elbow connecting sharply with my chest. When I doubled over, unable to breathe, she seized my throat once more. This time, she didn't let go.

She knew the rules of our game had changed.

Kill me, I whispered to her mind, unable to utter the words aloud. Goading her further, even as agony crescendoed in my lungs, pressure built behind my eyes. The capillaries there ruptured in little bursts of pain before healing once more. It didn't matter. I gripped her wrists and pressed closer with lethal purpose, staring into those sinister eyes. *Kill me, or I'll kill you.*

She snarled, squeezing harder, her own murderous impulse warring against her loyalty to La Voisin, who had told her not to kill me. Who had told her I was for Morgane.

She'll kill you if you do, I hiss. *I'll kill you if you don't. Either way, you die.*

Choking against her rage, she bared her teeth and forced me to the blood-soaked ground. I fed that rage. I fed it and stoked it and watched it consume her.

"She'll forgive us, yes," she breathed, wholly crazed. "Our mistress will understand—"

You stink with fear, Nicholina. Perhaps you were right—perhaps we are alike. Perhaps you fear death too. I forced a grin despite the blinding pressure in my head. Cords hung between us like the strings of a marionette—because Nicholina *was* a marionette. If I cut her free, she would fall. She would drown. The words raked up my battered throat like shards of glass. Like knives. I forced them past my swollen tongue, gasping, "You'll soon . . . join Mathieu . . . in the Summerland."

At his name on my lips, Nicholina made a guttural sound, forgetting her mistress, forgetting everything except her own bloodlust. Pressing her knee into my stomach, she leveraged her entire body, all her strength, against my throat. Her elbows locked.

And I had won.

Bridging upward with all my strength, I punched her arms at the elbow, breaking her grip, and hooked a foot outside hers. Air returned in a dizzying wave as I rolled atop her. I struck her face once, twice, before shoving off her chest to my feet. When I stumbled backward, heaving, La Voisin dropped to one knee beside the unconscious woman. She gripped the woman's chin hard and lifted her face.

I nearly lost my footing.

Coco stared back at me.

I shook my head incredulously, still reeling from lack of oxygen. It couldn't be Coco. It had to be someone else—someone nearly *identical*—

Nicholina tackled me from behind without warning, and we plummeted back into the icy churn of waters. With a high, maniacal laugh, she forced us down an even colder current. I tensed instinctively, fighting the pull, but it was too late.

We landed in a battered bedroom of Chasseur Tower. Bits of broken furniture littered the ground around us. I seized a shard of bedpost as we rolled. When I thrust it at her chest, she lurched sideways, and it lodged in her arm instead. Relentless, I twisted it, relishing her shrieks. "Give up." I lunged for another piece of wood. "You're *alone*. Your lover, your son—they're *gone*. They're *dead*. Josephine is going to kill you too, and if she doesn't, Morgane will. You're in over your head—"

She wrenched the wood from her arm and used it to block my strike. "We are not alone, little mouse. We are *never* alone." Giggling softly, she flicked her eyes behind me. "Not like you."

I wouldn't give her the satisfaction. I wouldn't look. I *wouldn't*—

Like a moth to a flame, my gaze drifted over my shoulder, following Reid's voice. I dreaded the sound of it. The look on his face. Nicholina cackled without moving to attack.

She'd already chosen her weapon.

She was trying to drown me too.

Reid towered over my pitiful form, his voice loud and angry and hurt. Estelle's sister still cooled at our feet, but neither of us looked at her. We had eyes only for each other. "I'm a Chasseur!" he roared, wringing his hands. His knuckles clenched white. "I took an oath to hunt witches—to hunt *you*! How could you do this to me?"

"You—Reid, you also made an oath to *me*." I listened to my own impassioned plea with bitter regret. "You're my husband, and I'm your wife."

His expression darkened, and my stomach rolled. An ache

built at the back of my throat.

"You are not my wife."

Cold, familiar despair chilled my bones at his words. How often had I heard them? How often had this exact scene plagued my nightmares?

"You see?" Nicholina crept closer, blood dripping in her wake. The puncture in her arm, however, had already vanished. I tore my gaze from Reid to study the smooth alabaster skin there. The waters had healed her. Nicholina realized it at the same moment I did, and a heinous grin split her face. She twirled the bloody shard of wood between her fingers. "Lucky you tricked him, really. Lucky, lucky, *lucky*."

I picked up my own shard to match, lifting it high. "He would've loved me anyway."

Then we were drowning again, caught up in fresh currents. When she tried to drive her shard into my skull, the wood burst in a geyser, spraying her face as we left the previous memory. Burning her. She shrieked again, and in that moment, I saw another scene flash: a dark tent and cloaked figures, my mother and La Voisin. They shook hands amidst the smoking sage while Nicholina hovered in the corner. Her heart rioted.

"We cannot do this," she muttered, following her mistress from the tent. Her face and shoulders twitched in agitation. "Not the children."

La Voisin turned without warning and slapped her roundly across the cheek. "We do what is necessary. Do not forget your place, Nicholina. You wanted a cure for death, and I gave you one. My benevolence extends only so far. You will follow me, or I will revoke my gift. Is that what you want?"

Nicholina thrashed in humiliation and hurt, tearing us from the memory. *You see?* My voice echoed cruelly even to my own ears. But we couldn't continue this way forever. The time had come for one of us to end—and one of us *would* end. I would die before I returned to the surface with Nicholina. *She doesn't love you. She isn't a sister or mother or family at all. You mean nothing to her. Give up, and go peacefully. You have nothing to fear in death, Nicholina. Mathieu will—*

She lashed out viciously then, pulling me along the coldest current of all.

Glittering masks.

A cavernous open space.

And—and Ansel.

My stomach bottomed out at her intent. My nails bit into the skin of her arm. No longer to harm her, but to *escape*. Every fiber in my being recoiled from the memory, but it didn't matter. I couldn't stop it.

And I would drown, after all.

She alighted, catlike, at the bottom of the amphitheater, and I landed sprawled at her feet. Dazed, I scrambled away before she could touch me, before she could force my gaze to the group at the center of the primitive stage. But I couldn't look at them. I couldn't spend these last precious moments staring at myself, at Coco or Beau, even at Reid—at the hideous relief on all our faces. We'd thought we'd won. We'd thought Claud had swooped in to save us, that we'd eluded Coco's prophecy, that we'd defeated my mother at last.

We'd thought so many things.

Morgane inched toward the back tunnel, where Ansel stood near. Too near. His beautiful face contorted with concentration as he looked from her to Claud to me.

He'd looked to me, and I hadn't seen it.

I bolted toward him now.

Rationally, I knew this memory would play out regardless of my presence, my interference. My feet, however, weren't rational. My heart wasn't either. Both carried me forward with foolish urgency as Morgane began to applaud. Skidding to a stop in front of him, I looked around wildly for anything I might use to shield him, to protect him. My eyes landed on the fallen knife. I bent to snatch it up, triumphant, but my fingers passed through the hilt, billowing into smoke before re-forming.

"No." I stared down at them. This didn't make sense. I'd—I'd touched the wood in Chasseur Tower. I'd stabbed Nicholina, for Christ's sake. "*No.*" At my vehement refusal, Claud's eyes seemed to flicker in my direction before finding Morgane once more.

"We can't change the past, little mouse, even in our memories. Not truly." Nicholina pursed her lips in saccharine pity. Her silver eyes glittered. "We can't save him, no. He is dead. He is dead, he is dead, with *that* knife in his head." She inclined her chin to the knife, which remained firmly upon the ground. Nicholina sauntered forward as Morgane inched backward. "Such a pity." When she reached out to stroke his cheek, I knocked her hand away, widening my stance between them. She grinned. "Such a pretty pity. He was *your* family, wasn't he, Louise? The only one who never betrayed you."

I scowled without looking at her. My attention remained on Morgane, who blithered about rules and games, still creeping backward. "Coco hasn't—" But Nicholina held knowledge that I did not, secrets of Coco and—and her mother. Nicholina laughed at my wide-eyed expression, at my slack jaw, as those secrets became my own. "No." I shook my head, a cold wave of shock washing over me. "Coco would have—"

Morgane lunged, and I could only stand there, immaterial between them, as she plunged her knife through me. My form rippled at the contact. Bone crunched. When Ansel crumpled to his knees, I went with him, trying and failing to catch his broken body, wrapping invisible arms around him to cushion his fall. Still stunned. Still numb. His blood soaked my dress, and my mind simply . . . fled. "Perhaps you didn't deserve your mother's ire," Nicholina mused, circling us idly as Morgane darted into the tunnel, as my own screams shattered the night, "or your huntsman's hate. But *this*"—she bounced excitedly on the balls of her feet—"this you earned, Louise."

Cutting my own strings mercilessly, she repeated the words I'd told him.

"You wreck everything you touch, Ansel. It's *tragic* how helpless you are." Snip. Snip. "You say you're not a child, Ansel, but you *are*." Snip. "You're a little boy playing pretend, dressing up with our coats and boots. We've let you tag along for laughs, but now the time for games is done. A woman's life is in danger—*my* life is in danger. We can't afford for you to mess this up."

Snip, snip, snip.

As if my life had been worth more than his.

As if his life hadn't been worth all of ours together.

I'd known it, even then. I'd known how much better he was than us. I stared down at his profile now, his eyes wide and unseeing. Blood matted his hair. It slicked down his graceful neck, stained the back of his coat. "Did you *love* him, Louise?" Nicholina echoed my mother's jeer. "Did you watch as the light left those pretty brown eyes?"

Why hadn't I told him? Why hadn't I hugged him one last time?

Closing my own eyes, I crumpled to my knees, pressing my forehead against his cheek. I couldn't feel him, of course. Couldn't feel anything. Was this what it was to drown? How strange. I couldn't even bring myself to cry—not when Coco wrenched the knife from his skull, not when Reid pried his lips apart. Not when Nicholina loomed over me, the discarded knife in hand.

She wouldn't be changing the past by killing me.

Part of me had died here already.

WHAT IT IS TO SWIM

Reid

I didn't pause to unlace my boots, unfasten my coat. When she hit the water, I moved to follow, already ankle-deep.

A low growl rumbled from behind.

Stiffening, I turned. Amber eyes reflected back at me. White fur gleamed in the moonlight.

I swore softly.

The *fucking* dog.

It paced along the path, hackles raised and teeth bared. Snorting, it shook its head before whining once. Twice. Its eyes bored into mine as if trying to . . . to communicate something. When it inched closer, I drew a knife. Unsettled. "Not another step," I said darkly. Flattening its ears, it snarled again, louder now, vicious, and did just that. To Coco, I asked, "How did it get here? Where is Constantin?"

"Leave it." She watched our standoff while hastily shucking off her own boots. "It isn't harming anything."

"Every time something catastrophic happens to us, that dog is there. It's an *ill omen*—"

"Lou is probably *drowning*." Her fingers moved to the laces of her bodice next. I looked away hastily. "Get your ass in there before—"

We both froze, scenting it at the same time: sharp yet sweet, barely there on the breeze. My nose still burned with its familiar scent.

Magic.

Not mine and not hers. Someone else's. Which meant—

Célie's scream split the night. The dog's ears pricked forward in response, but instead of turning toward it, he stared fixedly at a point within the waters. My blood ran cold. Torn with indecision—rooted in fear—I didn't move fast enough. I couldn't block it.

With preternatural speed, the dog careened past me, straight into the heart of the Wistful Waters.

The decision came easily then.

I dove in after it.

THE FINAL VERSE

Lou

Nicholina didn't strike right away. Though I kept my eyes closed, the scene still burned through our shared consciousness. Leisurely, she lifted the knife through the smoke, admiring Ansel's blood along the blade, while I remained bowed over his corpse, my hands clenched desperately around his shoulders. Through her eyes, I saw how pitiful I'd become. And she relished it. She relished this hideous pain inside me, this dark and noxious poison. It was exactly like hers.

I should've forced myself to my feet then—to fight, to flee, to *something*. And if I couldn't have stood, I should've crawled. I should've lifted my fists and raged through the ringing in my ears, should've spat in her face before she drove her knife into my back.

But I couldn't do any of it. I couldn't even lift my head.

"It isn't my birthday until next month," he said sheepishly, but he clutched the bottle to his chest anyway. The fire cast flickering light on his quiet joy. "No one's ever—" He cleared his throat and swallowed hard. "I've never received a present before."

He'd never received a birthday present.

"I'm sick and tired of everyone needing to protect me. I'd like to protect myself for a change, or even——" When my frown deepened, he sighed and dropped his face into his hands, grinding his palms into his eyes. "I just want to contribute to the group. I don't want to be the bumbling idiot anymore. Is that so much to ask? I just . . . I don't want to be a liability."

A liability.

"She keeps looking at you." Ansel tripped over a stray limb, nearly landing face-first in the snow. Absalon leapt sleekly from his path.

"Of course she does. I'm objectively beautiful. A masterpiece made flesh." Ansel snorted.

"Excuse me?" Offended, I kicked snow in his direction, and he nearly tumbled again. "I don't think I heard you correctly. The proper response was, 'Goddess Divine, of course thy beauty is a sacred gift from Heaven, and we mortals are blessed to even gaze upon thy face.'"

"Goddess Divine." He laughed harder now, brushing the snow from his coat. "Right."

Gasping now, half laughing and half sobbing, I rocked back and forth, unable to stand it for a single second longer—this great, gaping hole in my chest where Ansel had been. Where Estelle and my mother and Manon and my father and Coco and Beau and even Reid had been. *I* had once been there too. Happy and whole and safe and sound. What had *happened*? What had led us here? Surely we'd done nothing to deserve this life. If someone like Ansel had received only neglect, loneliness, and pain for his efforts, for his *goodness*, what hope could the rest of us have? I'd lied, killed, and cheated—I'd shredded the very fibers of my soul—yet here I was, still standing. He deserved better. He deserved *more*, so much more than he'd ever been given. In another time, I would've screamed and raged at the injustice of it all, at the senselessness, but no amount of anger would change anything now. This was life.

And Ansel was dead.

In another day, another week, another month, this would be Reid's lifeless body I inevitably held, or Coco's. Beau's own father would probably kill him, as my own mother would eventually kill me. There really *was* only one way this story could end. I'd been so foolish to think otherwise. So stupid and naive.

"It'll be quick," Nicholina lied in a whisper, bending over me. Her fingers caressed the back of my head, and her hair tickled my cheek. Around us, the entire cavern succumbed to black flame. "Painless. You will see him soon, little mouse. You can tell him exactly what he meant."

But if I died now, his death would mean nothing.

My eyes snapped open at that cruel reality, and I stared numbly at the flames in front of me. Ansel deserved better. He deserved more than my self-pity. Summoning the final dregs of my strength—the absolute last of them—I lifted my head. She lifted her knife. Our eyes met for one synchronized beat of our hearts.

Then something moved in the tunnel.

Confusion flashed through us both before we turned. Coco's fire had driven everyone in memory into that tunnel, and none should've reappeared. We'd all fled straight to Léviathan after La

Mascarade des Crânes. Could someone have crept back? Could they have returned for Ansel's body? I instantly quelled the thought. Even if someone *had* miraculously traversed the cursed fire, this was *my* memory. It should've ended the moment I'd disappeared in pursuit of Morgane. Why hadn't it?

Through the smoke, a white dog emerged.

Nicholina bared her teeth at it, blasting awareness through me the second before the dog transformed. If I'd been standing, my legs would've buckled. As it was, I rose slowly to my knees, the ringing in my ears deepening to a rushing sound. A roar of blood and hope and fear. This couldn't be happening. This couldn't be *real*.

Ansel ambled toward me.

"Hello, Lou." At my dumbstruck expression, he grinned, the same sheepish grin he'd given a thousand times and the same sheepish grin of which I wanted a thousand more. He wore a pristine powder-blue coat with golden tassels and buttons—my heart ached at the familiarity—with his hands shoved deep into the pockets of his pants. An eternal initiate. No blood marred his person, not his hair or his skin, and his brown eyes sparkled even in the dark. "Did you miss me?"

I stared at him for a second too long, swallowing hard. And then—

"Ansel." My voice broke on his name.

His gaze softened as he came to stand beside me, extending a slender hand to help me to my feet. Hardly daring to breathe, I accepted it tentatively and marveled at its warmth. When he glanced down at his broken body, his smile dimmed slightly, and he shook his head. "What are you doing here, Lou?"

I still didn't have an answer.

It didn't matter, however, as Nicholina's shock had worn off. She whooped with crazed hysteria, reeling backward in glee. "Oh, the baby mouse. The little pinkie, little pup." Her expression hardened. "The boy who doesn't know when it's time to give up."

He met her glare with an equally hostile one, his fingers still bracing mine. "No one is giving up here."

She charged without warning, stabbing her knife at him, and he vanished with a wink in my direction. My heart seized at his absence. When she whirled to find him—slashing her knife through the smoke and spewing a torrent of curses—he reappeared behind her without a sound and tapped her shoulder. She nearly leapt out of her skin.

A snort burst from me unexpectedly.

Ansel grinned again.

Recovering quickly, Nicholina struck out once more, harder and faster this time. Ansel didn't move, but allowed her blade to pierce him—except it didn't pierce him at all. It simply *stuck* an inch from his chest, jammed midair as if she'd plunged it into an invisible brick wall. His grin widened. "You can't kill me. I'm already dead."

"I do not fear the dead," she snarled.

He leaned closer. "You're probably the only one who should. I've recently met some of your enemies, Nicholina—splintered souls and vengeful witches and even a few of the king's children. They're all waiting for you."

I stepped closer, looping my elbow through his and ignoring the chill down my spine at his words. The certainty in them. I focused instead on the euphoric tingle in my chest, the warmth spreading through my limbs. His arm felt solid in mine. Real. I couldn't have stopped my grin if I'd tried. Which I didn't. "I bet they have all sorts of fun things planned for you."

He inclined his head. "Fun is one word."

"You're *lying*." Nicholina lunged again, and he stepped in front of me, blocking her knife. The movement held a sort of grace, or perhaps confidence, he'd never achieved in life. Fascinated, morbidly curious—and something else, something that weighed heavy in my chest—I plucked the knife from midair, paced backward twice, and threw it at him.

He caught it without hesitation—without even *looking*, the cheeky bastard—and I laughed again, unable to help myself. That heavy sensation in my chest lessened slightly when he blushed. "This is an interesting development," I said.

"Lots of those going around." He lifted a brow before pressing the knife back into my hand. Though Nicholina sprang for it, she couldn't seem to move past him to reach me. The wall he'd erected held firm. He didn't acknowledge her efforts, so I didn't either. "The Lou I knew wouldn't have given up," he continued softly. My grin vanished. "She would've fought, and she would've won."

My own words were barely audible. I spoke through numb lips. "Not without you, she wouldn't have."

"You've never needed me, Lou. Not like I needed you."

"Look where that got you." I closed my eyes, a fat tear rolling down my cheek. "I'm so sorry, Ansel. I—I should've protected you. I *never* should've let you come with me."

"Lou."

My chin quivered.

"Lou," he repeated, voice soft. "Look at me. Please." When I still didn't, he turned his back on Nicholina completely, drawing me into a hug. My arms wrapped around his slender torso of their own volition, and though they shook, they held on tight. Too tight. Like they'd never let him go again. "I didn't *want* to be protected. I wanted to help you—"

"You did—"

"I know I did," he said firmly, squeezing me once before drawing back. My arms remained locked around him. Removing them one at a time, he disentangled himself gently, stronger now than before. Strong and graceful and confident. Another tear spilled over. "And I'm going to help you again." He nodded toward Nicholina, who thrashed against the invisible barrier. "You'll have to kill her."

"I've tried."

"Try harder." He squeezed my fingers around the knife's hilt. "A wound to the arm won't do it. The waters have healed you both of superficial injuries. You won't be able to drown her, either." He glanced over his shoulder to where she raged, all but invisible, and a flash of pity crossed his warm brown eyes. "She's lived too long with her emotions. She's numb to them now."

"She isn't numb to her son."

He turned back around to look at me. "You'd rather kill her slowly? Make her suffer?"

"No." The word rose to my lips unbidden. I frowned, realizing its truth. Despite the heinous things she'd done—to me, to Etienne, to God knew who else—I couldn't forget the sense of longing she'd felt in that lavender field with Mathieu, the despair and hopelessness and shame. The fear. *We cannot do this*, she'd said to La Voisin. *Not the children.* Loathing burned up from my stomach to my throat. She'd still done it. She'd still killed them. And perhaps that was punishment in itself.

Will I become a wraith too, maman?

Never.

"I think . . ." I said the words quietly, my thoughts tangling out loud. "I think she's suffered enough." My knuckles clenched around the knife. "But this won't kill her permanently, will it? She said her body is at the Chateau."

"Only one way to find out."

With a sweep of his arm, the barrier collapsed, but Nicholina didn't assail us right away. Eyes narrowed, suddenly wary, she skittered backward as I approached. She felt my resolve. It frightened her. Undeterred, I continued forward with purpose, shifting to block the tunnel, her easiest means of escape. Though she dodged with incredible speed—feinted even faster—we still shared our consciousness, and I matched her every step. Ansel watched our dance in silence, black smoke undulating around his lean frame.

It didn't take long. Not now. Not with him behind me.

Not with Nicholina so incredibly alone.

I anticipated her third bluff, catching her wrist and trapping her against the wall of rock. Flames licked up its face, but neither of us could feel their heat. I pinned my forearm across her throat. She tore at my face, but Ansel appeared, catching her hands and subduing them with ease. She arched off the wall in response, hissing, spitting—eyes bright and rolling with fear—but stilled unexpectedly when I raised the knife. Those eyes found mine and held, and one name radiated through our consciousness.

Mathieu.

I took a deep breath and brought the knife down.

It slid through her ribs in a sickening, viscous movement, and I left it there, protruding straight from her heart. She stared at me, unblinking, as her body collapsed in our arms. "I'm sorry," I said. I didn't know if it was true.

With one last, ragged breath, she clutched me and whispered, "The dead should not remember, but I do." Those eyes found mine again as the light finally left them. "I remember everything."

She slipped from our hold, fading into black mist, and was gone.

We both stared at the spot where she'd disappeared.

In those seconds, a mournful sort of blanket settled over us, deadening the crackling of flames and rumbling of stone. The entire amphitheater would collapse soon. I couldn't bring myself to care. A knot solidified in my throat as I glanced at Ansel, as he looked back with a sad little smile.

"Good riddance." Swallowing hard, I forced a laugh. "She was a huge pain in the ass."

And that was a huge understatement.

"Thank you," I continued, rambling now. "We should really look into procuring you armor for next time. Just imagine—you riding in on a white steed, undoing your helmet in slow motion and tossing all that glorious hair in the wind." I swallowed again, unable to dislodge the lump, and—also unable to look at him—glanced down. "Coco would love it. Hell, Beau probably would too." The fire had completely consumed his body now. Bile rose in my throat, and I tore my gaze away, fresh tears filling my eyes. Surely, *this* was Hell, yet I couldn't bring myself to leave. My feet had grown roots. An inexplicable tug unfurled deep in my stomach the longer we stood there, like an itch I needed to scratch, yet I resisted its pull. It would take me away from here. Away from him. I knew it as fundamentally as I knew that, one way or another, this moment would have to end.

But not yet.

He missed nothing, shaking his head in fond exasperation. "I'll ask again, Lou . . . what are you doing here?"

I bumped his shoulder with mine. "You should know. It seems you've been following us since—since—" The words withered on my tongue, and I tried again. "Since—" *Fuck.* I dropped my gaze once more before quickly regretting the decision. His body still smoldered at our feet. *Double fuck.*

"Since I died?" he supplied helpfully.

My eyes snapped to his, and my expression flattened. "You're an ass."

He bumped me this time, grinning anew. "You can say the words, you know. They won't make me any less dead."

I swatted him away. "Stop *saying* it—"

"Saying what? The truth?" He splayed his hands wide. "Why are you so afraid of it?"

"I'm not afraid."

He leveled me with a frank stare. "Don't lie to me. You can lie to everyone else, but I know better. You're my best friend. Even if I hadn't been following you for the past few weeks, I'd know you're one of the most frightened people I've ever met."

"Everyone is frightened of death," I muttered petulantly. "Those who say differently are drunk." Unable to help it, my eyes drifted back to his body. Fresh gorge rose. I had a finite amount of time left with Ansel, yet here I stood, arguing with him atop his makeshift pyre. Perhaps these waters hadn't healed me, after all. Perhaps whatever was broken inside me couldn't be fixed.

Despite his harsh words, his insistence at our new reality, he lifted my chin with a gentle finger. His brows furrowed with concern. Still Ansel. "I'm sorry. Don't look if it upsets you." He continued in a milder tone. "No one wants to die, but death comes for us all."

I scoffed. It was an angry, ugly sound. "Don't feed me that shit. I don't want platitudes."

"They aren't platitudes." Dropping his hand, he stepped backward, and I couldn't help it. I looked down again.

"Of course they are." Hot tears brimmed over my eyes, burning tracks down my cheeks. I wiped them away furiously. "Death isn't a happy ending, Ansel. It's sickness and rot and betrayal. It's fire and pain and"—my voice cracked—"and never getting to say goodbye."

"Death isn't an ending at all, Lou. That's what I'm trying to tell you. It's the beginning." Quieter still, he added, "You've lived in fear too long."

"Fear has helped me survive," I snapped.

"Fear has kept you from living."

I backed away from his corpse, from the flames, from the knowing gleam in his gaze. "You don't—"

He didn't allow me to finish, however, waving his hand. The scene before us dissipated—as simple as brushing aside the smoke—and another formed instead: a crackling hearth, a smooth stone floor, and a gleaming wooden table. Copper pans hung above it, and flowerpots of eucalyptus cluttered the far windowsill. Snowflakes fell beyond its panes, illuminated by starlight.

At the oven, Reid pulled forth a baking stone, and the sticky buns atop it sizzled and smoked. He'd burned them slightly, their tops a shade too brown, but still he turned to me—exorbitantly pleased with himself—grinning and flushed from the heat. Coco and Beau sat around the table, mixing what looked like cream. Vanilla and spice perfumed the air.

I sank into the chair next to them, limbs trembling. Ansel took the last free seat.

Rapt, I watched as Beau plucked a bun from the stone, dipped it straight into the cream, and shoved the entire thing in his mouth without a word.

"'eez a' burnt," he protested, face convoluting in distaste. Or perhaps pain. Steam still rolled from the buns, and as such, from his open mouth. Coco waved his breath from her face, eyes rolling skyward.

"You're disgusting."

"And you"—he swallowed hard and gripped the back of her chair, yanking her closer and leaning low with a smirk—"are beautiful." She scoffed and pushed him away, plating two buns for herself.

Ansel watched with a surprisingly contented smile.

"Where are we?" I breathed, glancing around the room at large. A black cat curled by the hearth, and in the distance— perhaps in the next room, perhaps in the next house—a woman and her daughter sang a familiar ditty. A game of ninepin bowling echoed upward from the street below, as did the children's shouts and laughter. "I've never been here before."

Still, this place felt . . . familiar. Like a dream I could almost remember.

Reid drizzled cream over two more buns with expert precision, his focus intent, before handing them to me. He didn't wear his Chasseur coat, nor a bandolier around his chest. His boots sat neatly by the front door, and there—on the third finger of his left hand—a simple gold band gleamed in the firelight. When I glanced down at the mother-of-pearl ring on my own finger, my heart nearly burst from my chest. "We're in Paradise, of course," he said with a slow, sultry grin. He even winked.

Verily I say unto thee, today shalt thou be with me in Paradise.

I stared at him incredulously.

Coco snatched up the buns before I could touch them, dumping half the dish of cream over his masterpiece. Smirking at his sudden scowl, she pushed them toward me once more. Her eyes no longer glinted with pain. With heartache. "There. I fixed them."

Ansel squeezed my hand under the table. "This is what you wanted, right? A home in East End, surrounded by family?"

My mouth might've fallen open. "How did you . . . ?"

"It's a bit tame for you, isn't it?" Beau narrowed his eyes at the room. "No naked men with strawberries and chocolate"—Reid shot him a murderous look—"no mountains of gold or fountains of champagne."

"That's your Paradise, Beau." Coco smiled sweetly. "And a hideously clichéd one at that."

"Oh, come on. Don't tell me you weren't expecting something outrageous like dancing bears and fire-eaters." Beau frowned when he spied the cat purring at the hearth. "Is that . . . ? Tell me that isn't supposed to be Absalon."

Bristling at his disparaging tone, I said, "What? I miss him."

Reid groaned. "He was a restless spirit, Lou. Not a pet. You should be glad he's gone."

Coco rose to extricate a pack of cards from a nearby hutch. The familiarity of the movement, the intimacy of it—as if she'd done this precise thing a hundred times before—unnerved me.

We'd never had a real home, the two of us, but here in this place, surrounded by loved ones, it felt dangerously close.

In a different world, I might've been Louise Clément, daughter of Florin and Morgane. Perhaps they would've loved each other, adored each other, filling our home in East End with sticky buns and potted eucalyptus—and children. Lots and lots of children. . . . We could've been happy. We could've been a family.

Family. It'd been an errant thought in the catacombs, surrounded by dust and death. It'd been a simple, foolish dream. Now, however, my chest ached as I glanced from Coco to Reid to Beau. To Ansel. Perhaps I hadn't found parents or brothers or sisters, but I'd found a family regardless. Sitting with them at my table—in my home—that dream didn't feel so foolish, after all.

And I wanted it. Desperately.

"You never know." Coco lifted a casual shoulder as she closed the drawer. "Maybe Absalon has found peace."

Peace.

With a long-suffering sigh, Beau helped himself to another sticky bun in response.

I couldn't shake the word, however, as Ansel's eyes locked with mine, and the levity of the scene fell away. Even the firelight seemed to darken. And that pull in my stomach—it returned with a vengeance. This time, however, I couldn't discern exactly where it led. Part of it seemed to tow me away from this place, away from Ansel, but the other part . . . I tilted my head, studying it closer.

The other part seemed to tow me *toward* him.

A siren's call.

With another sad shake of his head, he leaned forward. His voice dropped to a whisper. "No, Lou."

Beau lifted a finger, pointing it between us accusingly. "Stop it. No secrets allowed."

Coco returned to her seat and cut the deck. The cards snapped between her deft fingers. "I do hate when they whisper." Her eyes flicked to Ansel, and she added, albeit playfully, "*I* am her best friend, thanks very much. If she's going to whisper with anyone, it should be me."

"It *should* be me." Reid crossed his arms, eyes sharp on the deck in her hand. "And I saw that."

She flicked the card from her sleeve, grinning without remorse.

"I'm okay, Lou," Ansel continued softly, ignoring them. He didn't so much as glance in their direction as the protests began anew. When my chin began to quiver—when the room blurred through my tears—he lifted a hand to stroke my back, consoling me. "I'm okay. You're going to be okay too."

The tears fell thick and fast now, salty on my lips, and my entire body trembled. I forced myself to look at his face, to memorize him—the color of his eyes and the shape of his smile, the sound of his voice and the scent of his clothes, like sunshine. Pure sunshine. That was Ansel. Always the warmest of us all. "I don't want you to go."

"I know."

"Will I ever see you again?"

"Not for a long time, I hope."

"Can't I come with you?"

He looked to Reid and Coco and Beau then, who'd just started up a game of tarot. Beau cursed roundly when Coco took the first trick. "Is that really what you want?" he asked. *Yes.* I choked on the word, face hot and wretched, before shaking my head. He smiled again. "I didn't think so." Still he made no move to rise, content to remain sitting with me for as long as I needed. He wouldn't force me to go, I realized. It would have to be my decision.

The tug in my stomach grew stronger, more insistent. I clenched my fists against it and bowed my head in response, shoulders shaking. Not yet. *Not yet not yet not yet.* "I can't just *leave* you, though. I can't do it. I—I'll never see you blush again. I'll never teach you the rest of 'Big Titty Liddy,' and we'll—we'll never go to Pan's or sneak spiders into Jean Luc's pillow or read *La Vie Éphémère* together. You promised to read it with me, remember? And I never showed you the attic where I lived. You never caught a fish—"

"Lou." When I looked up, he was no longer smiling. "I need to find peace."

Peace.

I swallowed hard around the word, my eyes wet and swollen.

Peace.

It felt foreign and strange on my tongue. Bitter.

Peace.

But . . . the ache in my chest expanded to thrice its size. It also felt right. Exhaling softly, I closed my eyes in resolve. I couldn't count the number of times I'd done wrong in my life—and I regretted few of them—but I would do right by Ansel. He wouldn't spend another moment following me, restless, trapped in a world where he no longer belonged. He would fix my mistakes no further. I didn't know how he'd managed to stick around in the first place—whether it'd been his choice or mine—but I couldn't keep him here. I'd finally give him what he needed. What he deserved.

He deserved peace.

Nodding, numb, I allowed the tug in my stomach to pull me to my feet. He rose with me, and the scene around us began to swirl and shift in waves. "Was any of this real?" I asked as Reid, Coco, and Beau continued their card game, oblivious to the waters. Pressure pinched at my shoulders. "Or did I drown and imagine everything?"

Ansel's eyes twinkled. "A little bit of both, I think."

We stared at each other, neither willing to move.

"I don't think—"

"It's funny—"

"You first," I insisted.

A touch of wistfulness entered his expression. "Do you think . . . before you go . . . you could sing me the last verse?" He rubbed his neck, sheepish once more. "If you feel like it."

As if I'd ever had a choice.

"*Their babe they named Abe*," I sang on a watery chuckle, "*his brother Green Gabe. Then Belle and Adele and Keen Kate. Soon dozens came mewling, but still they kept screwing, even outside the pearly gates.*"

His face burned so vivid a scarlet it rivaled my every memory, but he grinned from ear to ear regardless. "That's indecent."

"Of course it is," I whispered. "It's a pub song."

His eyes shone too brightly now, brimming with tears of his

own. Still he grinned. "You've been to a pub?" When I nodded, smiling so hard it hurt, my chest aching and aching and *aching*, he shook his head in horror. "But you're a *woman*."

"There's a whole world outside this church, you know. I could show you, if you wanted."

His grin faded slowly, and he touched my cheek, bending to brush a kiss across my forehead. "Thank you, Lou. For everything."

I clutched his wrist desperately as the last of the house darkened, as the tug in my stomach deepened to a burn. The pressure at my shoulders increased, and my ears popped. Shouts penetrated the thick haze of my consciousness, echoing all around as if from underwater. "Where will you go?"

He glanced back to where Coco had sat at our table, shuffling cards and laughing. The wistfulness in his expression returned. "I have one more goodbye to make."

The burn in my chest became near unbearable. Icy needles pierced my skin. "I love you, Ansel."

My vision clouded as the waves truly descended, shocking and brutal. Though they pulled me away from him, I'd remember his smile until the day I died. Until the day I saw it again. His fingers slipped from mine, and he drifted backward, a beacon of light in the darkness. "I love you too."

With a powerful kick of my legs, I surged upward.

Toward fear.

Toward pain.

Toward *life*.

ANOTHER PATTERN

Reid

We broke the surface together. Water sluiced from her face, golden and freckled, and her hair, long and brown. She clutched my shirt as she gasped, spluttered, before tipping her face to the sky and grinning. Those clear blue-green eyes met mine, and she finally spoke. "Do you have something in your pocket, Chass, or are you just happy to see me?"

I couldn't help it. I threw back my own head and laughed.

When I'd found her drifting beneath the surface—her body limp and cold, her white hair floating eerily around her—I'd feared the worst. I'd seized her. Shaken her. Kicked to the surface and shouted her name. Nothing had worked. In a fit of rage, I'd even dived back down to find the white dog, but it'd vanished.

As we'd risen the second time, however, something had changed: her legs had started to move. Slowly at first, then swifter. Stronger. They'd worked in synchrony with mine, and I'd watched, amazed, as her hair had grown longer with each kick, as the color had returned to each strand. To her skin.

She'd healed before my very eyes.

Crushing her to me now, I spun us in the water. It didn't ripple with the movement. I didn't care.

"Lou." I said her name desperately, pushing the long locks from her face. "Lou." I kissed her mouth, her cheeks, her throat. I kissed every inch of her I could reach. Still laughing. Hardly able to breathe. She laughed with me, and the sound sparked in my bones. Light. Bright. If I stopped swimming now, I would've floated. I would've *flown*. I kissed her again. I'd never stop kissing her. "Lou, are you—?"

"I'm all right. I'm me." Her arms wove around my neck, and she tugged me closer. I buried my nose in the crook of her shoulder. "I feel—I feel better than I have in ages, honestly. Like I could fly or wield an axe or—or erect a statue in my honor." She wrenched my head up to kiss me once more. When we broke apart, gasping for breath, she added, "It'd be made of sticky buns, of course, because I'm *starving*."

My cheeks hurt from smiling. My head pounded in rhythm with my heart. I never wanted it to stop. "I have one in my—"

Coco's shout at the shore caught us both unaware, and we turned as the world rushed back into focus. She'd sunk to her knees, staring into the waters like she'd seen a ghost. "Ansel," Lou whispered, loosening her grip to better tread water.

I frowned. "What?"

"He wanted to say goodbye." Smiling softer now, she kissed me again. "I love you, Reid. I don't say it often enough."

I blinked at her. Warmth cracked open in my chest at her

words, spreading to the tips of my fingers and toes. "I love you too, Lou. I've always loved you."

She scoffed playfully. "No, you haven't."

"I have."

"You didn't love me when I plowed into you at Pan's—"

"I absolutely did," I protested, brows shooting upward. "I loved your god-awful suit and your ugly mustache and—"

"Excuse you." She leaned back in mock outrage. "My mustache was *magnificent.*"

"I agree. You should wear it more often."

"Don't tempt me."

I leaned closer, brushing my nose against hers. Whispering against her lips. "Why not?"

Her eyes gleamed wickedly in response, and she wrapped her legs around my waist, nearly drowning us both. I couldn't bring myself to care. "You've corrupted me terribly, Chass." With one last maddening kiss—slow and deep—she disentangled herself and flicked my nose. "I'll wear my mustache for you later. For now, we should—"

Then Coco screamed again.

I knew immediately this scream wasn't like the last—knew it before a man's body thudded to the beach, knew it before Lou released me abruptly. I reached for her again, drawing her into a protective embrace.

Because I recognized the man's body.

And Constantin—an immortal being made of water and mist—was dead.

Coco sprinted forward with another cry. "Constantin!" Her hands fluttered over him helplessly while Lou and I treaded water in silent horror. Ice crept up my spine at his wide-open eyes. His slack mouth. The bloody hole in his chest. "Constantin!" Coco shook him fiercely now, clearly unable to process. Her shock, no, *denial*, mirrored my own. Constantin couldn't have died—the melusines had cursed him eternal.

No one is safe here, Cosette.

Lou's knuckles turned white on my arms. "How is this possible?"

My grip tightened on her waist. "I don't know."

When Coco continued to shake him, her hysteria rising, Lou swam forward determinedly. "Right. We can fix this. The waters restored him once, which means—"

I caught the back of her chemise. "Wait—"

A high, chilling laugh echoed over the cliffs, down to the shore, and Morgane le Blanc stepped from the path onto the beach. A dozen witches followed. They fanned out behind her in a defensive formation, eyes sharp and mouths hard. Resolute. Coco scrambled backward into the water, dragging Constantin's body with her.

"Well, isn't this sweet." Hair gleaming in the moonlight, Morgane clapped her hands in applause. Her gaze flicked from Lou and me to Coco, who lifted a silver chalice to Constantin's lips in a final attempt to revive him. Her lip curled. "You must be so proud, Josephine. Look how your darling niece frets over the guardian." To Coco, she said, "He's dead, *mon petit chou*." She lifted her stained fingers. "Surely you know magic cannot live without a heart?"

"How—how did you—?" Coco's voice stuttered as she stared helplessly at Constantin. "He's the *guardian*. How did you kill him?"

Morgane arched a brow. "I didn't."

La Voisin stepped into view. A dark substance coated her hands. It matched the hole in Constantin's chest. "I did."

Coco rose slowly to her feet.

"Foolish man. We presented our black pearls, of course, but still he put up quite the fight." Though Morgane tutted, the sound lacked her signature melodrama. Deep purple shadowed her eyes, like she hadn't slept in days. Her skin was paler than usual. Burns riddled her face and chest, and her hair appeared singed in places. "Unfortunately for Constantin, we are the two most powerful witches in the world. Now, I will admit, the dragon gave us pause. It stole my broken toys, nearly razed my dollhouse to the ground, but no matter. The dragon has gone, and we shall not be caught unprepared again." She glanced out at the waters, clearly displeased. "We are here now."

"A dragon?" Lou whispered. "Who . . . ?"

"Zenna."

She'd saved the others, after all. She'd flown back to Cesarine.

Coco could've been carved from stone. "What have you done, *tante*?"

La Voisin met her niece's hard stare, impassive. Her expression revealed nothing. With the dip of her chin, however, three blood witches marched forward. Between them floated two gagged and bound figures. Eyes wide, both thrashed against the magic holding them to no avail.

Beau and Célie.

Lou cursed softly.

"What I must," La Voisin said simply.

A beat of silence passed as they stared at each other.

"No." Coco's eyes burned at the word, her hands curling into fists. She took a small step forward, and the waters—they rippled beneath her foot. La Voisin's eyes tracked the movement, narrowing infinitesimally. "That isn't an answer, and neither is Morgane le Blanc. How many times did we ask for her aid? How many of our kin have perished from cold and disease? How many of them have *starved* while she stood idly by?"

La Voisin arched a brow. "As *you* have stood idly by?"

Coco didn't so much as flinch. "I'm not standing idly by now."

"No. You are *actively* standing in my way."

"You betrayed us."

"I am losing patience," Morgane said with quiet malevolence. Her fingers twitched.

"Foolish child." La Voisin spoke as if she hadn't heard her. "You would have us continue to sicken and starve. Why?" Her black gaze found Lou and me. "For them?" Lip curling, she shook her head in a slow, winding movement, like a cobra preparing to strike. "You are the Princesse Rouge. Once, I would have encouraged your voice. I would have respected your opinion. But now your empathy rings hollow. You do not care for our people. You do not claim them as kin. You may protest my betrayal, Cosette, but you betrayed us long before this. Morgane has promised our coven safety in Chateau le Blanc"—her eyes seemed to harden at the name—"in exchange for Louise. I would do far worse than betray you to procure it. The time has come to choose your side."

She stepped beside Morgane at the last, tall and unyielding. Together, the two formed a striking image. Both regal, both beautiful. Both queens in their own right. Whereas Morgane possessed a dark sort of glamour, however—ever the showman— Josephine boasted no decoration. She was stark. A study in harsh reality and bleak truth. The malice in the former's eyes looked comically bright next to the flat, cold cunning of the other. The honesty. She didn't try to hide it.

La Voisin loathed Morgane.

"The ends justify the means," she finally murmured. "If we don't stand together, we will fall."

Coco stared at her aunt as if seeing her for the first time. "You're right." The Dames Rouges on the beach stilled at Coco's unexpected response. I recognized a few of them from our time together in Léviathan. "I *was* a child," she continued, her voice growing stronger with each word. Impassioned. "I was a child scared of my own birthright—of leading everyone, of failing any-one. Of disappointing *you*. I feared the responsibilities such a life would entail. Yes, I ran, and I am sorry for that."

She looked to her kin then, bowing her head, accepting her culpability in their hardship. They regarded her with a mixture of suspicion and admiration. "I am no longer that child. You *are* my kin, and I want to protect you as much as my aunt does. But *her* life"—she pointed a finger in Lou's direction—"is worth just as much as yours." She turned back to her aunt. "Morgane has been hunting the king's children. We found Etienne—the king's son—butchered in our own camp, and Gabrielle disappeared shortly after. Morgane was responsible, *tante*. But you already know that, don't you? Did you offer them up yourself? Your own people?" When Josephine said nothing, confirming her suspicions, Coco exhaled harshly, moving to stand between us and her aunt with deliberate care. "I've chosen my side."

Lou went still at her words. The blood witches, however, stirred. Murmurs rose from a few of them. Whether in support or dissent, I couldn't tell.

La Voisin's expression didn't change at her niece's declaration. Instead, she jerked her head to the witches nearest her. "Take her." When they hesitated, shooting anxious glances at Coco, La Voisin slowly turned to face them. Though I couldn't see her expression, they hastened to obey this time.

Coco skittered backward as they approached, and the waters rippled again. Kept rippling.

The witches halted at the shore, reluctant to follow, until the bravest took a tentative step forward.

When her toe touched the waters, her entire body jolted, and—as if a spectral hand had reached forth to snatch her foot—she slipped, vanishing into their depths. They swallowed her scream without even a ripple. Sinister and still in the moonlight.

The witch might've never existed.

Morgane tsked as the other witches balked. Her voice rang out hard. Ruthless. "I suppose rules are rules, aren't they? Dreadful things. As if any one of us had time to *speak our truth*. Never fear, though, *tata*," she said to Josephine, whose jaw clenched at the diminutive epithet. "The poor dears will have to come out eventually, and we have all the time in the world." She snapped her bloody fingers, and Beau and Célie dropped to their feet. "*These* two, however, don't have much time at all. What say you, darling?" she called to Lou. "How shall I play with them?"

"You're sick," Beau snarled, the veins in his throat bulging as he fought to move.

She only smiled. It held no warmth. From her cloak, she extracted Célie's injection, hurling the syringe into the water. "Though perhaps I tire of play altogether. Come here, Louise, or I shall kill them. Our game is done."

Lou started forward instantly, but my fingers caught her chemise. I didn't let her go. Couldn't let her go.

"Reid, don't—"

Baring her teeth, Morgane snapped her fingers again. Swords appeared in Beau's and Célie's hands. Another snap, and Beau lunged forward, his blade slicing through Célie's side. Blood welled in its wake. With the flick of Morgane's finger, Célie retaliated with a sob, her sword lodging deep in Beau's shoulder. Toy soldiers. "I'm sorry," she gasped, arms trembling as she attempted to combat Morgane's magic. "I'm so sorry—"

"I'm fine." Beau desperately strove to comfort her as he countered her strikes, teeth gritted. Breath shallow. "We're going to be fine—"

Célie stabbed again, this time in his thigh.

Blood poured.

With a wild cry, Coco surged forward as Lou twisted in my arms. Morgane waved a hand, however, and when Coco cleared the water, a glass cage descended around her. She pounded against its walls, furious, and strings wrapped themselves around her wrists and ankles.

Baring her teeth, La Voisin darted forward to intervene.

"The ends, Josephine." Morgane waved another hand, and the strings tightened, stretching Coco's limbs taut to the point of pain. A doll in a box. "They justify the means. Is that not what you said?"

La Voisin stopped dead in her tracks. Her body quivered with fury. "My niece remains unharmed."

"She *is* unharmed." Those glittering emerald eyes found Lou. Beau and Célie continued battling behind her, their blood splattering the sand. "For now."

"You have to let me go, Reid," Lou pleaded. "She won't stop—"

"No." I kept my voice low, shook my head fervently. Tried to ignore my own mounting panic. There had to be another way. My eyes swept over the witches again, assessing. Thirteen in all—six Dames Rouges, judging from the scars on their skin, and seven Dames Blanches. The former would need physical contact to harm, but the latter could attack at any moment. My mind searched wildly for an advantage. *Any* advantage. Could L'Eau Mélancolique affect our magic? Repress it? If we could somehow lure Morgane into the waters . . . I tested my own patterns. The golden cords rose instantaneously. *Shit.*

Worse still, one cord continued to shine brighter than the rest, pulsing with insistence. The same cord that had answered at the lighthouse. The same cord I couldn't pull. I *wouldn't* pull.

Save her, the magic whispered. *Save them all.*

I continued to ignore it.

Coco cried out as her strings tightened, and Lou took advantage of my distraction, finally twisting free. "Look, *maman*, look." She waved her hands in a placating gesture. "I'll play with you now. I'll even trade toys: me in exchange for Beau and Célie." Though I still shook my head, reaching for her, she kicked away and continued determinedly. "But you can't harm them again. I mean it, *maman*. Any of them. Beau, Célie, Reid, Coco—they're all safe from this point onward. No one touches them."

The pattern pulsed. My head continued to shake.

Morgane didn't seem particularly surprised by Lou's request, nor did she laugh or dance or goad as she once would have. "You can see how that might present a problem, daughter. With your death, the prince and huntsman will also perish."

"You assume I'll die."

"I *know* you'll die, darling."

Lou smirked then, and the sight of it struck me like a physical blow. Only days ago, I'd feared I would never see that smirk again. My body tensed with barely controlled restraint. "I guess we'll have to play to find out," she said.

She started for shore once more.

"No." I caught her arm. She hadn't suffered this long—she hadn't sacrificed everything, walked through literal fire, exorcised a fucking *demon*—to give up so easily now. Coco had said one life wasn't worth more than another, but she'd been wrong. Her life meant more. Beau's and Célie's lives meant more. And Lou—her life meant most of all. I would ensure she lived it. I would ensure they *all* lived. "You can't do this."

She kicked upward to kiss me in one last desperate plea. "I can't kill her if I keep hiding, Reid," she breathed against my cheek. "Remember what your mother said—closing my eyes won't make it so the monsters can't see me. I have to play. I have to *win*."

"No." My jaw locked. I couldn't stop shaking my head. "Not like this."

"Either I kill my mother, or my mother kills me. It's the only way."

But it wasn't. It wasn't the only way. She didn't know that, of course. I'd refused to speak the alternative aloud, refused to acknowledge it even in my own thoughts. The golden cord quivered in anticipation.

Lou had already given so much. She'd journeyed to Hell and back to save us, shattering herself in the process. She couldn't die now. And if she didn't die—she spoke of killing her mother lightly, as if matricide wasn't an unspeakably heinous act. As if it wasn't unnatural. As if it wouldn't break her all over again.

"No."

My purpose resolved as I clutched her face. As I brushed the water droplets from her lashes.

So beautiful.

"You test my patience, children." Morgane flicked her hand, and Beau, Célie, and Coco all crumpled in identical movements—like toys crushed underfoot. Beau and Célie lost consciousness completely, and Coco bit her lip around a scream. Morgane's emerald eyes filled with spite. "Perhaps you're right, little blood witch. Perhaps I'll kill all of you instead."

"Do not be foolish," La Voisin snapped. "Accept the terms. The prince and girl mean nothing. They will die soon enough."

Morgane whirled to face her. "You *dare* command me—?"

Faintly, I heard their voices escalate, but my entire world had narrowed to Lou's face. To the golden pattern. It vied for my attention, nearly blinding now, pointing straight and true at its target. Connecting us. Demanding to be seen. Hope and despair warred deep in my chest. Neither existed without the other.

I would find my way back to her. I'd done it once. I could do it again.

And she'd finally be safe.

"I'll find you again, Lou," I whispered, and her brows puckered in confusion. I kissed them smooth. "I promise."

Before she could answer, I clenched my fist in her hair.

The pattern burst in a shower of gold.

I saw no more.

PART III

C'est l'exception qui confirme la règle.
It's the exception that proves the rule.
—French proverb

DOUBT CREEPS IN

Nicholina

The pain fades without a body, as does all sense of touch, of smell, of taste. There is no blood as we spiral from sea to sky. There is no magic. No death. Here we are ... free. We are a gust of wind. We are the winter cold. We are a flurry of snow on the mountainside—swirling, twirling, whirling—nipping the noses of witches below. Our mistress walks among them. She calls them by name.

She does not call ours.

Anxious now, we sweep onward, up, up, *up* the mountain as snowflakes flit to and fro around us, within us. *It isn't here*, they flutter, they mutter. *We cannot find it.*

Our body, our body, our body.

Our mistress will not have forgotten us.

We move faster now, searching, gusting through the trees. The castle. She will have brought our body to the castle. But there is no castle, only snow and mountain and pine. There is no bridge. There is no one to welcome us, no one to grant us entry. If *she* would've stayed—the one with the nasty words, the one with the golden patterns—if her spirit would've fragmented, we would have found the castle. We would have found our body.

But she did not fragment. She did not stay.

Now she is alone.

You've failed, Nicholina.

Nasty words.

Your mistress needs her more than she needs you.

Our mistress has not forgotten us.

Perhaps your body won't be there at all. Perhaps you will *die.*

We spiral again in agitation, in fear, and streak the mountainside. Already, we feel ourselves spreading, drifting, losing purpose. We cannot linger long without a body, or we will become something else. Something helpless and small. A cat or a fox or a rat. There are many ways to become a matagot, oh yes, but we will not become one. Not us. We are not forgotten.

Something scurries through the foliage, and we dive, eliciting a shriek of fear from the creature. It matters not. We need a body until our mistress returns. Until *her* mistress shows us the way. Nasty woman, like her daughter. Nasty witch.

We crouch inside the mink's body and wait. Time passes differently to animals. We track shadows instead, quivering within the roots of a tree. Hiding from eagles. From foxes. We smell our mistress before we see her, and we hear her sharp, impatient words. She argues with Morgane. She speaks of Morgane's daughter.

We leave the mink and follow behind as towers and turrets

take shape. A bridge. Fire has ravaged each structure. All around, white ladies knit and weave their invisible patterns into stone. Into wood. Into windows and arches and shingles. We do not care about castle reparations. We sweep for the entrance, hiding from their prying eyes, curling through the smoke. We feel the pull of our body now. We feel it here.

Our mistress hasn't forgotten us after all.

Up the stairwell, down the hall, into the small, sparse bed-room. Our body isn't on the bed, however. It isn't on the pillow. *The bed is empty,* we cry in dismay. *The bed is bare.* We draw short, quivering, as we search. As we follow our body's pull. As we find it on the hard stone floor. *But the bed is empty.* Confusion swirls. *The bed is bare.*

Our body looks as a corpse in the shadows of the corner. Sickly and pale. Scarred. We hover above it, regret wafting through us now. A tendril of hurt. No fire warms the chamber. No candle-light. But it matters not. We feel no cold, no, and our mistress knows this. She knows. She knows pain is fleeting. She will relish our greeting.

You've failed, Nicholina.

It matters not.

Your mistress needs her more than she needs you.

Pain is fleeting.

You've chosen the wrong side, Nicholina. But it isn't too late. You could ally with us before they betray you. Because they will *betray you. It's only a matter of time.*

Our mistress would never betray us.

Slowly, we sink into ourselves, first a finger, a toe, then a leg and an arm and a chest until our entire body settles in on itself with a heavy breath. Heavy. So heavy. So weary. Images of lavender and wraiths and sickly, corpselike little boys flicker. Memories of family. The word tastes different now than it did then. Once, it tasted of comfort, of love, of warmth. We do not remember what warm feels like now. We do not remember love. Within *her* we'd felt it—a brief flicker in the shadows, in the dark. She'd felt it so strongly. We hold on to it now, that memory. We hold on to that warmth we'd felt when she looked upon her huntsman, her family.

Our own eyes do not open as we lie upon this hard, cold stone. We do not move to the bed. Our mistress did not want us there.

Sometimes we think our mistress does not want us at all.

ANGELICA

Lou

Without warning, Reid collapsed face-first into the water, and that—

That is when I lost my shit completely.

Fresh shouts erupted from shore as I dove toward him, slinging an arm across his shoulders and spinning him to his back, looping his elbow through mine and cradling his head against my shoulder. The sharp, potent scent of magic clung to him. Though his chest still rose and fell, the movement seemed shallow, harsh, as if he was in terrible pain. "Reid!" I shook him desperately, struggling to stay afloat. We both went under. Water burned my throat, my eyes. Choking on it, I kicked harder, propelling us above the surface for a few precious seconds. I could swim, yes, but towing a limp two-hundred-and-something-pound man was something else entirely. *"Reid!"*

The shouts around us escalated, and I glanced to shore. My heart lodged in my ravaged throat.

Morgane had lost consciousness with Reid.

Whatever magic he'd done, it'd affected her too, and absolute chaos reigned. The Dames Blanches nearest her shrieked and rushed forward, pulling her away from Josephine, from Coco, from us. "Do not be foolish!" Josephine's vehement shouts cut through the mist, which had descended with a vengeance once more. "This is our chance! Get the girl!"

But even the blood witches wouldn't step foot in the waters again—not when they continued to ripple.

Not when Coco rose, her binds having vanished after Morgane's collapse.

Not when she stepped back into the waters, nor when she lifted her hands. Her dark eyes fell first to Constantin, then to Beau and Célie—still blood-soaked and unconscious—and they burned with retribution. "You should've known better than to follow us here, *tante*. I was born in these waters. Their magic is my own."

I foundered beneath the waves, surging up in time to see Josephine clench her fists.

"Their magic is *hers*," she spat. "Not yours. Never yours."

"I am part of her."

"You are *mine*." The last shred of Josephine's control seemed to snap, and she swept a long, crooked dagger from her cloak. Her hands shook. "She abandoned you. She abandoned *me*. She—"

"—is on her way," Coco finished grimly, eyes flicking to her own uplifted hand. A fresh wound I hadn't noticed sliced her palm. Blood dripped from it into the waters, and with a start, I realized Coco's steps hadn't woken L'Eau Mélancolique at all.

Her blood had.

And the waters weren't merely rippling now.

They were *moving*, parting down the center as if the heavens had drawn a line from Coco to the horizon. They swelled on either side of that line, growing and growing and *growing*—like twin tidal waves—until a footpath along the rocky seafloor appeared. Small enough for a single person to walk unhindered. I clung to Reid as the waves battered us, the currents dragging us under before thrusting us upward once more. When I shouted Coco's name, coughing and spluttering and desperately kicking for shore, she turned to look at us. Her eyes widened with panic before we went under again.

When we reemerged, another current swept us up between one breath and the next. This one, however, seemed determined not to drown us, but to deliver us to Coco. I didn't fight or question it, focusing all my attention on keeping Reid's head above water. My arms shook with the effort. My legs seized. "Come on, Chass." I pressed the back of his head into the crook of my neck once more. "We're almost there. Stay with me. Come on, come *on*—"

The current dropped suddenly, and we plummeted with it, straight through the icy water to the seafloor path. When we landed, stunned and shivering, Coco sprinted out to meet us, pulling at my arms, my hands, pushing Reid's soaking hair out of his face, checking his pulse. She ignored Josephine and the blood witches completely. They still didn't dare enter L'Eau Mélancolique, even on the path. "Are you hurt?" Coco demanded, checking every inch of me in harried, clumsy movements. "Are you—?"

I caught her hands and grinned. "You look like shit, *amie*. Those eye bags are as big as Beau's head."

Coco dropped her forehead to our joined hands, exhaling in relief. "You're you."

"I'm me."

"Thank god."

"Thank *Ansel*."

She chuckled on a weak exhale, lifting her head—then froze. Her stare fixed on something over my shoulder, something farther up the footpath. Its silver reflection, just a speck in the darkness, shone bright in her eyes. Whoever or whatever it was, it approached not from shore, but from the depths of L'Eau Mélancolique. I tensed instinctively. A face drifted in my mind's eye from Nicholina's memories, and suspicion lifted the hair at my neck. Gooseflesh rose on my arms.

When Josephine turned ashen, however, I knew. When she stumbled—actually *stumbled*—back a step, I clutched Reid tighter in my lap, my heartbeat thundering in my ears. Several of the blood witches fled without a word. My gaze remained locked on Coco as the silver speck in her eyes grew larger. Nearer. Too near now to ignore.

I twisted to look over my shoulder at last.

And there she was.

A full-body chill swept through me at the sight of her: tall and statuesque with thick black curls and rich brown skin, nearly identical to Coco in every way. Except for the eyes. At some point between Nicholina's memory and now, they'd turned a pale, icy shade. Her gown matched the peculiar color—the iridescent fabric swirling between white and green and purple and blue—and rippled in the breeze as she approached. Like a goddamn fairytale princess.

She stopped a pace behind me. I might've gaped. My mouth might've fallen open like a bug-eyed fish. Up close, she appeared even more beautiful than from afar: her face perfectly heart-shaped, her lips perfectly bowed. Silver powder dusted her cheeks and nose, as well as her brow and collarbones, and ornate moon-stone jewelry gleamed from her fingers, her wrists, her ears, her throat. She'd braided her hair around a teardrop opal headpiece. The precious stone glittered against her forehead.

Her dress and hair continued to undulate gently, even after the breeze waned.

She smiled down at me.

"Angelica," I whispered in awe.

"Sister," Josephine hissed.

But it was Coco's whispered accusation that changed everything. "Mother."

With the graceful incline of her head, Angelica nodded. She stood with impeccable posture, unearthly stillness, her shoulders back and her hands clasped at her waist in a familiar position. How many times had I seen Josephine hold herself that way? How many times had I yearned to wring that long, elegant neck?

It was uncanny how two people with the same features could look so different.

I glanced at Coco.

It was haunting when there was a third.

"*Sœur.*" With a voice smooth as silk, Angelica spoke with calm assurance. "*Fille.*" She lifted a hand as if to touch Coco's cheek before thinking better of it. She let it fall to her side instead. Bereft. "I have missed you."

Though Coco said nothing, her eyes spoke volumes. They glittered with unshed emotion in the moonlight.

I frowned, my own eyes narrowing, and the glow around Angelica's face dimmed slightly.

More than slightly.

I might've even called her hideous now.

Then again, mothers abandoning their children to cruel relatives might've been a sore spot for me. Madame Labelle had left Reid, and he'd ended up with the Archbishop as a father. Morgane had tried to kill me, and somehow, I had too. Though beautiful, Angelica had left Coco in the hands of her aunt. She was no different from them, really. She was rotten inside.

In her case, rot just happened to smell like lilies.

Accepting that her daughter wouldn't or perhaps *couldn't* answer, Angelica returned her gaze to Josephine, who had inched toward Beau and Célie. Those perfect lips pursed. "Do not harm the children, Josie. Your quarrel is with me."

Josephine glowered as she lifted Célie's head. Her hands weren't needlessly cruel, but careful and steady as she held

Célie's neck firm. No. Not careful. Practical. Efficient. She would kill Célie if necessary, just as she'd killed Etienne. "What will you do?" she asked her sister. "You cannot leave the waters."

Coco and I shared a brief, confused look.

Angelica only flicked a jeweled dagger from her thigh sheath—her *thigh sheath*—and sighed. "Must we do this, *sœur*? We both know the damage I can inflict from here." To illustrate her point, she placed the dagger against her chest and sliced down, directly between her breasts, without hesitation. The blade tore through fabric and skin as butter, leaving a thick line of blood in its wake.

Josephine hissed, and her hand flew to her own chest, where an identical wound had formed.

My confusion deepened as I stared at it. Nicholina's memories hadn't revealed anything like this. Not that I'd known to look for it.

"What the hell is happening?" I breathed to Coco. Josephine and Angelica still glared at each other, bleeding, in a silent stand-off. "You said your mother was dead."

"I said my *aunt* said she was dead."

"And now?"

She shrugged stiffly. "Now it looks like they're blood bound."

"Blood bound?"

"It's a dangerous spell between Dames Rouges. It binds their lives together. Their magic."

I looked again at their twin wounds. "Oh shit."

She nodded. "That about sums it up."

On the heels of that unpleasant realization, however, came another. "Does that mean we can't—we can't kill your aunt without killing your mom?"

"Apparently."

My stomach plunged as Josephine readjusted her grip on Célie, pressing the dagger to the back of her head. "Your threat is empty as always, *sœur*," she said, "while you clutch at others' skirts and hide where I cannot reach you." She laughed harshly. The only time I'd heard her laugh at all. "No. You will not inflict real harm on yourself to hurt me, or you would have done so centuries ago."

Right. I couldn't kill her, then. Testing my patterns swiftly, I followed each one to their sacrifice. I just needed to knock the knife from her hand—something simple. A gust of wind, perhaps. A spasm of her fingers. "Wait," I whispered to Coco as I searched. "If you thought your mother was dead, why were you trying to summon her?"

"I wasn't trying to summon her. I just—the waters spoke to me. I listened."

"You gave them your *blood*"—I cut an incredulous glance at her over my shoulder—"because they asked nicely? Did they at least say please?"

"I was born of them," she muttered defensively.

"Surrender Louise," Josephine insisted, ignoring our low, fervent conversation. Angelica kept her blade loose at her side. Her blood dripped from its tip to the seafloor, and black pearls formed from each drop. I glanced again at Constantin.

"Surrender Cosette"—Josephine's fingers tightened around her own dagger—"or I will dispose of this pathetic child. I will dispose of the mortal prince."

Like hell.

Gritting my teeth in a sharp burst of hatred, I clenched my fist, and my anger sparked along a pattern. I watched as it sizzled between us, feeling the heat of it leave me. The cord disintegrated to golden ash as Josephine yelped, dropping her dagger and clutching her burned hand. I grinned in satisfaction and wiggled my fingers. "It's time for you to go, *Josie*."

Angelica lifted her own hand in emphasis, and the waters responded, surging past the shoreline to reclaim Célie and Beau, depositing each of them at our feet. But they didn't stop there. They continued to flood the sand, to reclaim the beach, sweeping away the silver chalices. They chased Josephine's hem with sentient determination, and she had no choice but to back away quickly. Just as Nicholina had feared the dark, it seemed Josephine feared the strange magic fortifying these waters.

She still refused to cede.

When she turned to shout orders to the remaining Dames Rouges, however—commanding them to hold their ground—her eyes widened, and she finally saw the battle had been lost. The blood witches had already fled into the cliffs. Josephine stood alone.

"Leave this place, *sœur*," Angelica said. From the steely edge to her voice, I knew this was her final warning. "And never return. I cannot promise your safety if you continue to provoke Isla."

"*Isla.*" Josephine's face twisted at the name. The waters kept coming, however, forcing her back until she stood atop the first rocks of the path. Her black eyes bored holes into Angelica's beautiful face. "The Oracle. Your *mistress.*"

"My *friend.*" With another wave of Angelica's hand, the waters climbed higher, and Josephine leapt backward, away from them. She moved with surprising agility for a thousand-year-old hag. "You would do well to respect her," Angelica continued. "Though she rules below, she has not turned a blind eye to the war above. You do not want her as an enemy." A peculiar light built in those pale eyes as her gaze turned inward. "Though it seems you've already displeased her siblings." For our benefit, she added, "The Triple Goddess and the Wild Man of the Forest."

Do you have a family, Monsieur Deveraux?

As a matter of fact, I do. Two elder sisters. Terrifying creatures, to be sure.

"All these years, I have watched you, Josephine." Sadness softened Angelica's voice, and the ethereal glow slowly faded from her eyes. "I have hoped for you. You think me a coward, but you are a fool. Have you learned nothing from our mistakes?"

Josephine didn't visibly react to her sister's piteous words. She merely continued to walk backward, her face inscrutable, her eyes burning like twin flames in the darkness. "There are no mistakes, sister." She smiled at each of us in turn. "We shall see each other soon, I think."

Then she turned, cloak billowing behind her, and disappeared into the night.

A LIE OF OMISSION

Lou

I collapsed at Reid's side the next moment, and Coco followed suit with Beau and Célie. To my surprise, Angelica knelt too, brushing Constantin's cheek with the back of one slender hand. Unlike her sister, she wore her emotions proudly for all to see. This one looked akin to . . . wistfulness.

I gestured to the floodwater on the beach, both irritated and impressed. "Maybe lead with that next time."

She laughed softly.

Shaking my head and grumbling—her laughter sounded like a goddamn bell—I pressed my ear to Reid's chest to listen to his heart. It beat strong and steady. When I checked his temperature, his skin felt warm—but not too warm—beneath my wrist. I lifted his eyelids next, sparking a light on the tip of my finger with residual anger. His pupils contracted like they should've. Right. I sat back in relief. He was perfectly healthy, just . . . asleep. He'd probably claimed Morgane's consciousness to give us time to flee, sacrificing his own in the process. I only needed to wake him up. As I searched for a pattern to do that, however, I couldn't quash my curiosity. Glancing at Angelica and Constantin, I asked, "Didn't he betray you?"

Her pale eyes rose to mine. "He did."

Coco didn't look up. Tension radiated from her clenched jaw, her taut shoulders. She snatched my dagger to reopen the cut on her palm. Like me, however, she couldn't seem to help herself. "And you still loved him?"

"You needn't do that, darling." Angelica's gaze flicked to the wall of water on our right. In response, a thin stream twisted toward us like a serpent. It reached first for Beau, touching the deep puncture in his leg and flowing into his very skin. The wound closed almost instantly, followed by the one on his shoulder. A second tendril unfurled toward Célie, and a third stretched to Angelica. All of their injuries vanished.

"You see?" Angelica smiled, and my breath might've caught in my throat a little. I forced a scowl to compensate. "Do not fatigue yourself." She looked again at Constantin's lifeless body, her gaze lingering at the hole in his chest, before swallowing hard. The movement made her seem almost human. "But yes, Cosette. I loved him the way we all love things we shouldn't—to excess. He hurt me in the way those things always do." That palpable sadness crept back into her voice. "I am sorry he is dead."

I am sorry he is dead. Just like that, she became something strange and foreign once more.

Coco's hands clenched around Beau's collar as his eyes fluttered open. She didn't thank her mother for healing him. I didn't blame her. Instead, I scooted closer, pulling Reid with me, and braced my shoulder against hers in silent support. She leaned into the touch, dropping Beau's shirt as he sat upright. "What happened? Where's Mor—" His eyes widened when he caught sight of Angelica. To his credit, he only blinked stupidly for about three seconds before turning to Coco. Then he blinked a few times more. "Is this . . . ?"

Coco nodded curtly. When her hand rose to clench her locket in a death grip, Angelica's eyes followed, widening in disbelief. "You . . . wear my locket," she said. It sounded like a question.

"I—" Coco stared at the ground with ferocious intent. "Yes."

A fierce sort of protectiveness pricked my chest at her obvious discomfort. Perhaps I should've been angry with her for never telling me about her mother. How many times had we talked about Angelica together? How many times had she chosen not to tell me? A lie of omission was still a lie. Hadn't I learned that the hard way?

Nicholina had called it a betrayal. Perhaps I should've been upset, but I wasn't. We all had our secrets. I'd certainly kept my fair share. Though I didn't know why she hadn't confided in me, I *did* know Coco had been six years old the last time she'd seen her mother. I knew she didn't need an audience for this reunion. What she *needed* was time to process, time to decide what she wanted her relationship with Angelica to look like. To decide if she even wanted that relationship at all.

Resolute, I settled on a pattern to wake Reid, flicking his nose to wield it, eager to distract the others from this painfully awkward situation. One night of my own sleep in exchange for his consciousness now. Simple, yet effective. Nothing too harmful. With Reid awake, we could move on. We could gather our allies to march on Chateau le Blanc or return to Cesarine or—well, I didn't know exactly, but we could do *something* other than gawk.

I flicked Reid's nose once more, waiting for the pattern I'd enacted to dissipate. It didn't budge. I tried again, clenching my fist this time. It actually recoiled, twisting into a different pattern altogether. And the other patterns in my web—they did too. They grew hopelessly knotted in a way I couldn't trace or understand, as if the magic itself had grown confused.

I frowned down at him.

What the hell had he *done*?

Distracted by my nonsensical patterns, I didn't see or hear Angelica move behind me. Her hand landed on my shoulder. "He will not wake," she said gently. "Not until he is ready."

I shot her an irritated look, shrugging away from her touch. "What does that mean?"

"His mind needs time to heal." She dropped her hand without insult, lacing her fingers together in a maddeningly calm pose. "He is lucky to be alive, Louise. This spell could have done irreparable damage to more than his mind."

"*What* spell?" When she didn't answer, my frown deepened to an outright glower. I pushed to my feet, my cheeks hotter than usual. Claud, Constantin, Angelica—what was the *point* of omniscience, of omnipotence, if one didn't use it? I shook my head. "If his mind has been harmed, why can't you heal him? You healed everyone else!"

She only smiled again, a horrible, pitying smile. "Only he can heal himself."

"That's horsesh—"

"Do not worry, Louise." A hint of that unnatural glow reentered her eyes, and I stepped back despite myself. "His injuries are not fatal. He will wake—of that, I am certain. His path forward, however, cannot yet be seen."

The waters see things we cannot see, know things we cannot know. Constantin's warning repeated in my mind. *Angelica was a seer, and her magic shaped them.*

"Your path, on the other hand, is clear." She gestured down the narrow split in the waters. It led straight into the heart of L'Eau Mélancolique. In the silver light of the moon, the mist from its flowing walls sparkled like flecks of diamond. She looked almost apologetically to Coco. "I am sorry, *fille*, that our reunion is fraught with such complication. When you summoned me—"

"I didn't know I was summoning you," Coco interjected.

Angelica nodded, though something like pain flashed through her eyes. "Of course. When you called upon the *waters*, I heard it. I felt your need, and I—well, I needed to answer it." Her voice gentled as she continued, though she spoke with no less certainty. "There is much you don't understand, Cosette. I know you are angry with me—as you well should be—but we do not have the luxury of time for lengthy explanations and apologies."

Coco stiffened at the straightforward words, and I squeezed her arm. Angelica was right, however; this wasn't the time or place for this conversation. Not with Morgane and Josephine roaming near, not with a corpse at our feet, trapped between colossal walls of water. I eyed them nervously as a long silver fin flicked past.

"To do so," Angelica continued, recapturing my attention, "you must understand three things. First, I am no longer safe outside these waters. Isla's benevolence protects me, and she risked much in allowing me to come here. My sister lives in fear of my magic—in fear of Isla herself—but if Josephine had tried to enter these waters, I would not have been able to stop her. For as much as this magic is yours through birth, it is also hers because of our blood bond."

She didn't give us another chance to interrupt. "Understand this second: all of your life, Cosette, I have watched you." Those blue eyes eddied with white, and fresh gooseflesh lifted the hair on my arms. It lifted Coco's too. "I know where you have been and who you have loved. I know you have scoured the kingdom—from La Fôret des Yeux to Le Ventre to Fée Tombe—for allies against Morgane. You have befriended the Beast of Gévaudan and the Wild Man of the Forest. You have entranced dragons and witches and werewolves alike."

For the first time, she hesitated, the white in her eyes flaring brighter. To me, she said, "You still wish to defeat your mother?"

"Of course I do, but what—?"

"Isla would make a powerful friend."

Coco clutched my arm so hard that I nearly lost sensation in it. But her voice didn't falter. "Whatever you're trying to say, *maman* . . . say it."

"Very well." She waved her hand at the waters once more, and streaming tendrils shot forth, weaving midair to form a liquid lattice. They looked much like the roots of a glass tree, clear and bright and shining. Twining beneath Reid, they lifted his body and suspended it at waist level. I reached out to seize his hand with my free one. When Angelica motioned him down the path, the waters obeyed. He floated away from us, and I darted to keep up, dragging Coco along with me. "Stop it! What are you—?"

Her mother spoke in a strained voice. "I wish I could offer you a choice, *fille*, but truthfully, you have already made one. When you called upon the waters, you asked of them a favor. Now we must ask one of you."

Coco dug in her heels, incredulous. "But I didn't know—"

The waters began to close behind us, blocking our path to the beach. We stared at them in horror. "Isla wishes to speak with you in Le Présage, Cosette—you and your friends." Angelica's beautiful face pinched with regret. "I'm afraid you must all come with me."

A MAGPIE'S NEST

Lou

Le Présage.

I'd heard the name once, spoken amidst breathless giggles at the maypole. Another witchling had suggested we seek it out as we'd twirled and danced in the sweltering midsummer heat. Manon had refused, repeating a story her mother had told her about melusines drowning unsuspecting witchlings. We'd all believed it at the time. Melusines *were* bloodthirsty, after all. Treacherous and uncanny. The boogeyman hiding beneath our beds—or in our backyard, as was actually the case. Some days, I'd been able to see the mist from their shore through my window at sunrise. It wasn't until I'd first played with Coco that I'd realized melusines posed no real threat. They held dominion over an entire world below—a world apart from the rest of us, greater and stranger than our own. They had little interest in the affairs of witches.

Until now, it seemed.

I shot surreptitious looks at the black waters as we trudged along the footpath. They twined beneath Reid, towing him forward, while more water flooded the path behind, forcing us deeper along the seafloor. Within the waves on either side, shadows moved, some small and innocuous and others alarming in their size and dexterity. Beau appeared to share my disquiet. He nearly clipped my heel in his haste to flee the serpentine faces pressing in on the pathway. "Fish women, eh?" he muttered at my ear.

"Legend says they could once walk on land, but I've never seen it in my lifetime."

He gave a full-body shudder. "I don't like fish."

Another silver face flashed through the waters, sticking her forked tongue out at him.

Angelica glanced over her shoulder as she continued to glide forward. "Whatever you do, do not insult them. They're incredibly vain, melusines, but never vapid. They value beauty almost as much as gentility—manners are of utmost importance to a melusine—but they have vicious tempers when provoked."

At Beau's alarmed expression, Coco added, "They love flattery. You'll be fine."

"Flattery." Beau nodded seriously to himself, tucking the knowledge away. "Right."

"Are they very beautiful, then?" Célie asked, clutching her leather satchel over her shoulder with both hands. Dirt was caked beneath her cracked nails, and her hair spilled haphazardly from her chignon. Blood and grime stained her porcelain skin, the once-rich velvet of her trousers. The lace trim at her sleeves now trailed gently behind her in the wind. "Since they value beauty?"

"They are." Angelica inclined her head with an almost impish smile. "They are not, however, human. Never forget that, child— beautiful things can have teeth." Célie frowned at the words but said nothing more, and Angelica turned her attention instead to Coco, who studiously ignored her. She stared at her daughter for a long moment, deliberating, before clearing her throat. "Are you well, Cosette? Have your own injuries healed?"

"It's Coco." She glared at a beautiful fish flitting past, its golden fins rippling behind it. "And I've survived worse."

"That isn't what I asked."

"I know what you asked."

An awkward moment passed before Angelica spoke again. "Are you warm enough?"

"I'm fine."

Then another.

"Your hair looks lovely, I must say," she tried again. "Look how long it's grown."

"I look like a drowned rat."

"Nonsense. You could never look like a rat."

"Though you do look a bit peaky," Beau interjected helpfully. "A bit limp."

They both turned cold gazes upon him, and he shrugged, not at all contrite. When they turned away once more, I elbowed him in the ribs, hissing, "You ass."

"What?" He rubbed the spot ruefully. "That's likely the first time they've ever agreed on something. I'm trying to help."

After a handful more feeble attempts at conversation—which Coco shut down with an ease and efficiency I admired—Angelica cut straight to the heart of it. "We have a long walk ahead of us to Le Présage, daughter. I should like to know you better, if you are willing."

Coco scoffed and kicked an algae-covered rock. It plunked into the water, splashing my ruined hem. "Why? You said you've been watching me. You should already know everything."

"Perhaps. I don't know your thoughts, however." Angelica tilted her head to the side, lips pursed, as if debating something. After another few seconds, she said, "I don't know why you wear my necklace, for example."

Subtle as a brick.

"I wonder what that's like," Coco mused bitterly, still watching the golden fish. "Wanting an explanation and never receiving one. It'd be horribly frustrating, don't you think?"

Angelica didn't force any more horrendously awkward conversation after that.

As for myself, I tried not to think. Angelica had said Reid's injuries weren't fatal. She said he would wake. And Isla—though I knew little about the mysterious woman they called the Oracle, she *would* make a powerful ally against Morgane and Josephine. With our other allies occupied, it made sense to indulge Isla. Josephine clearly feared her.

I didn't know how much time passed before my heels began to ache. It could've been moments. It could've been hours. One second, the moon shone directly overhead, limning Reid's silhouette in silver, and the next, it had dipped below a wall of water, bathing us all in shadow. Only then did I notice the strange phosphorescent glow emanating from the waters.

"What is that?" I whispered.

"A special kind of plankton," Angelica said, her voice equally soft. "Though here we call them sea stars. They light the waters around the city."

The bluish glow reflected in Célie's wide eyes. She reached out to the wall nearest us, where thousands of nearly indiscernible specks of light swirled together to form one bright, pulsing wave. "They're like fireflies."

Angelica smiled and nodded, lifting her chin for us to look down the footpath. What appeared to be a golden gate bisected it, colossal and ornate, expanding into the empty plains of water on either side and rising to the sky. If not for the algae growing along its whorls and spikes, it could've been the gate to Heaven.

Beyond it, there seemed to be no water at all.

"Behold—Le Présage." Angelica's smile widened as we drew to a unanimous halt. "And there, in the center, Le Palais de Cristal."

We all stared, necks craned, at the orb of dry, mountainous terrain in the heart of L'Eau Mélancolique. Huts had been carved into the rock along the city's edge, into the very mountainside, as the seafloor rose to one tumultuous peak. At the top of that peak, spires of sea glass rose—cruel and sharp and beautiful— from the ruins of an enormous sunken ship. Its broken masts and shredded sails glowed blue in the light of the sea stars.

"Is it—is that dry land?" Beau glanced from Coco to me and

back again in search of an explanation, but Coco didn't seem to notice; her mouth had parted slightly as she gazed up at the city, and her free hand had risen to grasp her locket once more.

"I . . . I remember this place," she breathed. Those dark eyes sought mine, brimming with sudden certainty. With hope. Grinning, I released her arm, and she took a stumbling step forward. "I've been here before. Le Présage." She said the words as if tasting them, returning my smile. Her anger, her resentment momentarily forgotten. Memory was a strange and wonderful thing. "The Oracle City. Le Palais de Cristal."

Angelica shadowed her movements, close enough to touch. She still didn't dare. "You were born there."

Coco whirled to face her, nearly breathless in her anticipation, and the dam finally burst. "How? How was I born here if you can't leave? Is my father a merman? Is my father Constantin? Why is the Oracle City built on dry land? How is there dry land in the middle of the Wistful Waters?"

Angelica laughed at Coco's outburst—it really *did* sound like bells—and gestured us onward toward the gate. The sea stars followed in our wake. Though they didn't speak, though I could hardly see them, they seemed almost . . . *curious*. Sprite-like. "It isn't always dry," she said. "I told you. Melusines are courteous to a fault. They wouldn't want their guests to feel uncomfortable."

"So they drained their entire city?" Beau asked incredulously. "Just for us to breathe?"

Even Angelica's shrug articulated elegance and grace. "Why not?"

"Does that mean they *can* walk on land?" I asked, sticking a finger into the waters on impulse. The sea stars clustered around my knuckle, illuminating the shape of my bone through my skin. I flexed it in fascination, watching as they swirled and eddied, desperate to touch me. They left a cold, tingling sensation in their wake.

Angelica's smile vanished, and she slapped my hand away. "Stop it." She lifted my finger to eye level, revealing thousands of tiny bloodred pricks. Teeth marks. "They'll eat you if you let them." I snatched my hand away with an outraged sound, wiping my blood on my chemise and glaring at the carnivorous little beasts. "And we are *not* on land," she continued, resolute. "Make no mistake. We remain on the seafloor, where melusines are free to grow legs."

"Grow legs?" Beau's face twisted in disgust as a handful of humanoid shadows swam toward us from along the gate, their metallic tails flashing. I inched closer to Reid. "Like frogs?"

Angelica's expression grew stony as the melusines' faces took shape through the waters. Three women and two men. Though their bodies ranged in shape—from broad and coarse to fine and delicate—they all seemed somewhat longer than human, as if their limbs had been stretched, and each moved with a sort of liquid grace. Their colors varied from the palest of silver to the deepest of ebony, but all shimmered slightly, monochromatic and dusted with pearlescent scales. Their webbed fingers wrapped around what could only be described as spears. Perhaps tridents.

Whatever they were, they gleamed wickedly sharp in the

phosphorescent light, and I had no interest in meeting the receiving end of them.

"Beau," I murmured, smiling pleasantly at their hostile faces as they swam closer. Closer still. "Apologize, you blithering idiot."

He backed into me, nearly breaking my foot. I stomped on his toes in return. He swore roundly, snarling, "They couldn't have heard me."

Coco spoke through her own fixed smile, imitating Célie, who curtsied low, and elbowed Beau when he didn't do the same. "Good idea. Let's risk it."

"It was an honest question—"

The melusines didn't pause at the walls of water, instead gliding seamlessly through them and stepping—actually *stepping*—onto the footpath, their split tails transforming to legs before our very eyes. The scales on their fins disappeared, and glistening skin wrapped around feet, ankles, calves, thighs, and—

A beat of silence passed as Beau's alarm promptly vanished, replaced by a wide, shit-eating grin.

They were naked.

And, contrary to Angelica's assertion, they looked *very* human. Célie gasped.

"*Bonjour, mademoiselle,*" Beau said to the one in front, bending to kiss her long-fingered hand. He hesitated for only a second when he saw she had one extra knuckle per finger. Each clenched around her spear as she pointed it at his face, hissing and revealing a pair of thin fangs.

"You dare to touch me without permission?"

The male nearest her lifted his trident to emphasize her words. Unlike the female, he wore a thick golden rope around his neck, its emerald pendant the size of a goose egg. Matching twin emeralds glittered at his tapered ears. "He likened us to amphibians as well." When he tilted his head, the movement was predatory. His silver eyes glittered with menace. "Do we appear as amphibians?"

Angelica swept into a deep, immaculate curtsy. "He meant no offense, Aurélien."

Beau lifted placating hands, nodding along hastily. "I meant no offense."

The female slanted her black eyes at him. Against her narrow silver face and her long—*long*—silver hair, they appeared . . . disconcerting. And far too large. Indeed, everything about her and her kin's features seemed disproportionate somehow. Not wrong, exactly. Just . . . strange. Striking. Like a beautiful portrait meant to be studied, not admired. She didn't lower her weapon. "Yet still I hear no apology. Does the human prince think us ugly? Does he think us strange?"

Yes.

The answer rose to my lips, unbidden, but I bit my tongue at the last second, frowning and averting my gaze. The movement attracted the melusine's attention, however, and those black eyes turned to me, flicking over the planes of my face. Studying me. She grinned with dark cunning, and my stomach dropped with realization.

The women who dwell here are truth tellers.
Drink of the waters, and spill their truth.

Oh god.

Beau, who'd quashed his own answer with a strangled sound, cast me a panicked look. I returned it full measure. If we couldn't lie, if we'd been forced into a kingdom of *literal* truth—

If he didn't kill us, I certainly would.

Either way, we'd all be dead by night's end.

Beau tried to speak again, keeping his eyes trained carefully on the melusine's face. His throat bobbed against the tip of her spear. "Of course you do not look like a frog, *mademoiselle*, and I am grievously sorry for the implication. Indeed, you are quite—" The lie stuck in his throat, and his mouth gaped open and closed, like the fish who'd gathered to watch our inevitable demise. "Quite—"

"Lovely," Célie finished, her voice earnest and firm. "You are lovely."

The melusines regarded Célie with open curiosity, and the silver-haired female slowly lowered her spear. Beau swallowed visibly as she inclined her head. The others followed suit, some bowing deeply, others curtsying. The one called Aurélien even extended his hand to her, pressing an emerald earring into her palm. "You are welcome here, Célie Tremblay." The silver-haired melusine's lip curled as she glanced back at Beau. "More so than your companions."

Célie curtsied again, smaller this time. "I am pleased to make your acquaintance, Mademoiselle . . . ?"

"I am Elvire, the Oracle's Hand." The melusine smiled in approval at Célie's impeccable manners, and another of her companions looped a strand of pretty white pearls around Célie's neck. They looked ridiculous against her tattered gown, but Célie didn't seem to mind.

"Thank you." She lifted a hand in surprise, stroking them gently, before pushing the single emerald stud through her pierced earlobe. She looked like a magpie. "I shall treasure each one."

Beau stared at her incredulously.

"They suit you." Elvire nodded before gesturing toward her companions. "We are here to escort you into the Oracle City. This is Aurélien"—she pointed to the bejeweled but otherwise naked merman—"Olympienne"—another mermaid, this one the palest lavender with diamonds adorning her teeth—"Leopoldine"—a third with thin golden chains sparkling along her charcoal torso—"Lasimonne and Sabatay." She finished with two onyx mermen. One boasted rubies in his nipples, while the other's eyes glowed milky white. Seaweed wound through his braided hair. "We are simply enchanted to meet you. If you would be so kind as to walk beside me, Mademoiselle Célie, I would much appreciate your company."

When Célie nodded, Elvire extended an arm, and the two joined elbows, as prim and polite as any two aristocrats strolling through the park in Cesarine. Sabatay gestured for Angelica and Coco to fall in behind them while Leopoldine and Lasimonne flanked Reid on either side. Aurélien stepped in behind without a backward glance. Only his barnacle-crusted trident even glanced in our direction, waving us forward.

And *that* was how Beau and I found ourselves at the rear of the procession into the city.

Le Présage was unlike anything I'd ever seen. Just as I'd suspected, the melusines lived like magpies, building their homes from the remnants of sunken ships, from coral, from stone, hoarding sunken treasure to decorate their windows and lawns. A weathered marble bust sank deep into the silt of a kelp-filled garden at the edge of the city. The owner had affixed diamonds to each eye. Farther in, officials ushered melusines to the side of a bustling thoroughfare. Instead of brick or cobblestones, the road had been paved with mismatched coins—gold, silver, and bronze *couronnes*, as well as foreign coinage I didn't recognize. The occasional gemstone. An errant shell.

"Is it always this . . . crowded?" Beau asked, brows raised. Scores of melusines gathered to watch us pass, their eyes luminous and skin lustrous. Many wore gowns hundreds of years out of fashion—ostentatious and ornate—while others, like our guards, wore nothing at all. A merman with a bone necklace and pearl hood winked at me from afar. His companion had painted her entire body gold, donning only a fork in her intricately braided chignon.

The only thing every melusine had in common, it seemed, was their legs.

"We have not walked for many years," Aurélien said as means of explanation.

From around the bend of the street, a team of sienna-colored octopi surged into view, pulling a gilded carriage behind. Except its paint had disintegrated in the salty water, and its wood had mostly rotted, caving in half the roof. Still, the melusines nearest it clapped gleefully, and the couple inside—one wore a monocle, for Christ's sake—waved as if royalty. And perhaps they were. Perhaps kings and queens in the world below owned octopi and carriages. Perhaps they also sewed shark teeth into veils and wore golden cutlery in their powdered wigs.

The entire city glittered with the air of ludicrous opulence gone to seed.

I adored it.

"I want a wig." I couldn't see enough as we marched past little shops of stone with planter boxes of red algae. One melusine walked his pet spotted turtle on a gold-threaded leash. Another lounged in a claw-footed tub at the street corner, pouring water from a pitcher onto her legs. They transformed back into obsidian fins before our very eyes. Merchants hawked wares of everything from conch fritters and crab legs to oyster-and-pearl earrings and music boxes. The light of the sea stars undulated eerily across each face, the only illumination in the entire city. "*Why* do melusines own wigs?"

"And gowns?" Coco asked, eyeing the couple nearest us. They both wore heavy trains of brocade velvet and . . . corsets. Just corsets. No bodices. No chemises. "How do you wear them with fins? Wouldn't skirts weigh you down in the water?"

"Can a melusine drown?" I asked curiously.

Olympienne tilted her lavender head between us in consideration. She pursed her lavender lips. "Do not be silly. Of course melusines cannot drown. We have gills." She bared her neck, revealing pearlescent slits along the side of her throat. "And lungs." She inhaled deeply. "But yes, unfortunately, such handsome attire can prove quite troublesome underwater. We have much anticipated your arrival for just this reason."

"To wear dresses?" Beau frowned as a young boy strode past in scarlet breeches and billowing cloak. He bared sharp teeth at us. "You drained the entire city to wear . . . dresses."

"We drained the city because we are courteous hosts," Lasimonne said, his voice unexpectedly deep. "That we should also wear our treasure is a pleasant inclusion."

Wear our treasure. Huh. It made sense. Where else would a melusine trapped below water find such sumptuous clothing but sunken ships? Perhaps Lasimonne's ruby nipple rings had come from the ship we approached at this very moment, splintered at the base of Le Palais de Cristal.

"How long does it take to drain an entire city?" I peered down a darkened alley that seemed to drop straight into an abyss, where I swore I saw an enormous eye blink. "And what's down there?"

"A giant squid. No, do not provoke it." Aurélien steered me back onto the main road with the tip of his trident.

"Isla foresaw your arrival months ago." Sabatay tossed his braid over a sculpted shoulder and gestured for us to keep moving. The palace loomed directly ahead of us now. "From the moment you chose to marry the huntsman rather than flee or allow the authorities to lock you away."

Beau cleared his throat, glancing up at the waters far above. The sea stars' reflection pulsed faintly in his dark eyes. "Yet Constantin was quite adamant that Célie and I *not* enter this place.

Indeed, he said humans who drank of the waters would go mad."

Elvire looked at us from over her shoulder. "And *did* you drink of the waters?"

"I—" Beau frowned and looked at Célie. "Did we?"

She shook her head slowly, brow creasing. "I don't know. I did have a rather disturbing dream while unconscious, but I thought . . ."

Elvire patted her arm knowingly. "Dreams are never dreams, Mademoiselle Célie. They are our deepest wishes and darkest secrets made true, whispered only under cloak of night. In them, we are free to know ourselves."

Beau's skin appeared sallow in the ghostly light, and he swallowed, visibly disturbed. "I didn't speak any truth."

Elvire arched a silver brow. "Didn't you, *Your Highness*?" When he didn't answer—merely stared at her in confusion and dismay—she chuckled softly. "Never fear. You shall not go mad from it. You entered the waters under the Oracle's invitation, and she will protect your mind for the duration of your stay."

My own frown deepened as more guards lowered a rotten gangway for us to board the ship. "The only human entrance into Le Palais de Cristal," Aurélien explained, prodding us forward. Tentatively, we followed the others atop the soft wood. It bowed beneath our weight.

A buxom melusine waited for us above, her silver hair elaborately coiffed and her gray eyes clouded with age. Fine smile lines crinkled the corners of her mouth. "*Bonsoir,*" she greeted us with a deep curtsy, her train sparkling behind her on the deck.

She wore no forks or monocles, instead looking every inch the consummate human aristocrat. Even the color and fabric of her gown—aubergine silk embellished with golden thread—would've been the height of fashion in Cesarine. "Welcome to Le Palais de Cristal. I am Eglantine, the Oracle's personal handmaid and lady of this palace. I shall be attending you during your stay in our home."

With the same impeccable grace and innate confidence as Angelica, she turned toward the colossal doors to our left. By some miracle, water hadn't eroded the structure beyond—perhaps the captain's quarters?—as it had much of the quarterdeck. Some boards had splintered or rotted completely, leaving gaping holes through which candlelight flickered from below. Music too. I strained to hear fragments of the haunting melody, but Aurélien prodded me forward once more, through the doors and onto a grand staircase. Covered in moldy carpet and lit by gilded candelabra, the stairs seemed to descend into the belly of the ship.

I glanced at the crystal spires above our head. "Are we not going up?"

"Guests are not permitted in the towers." Aurélien poked me more insistently now. "Only the Oracle and her court inhabit them."

"Are you part of her court, then?"

He puffed out his muscled chest, a peculiar shade between white and gray. Like fog. "I am."

I patted his trident. "Of course you are."

Reluctantly fascinated, I followed Beau down the stairs. The walls had once been papered, but time and water had disintegrated all but scraps of the striped design. The carpet squelched softly underfoot. "When will we meet with Isla?" I asked, grinning as Leopoldine trailed a long finger through the candle flame. She drew it back sharply a second later, examining the fresh burn there with a frown. "Will there be food?"

Though the guards stiffened as if insulted by the question, Eglantine chuckled. "Of course there shall be food. As much as you could possibly eat." My stomach rumbled its appreciation. "A special banquet has been prepared just for you. After you wash, we shall join Isla to dine."

"*Just* her?" Coco asked, eyes narrowed in suspicion.

A knowing gleam entered Eglantine's eyes. "Well, I would be remiss if I didn't mention how eager the entire court is to meet all of you. Especially you, Cosette." She winked at Coco in a conspiratorial fashion, and I decided instantly that I liked her. "Look how you've grown! You've always been beautiful, *chérie*, but I must say your breasts are an exquisite addition."

I definitely liked her.

Coco straightened her shoulders in pride—or defiance—pushing said additions front and center as the guards prepared to leave us. To Célie, Elvire asked, "Won't you sit with us at tonight's feast, Mademoiselle Célie? We would so enjoy your company."

Célie blinked once, glancing between each of their hopeful faces, before smiling wide. "I would love that."

"Excellent." Olympienne flashed her diamond teeth while

Leopoldine unclasped a golden chain from between her breasts, refastening it around Célie's waist. Sabatay tucked a strand of seaweed into her chignon, and Beau, Coco, and I—well, we all watched Célie become a bird's nest in unabashed bewilderment. "Until later, *mon trésor*."

They left us under Eglantine's watchful gaze. "Your chambers are just around the hall—one for each of you, of course. Unless you and the human prince would like to share, Cosette?"

Beau smirked as tension bolted down Coco's spine. "That won't be necessary," she said tersely. Angelica turned away to hide her smile behind her hand. "Thank you."

"Very well. I shall leave you here." Eglantine halted outside another decaying door. A burgundy curtain had been draped over the threshold, shielding the room from the hall. "This entire wing is completely your own." She nodded to the other doors lining the way. "Ring the bells when you've finished with your wash, and I shall collect you. Might I bring anything else to make you more comfortable?"

Célie reluctantly glanced at her ruined trousers. "Perhaps a clean nightgown?"

"Oh! How silly of me." Eglantine brushed the burgundy curtain aside, pointing to the tarnished armoire beside a hammock of nets. "Each room has been stocked with clothing of all shapes and sizes, hand selected by the Oracle herself. Consider each piece yours."

THE GREEN RIBBON

Lou

Coco followed me into the curtained room while Beau and Célie wandered down the corridor in search of privacy. Already, steam curled from a golden tub in the corner. What had probably once been a silk dressing screen stood furled beside it, but the fabric had decomposed long ago. They'd woven seaweed into the panels instead.

Yawning, Coco unlaced her blouse before stripping it over-head. Though I moved to Reid's side, I didn't bother shielding his eyes. He hadn't so much as stirred since we'd entered Le Présage, and if the sight of even Coco's exquisite assets couldn't tempt him to wake, we might've been in more trouble than I thought.

I snatched a bowl from the dressing table, filling it with bath-water.

Then again, this *was* Reid. If he'd opened his eyes just now, he would've fainted all over again.

He was going to be *fine*.

Coco eyed the bowl as she shimmied from her pants and

plucked a scarf from the armoire, wrapping it around her hair. "Are you bathing him?"

"Nope." Thrusting my shoulder into his, I rolled him onto the hammock, and his magical bed burst beneath us, soaking the carpet once more. "Not yet anyway." She arched a brow and slipped into the tub, scooping sea salt from the pot beside it and scrubbing the gritty substance onto her skin. When I lifted Reid's wrist to submerge his hand in the bowl, she shook her head and sighed.

"Tell me you aren't doing what I think you're doing."

I shrugged. "Your mom said he would wake. I'm just helping him along."

"She said he would wake *when he's ready.*"

"And?" I watched his pants intently, settling into the hammock beside him, my back against the musty wall. My *magic* wouldn't work, but . . . "Perhaps he's ready."

Her lips twitched slightly as she followed my gaze. His chest still rose and fell rhythmically, but otherwise, he didn't move. "Perhaps he's not," she said.

"Well, we'll know in a few minutes, won't we?"

"I expected you to be more worried about this."

"I've spent the entirety of my life worried, Coco. Nothing has changed."

Except it had. Everything had changed. I'd made a promise to Ansel—to myself—when I'd left him in those waters. I wouldn't allow fear to control me for another moment. No. Not even for another second.

Coco's lips twitched harder as she scrubbed her skin. "He'll be furious when he wakes."

When he wakes.

I arched a devilish brow. "Dare I say he'll be . . . pissed?"

She cackled outright now, leaning over the tub to better see the proceedings. "Oh my god. That was *terrible*."

"That was brilliant, and you know it." Absurdly pleased with myself, I pushed to my feet just as a veritable army of maids bustled through the curtain. Each carried pitchers of fresh, scalding water in tow.

"Are you finished, milady?" one of them asked Coco. When she nodded, the maid held out a silk robe, and Coco—shooting a quick, dubious glance in my direction—hesitated before stepping into it. I hid a smile behind my hand. I couldn't speak for Coco, but I hadn't been waited on since I'd left the Chateau at sixteen. Had anyone ever pampered her? My grin spread as another maid presented her with bottles of perfumed oils for her skin and hair. The others set about emptying the tub and refilling it with fresh water.

"From the geysers below the palace," one explained through the steam. She selected a gown for Coco, draping it across the ornate—albeit mildewed—chair in the corner. "We often visit them to bathe ourselves, yet this is our first opportunity to use their waters in such a fashion. How did you find your bath?" she asked Coco. "Was it pleasant?"

"Very." Slowly, Coco trailed her fingers along the lace of her nightgown. "Thank you."

The maid smiled. "Very good. Is there anything else you require?"

Coco touched a tentative hand to her stomach. "I'm actually feeling a little sick."

"We shall send for some ginger tea. Just harvested from a ship on route to Amandine. It will settle your stomach."

I waited until they'd left before shucking off my bloody chemise and sinking into the tub. The water nearly scalded me, but I relished the heat of it, the catharsis. Dipping my head back, I scrubbed at my scalp, loosening the sand and dirt there. I couldn't remember the last time I'd been truly clean.

I glanced again at Reid, who hadn't wet himself and hadn't woken.

Coco removed his hand from the bowl. "We need to get creative. You could—"

A light knock sounded from the threshold, and we both turned. "It's me," Célie said softly. "May I come in?"

At the sound of her voice, Coco and I both froze, exchanging a panicked look. It wasn't as if we *disliked* Célie. Indeed, we'd risked life and limb to save her, but we hadn't . . . spent time with her. Not really. We hadn't bonded outside of La Mascarade des Crânes. We weren't *friends*.

Coco gestured toward the curtain. *Go on*, she mouthed. *Answer her.*

I waved an agitated hand down my naked body.

Coco shrugged, the corners of her mouth lifting. *Who cares? You're hot as f—*

"Come in!" I called, flinging wet sea salt at Coco's smug face. It landed with a *splat*, soaking her robe, just as Célie poked her head into the room. "Hi, Célie. Is something wrong?"

A pretty pink blush spread across her cheeks at the question. She too had bathed, and she wore her own dressing robe, ruffles rising to her chin. "No." Moving the curtain aside tentatively, she stepped forward without looking at either of us, concentrating on the ostentatious gold-and-glass serving tray in her hands. A chipped china set perched atop it. "I just . . . heard you talking. Here"—she thrust the tray toward us abruptly—"I passed a maid in the hall. She ground ginger for your stomach pains, and I—I offered to bring it to you."

Coco cut her gaze to me, clearly waiting to follow my lead. I scowled at her. It made sense, of course, as Célie wasn't *Beau's* clinging ex-paramour, but still . . . how did one react in this situation? Célie had nowhere to go. She had no friends to speak of, and the horrors she'd endured . . . I sighed. The last time I'd spoken to her, she'd loathed my very name, accusing me of stealing Reid away from her with magic. That same night, she'd fled into my arms.

No. Realization twisted my already knotted stomach. Into Reid's.

She'd fled into *Reid's* arms, not mine. She probably still thought me a whore. She'd said as much once, right before kissing my husband at the Saint Nicolas Day ball. The knot in my stomach tangled further, and the silence lengthened as I stared at her, as she stared at anything but me.

Right. I sat forward in the tub, loathing the awkwardness between us. There was nothing for it. I'd have to ask her.

Coco sighed hard through her nose before I could speak. Flicking an impatient look in my direction, she started to say, "Thank you," at precisely the same moment I said, "Are you still in love with Reid?"

Startled, Célie finally looked up, and the blush on her cheeks fanned to an open flame upon seeing me naked. She stumbled back a step, and the tray slipped from one hand. Though she did her best to right herself, one hand still flailed wildly, finding purchase against Reid's—

Oh shit.

My eyes flew wide. With a small cry, she snatched her hand away from him, and the tray went flying, china shattering against the wall, the carpets, while tea sprayed in every direction. It dripped from her beautiful dressing robe as she dropped to her knees, trying and failing to fix it. "I—I'm so s-sorry. How terribly clumsy—"

Guilt reared her ugly head like a bitch, and I swung my legs over the tub, searching for something with which to cover myself. Coco threw another robe my way. I hurried to tie it as Célie continued spluttering on the sodden carpet, collecting the shards of china in vain. "I didn't mean—oh, the maids will be so upset. And your poor stomachs—"

I knelt beside her, stilling her hand before she cut herself. Her gaze swung upward and locked on mine. Tears welled in her eyes.

"Our stomachs will be fine, Célie." Gently, I took the shards from her and deposited them back on the floor. "We'll all be fine."

She said nothing for a long moment, simply staring at me. I looked back at her with feigned calm and waited, though I longed to rise, to seek the ease and familiarity of Coco's presence amidst this painfully awkward situation. Célie had no such person to comfort her. She had no familiarity here. And though we weren't friends, we weren't enemies either. We never had been.

When she spoke again, her voice was a whisper. Barely discernible. "No. I am not in love with him. Not anymore." Some of the tension left my shoulders. She spoke truth. The waters wouldn't have allowed the words otherwise. "And I'm sorry." Her voice fell quieter still, but she didn't lower her gaze. Her cheeks shone brilliant scarlet. "You aren't a whore."

Coco knelt beside us now, a clean robe in hand. She snorted, puncturing the unexpected sincerity of the moment. "Oh, she is, and I am too. You don't know us well enough"—she extended the robe, arching a meaningful brow—"yet."

Célie glanced down at herself, as if just realizing she'd been doused with tea.

"Take it." Coco pressed it into her hands before motioning toward the dressing screen.

Célie blushed again, looking between us. "You probably think I'm a prude."

"So?" I waved a hand over the broken china set, and the golden pattern connecting each shard dissipated. Sharpness pierced my chest as the pieces knit themselves back together. I lifted a hand to rub the spot, torn between sighing and wincing. Forgiveness was a painful thing. A sacrifice in itself. "You shouldn't care what we think, Célie—or anyone else, for that matter. Don't forfeit your power like that."

"Because who cares if you're a prude?" Coco pulled Célie to her feet with both hands. She gestured to me. "Who cares if we're whores? They're just words."

"And we can't get it right no matter what we do." Winking, I slipped a satin ribbon from the armoire, tying it around my throat before falling into the hammock once more. Reid swayed beside me. I ignored the knot of panic in my chest. He hadn't so much as stirred. Instead, I flicked his boot and added, "We might as well do it our own way. Being a prude or being a whore are both better than being what they want us to be."

Célie blinked between us, eyes huge, and whispered, "What do they want us to be?"

Coco and I exchanged a long-suffering look before she said simply, "Theirs."

"Be prudish and proud, Célie." I shrugged, my hand curling instinctively around Reid's ankle. "We'll be whorish and happy." He would wake soon, surely. And if not, Isla—the Oracle, Claud's sister, a *goddess*—would help us fix everything. We just needed to dine with her first. I glared at the brush on the dressing table. Following my gaze, Coco seized it before I could melt its golden handle into ore.

Planting one hand on her hip and grinning in challenge, she said, "It's time, Lou."

I glared at her now. "Everyone knows not to brush wet hair.

The strands are weaker. They could break."

"Shall we summon a maid for a fire, then?" When I didn't answer, she waved the brush under my nose. "That's what I thought. *Up*."

Rolling my eyes, I slid from the hammock and stalked toward the mildewed chair. It sat before a full-length, gilded vanity mirror that had clouded with age. Golden serpents twined together to form its frame. I stared peevishly at my reflection within it: cheeks gaunt, freckles stark, hair long and tangled. Water still dripped from its ends, permeating the thin silk of my robe. I didn't shiver, however; the melusines had cast some sort of magic to keep the air balmy and comfortable.

Before Coco could lift the brush—I suspected she secretly enjoyed tormenting me—Célie stepped forward tentatively, hand extended. "May I?"

"Er—" Coco flicked her gaze to mine in the mirror, uncertain. When I nodded once, part curious—mostly curious—she handed Célie the brush and stepped aside. "The ends tangle," she warned.

Célie smiled. "So do mine."

"I can brush my own hair, you know," I muttered, but I didn't stop her as she lifted a small section and began working the brush through the ends. Though she held the hair firm, she moved with surprising gentleness.

"I do not mind." With the patience of a saint, she set about untangling two gnarled locks. "Pip and I once brushed each other's hair every night." If she felt me still, she didn't comment. "We dismissed our maid when I was ten. Evangeline was her name. I couldn't understand where she'd gone, but Pippa—Pippa was old enough to realize what had happened. We often snuck into our father's safe as children, you see. Pippa liked to steal his ledger, sit at his desk, and add his sums, pretending to smoke his cigars, while I played with our mother's jewels. She knew our parents had lost everything in a bad investment. I didn't know until all of Maman's diamonds disappeared."

Successfully untangling the knot, she moved on to another section of hair. "Père told us not to worry, of course. He said he would make it right." Her smile twisted in the mirror's leaden reflection. "He did just that, I suppose. Slowly but surely, Maman's jewelry returned, along with all manner of other strange and unusual objects. He changed the lock on his safe shortly thereafter—an impossible lock even I could not pick. Not then, anyway."

"Did Evangeline return?" I asked.

"No." She shook her head ruefully. "Evangeline wouldn't so much as step foot through our door after that. She said we were cursed. Another maid took her place, but Pip insisted on brushing my hair regardless. I think she wanted to distract me. Père's contacts always visited at night."

"She sounds like a wonderful sister."

Her smile turned warm and genuine. "She was."

We descended into silence for only a moment—Célie continuing to stroke my hair with expert precision—before Coco surprised me by speaking. "And your mother?"

Célie spoke without hesitation, matter-of-fact, as if Coco had asked her not an exceptionally personal question, but the color of the sky. "My mother tried. She was not particularly maternal, but she gave us what she could: gifts, mostly, but on occasion she'd join us in the parlor while we sewed or played pianoforte. She would read us stories. She could be severe at times, of course—especially after Pippa's death—but . . . it was how she expressed her love."

Coco no longer pretended to be interested in her reflection. "Do you think she misses you?"

"I certainly hope so." Célie shrugged delicately, setting the brush atop the vanity. She swept my now-tidy hair down my back. "But I will see her again soon. Who knows? Perhaps she'll be proud I helped rid the world of Morgane."

Coco and I locked gazes in the mirror. The heartbreak in hers shone clear.

My mother tried.

It shouldn't have been a glowing commendation, yet it was. Célie's mother had tried, and in doing so, she'd given more to her daughter than either of our mothers had given us. Unbidden, my hand crept upward to the satin ribbon around my throat. A mark of my mother's love.

"Why do you hide it?" Célie asked abruptly. I glanced up to find her staring at me—at my scar. Even Coco seemed to return from her thoughts, eyes sharpening on the emerald ribbon. She arched a brow, and Célie nodded to her. "Coco shows her scars."

"Coco's scars aren't shameful." I tilted my head, fixing her reflection with a narrow gaze. "Why don't you show *your* scars, Célie?"

She looked away then. "I don't have any scars."

"Not all scars are visible."

"You are avoiding the question."

"So are you."

Sighing, Coco joined Célie behind me, her hands threading through my hair. Comfortable and familiar. She leaned down, her cheek hovering beside mine, and our reflections met once more. "How many times have I told you? No scar is shameful." Mouth set with determination, she plucked at the end of my ribbon, and it fell from my throat, revealing my scar. Except it wasn't my scar any longer. At least, it wasn't the scar I'd always known.

Gasping, I traced the fine lines with my fingertips, following the graceful curve of leaves, the delicate whorls of petals. Like a silver necklace, it transformed the column of my throat into something rare and beautiful. Something exquisite. When I swallowed, the leaves seemed to wink at me in the candlelight. "When did this happen?"

"When we learned you'd been possessed." Coco straightened, pulling a small stool over beside my chair. From the pile of its fabric, the upholstery had once been velvet, though the original color and pattern had long been lost. It was simply gray now, its curving legs as rotted as the rest of this place. Coco gestured for Célie—who appeared paler than before, her hands knotted together in apprehension—to sit. "When I decided to hope regardless. My tears transformed it."

Hope isn't the sickness. It's the cure.

Coco slipped her hands into Célie's unbound hair next, surprising me yet again. Judging by the way Célie straightened, the way her eyes flew wide, Coco had surprised her too. She wove the black strands into a single plait down Célie's back, tying the end with my ribbon, looping the emerald satin into a perfect bow. "You should both show your scars," she murmured.

Célie dragged her braid across her shoulder to stare at it, fingering the tails of the ribbon in quiet wonder. Coco plopped her cheek atop my head, and her familiar scent—earthy yet sweet, like a freshly brewed cup of tea—engulfed me. "They mean you survived."

THE ORACLE AND THE SEA URCHIN

Lou

Clad in a gown of marigold chiffon with floral appliqué, each rose dark and glittering as gunpowder, I followed Eglantine through a labyrinth of passages that night. Coco walked beside me. Her own gown of ivory satin—slimmer in skirt than my own, with a fitted bodice and golden thread spun into delicate filigree—trailed behind us for miles. The dress of a true *princesse*. Célie glided forward on her other side, regal and elegant and completely in her element. The soft petal pink of her bodice brought color to her porcelain cheeks, and the crawling juniper vines adorning the skirt flattered her slender form.

We cut quite the striking figure, the three of us. More than one head turned as we passed.

Even Beau did a double take as he stepped from his cabin, eyes flitting from the pearl headpiece in Coco's hair to the emerald earring in Célie's ear, the matching ribbon on her wrist.

"Lord help us all." Beau shook his head and stepped behind us, plunging his hands into the pockets of his velvet pants. He whistled low. "Though Heaven never created such a view."

"We know." Coco arched a brow over her shoulder, each step revealing a bit of smooth thigh through the slit in her skirt.

Like the rest of the ship, the hall boasted extravagance with its once-gilded panels and glittering, albeit broken, chandeliers. Unlike our cabins, however, this room rose high above us, the painted ceilings towering unnaturally tall for a sea vessel. The air here smelled not of mildew but of magic, sweet and pleasant and sharp. A golden banquet table ran the length of the enormous room, and atop it, dishes and platters of a strange variety covered every inch. At the door, a liveried melusine bowed deeply and nearly sent his wig tumbling to the floor.

"*Bonjour, mes demoiselles.*" He straightened with the cool hauteur of an aristocrat. On one powdered cheek, he'd drawn a tiny black heart. "Please, allow me to escort you to your seats."

Eglantine winked at us before retreating from the room.

We followed the butler in a single-file line until we reached the head of the table, where a veritable throne of seashells and pearls sat empty, along with two seats on either side. The butler seated Coco and Célie together with practiced efficiency before turning to me. He ignored Beau altogether. With another low bow, he murmured, "The Oracle will join us shortly. She kindly asks for you to sample the salted sea lettuce." He paused to sniff through his long nose. "It is her very favorite."

"Remember"—Célie spoke in a low voice, keeping her expression pleasant as the butler stalked back to his post—"to mind your manners." She smiled at the aristocrats down the table. They watched us openly, some returning her smile, others whispering behind painted fans. "We would not want to disrespect our host."

Elvire appeared without warning at her shoulder. No longer naked, she wore a dress fashioned from faded sails, complete with a belt of rope and a tiara of emeralds. The latter matched Célie's earring. I suspected it wasn't a coincidence. Touching it reverentially, Elvire inclined her head. "*Bonjour*, Mademoiselle Célie. Your gown is exquisite."

Behind her, Leopoldine and Lasimonne leaned forward with comical interest to hang on Célie's every word. Without preamble, the melusines sitting beside Célie rose politely and offered their seats to the guards, who accepted with equal courtesy. It was all very civil. Almost saccharine. "You must try the sargassum," Lasimonne insisted, spooning the yellowish leaves onto Célie's plate and drizzling green sauce over them. "It is the Oracle's favored dish."

I eyed her plate suspiciously, feeling very much like I'd failed to prepare for a schoolroom test. "I thought the salted sea lettuce was her favorite?"

He blinked at me before turning to Leopoldine, who nodded gravely. "It is true. Sargassum was her favored dish *yesterday*."

Oh god.

"Dear me." Lasimonne lifted a horrified hand to his chest before bowing deeply over Célie's plate of sargassum. "My apologies, *mademoiselle*. Of course you must sample the salted sea lettuce instead. Good gracious. The Oracle would not have forgotten such a slight."

Beau and I exchanged wide-eyed glances.

Without another word, I heaped salted sea lettuce onto first my plate, then Beau's. "To the right of the dinner fork," he muttered discreetly as I studied the mismatched cutlery on either side of my plate. I speared a leaf with the tiny fork, but before I could lift it to my mouth, Beau stopped me with the curt shake of his head. "Cut it first. Were you raised in a barn?"

Heat licked at my cheeks as I returned the leaf to my plate, searching for the proper knife.

Elvire sipped at the effervescent liquid in her flute as Célie cut her own lettuce into exemplary pieces. "Yes," the former said, "the Oracle positively banished Guillaumette for the gaffe last week."

"An insipid woman," Leopoldine added conspiratorially. "I never cared for her."

Elvire fixed her with a cool stare, lifting a silver brow. "Verily? Is she not the godmother of your daughter?"

Leopoldine abruptly busied herself with her own drink, unable to answer.

"Where is Angelica?" I focused on cutting my sea lettuce into perfect squares, lest Elvire or Leopoldine or the octopi in the street take offense and feed me to the giant squid. "Will she be joining us?"

Lasimonne stared at me as if *I* were the giant squid. "Of course she is." Though clearly vexed that I'd spoken at all, he didn't hesitate to pour me a flute of the effervescent liquid. So polite. So fascinating. If I spilled my plate in his lap, would he thank me?

"She is the most treasured of the Oracle's companions. I daresay she will arrive with Our Lady herself."

I bit my tongue before I could ask *when* that would be—then ran it over my teeth to check for bits of sea lettuce, just in case. Apparently, tardiness wasn't as heinous a gaffe as forgetting Her Ladyship's favorite food. Lifting the flute to my lips instead, I simply nodded. Then choked.

It was seawater.

With a forced smile, Beau patted my back as I spluttered, pressing his foot atop my own under the table. "There, there." He handed me a folded napkin before saying to the others, "Please pardon my dear sister. She must have a sensitive gag reflex."

I snorted again, unable to help myself, and kicked Beau's foot from mine.

Two more liveried melusines stepped into the banquet hall then, each holding an enormous conch shell. As one, they lifted the shells to their lips and blew. The call reverberated through the chamber, rattling china and chandeliers, as the melusines around us swept to their feet.

The Oracle followed a moment later.

I could only stare at her.

Quite simply, she was the most beautiful woman I'd ever seen.

Her hair rippled like water down her shoulders as she floated into the room, casting her ethereal silver gaze in our direction. When her eyes met mine, I saw not iris and sclera but tranquil moonlight on the sea, silken foam along the shore. I saw cresting waves and flashing scales—primordial creatures of teeth and shadow who awoke with the darkness. I saw tempests to tear apart kingdoms, secrets bared and secrets kept. Secrets drowned in boundless depths.

Then she smiled at me, and a shiver skittered down my spine. In that smile, I saw chaos.

Pure, unadulterated chaos.

Angelica walked behind her, head bowed and hands clasped. She caught Coco's eye as they approached, winking covertly, before resuming her pious stance. The Oracle looked only at me. I straightened as furtively as I could, painfully aware of my damp palms, but otherwise, I didn't cower. Claud had once described himself as the Wild, and in his true form, I'd believed it. The Oracle didn't need to assume her true form for me to understand. From the misty, nameless color of her hair and skin to the liquid movement of her body, she *was* the sea. And the sea drowned those who couldn't swim.

"*Je vous voir*, Louise." To my great surprise, her voice held a calming, tranquil note, like still waters at dawn. "*Bienvenue* to the Crystal Palace. I have long awaited your arrival."

I curtsied with the others. "I'm happy to be here. Thank you for interfering at the beach."

Her silver eyes—so like Angelica's, yet so different—sparkled with amusement. "Ah. The beach. We shall speak at length about that happy coincidence later. First, we must dine." She nodded to another liveried melusine, who hastened to pull back her chair. Her gown—crafted entirely from long, gleaming strands of pearls—clinked softly as she sat. The rest of the court seated themselves with her. When she snapped her fingers, the aristocrat on Coco's right vaulted to her feet without a word, ceding her seat to Angelica. "You have sampled the salted sea lettuce, yes?"

"Yes, my lady." I too returned to my seat, wiping my palms on my thighs beneath the table. "It was . . ." The waters prevented me from lying. I tried again. "A special experience."

"Come now." Her smile broadened, and unbidden, the image of a hungry shark rose in my mind's eye. I clenched my skirt between two fists, mentally chastising myself. "There is no need for clever language amongst friends. How did you find it, truly?"

"I'm glad to have tasted it."

"Glad." She said the word slowly, curiously. "There are uglier designations, I suppose. *I* am glad you found it . . . what clever word did you use?" She tapped her lips. "*Special.* Now"—she snapped her fingers again—"clear it away. I tire of its stench." The servants bustled to remove every plate of salted sea lettuce from the table. "*S'il vous plaît,*" she continued before they'd finished, "I crave heavier fare tonight. Bring the *neige marine* for our *special* guests."

Perhaps not so calming at all.

My palms continued to sweat.

We sat in distinctly uncomfortable silence as more dishes were passed down the table. Isla didn't seem to notice. She merely continued to smile as servants spooned small amounts of gray, sticky substance onto each plate. When she lifted a bite to her lips, she paused, appraising the room to ensure she held everyone's attention. She did, of course. Every melusine's face turned toward her as if she were their very sun. She waved an elegant hand with a laugh. "Eat, *mes enfants*, and be merry."

Her children obliged, and the gentle sounds of clinking cutlery and soft voices soon filled the silence. Elvire, Leopoldine, and Lasimonne immediately engaged in conversation with Célie—and Angelica with a resigned Coco—leaving Beau and me to suffer the weight of Isla's stare alone. "Tell me," she crooned, leaning across him to grasp my clammy hand. He stiffened but didn't complain. "What were your last words to Reid?"

I looked up from my *neige marine* in surprise. "Pardon me?"

"The last words you spoke to your lover—what were they?"

"I—" Glancing at Beau, I frowned. "I don't remember."

Her smile turned positively wicked. "Try."

Feeling increasingly unsettled, I concentrated on recalling the memory, exhaling hard as the threads of our conversation returned. "I said 'Either I kill my mother, or my mother kills me. It's the only way.'"

That smile. Those eyes. Not tranquil water at all, but the calm in the eye of a hurricane. Perhaps the hurricane itself. Inexplicably, I knew the pleasantries had ended. She released my hand and returned to her seat, dabbing her mouth with a napkin. "Is that so?"

"I wouldn't have been able to say it otherwise."

Beau pressed his foot over mine again.

"And . . . do you remember his last words to you?" she asked slyly.

These words I didn't struggle to remember. "He promised he would find me."

"Find you?" When she batted her lashes as if—as if goading me—unease lifted the hair at my neck. Surely this wasn't appropriate table conversation? We'd only just met, and melusines valued etiquette. My suspicion only deepened when she asked, "He sleeps belowdecks, does he not?"

"He does." I forced my voice to remain calm and collected— pleasant even. Still, I couldn't help but search her features for some of her brother's warmth. His good humor. "I've tried to wake him to no avail. Actually . . ." I cleared my throat as delicately as possible, throwing caution to the wind. "I was hoping you might . . . speed along the process."

Inexplicable triumph flashed in those nameless eyes. "Oh?" Though her voice remained light, conversational, her words belied the tone. "You *hope*, or you presume?"

My brows furrowed at the word. "I would never *presume*—"

"No?" Idly, she lifted a hand, and a servant hurried to fill her flute. "Do my mirrors lie, *l'oursin*? Do you not secretly scheme for an alliance?"

"I—" Incredulous, I met Coco's eyes across the table. She didn't intervene, however. She didn't dare interrupt. "I don't *scheme* for anything, my lady. While I would've *liked* to secure your friendship during our visit, I don't expect it."

"*Would've?* Does this mean you no longer desire my friendship?"

"No, my lady. I mean *yes*. It's just"—I splayed my hands

helplessly—"this doesn't seem to be going terribly well."

"What do you *expect*, Louise, when you treat gods and goddesses as your personal attendants?" She sipped at her seawater, still studying me. "To be frank, I cannot fathom what my siblings see in you, nor why they indulge your arrogance. When I sent Angelica to fetch you, I expected . . . some sort of grandeur—a magnetism, perhaps—but now, having met you, I see you possess neither. Aurore has bestowed her blessing on a sea urchin."

The first spark of anger lit in my chest. *Aurore's blessing? A sea urchin?* "Is that why you invited me here? To satisfy your curiosity?"

She didn't answer, instead turning to Beau. "What about you, princeling? Do you find Louise intelligent?"

He carefully returned his spoon to his plate before answering. "I do."

"Do you find her extraordinarily intelligent?"

"Y—" His reply caught in his throat, however, and his gaze cut to mine, abruptly panicked. Rueful. My anger spiked in response. He couldn't lie—not here, not caught in Isla's web of magic—even to spare my feelings. The knowledge hurt, but it didn't cut deep enough to scar. I might not have been *extraordinarily intelligent*, but I had intelligence enough to know Isla wanted to hurt me. To shock and awe me. I just didn't understand why.

"As I thought. Tell me, princeling, do you find her extraordinarily beautiful, then?"

He frowned, eyes still darting between us. Her gaze, however, still didn't stray from mine. It bored into me with disturbing intensity. With disturbing *clarity*. Beau tugged at the collar of his shirt before muttering, "Of course I find her pretty. She's my"— his throat worked again, failing to form the words—"she's *like* my sister."

"How quaint. I asked if you find her beauty *extraordinary*, however. Is Louise among the fairest you've encountered?" When he didn't answer right away, she inclined her head. "Just so. Do you consider her extraordinarily brave instead?" Again, he didn't answer. "No? Extraordinarily true, perhaps? Extraordinarily just?" Still Beau said nothing, swallowing hard around words that couldn't come. Sweat beaded along his forehead at the effort. His foot pressed against mine with enough force to crack my bones.

A peculiar hum started in my ears at the pressure, and my vision tunneled on Isla's superior expression. How *dare* she treat us this way? We were guests in her realm. She'd *invited* us here—and for what? To torment us? To poke and prod until we snapped? An almost childlike indignation flooded my system at the injustice.

Isla was supposed to be an ally.

"I don't—why do you ask such questions?" Beau ground out.

She ignored his struggle, continuing ruthlessly. "Is Louise a leader, Beauregard? A visionary?"

"She—not as such—"

"Has she offered you riches in exchange for your loyalty? Has she offered you magic?"

He nearly choked on his answer.

"Is she extraordinary in *any* way?"

"She—" He looked to me, helpless, color rising in his cheeks. Across the table, Célie shot us covert looks, still pretending to listen to Elvire. Coco didn't pretend at all. She glared at Isla with eyes that blazed with hatred while the hum in my ears grew louder.

"—is just as I feared," Isla finished for him. "She is ordinary. Painfully, intolerably ordinary, yet she inspires the loyalty and devotion of my sister, my brother, *you*." Scoffing, she shook her head and signaled for another course. "A wasted blessing, to be sure."

"I am not blessed."

"You don't even realize, do you? I shouldn't be surprised. Aurore may say what she likes about Morgane, but at least your mother possesses a modicum of awareness."

My fingers shook at the comparison. At the insult. I curled them into fists, staring at the pan-fried dulse without seeing it. "Why did you summon us here?"

Again, she ignored my question, reaching across Beau to seize the diamond pin in my hair. "Help me understand, Louise. Why do they follow where you lead? I have only ever watched you fail—watched you murder, watched you lie, watched you cheat. Indeed, like a sea urchin, the only feat you've managed in all your life is survival. In doing so, you have harmed every person in this beloved family of yours, yet each one remains. Why?"

"Perhaps it's my extraordinary sense of humor." The words fell heavy from my lips. Hard. Heat rippled from my chest through my limbs now, and my entire body trembled. White edged my vision. *Ordinary*. She'd said it as an expletive. Something basic and coarse, something inferior.

"No." With an errant flick of her wrist, my diamond pin clattered to the floor. Vaguely, I realized the table had stilled around us. Every eye had turned in my direction. "I do not think so. Even with Aurore's blessing—even with your precious allies—you are not equipped to win this war, Louise le Blanc. Quite simply, my sister chose wrong."

That heat kept spreading. Hotter than anger now. Hotter than embarrassment. Brows furrowing in alarm, Beau stared at my hand when I slammed it atop the table. "You speak of blessings," I said, the words spilling forth wildly and with abandon, "but what good are the *loyalty* and *devotion* of the Wild Man of the Forest and the Triple Goddess? My mother—my own *mother*, the person who should've loved me most in the world—has tried to kill me three times. She murdered my best friend in front of me. Since then, I've spent days, perhaps *weeks*, possessed by Nicholina. Earlier tonight she almost drowned me in these wretched waters, where my mother also tried to kill me. *Again*. Now Reid sleeps under an enchantment I cannot break while you insult me in front of your entire court." My chest heaved. "If this is the *blessing* of a goddess, I'd hate to see her curse."

Isla only smiled.

With a single finger, she pushed the dish between us—still covered—in my direction. The flippant gesture only enraged me further. I shoved to my feet, prepared to stalk from the hall, to seize Reid's body and *leave*, when my eyes dropped to the silver cloche. To my reflection there.

Too late, I registered the sharp scent of magic.

Coco's eyes held wonder, fear, as she too pushed from the table. "Lou?"

But I didn't recognize my reflection. Round brown eyes stared back at me, and straight, wheat-colored locks replaced my own. Pink cheeks replaced freckles. My gown hung from diminutive shoulders, the excess fabric pooling at my feet. As I stared at it, the heat in my chest morphed slowly to something else—something innocent, youthful, inquisitive, *alive*.

Without realizing, I'd transformed into the Maiden.

When Isla stood to stroll toward me, her entire court stood too. She trailed a casual finger across my throat. Scarless now. "You were saying?"

I swallowed hard against her nail, refusing to look at anyone. Especially my reflection. "How—how is this possible?"

"Claud warned Morgane. He told her what would happen if she continued to defy us. Morgane arranged your possession regardless."

"But that"—Beau pushed his plate away with a slack expression—"that means—"

"Yes, princeling." Isla moved behind me, fanning my hair across my shoulders. "The sea urchin has become La Dame des Sorcières. A pity, if you ask me, but admittedly a useful one."

"Does Morgane know?" Coco asked sharply.

In answer, Angelica tensed, her eyes eddying until she no longer saw the room but something else. *Somewhere* else. "Yes." She returned to us after another moment, shaking her head and wincing. "She is not pleased."

I spoke through numb lips. "Why did you bring us here?"

Her hands tightened on my neck, and at last—at *last*—she answered. "My darling Angelica believes we should ally ourselves with you in this tedious struggle against Morgane." I felt her shrug, as if we discussed the weather and not my very life. "I must confess, I care not for it. Neither your death nor your mother's will affect us here." She moved beside me then, offering a hand. I had no choice but to accept it. Tucking my arm in hers, she led me about the room while the others tracked us with their eyes. No one dared resume eating.

"I am not, however, a fool."

I didn't correct her.

"You present a unique opportunity for me and my people— and most of all for Angelica. I treasure her, you know," she added. The woman in question kept her head bowed and her hands clasped, as all the melusines did. "Twenty years ago, a ring of hers was stolen while she dallied above water, creating your rather beautiful friend." Isla waved a vague hand toward Coco. "You have heard of this ring. You have called it by name." Reaching around me, she lifted my right hand to stroke my empty ring finger. "You have even wielded its magic. You do not, however, know it as we do. It is not a simple ring of immunity and invisibility, as your foolish kin believe. More importantly, it does not belong to them. It does not belong to *any* of you. It is Angelica's Ring—it is her very power—and we shall have it back."

Vindicated, I almost laughed at the realization. At the hard, delicious truth. For all her extraordinary intelligence, beauty, and bravery, here she was . . . in need of me. A sea urchin. "If you know I've used it, you also know I don't have it any longer. My mother does. It's kept under lock and key at Chateau le Blanc."

"Precisely."

"I don't quite grasp what you're implying. Ordinary brain, you know. If her ring is so important, surely you can retrieve it yourself?"

When she turned me to face her abruptly, her smile shone hard and bright, and her nails dug painfully into my forearm, longer and sharper than before. She lifted a finger to my lips when I tried to protest, and the metallic taste of blood followed. *My* blood. "Ah, ah, ah." Her eyes dipped to my lips, to her finger, before flicking back to my own. "Do not disrespect me, or you shall never hear my proposition."

I glared at her in mutinous silence.

She arched a devilish brow. "I cannot retrieve the ring myself because I cannot directly intervene. My melusines cannot do it for me because they cannot leave the waters without it. Do you understand now, *mon pouffiasse*? It is, as you say, a mutually beneficial arrangement."

Her words rang in my ears as the rest of her fingers curled around my face, squeezing my cheeks hard enough to bruise. "Tomorrow, you shall return to the surface, and you shall steal back Angelica's Ring from your mother. Then—and *only* then—will my people join you against her."

THE MOST BEAUTIFUL SHADE OF BLUE

Lou

On deck a scant hour later, Angelica pulled Coco aside as Auré-lien, Olympienne, and Sabatay hovered around Célie, bidding her tearful farewells. Truly. Actual *tears* dripped down Olympienne's lavender cheeks. Scoffing, Beau readjusted his pack and started down the plank. Halfway to the seafloor, he turned to jerk his chin at me. "Come on."

I hoisted my own pack over my shoulder. After dinner, Isla had wasted no time in expelling us from her realm. She might've been the most conceited creature alive, but she *had* gifted us supplies for the journey ahead, at least. That included fresh clothes. Sensible ones, this time, and warm ones too. I'd also slipped a new sheath around my thigh, just in case.

Reid drifted along behind, still comatose, as Elvire and Leopoldine escorted us from the city. With each step, the unease I'd been avoiding grew impossible to ignore. It set my teeth on edge, pulsing painfully in my right temple.

Despite my pleas, Isla hadn't woken him. She'd insisted she couldn't intervene. I'd insisted we couldn't rob Chateau le Blanc with a six-and-a-half-foot, two-hundred-pound, *unconscious* man in tow.

Truthfully, I'd expected him to wake by now. He'd been unconscious for hours.

Do not worry, Louise. His injuries are not fatal. He will wake—of that, I am certain.

My head continued to throb.

The others walked toward the gates in silence, seemingly oblivious to our rather giant problem, except for Beau. He threw more than one anxious glance my way.

I assumed he expected me to transform into the Maiden at any moment. I half expected it myself. Even now, I wasn't sure how I'd done it, but I took care not to think too long or too hard about that shiver in my skin—that heady sensation of wild abandon. Curiously enough, it reminded me of . . . rooftops. If I closed my eyes, I could almost *feel* the wind tangling in my hair, my arms stretching wide, as I propelled myself upward, outward, from shingles into empty air. Exhilaration swooped low in my stomach for those precious seconds. Those precious seconds when I might've flown.

When my hands began to ripple, my eyes snapped open.

Beau still stared at me.

"What is it?" I snapped. "Spit it out."

"Are you okay? With"—he jerked his chin toward my hands—"that?"

I eyed him suspiciously. "Are *you*?"

He tipped his head, considering, before a fierce smile broke across his face. "I think it's the most impressive fucking thing I've ever seen. You're a . . . Lou, you're a *goddess* now."

"Goddess Divine." I matched his smirk with one of my own, despite Isla's words ringing loud and true in my ears. *My sister chose wrong.* "Queen of the sea urchins."

His smirk vanished at the last, and he stared resolutely at the back of Elvire's head. "About that. I . . . want to apologize." He cleared his throat. "For earlier."

"Ah." I exhaled with a soft chuckle. "There's no need."

"There is a need—"

"You told the truth."

"It *wasn't* the truth." He shook his head in agitation. "That's what I'm trying to tell you. Isla, she—she twisted my words—" Clearing his throat, he tried again, lowering his voice so the others couldn't hear. "I *do* find you extraordinary. Perhaps not extraordinarily brave or just or true, but extraordinary none-theless." When I rolled my eyes, politely skeptical, he stepped in front of me, forcing us both to a halt. "Who else would have accepted the spoiled son of a king? The misused aristocrat? The sacrilegious huntsman? In the eyes of the kingdom, we are noth-ing." His voice dropped lower still. "You've given us all a place, a purpose, when before we didn't have one. *You* are the reason we're here, Lou. And I don't care about the waters' truth—you *are* my sister. Never forget it."

He sped up to walk beside Coco and Célie without allowing me to answer. Probably for the best.

I couldn't speak around the emotion in my throat.

When we finally reached the shores of L'Eau Mélancolique, the water supporting Reid burst—the last of Angelica's magic falling away—and he collapsed upon the sand. I immediately dropped to my knees beside him. "Shit." I checked his pulse again, pried open his eyelids to assess his pupils. All sounded and looked perfectly healthy.

Exhaling harshly, I poked him in the ribs. Nothing. I flicked his nose. Nothing again. I blew in his face, his eyes, unlaced his boot to tickle his foot, even slapped him smartly across the cheek. Nothing, nothing, *nothing*. My chest tightened with frustration as I dragged him to the water's edge. When splashing his face yielded no results, I swore viciously and prepared to dunk his entire head—his entire *body*, if necessary—but Beau stopped me with an impatient hand. "I don't think drowning him is an option."

"It worked for me—"

"You've tried magic, I assume?" His eyes darted up the path and into the mountains. I didn't blame him. Morgane and Josephine could've been watching us at this very moment. Still . . . as much as Isla had insisted she wouldn't get involved, I doubted she'd forgive an attack on her people so quickly. Constantin had been under her protection. It would be a very brave witch indeed—or perhaps a very stupid one—who trespassed on these shores again. Morgane and Josephine were neither brave nor stupid.

Here, we were safe. For now.

"The patterns are in a knot." I resisted the urge to snap at Beau again in light of his confession. It must've been hard to admit such things aloud. I appreciated them. "I can't make any sense of it."

Coco approached tentatively. "I could take some of his blood."

My mind immediately recoiled from the idea. The last time Coco had taken blood, she'd foreseen Ansel's death, and I'd had quite enough of misinterpreting the future.

"Angelica said—" Célie started, but I interrupted impatiently. "We don't have time for cryptic advice. He needs to wake *now*."

Célie crouched beside me in response, placing a comforting hand on my back, and I felt like the world's greatest ass.

"Sorry," I muttered. "I just don't know what to do. If we don't wake him, we can't steal Angelica's Ring, and if we don't steal Angelica's Ring, we can't count on the melusines to join us against Morgane. Without the melusines—"

"I understand." Her hand drew soothing circles. "At least Reid is all right. He is. Look at him." Forcing my eyes open, I watched him breathe, each swell and fall of his chest a small comfort. Célie smiled. "Truly, he could be only sleeping. An enchanted sleep, perhaps, but—"

Her eyes flew wide.

"What?" I lurched upright. "What is it, Célie?"

"One of the stories my mother used to read me," she said breathlessly, clapping her hands together. "It was about a princess cursed with eternal sleep. The only way to break the spell was the kiss of true love."

Coco scoffed and threw herself on the sand. "That's a fairy tale, Célie. It isn't real."

"We just bathed and dined and conversed underwater in the royal palace of melusines, where octopi walked on leashes and the Goddess of the Sea served us salted *sea lettuce*." Célie's cheeks burned pink. "None of this should be real."

Beau arched a brow. "She makes a fair point."

"Fine." With a sigh of fatigue, Coco fell to her back, folding her hands on her chest. "Kiss him, then. Kiss him good. Just do it quickly. And when that inevitably fails, I'll prick his finger, and we can make real progress."

I looked between each of their expectant faces, feeling utterly ridiculous. *True love's kiss.* Célie had apparently mistaken this nightmare for a sweeping romance, complete with the white knight charging in to save his fair maiden. I glared at Reid's lips. To be fair, it *had* started that way, once upon a time. He'd crossed the entire kingdom to save me from Morgane's sacrificial altar. Perhaps the roles could be reversed now that he was in need. And what real harm could there be in a kiss?

Exhaling hard through my nose, I gripped his shoulders and leaned over him.

Here goes nothing.

My lips brushed his in a light caress, and I parted them slowly, touching his tongue to mine. Just for a second. Just a single breath. My eyes fell closed at the simple joy of it—of kissing Reid. God, I missed him. For too long, our lives had been tangled yet separate, intrinsically linked yet forever apart. It was my fault. It was his too.

But mostly, it was Morgane's.

He didn't wake.

Sighing in defeat, I rested my head against his chest and listened to his heart. How many times had I lain in this exact position, counting each beat? He'd often stroked my hair, traced my spine, even when things had been strained between us. When things had been good, however, he'd wrapped his strong arms around me and—

A heavy hand fell upon my back.

My eyes snapped open.

Behind me, Célie gasped, Coco gasped—even *Beau* gasped—as I scrambled to my elbows, staring down at Reid's face in shock. He blinked back at me, and those eyes—they were the most beautiful shade of blue. Giddy laughter bubbled up my throat at his frown. "Sleeping beauty awakes."

His hands landed lightly on my waist. "I beg your pardon?"

Skimming a fingertip along his dark lashes, I leaned down to kiss him once more. He drew back before I could. "You slept for a while, Chass. We worried you wouldn't wake up." I chuckled and brushed my nose against his. His brows puckered. "You aren't going to *believe* where we've been." I didn't pause for him to guess. "We went underwater, Reid. To the seafloor of L'Eau Mélancolique. You were there too, of course, just unconscious." My thoughts whirled in an incoherent blur of excitement. Where to begin? So much had happened in such a short period of time. "We walked with melusines in Le Présage—did you know they can grow legs?—and we dined with the Oracle in Le Palais de

Cristal. The Oracle is Claud's sister, remember? Isla. We met Isla, and she was the world's biggest *bitch*—"

He stiffened abruptly, and his frown deepened to an outright scowl. "My apologies, *mademoiselle*, but I think there's been a misunderstanding. Please"—he lifted me from his lap, depositing me firmly onto the sand beside him—"allow me to introduce myself. I am Captain Reid Diggory." He cleared his throat pointedly. "And I'd appreciate if you'd refrain from using such coarse language around me in the future."

I snorted in disbelief. "That's rich coming from *you*, Monsieur Fuck." His eyes widened comically at the expletive, and I laughed out loud. He didn't. "Fine," I said, still light with giddiness. His prickliness couldn't puncture it. He was awake, I was awake, and we were together. Finally. "I'll play along with this . . . whatever this is. Some sort of foreplay?"

Pushing to my feet, I offered him a hand. He stared as if it might bite him. Shrugging, I brushed off the seat of my pants instead. If his eyes had been wide before, they nearly burst from his face now. "*Bonsoir*, Captain Diggory." Laughing again, I dipped in a theatrical bow. "My name is Louise le Blanc, daughter of the infamous Morgane le Blanc, and I am positively *chuffed* to make your acquaintance. I see you're missing your official uniform, but no matter. Shall we light the stake now, or—?"

His eyes sharpened on my face, and without warning, he launched to his feet. "What did you say?"

My smile slipped at the sudden fierceness in his voice. I glanced at Coco and Beau, who both looked back in bewilderment. Célie rose slowly behind me. "My name is Louise le Blanc," I repeated, less theatric now. For someone as stoic as Reid, he could play-act much better than I'd anticipated. "And I'm chuffed to make your—"

"You're the daughter of Morgane le Blanc? A witch?"

Alarm bells began pealing in my head. "Well, yes—"

He tackled me before I could finish.

We hit the ground hard, rolling, and his forearm collided with my throat. My breath left in a painful rush. "Um—*ow*." Gasping, I shoved at his chest, but he didn't move. His forearm remained. Combined with the weight of his body, I could scarcely breathe. "Okay, Chass, this role-play thing has officially gone too far—" He only pressed down harder until lights popped in my vision.

Right. This wasn't fun anymore.

Cocking my head back, I smashed my forehead into his nose, thrusting my knee into his groin when he recoiled. When he bent inward with a groan, I scrambled out from beneath him. "What the hell is wrong with you?" I snarled, clutching my throat. "Are you trying to kill me?"

He panted and bared his teeth. "You're a witch."

"Yeah? So?"

Ignoring me, he tore at his bandolier, unsheathing one knife and reaching for another—the one directly above his heart. But it wasn't there. Its sheath remained empty. He checked the others frantically, fingers seizing each one, before he realized what we'd already known. All emotion slid from his face. With deadly calm, he said, "Where is my Balisarda?"

I inched toward Coco. "Stop it, Reid. You're scaring me."

He stalked forward slowly, intently, matching each of my steps with his own. "Where is it?"

"A tree ate it." Coco gripped my elbow and pulled me to her side. We watched him approach together. "In the southern part of the kingdom. Bas and his bandits attacked on the road, and Lou threw your Balisarda to protect me." She paused, uncertain. "Don't you remember?"

"You." Recognition flared as he focused on Coco. "You're a healer in the Tower." His eyes dropped to where she clutched my arm, and his lip curled. "Are you in league with this witch?"

"I—" She stopped short when I shook my head, my stomach plunging with déjà vu. I'd had this exact conversation with Bas after he'd tried to kill me in La Fôret des Yeux. Had Reid—?

No.

My mind seized, unwilling to continue thought. He wouldn't have. He—he *couldn't* have. Could he?

"Who am I?" My voice shook as I stepped in front of Coco, toward him and his knife. The movement seemed to surprise him. He didn't strike right away. Instead, he stared at me with brows furrowed as I carefully pushed down his blade. "How do we know each other?"

He lifted it back to my face. "We don't."

No no no

"If this is a joke, Reid, it's gone far enough."

"I do not joke."

The truth of the words fragmented in my chest, and I exhaled deeply, absorbing their pain. No one was this good at playacting. Which meant . . . he had forgotten me. Just like Bas, he'd forgotten, only this time, I couldn't reverse the pattern. I hadn't cast it. But how far did it reach?

And *why* was he acting this way?

I searched blindly for an answer, remembering the way he'd collapsed in my arms. The way Morgane had collapsed with him on the beach. If he'd truly forgotten me, did that mean . . . ?

Holy hell.

"Are you sure?" I asked. "Think hard, Reid. Please. Just think. I'm Lou, remember? I'm your . . ." I glanced down at my empty ring finger, and the cracks in my chest splintered further. I'd returned his mother's ring. *Stupid. So stupid.* "I'm your wife."

His eyes hardened. "I don't have a wife."

"Easy." I jerked back as he swiped at me, lifting placating hands. "I *am* your wife. Maybe not *legally*, but in the biblical sense—"

Perhaps speaking of his holy book had been a mistake.

With a snarl, he charged again, and I sidestepped, kicking his knee from behind as he went. He didn't stumble as planned, instead pivoting with frightening agility. This time his knife caught my shirt, but I twisted at the last second. It shredded my sleeve instead. "God*damn* it." The fabric fluttered uselessly in the breeze. "Just once, I'd like to keep my clothing *intact*—"

He rushed again with unexpected speed, catching my torn sleeve and yanking me closer, lifting his knife to thrust it deep in my chest. I caught his wrist, but physically, I was no match for his strength. The blade plunged lower and lower, and—not for the first time in my life—I looked death straight in the eyes.

They were the most beautiful shade of blue.

Something hard thudded into Reid's back, propelling his knife the final inch. Blood welled as it pierced my skin, as Beau pounded at Reid's head with both fists. Coco soon joined him, hissing as she punched down on Reid's elbows, breaking his hold. When he turned—dragging Beau over his shoulder and throwing him to the ground—Coco wrenched a knife from his bandolier and sliced open her forearm. The bitter scent of blood magic coated the air. "We don't want to hurt you, Reid," she said, breathing heavily, "but if you don't stop being an asshole, I'll cut you a new one."

His nostrils flared. "Demon spawn."

She bared her teeth in a grin. "In the flesh."

He moved to attack her, but Beau caught his ankle. "Stop this now. I command it as your—as your crown prince," he finished lamely. Reid froze and frowned down at him.

"Your Highness? What are you doing here?"

"That's right." Beau choked on a cough, still struggling to breathe. He pointed to his chest. "I'm in charge. Me. And I'm telling you to concede."

"But you're"—Reid shook his head sharply and winced as if in pain—"you're my . . . are you my brother?" He touched a hand to his temple. "You *are* my brother."

Beau slumped on the ground. "Oh, thank God. You remember." He twirled a hand and coughed again. "Put your knife down, Reid. You're outnumbered if not outmanned, and I have no interest in seeing your second asshole." He turned to Célie, who stood apart from the rest of us, her face ashen. "Do you want to see his second asshole?"

It was Reid's turn to blanch. "Célie." Instead of dropping his weapons, however, he streaked to her side, his righteous anger deepening to outright rage. He pushed her behind him. "Stay back, Célie. I won't let them touch you."

"Oh, good lord," Coco muttered.

"Reid." Tentatively, Célie pushed at his back, but he didn't budge. His eyes found mine, and in them, hatred burned hotter than anything I'd ever seen. I could feel its heat wash over my skin, primal and visceral. Eternal. Like Coco's Hellfire. "Reid, this is unnecessary. These—Louise and Cosette are my friends." She tried showing him the green ribbon around her wrist. "See? They will not harm me. They will not harm you either. Just give us a chance to explain."

"What?" He whirled to face her then, seizing the ribbon and tearing it free. "You call them *friends*? They're *witches*, Célie. They killed your sister!"

"Yes, *thank* you for that kindly reminder." She snatched the ribbon back, scowling and stepping around him. "You'll be surprised to find my ears actually do work. I know who they are. More importantly, *you* know who they are, if you'd stop acting like a barbarian and *listen*."

"I don't—" He shook his head again, eyes narrowing. Confusion clouded his gaze, and stupid, *useless* hope lit in my heart. He sensed the truth in her words. Of course he did. Surely he could feel something had gone terribly wrong. Surely if he followed the thread of his thoughts, he would realize what had happened, and he would reverse the pattern. And he *had* to reverse the pattern. Forgetting me was one thing, but this—this wasn't Reid. This was a murderous *zealot*. He must've botched the magic somehow, perhaps pulled two cords instead of one.

As quickly as the thought came, I dismissed it, knowing in my heart it wasn't true. Reid hadn't botched anything.

He'd simply . . . forgotten me.

Forgotten him.

Forgotten everything.

"Remember, Reid," I whispered, tears thickening my voice. "Please. I don't know what you gained by doing this, but give it back. It isn't worth it." When I reached out to him, unable to stop myself, his knuckles tightened on his knives. He pushed Célie behind him once more.

"I don't know what you're talking about."

"The pattern." The sounds of the beach fell away as I wrung my hands, imploring him to look at me. To *see* me. "It's your magic. Only you can reverse it. You lost consciousness in L'Eau Mélancolique. Think back to that moment. Remember what you chose to forget."

"Lou." Coco shook her head sadly. "Don't."

"He needs to understand. I can help him—"

"He *did* understand. That's the point. He made a choice he felt was necessary. We need to respect it."

"Respect it?" My voice rose hysterically. "How can I *respect* it?

How can I respect *any* of this?" I flung my arms wide, danger-ously close to my breaking point. "If he doesn't love me—if he doesn't even *remember* me—what was the point in all this, Coco? What was the point in *any* of it? All the pain, all the sorrow, all the *death*?"

Tears limned her own lashes as she took my hands in hers. "He did this for *you*, Lou. If Morgane has forgotten, maybe you're—you're finally safe."

I tore my hand away from her. "I will *never* be safe, Coco. Even if Morgane *has* forgotten me, Josephine hasn't. Auguste and his Chasseurs haven't. How are we supposed to win this *war* if Reid can't separate friend from foe?"

"I don't know." She shook her head helplessly. "I really don't. I just know he saved our lives."

Reid wrapped an arm around Célie's waist then, pulling her away from us. I closed my eyes against the sight of it. The sight of them. He'd made a sacrifice for the greater good, yet again, my blood spilled upon the altar. "You're both insane," he said brusquely. "Come on, Célie. We need to go."

Célie's voice rose in protest. "But I don't want—"

"You're making a mistake, Reid," Coco said.

He chuckled darkly. "Don't worry. I'll be back for you, witch. And your friend. I'll even bring some friends of my own. Perhaps we'll build a bonfire."

"Oh, you'll be back all right, brother." Beau rose to his feet. "You have nowhere else to go. But you won't be taking Célie with you."

"With all due respect, *brother*—"

"All due respect means honoring the lady's request," Coco said. "She doesn't want to go with you, and *you* don't want to pick a fight with me, Reid. Not without your Balisarda."

The threat hung heavy in the air.

I finally opened my eyes.

Reid's throat worked with palpable distress as he weighed the situation: two witches against an unarmed huntsman with his blasphemous prince and childhood love caught in the crossfire. The Chasseur inside him—the part ruled by duty, by honor, by courage—refused to leave. The man inside him knew he must. Coco hadn't been bluffing; she *would* hurt him if necessary. He didn't know I wouldn't let her. He didn't know he could wield magic.

He didn't remember me.

Leveling his knives at our faces, he spoke softly, viciously. "I *will* be back."

I watched him disappear up the path with an overwhelming sense of emptiness.

Coco pressed my head upon her shoulder. "He'll be back."

STICKS AND STONES

Reid

My footsteps pounded in rhythm with my heart. Faster and faster. Faster still. My skin flushed with heat, with sweat, as I sprinted uphill, vaulting stone and fern. I'd only traveled this far north once. Right after taking my vows. My captain at the time, a weak-spirited man by the name of Blanchart, had been trying to prove his spine to the Archbishop. He'd heard rumors of melusines in the area, and he'd ordered my contingent to investigate. We hadn't even found the beach, instead wandering for days in this godforsaken mist.

If the freckled witch spoke truth, Blanchart had been right. There were melusines in the area. After I dispatched the demon in question, I'd return and—

Scoffing, I launched from the path.

She was a witch.

Of course she didn't speak truth.

Instead of plunging into the forest, I followed the tree line south. There'd been a hamlet nearby. My brethren and I had rented rooms there each night. Unbidden, I glanced down at my chest. My bandolier. The empty sheath above my heart. Pieces of memory swarmed and stung like insects. Leering faces. Bloodstained snow. Searing pain and painted wagons and bitter honey—

A *tree* had eaten my Balisarda.

I nearly stumbled at the realization. At the onslaught of images. They formed a picture riddled with holes, a puzzle with missing pieces. There'd been lavender hair. Starry cloaks. Troupe de Fortune. The words gored my mind with surprising pain, and this time, I did miss a step. I'd traveled with them, briefly. I'd thrown knives in their company.

Why?

Clenching my eyes against such riotous thoughts, I focused on the one knife that mattered. The one knife I *would* reclaim. I'd burn the whole forest if necessary. I'd hack the demonic tree down to the ground, and I'd dig until its roots became kindling.

Bas and his bandits attacked on the road, and Lou threw your Balisarda to protect me. Don't you remember?

Oh, I remembered. I remembered the scarred witch, who'd slithered into our mists as a healer. I remembered the disgraced Bastien St. Pierre, and I remembered my own gruesome injury. I did *not*, however, remember their coconspirator—the freckled witch. The one who'd looked at me as if someone had died.

I'm your wife, she'd said, her eyes glistening with unshed tears. *In the biblical sense.*

Remember, Reid. She'd known my name. *Called* me by name.

If he doesn't love me—if he doesn't even remember *me—what was the point in all this, Coco?*

Blistering rage further quickened my step. The wind rushed past me now, burning my cheeks and numbing my ears. As if I'd ever debase myself with a witch. As if I'd ever marry *anyone*, let alone a bride of Satan. "*Lou.*" I sneered the name aloud, my breath catching around it. A hideous name for a hideous being, and Célie—

My God.

I'd left Célie alone with them.

No. I shook my head. Not alone. The crown prince, my *brother*—he'd been there too. He'd even shared some sort of absurd camaraderie with the creatures, as if they three were family instead of him and me. Perhaps he could protect Célie. Then again, perhaps he couldn't. Regardless of how he felt toward them, witches held no family. I couldn't risk it. Not with her.

I hurtled around the bend, and sure enough, a familiar hamlet rose to meet me. If one could even call it that. Comprising a single street, it boasted a parish and an inn, complete with pub underneath. The entire settlement had risen only to accommodate sailors in need of work, passing from one port city to the next. A handful of them stared as I hurtled past. It mattered not.

Without breaking stride, I headed toward the parish at the end of the road. My fist nearly leveled the door. Once. Twice. Three times. At last, a tall, spotted boy peeked his head out. His eyes widened at my ruddy cheeks, my towering frame. My palpable fury. He let out a squeak before trying to slam the door in my face. Incredulous, I caught it and wrenched it back open. "I am Captain Reid Diggory, and—"

"You can't be here!" His feeble arms trembled with the effort to shut the door. I held fast. "You—you—"

"—require your services," I finished roughly, losing patience and flinging the door wide. It banged against the weathered stone wall. Men outside the pub turned to stare. "There are witches in the area. Summon your priest. If no Chasseurs are near, I'll need a contingent of able-bodied men to—"

The boy planted himself in the threshold when I moved to step inside. "Father Angelart ain't here. He's—he's in Cesarine, sittin' in on the conclave, isn't he?"

I frowned. "What conclave?" But the boy merely shook his head, swallowing hard. My frown deepened. Though I attempted to pass once more, he flung his arms wide, barring entrance. Impatience roused the anger in my gut. "Step aside, boy. This is urgent. These witches hold both the crown prince and a lady of the aristocracy hostage. Do you want the lives of innocents on your conscience?"

"Do *you*?" His voice cracked on the challenge, but still he didn't move. "Go on. Get!" He jerked his head down the street, waving his hands to shoo me away like I was a mangy dog. "Father Angelart ain't here, but I—I got me a knife too, right? I'll gut you, I will, before the huntsmen arrive. This is a sacred place. We don't—we won't tolerate your sort here!"

I clenched my fists, resisting the urge to knock his hands aside. To force my way through. "What sort is that?"

The boy's entire body trembled now. With anger or fear, I couldn't tell. "Murderers." He looked as if he wanted to spit at me. Anger, then. "*Witches.*"

"What are you talking—" My own angry words broke as the memories rose. A temple. The Archbishop. And—and me. I'd stabbed him to death. Sickening cold swept through me at the realization. It extinguished my rage. My mind continued to skitter over the images, however, leaping from one to the next before scattering. I stumbled back a step. Lifted my hands. I could still feel his blood there, could still feel its slick warmth on my palm.

But it—it made no *sense.* I'd felt nothing but love for my patriarch. Nothing but respect. Except . . . I focused harder on the memory, the parish in front of me falling away.

I'd felt vengeful too. Bitter. The emotions came to me slowly, reluctantly. Like shameful secrets. The Archbishop had lied. Though I couldn't recall it—though the memory rippled somehow as if distorted—I knew he'd betrayed me. Betrayed the *Church.* He'd consorted with a witch, and I—I must've killed him for it.

I was no longer a Chasseur at all.

"Is there a problem here?" A brawny sailor with a beard pressed his hand on my shoulder, jerking me from my thoughts. Two companions flanked him on either side. "Is this man bothering you, Calot?"

Instead of relief, fresh panic widened the boy's features. He looked from the sailor's hand on my shoulder to my face, where my jaw had clenched and my mouth had flattened. "Remove your hand, sir," I said through my teeth. "Before I remove it for you."

The man chuckled but complied. "All right." Slowly, I turned my head to look at him. "You're built like a tree, and I don't want any trouble. Why don't you and I head on up for a pint and leave poor Calot here alone?"

Calot pointed to something beside us before I could answer. A piece of paper. It fluttered in the evening breeze, tacked to the message post beside the door. I looked closer. A picture of my own face glared back at me.

REID DIGGORY

WANTED DEAD OR ALIVE

UNDER SUSPICION OF MURDER, CONSPIRACY, AND WITCHCRAFT.

REWARD.

The sick feeling in my stomach increased tenfold.

It couldn't be true. Though my memory felt—*off*, surely I would know if I—if—

I swallowed bile. There were too many gaps. I couldn't be sure of *anything*, and these men—their amicable nature vanished instantly. "Holy shit," one breathed. His companion hastened to yank the sword from his scabbard. I lifted my hands in a conciliatory gesture.

"I don't want any trouble either. I came to gather men. There are witches three miles up the road. Two of them. They—"

"We know who they are," the bearded man growled, jabbing

a finger at the other posters. More men from the pub headed toward us now. They drew weapons as they came. Calot shrank into the shadows of the foyer. "You travel with them. They even say one is your wife. Mort Rouge and Sommeil Éternel, they call you." He too drew a set of knives from his belt. They gleamed sharp and polished in the setting sun. Well used. "You killed the Archbishop. You set the capital aflame."

My eyes narrowed. A tendril of old anger unfurled. Of disgust. "I would never marry a witch."

"Is this some sort of hoax?" his friend asked uncertainly.

The bearded man jerked his chin. "Ride to Hacqueville. See if that Chasseur is still there. We'll hold him."

"That Chasseur?" My voice sharpened. "Who?"

Instead of answering, the man charged, and the anger simmering in my gut exploded. We collided with bone-shattering impact, and Calot squeaked again before slamming the parish door shut. I threw the bearded man against it. "This is ridiculous. We're on the same—"

His unharmed friend leapt atop my back, wrapping an arm around my neck. Fisting his hair, I wrenched him over my shoulders and drew a knife from my bandolier. Each dove out of reach as I slashed it in front of me. "Fine. You want to challenge me? You'll lose. I'm the youngest captain of the Chasseurs in history—"

"*Were.*" The bearded man stepped around me in a circle. His friend stepped behind. "You *were* a captain of the Chasseurs. Now you're a witch."

"Call them." With a snarl, I unsheathed another knife, pointing one at each of them. Backing into the parish wall. "Call them all. There are witches near, and they've taken someone I—"

They dove at me simultaneously. Though I dodged the bearded man, his friend's sword clipped my side. Gritting my teeth, I blocked his counterstrike, but others joined now—too many. Far too many. Blades glinted in every direction, and where one failed, a fist connected. A boot. An elbow. A scabbard smashed into my skull, and stars blurred my vision. When I doubled over, someone drove a knee into my face. Another my groin, my ribs. I couldn't breathe. Couldn't think. Wrapping my arms around my head, I attempted to bowl through the mob, but I crashed to my knees instead, spitting blood. The blows kept coming. Violent, frenzied shouts echoed from everywhere at once. My head swam with them.

A strange, whispering energy thrummed in my chest, building and building until—

"That's enough!" A familiar voice cut through the din, and the foot on my back vanished. "Stop it! Let him go!" I felt rather than saw him approach. My eyes had swollen shut. Still, two hands gripped under my arms and heaved until I stood vertical, and his arm wrapped around my bloody waist.

"Jean Luc," I croaked, prying my right eye open. Never before had I been so pleased by his presence.

"Shut up," he said harshly.

Perhaps not.

He swung his Balisarda wide, and those nearest us lurched

back with sounds of protest. "This creature belongs to the Church now, and we shall deal with it accordingly—on a stake in Cesarine. Did you think your fists could kill it? Did you think a sword to the heart would do?" He sneered derisively like only he could. "Witches must *burn*. Here now, watch me subdue the creature!" When he lifted a syringe, I pushed away from him, lunging for my fallen knives. He laughed coldly and kicked my knees. I sprawled into the snow. Bearing down on me, bending low, he pretended to stick the needle in my throat and whispered, "Play along."

My muscles sagged in relief.

He rolled me to my back with the tip of his boot. "You there"—pointing to the bearded man, he jerked his chin toward his horse—"help me move the body. It shall burn within the fortnight." Hastily, the man complied, and together, the two heaved my body upward. "Onto the saddle," Jean Luc commanded.

The man hesitated in confusion. "Sir?"

Jean Luc's eyes narrowed as he realized his mistake. "I meant tie him *to* the saddle. I'll drag him behind to Cesarine."

"Him?"

"*It*," Jean Luc snapped. "I'll drag *it* to Cesarine, you impertinent clot. Perhaps you'd like to join?"

They dumped me behind the horse without another word. No one spoke as Jean Luc tied a length of rope around my wrists, as he hoisted himself into the saddle. I watched him in disbelief. "You all can clear off now." He kicked his horse into a trot, and my body rioted with pain as I staggered to my feet. At the last second, Jean Luc called, "Thank you for your service in apprehending this criminal. I shall inform the king of your"—he craned around to look at them—"what is the name of this foul place?"

"Montfort," the bearded man called back angrily.

"What about our reward money?" someone else shouted.

Jean Luc ignored them both, dragging me into the forest.

"You enjoyed that too much," I said darkly.

Rougher than necessary, Jean Luc untied the rope from my wrists outside the village. "Entirely too much." He didn't smile, instead shoving my chest with a murderous expression. "What the hell is wrong with you? Where's Célie?"

I rubbed my wrists, instantly alert. My head still pounded. "She's with the witches."

"What?" Jean Luc's roar shook the birds from the nearest trees, and he advanced on me again. "What witches? *Who?*"

Under normal circumstances, I wouldn't have retreated. As it was, however, I'd sustained two broken ribs, a concussion, and a shattered nose. My pride was bruised enough already. It needn't suffer another defeat at the hands of Jean Luc. "I don't know. Two of them." I started north, careful to navigate *around* Montfort. "Coco and—and Lou. The crown prince was there too. I tried to bring her with me, but she refused. She likes them."

"She *likes* them?" Jean Luc hurried to catch up. "What does that mean?"

"How did you know I was here?" I asked instead.

"I didn't. I've been tracking Célie since she hatched this demented scheme. Did you know she stole her father's carriage?"

"After robbing his vault," I added, surprising even myself.

"She robbed him?" Voice faint, Jean Luc shook his head. "You've been a terrible influence—you and that witch. I can't *believe* you left Célie." He flung his hands in the air, outpacing me in his agitation. "You are the *only* reason I allowed her to go. This place—this entire fucking kingdom—it's dangerous. You were supposed to *guard* her. Now she's God knows where with only an idiotic prince for protection." He exhaled hard, shaking his head frenetically. "This just might be the stupidest thing you've ever done, Reid. I shouldn't be surprised. You haven't thought straight since the moment you met—" He clenched his fists mid-air, apparently overcome. He took a deep breath. Then another. "Whenever *she's* around, it's like every single coherent thought flies out of your head."

"Who? Célie?"

He whipped around to face me, eyes murderous. "No. *Not* Célie. Lou. Your *wife*."

My wife. I snapped at the repulsive words, stooping to pick up a stone and hurling it at his face. Eyes wide, he ducked, narrowly missing it. "Stop *saying* that," I snarled.

"What the hell is wrong with you?" He scooped up his own stone then, launching it back at me. I didn't dodge in time. When it grazed my shoulder, I groaned, but he merely reached for another—a stick this time. "Saying *what*? That she's your wife? She *is*. I watched the inane ceremony myself—"

"Shut up!" I tackled him around the knees, and we both went tumbling in the snow. "Shut! Up! I would *never* tie myself to such a creature." We rolled, neither of our blows fully landing. "I would never deign to even *touch* one—"

"You've touched her plenty from what I gather." He bared his teeth and pushed a palm against my face, scrambling free. "What's the matter, Reid? Trouble in paradise? I could've told you it would never work, but you wouldn't have listened. You've been completely obsessed with her—and still are, by the sound of it. Oh no, don't try to deny it, and don't get any ideas about you and Célie either. You made your choice. She's moved on—"

I snorted and shot to my feet. "You're pathetic. You think she *belongs* to you? You think you *allowed* her to come here? You don't know her at all, do you?" When he seized my coat front, enraged, I broke his grip, resisting the urge to break his nose too. "She isn't an object. She's a person, and she's changed since you last saw her. You better prepare yourself."

"If you—"

I elbowed past him. "You don't have to worry about me." The truth in the words shocked me. Where once there had been attraction, even infatuation, when I thought of Célie now, I felt only a familial sort of affection. Frowning, I tried to pinpoint the source of the change, but I couldn't. Though I'd tried to deny it, to rationalize it, something had clearly happened inside my head. Something unnatural. Something like witchcraft. I stormed north, determined to fix it no matter the cost. The witches would know. They'd probably cursed me themselves. Their last act on earth would be undoing it. "Worry about yourself, Jean. Célie won't be happy to learn you've been following her. It implies a lack of trust. A lack of confidence."

He grimaced and looked away. Good.

"Now," I said, taking advantage of his silence, "we should strategize for when we meet them. I don't have my Balisarda, but you do. You'll need to incapacitate the freckled one." I frowned. "Coco's magic is different. She needs to touch us to inflict harm, so I'll handle her. I should be able to disable her before she can draw blood."

Jean Luc shook his head, nonplussed. "Why would we need to incapacitate either of them?"

"Because they're witches."

"So are you."

It was my turn to grimace. "Just stick to the plan."

He squared up to face me at last, straightening his shoulders. "No."

"Excuse me?"

"I said *no*." Though he shrugged, old spitefulness glinted in his pale eyes. "I hate your plan. It's a terrible plan, and I won't be doing any of it. I'm only here to collect Célie. Why would I pick a fight with two witches, one who nearly killed me during our last encounter?"

"Because you're a Chasseur," I ground out. "You swore an oath to eradicate the occult."

"Does that mean I should eradicate you?" He stepped closer, cocking his head. "When shall I do it, Reid? How? Would you prefer I drag you back to Cesarine, or shall I behead you here and now, burning your body to ash? It'd certainly be easier." He took another step, nearly chest to chest with me. "How is that for a plan?"

Red washed over my vision—whether at him or at myself, I didn't know. I inhaled deeply through my nose. Exhaled hard. I concentrated on each breath, counting to ten. Finally, forcing my voice to remain even, I said, "We can't simply let them live. They—they did something to me, Jean. My head, it isn't right. I think they've stolen my memories. Pieces of my life. And the freckled witch, she—"

"Lou," he corrected me.

"*Lou.*" The name tasted sour on my tongue. "I think she's the one who did it."

He rolled his eyes and started forward once more. "She'd die before she'd harm you. No, don't"—he lifted a hand to stop my protest—"don't start. Clearly, something *is* wrong, but killing Lou and Coco won't solve it. It *won't*, Reid. They're the only people who like you. No, I *said* don't interrupt. If you kill them and return to Cesarine, the huntsmen will inevitably find and execute you. You saw the wanted posters. You're one of the most notorious outlaws in the entire kingdom, second only to Lou. It's too dangerous for you to wander the countryside alone—a point you've just proven, by the way—which leaves only one option: you stay with the witches."

"I don't—"

"You stay with the witches," he continued in a hard voice,

"and they will protect you. Perhaps they'll even help undo whatever has gone so *critically* wrong inside your head. Of course, you might need to conduct yourself with a bit more charm to persuade them. A near impossible task, I know—"

"They'll undo it either way," I growled.

He stopped again, turning to face me with an impatient sigh. "You still don't seem to understand, so allow me to make this perfectly clear. You can't kill them. Simply put, I won't let you. You're a dead man walking without them, and beyond that, you'll hate yourself later if you do. Despite what you think now, those women are your friends. Your family. I've watched you all together, and I—" He broke off abruptly, eyes tightening, before turning to stomp through the snow once more. "You're an idiot."

I glared at the back of his head, but I no longer tried to argue. He'd painted a clear enough picture. Yes, perhaps I had nowhere else to go at present. Perhaps my brethren would kill me if they found me. Perhaps I *did* need these witches—to reverse the hex on my mind, to ensure Célie and the crown prince survived. But Jean Luc had been wrong about one thing: I *could* survive alone. I'd been unprepared before. It wouldn't happen again.

And I would kill Lou and Coco at the first opportunity.

THE WAGER

Lou

Coco allowed me to wallow in misery for approximately three minutes—hugging me all the while—before pulling back and wiping my tears. "He isn't dead, you know."

"He loathes me."

She shrugged and rifled through her bag, extracting a bottle of honey. "I seem to remember him loathing you once before. You both rose to the occasion." She combined the amber liquid with blood from her forearm before swabbing the mixture over the wound at my chest. She turned to examine Beau's injuries next. "We might as well be comfortable while we wait."

"Wait for what?" Beau asked mulishly. Sporting a terrific shiner from Reid's ministrations, he swallowed the blood and honey. The swelling disappeared almost instantly.

"For Reid to crawl back with his tail between his legs. It shouldn't take long." She shooed him down the beach. "Now go find some driftwood for a fire. It's colder than a witch's tit out here."

"*Why?*" Though Beau complied, snatching up a stick by our

feet, he glanced around nervously. "Shouldn't we leave? Morgane could be lurking out of sight."

"I doubt it," Coco murmured, "if she doesn't remember Lou."

I jerked my sleeve back in place.

"Here." Célie smiled faintly, reaching into her own bag. She withdrew a needle and thread. "Let me help with that." I frowned as her delicate fingers threaded the eye, as she slowly, carefully reaffixed the fabric.

"We'll leave as soon as Reid returns." Coco walked to the path to gather rocks for a firepit. "If we go before, he might not find us again. We'll need him to help steal the ring before we can return to Cesarine." With an inscrutable look in my direction, she added, "That *is* the plan, isn't it? To rejoin Claud and Blaise with the melusines? Plot a final strike against Morgane? Rescue Madame Labelle from the stake?"

"More or less."

Beau scowled when she snatched his stick, speaking in an aggrieved whisper. "On that note, how on earth are we supposed to *steal* the ring? Chateau le Blanc is a fortress, and *again*— Morgane could be hiding behind that rock even now, listening to our every word."

"*Again*, without Lou in the picture, Morgane could be rallying forces to kill your father as we speak," Coco said pointedly. "Zenna said witches have been gathering at Chateau le Blanc en masse. I doubt they're braiding each other's hair. Perhaps they've already marched toward Cesarine. It'd certainly make our job easier."

"And if not? Couldn't we just . . . dispatch Morgane at the Chateau?"

"Like we could've dispatched her on the beach?" I watched as Célie moved to the gash at my chest. Though the fabric was still wet from my blood—from Coco's blood and honey—she didn't seem to mind. I, however, struggled to remain still. To remain *calm*. "It worked out so well for us the first time. I'm sure it'll be even simpler surrounded by witches en masse." To Coco, I said, "Why didn't we think of that?"

She shrugged. "Who needs gods and dragons, werewolves and mermaids, when we could've just done it ourselves the whole time?"

"Yes, all right." Beau scowled at each of us, stalking down the beach, as Célie finished mending my shirt. "It was just a thought."

He returned a few moments later with an armful of driftwood, dumping it at Coco's feet. She promptly scowled and stacked the pieces into a square. "Genuinely, how have you survived this long, Beauregard?"

"Here." I snapped my fingers, magicking the friction between them to the point of pain. The golden pattern vanished as a flame sparked. Delicious heat washed over me, a welcome reprieve to the icy cold in my chest. I glanced to the path instinctively.

He'll come back.

"Lou." As if reading my thoughts, Coco turned my chin with a single finger. "You forgot to include one key component in our plan: seducing Reid." She smirked at my deadpan expression. "Fortunately you happen to know a master in the art of seduction.

Don't worry, Célie," she added, winking. "I'll teach you in the process as well. Think of it as your first lesson in debauchery."

My heart sank miserably, and I shook my head. "We have more important things to worry about. Besides," I added, loathing the note of bitterness in my voice. "It won't work. Not this time."

"I don't see why not. He fell in love with you before." She dropped her hand. "And I would argue it's the *most* important thing."

"He didn't know I was a witch then. He thought I was his wife."

"Nuance. Your souls are bound. Magic can't change that."

"You can't really believe in soul mates?"

"I believe in you." At my incredulous look, she shrugged again, watching the flames crackle. "And *perhaps* I'm willing to make an exception when it comes to the two of you. I've been here this whole time, you know," she added. "I watched Reid take his forefather's life to save yours. I watched him throw his entire belief system out the window and learn magic for your sake—and wear leather pants in a traveling troupe. I watched you sacrifice pieces of yourself to protect him. He fought an entire pack of werewolves to return the favor, and *you* fought tooth and nail in these waters to return to him. You've befriended a god, swum with mermaids, and now you can even transform into a three-form shape at will. You can probably do a whole slew of other fun new things too." Her brows lifted with her shoulders. "I'm certainly not betting against you—unless you're too afraid to try?"

Nicholina's hateful voice filled my mind. *But you should feel lucky you tricked him, oh yes, because if you hadn't tricked him—such a tricky little mouse—he never would've loved you. If he had known what you are, he never would've* held *you beneath the* stars.

Goddamn it.

Beau, who'd been listening in silence, watched me too closely to be comfortable. He arched a brow. "I don't know, Coco. I don't think she can do it."

I glared mutinously at the fire. "Don't start with me, Beau."

"Why not?" His dark eyes searched my face and missed nothing. "You just said as much yourself. It won't work. He'll never love you again. I'm merely concurring with the sentiment."

"I'm not doing this."

"Yes, you've made that perfectly clear. Better not to try at all than to fail, right?" He shrugged dispassionately. "I couldn't agree more."

"Beau!" Célie's eyes widened in protest. Perhaps she was too naive to see Beau's manipulation, or—more likely—perhaps she insisted on being the voice of optimism despite it. "How can you say such wicked things? Of course Reid will love her. The bond they share is *true.* You saw their kiss—it woke him up despite the magic!"

"Oh, Célie, enough with this *true love* nonsense." He returned his cool attention to me. "You want truth, sister mine? I shall give you truth. You were right before. Without memories of your relationship, you are only a witch to Reid, and he hates you. You are no longer his wife. As far as he knows, you were *never* his wife. Indeed, he's probably plotting creative ways to kill you at this very moment." He leaned forward to whisper conspiratorially.

"My money is on strangulation. He never has been able to keep his hands off you."

Célie's eyes flashed. "*Really*, Beau, you shouldn't—"

I mimicked his movement with a black smile, leaning toward him until our noses nearly touched. "Let's sweeten the pot. I bet it'll be a knife to heart."

Coco rolled her eyes as Beau shook his head. "Not intimate enough."

"There's nothing *more* intimate—"

"Oh, I disagree—"

"You're both ridiculous," Célie snapped, shooting to her feet in a spectacular display of temper. "You want to sweeten the pot? I wager all the riches in my father's treasury that Reid *does* fall in love with you again, *despite* knowing you're a witch."

A beat of silence passed as she glared at me. Pink tinged her cheeks.

"I thought you stole all of your father's treasure?" Beau asked suspiciously.

"Not even close."

He pursed his lips, considering, while I quietly seethed. They were treating this like a game, all of them. But this wasn't a game. This was my *life*. And why did Célie care so much, anyway? Reid had wrecked their own relationship for the sake of *true love* with me. As if reading my thoughts, she whispered, "The two of you have something special, Louise. Something precious. How can you not fight for him? He has certainly fought for you."

You've lived in fear too long.

Fear has helped me survive.

Fear has kept you from living.

"I think I'd like to accept that wager, Mademoiselle Tremblay," Beau mused before turning to Coco. "What do you think, Cosette? Does the fair maiden stand a chance of seducing her gallant knight? Shall true love win the day?"

Coco carefully stoked the fire. "You know what I think."

"It would seem we have a wager." Beau held out a hand to Célie, clasping her wrist and shaking it. "If Lou fails to seduce her husband, you will give me all the riches in your father's treasury." His teeth flashed in a hard smile. "And if she succeeds, I will give you all the riches in *mine.*"

Célie blinked, the indignation in her eyes winking out. Her mouth parted in awe. "King Auguste's entire treasury?"

"Indeed. Unless, of course, our fair maiden objects?" He extended his free hand toward me, but I knocked it aside with a scowl. Ass. "As I thought." He tutted softly. "You *are* too afraid."

Paralysis crept up my spine as I looked between them all. Though I opened my mouth to speak—to *vehemently* object to this foolish game—the words caught, and different words altogether spilled out instead. Honest ones. "I'm not afraid. I'm *terrified.* What if he does try to strangle me or stick a knife through my heart? What if he doesn't remember at all? What if he doesn't . . ." I swallowed hard and blinked back fresh tears. "What if he doesn't love me?"

Beau wrapped an arm around my shoulders, pulling me close. "Then I will become a rich man."

"You're already a rich man."

"A *very* rich man."

"You're an ass, Beau."

He brushed a brotherly kiss across my temple. "Do we have a wager?"

I rested my head on his shoulder as noise sounded from the path, and Reid stormed into sight, right on time. Jean Luc followed at a wary distance. *Jean Luc.* It was a mark of the last twenty-four hours that I didn't bat an eye.

"Yes," I said. The word tasted like hope. It felt like armor. I allowed it to wrap around me, bolstering my spirit and protecting my heart. Reid *had* fallen in love with me once, and I still returned that love fiercely. It was special. It was precious. And I would fight for it. "Yes, we have a wager."

HOLES IN THE TAPESTRY

Reid

The witch called Lou stepped from the crown prince with a smirk as I approached. I did a double take. Whereas before her eyes had shone with grief—with near unfathomable loss—they now sparkled with wicked intent. I frowned as the other witch, Coco, stepped in front of her, breaking my line of sight.

Was she—I stared at them incredulously—was she pulling Lou's neckline down?

I averted my eyes, furious, but glanced back as Célie leaned over to pinch Lou's cheeks.

Beside me, Jean Luc broke into a jog. He didn't seem to notice Lou's décolletage. He saw only Célie. Spinning her around, he cupped her face and kissed her. Straight on the mouth. In front of us all. Though Célie's eyes flew open in surprise, she didn't protest. Indeed, she even wrapped her arms around his neck, smiling against his lips. "You're here," she said happily.

He returned her smile before resting his forehead against hers. I stared at them. I hadn't seen Jean smile since we were children. "I'm here," he breathed.

Something shifted in her expression. Her smile faltered. "You're here." She blinked up at him in confusion. "Why are you here?"

"Yes, Jean." I stalked forward, careful to keep one eye on Lou. She kept both on me. Unease snaked down my spine, further inflaming my fury. "Why *are* you here?"

Lou sauntered forward, still grinning. I refused to retreat a step. Not a single one. "I could pose the same question to you, Chass." She batted her lashes and trailed a finger across my chest. "Just couldn't stay away, could you?"

I caught her wrist and stepped closer. Baring my teeth. I longed for my Balisarda. "Hardly. You've clearly tampered with my memories, witch. I want them back."

She tilted her face toward mine, unperturbed. "Hmm. I don't think I can help you with that."

"You can, and you will."

"Only the witch who cast the enchantment can break it." Coco's hip knocked into Lou as she swept past us, pushing Lou flush against me. She winked. "In this case, that means *you*."

My jaw clenched, and I lifted my hands to Lou's shoulders to forcibly remove her. "You lie."

"Why would we lie? Trust us when we say you aren't exactly fun to be around—not like this anyway. If there was a way for us to reverse your memory, we would've already done it." Coco lifted a shoulder as she stepped on the path. "You'll need to do it, or no one will."

"A pity, that." Lou thrust her pack against my chest. I caught it instinctively. "Guess you'll have to stay with us until you figure it out." She followed Coco without a backward glance, swaying her hips as she went. My lip curled in disgust. She wore trousers. Fitted ones. Leather. They adhered to her delicate shape in a distasteful way—indecent, even. Shaking my head, I tore my gaze away to stare at the pack in my hands.

I suspected she was anything but delicate.

"Answer the question, Jean." Célie's voice reclaimed my attention. She scowled up at Jean Luc, fierce and unrelenting. "You said the priests—the *king*—requested your presence at the conclave."

"They did."

"You *disobeyed* them?"

"I . . ." He tugged at his collar. "I had to see you."

Her eyes narrowed in suspicion. "Why? Why are you here? Did you"—those accusing eyes cut to mine—"did he think I couldn't do this? Did he think I would die at the first opportunity?"

"You did almost fall from a cliff," Jean Luc muttered defensively. When Célie's face contorted in shock, in outrage, he added, "What? You *did*. I spoke with Father Achille."

"You spoke with Father Achille?" Célie's voice could've frozen water. Abruptly, she stepped away from him, her neck and spine snapping impossibly straight. Taut as a bow. "Have you been following me?"

"I—well, I—of course I have." He rubbed a sheepish hand across his neck. "How could I not?"

"For how long?"

He hesitated, clearly reluctant. "Since . . . since Cesarine."

Her expression emptied of all emotion. "You abandoned your post. You forsook the conclave."

"*No*." Jean Luc shook his head vehemently. "I delegated my duties before I left. I ensured the king and your parents would remain protected—"

"Do my parents know? Did you tell them that you planned to follow me?"

He looked deeply uncomfortable now. "Yes." At her intense, cold stare, he hastened to add, "We had to know you were safe, Célie. They—*I*—couldn't bear the thought of anything—"

She didn't allow him to finish. Instead, she bludgeoned him in the chest with her own pack, turning on her heel to follow Coco and Lou. He staggered beneath its weight. "Célie." When she didn't turn, his voice grew louder, imploring. "Célie, please, wait—"

She whirled suddenly, fists clenched. "I do not need a *keeper*, Jean. This may come as a surprise, but I can take care of myself. I may be a woman—I may be gentle and meek and refined, like a *pretty doll*—but I have survived more in my eighteen years than you and my parents combined. Do not mistake me for porcelain. Do not mistake me for *weak*."

She left without another word.

Struggling to hold her bag, Jean Luc tried to follow, but the crown prince clapped his shoulder, further upsetting his balance. He pitched forward with a curse. "Bad luck, man." Beau didn't lift a finger to set him right. "I think there might be actual bars of gold in there." He shrugged. "The melusines liked her best."

"She's wearing trousers," Jean Luc said incredulously, panting now. "*Célie.*"

Tension radiated across my face, shoulders, neck. I cared for none of this—the witches, their lies, their *clothes.* Tasteless wardrobes aside, however, the women had disappeared around the bend. We couldn't afford to lose them. *I* couldn't afford to lose them. Not with my memory at stake. Despite their deceit, they would help me restore my memories, or I would cut the very lies from their tongues. I just needed patience. Scowling, I hitched Lou's bag higher. "Where are we going?"

Beau started after them without waiting for either of us. "I believe to pillage a castle."

Jean Luc acquired two additional horses at the next village to speed our travel. When he extended a hand to Célie to help her mount his own, she knocked it aside and ascended herself. She now sat formal and straight in his saddle while he perched behind her.

That left four of us.

I glared at the witches, prepared to tie them behind as Jean Luc had tied me. Beau had a different idea. Without giving me a chance to speak—to protest—he ushered Coco astride the second horse, hoisting himself up after her.

That left two of us for the last horse.

And it was unacceptable.

"Give me the rope." I stomped to Jean Luc's side, seizing

his bag. The coil sat at the top. Right. Squaring my shoulders, I turned to face the witch. The others watched in rapt fascination. "Don't make this difficult."

Her eyes fell to the rope in my hand. Her smile faltered. "You're kidding."

"I don't kid. Give me your wrists. You can walk behind the horse."

"Fuck you."

Coco slid from her own horse now, coming to stand beside Lou. "Don't make us tie *you* to the horse, Reid." She lifted her wrist to place a thumbnail upon it. A threat. "If you talk to her like that again, it would be my pleasure."

My hands tightened on the rope. "Try."

Beau rolled his eyes. "Honestly, brother, will you insist on this asshattery at every turn? If so, it's going to be a very long trip."

"I'm not riding anywhere with that witch."

Without my Balisarda, I was virtually defenseless. She could attack me even now, and I wouldn't be able to stop her. As if sensing that thought, Lou snorted. "You aren't in any more danger on the horse." Stepping into the stirrup, she swung her leg over its back. "Don't be stupid, Chass. Climb up. You can tie me up later if you'd like, but I'm not walking anywhere."

I glared up at her. "I don't trust you."

Her answering smile was hard. "I don't particularly trust you either, which is why you should know"—she brushed the sheath at her thigh—"I'll gut you like a fish if you try anything."

I didn't move. Coco didn't either. Her eyes narrowed on my

bandolier. "Not good enough. Give me your knives."

"That isn't going to happen."

Lou tipped her face up to the sky, exhaling heavily. "It's fine, Coco. I've kicked his ass before. I can do it again."

"We're wasting time," Célie urged.

Jean Luc shot me an impatient look. "Just get on the horse, Reid."

Judas.

Reluctant, furious, I hoisted myself behind her, reaching around to take hold of the reins. She relinquished them freely. "Be very careful," I warned her, voice low. "You may have magic, but you aren't the only one who can gut a fish."

She turned her face toward mine. "I'm not the only one who has magic either." When I nudged our horse into a trot, following the others, she asked, "Have you heard them yet? The voices?"

I glared straight ahead. "I am sound of mind."

"For now."

I ignored the bait. Ignored her altogether. Until— "Beau said we're riding toward a castle?"

"Chateau le Blanc." She settled between my arms, heaving a terse sigh when I shoved her forward once more. "My ancestral home."

"You're going to rob it?" I tried to keep my voice casual. Cold. Only a Dame Blanche could locate the infamous Chateau. Finally, I'd found one to lead me to it. How many years had my brethren searched? How many witches would I snare there, unsuspecting and defenseless? Would I unearth the great pythoness herself, La Dame des Sorcières? One could only hope.

If Lou couldn't return my memories, perhaps this was the next best thing.

"*We* are going to rob it." She didn't lean against me again. Unfortunately, her forward position fitted her backside more firmly between my legs. I gritted my teeth against the sensation. "It'll be locked in the treasury, up in the highest room of the tallest tower. That's where my coven hides all their relics—cursed books and eternal flowers and magic rings alike."

"Your father would shit a brick, Célie," Beau called over his shoulder.

"Shut up, Your Highness," Jean Luc fired back.

Célie spoke through her teeth. "I can speak for myself, Jean."

Lou chuckled before continuing. "My mother allowed me inside only once, and the door was guarded by a powerful enchantment. We'll have to break it somehow—if we even manage to reach it. Eyes surround the castle itself from all sides. Hundreds of witches live there year-round." She paused. "Even more now."

Hundreds of witches.

"You said only the witch who casts the enchantment can break it."

"That's right."

I clenched my jaw in irritation. In disappointment. "How will we break the enchantment on the door?"

She merely shrugged, her hair tickling my face. Long and thick and brown. Wild. Against my better judgment, I inhaled its scent. She smelled sweet in a way I almost recognized—like vanilla and cinnamon. A warm coat on a cold winter day. Snow on my tongue. I shook my head, feeling thoroughly stupid. "You have no strategy at all, do you?"

"I bottled several pints of L'Eau Mélancolique." The wind carried Coco's voice in an upward spiral. Lou strained forward to hear her, and I shifted away, cursing inwardly. Heat crept into my cheeks. My body didn't realize, of course. This wasn't a woman but a witch. "Maybe the waters will restore the door to what it was before the enchantment," Coco continued. "If not, my blood might. It's a different magic than yours."

Jean Luc didn't hide his scorn. "It's a door. We break it down."

I scarcely heard the exchange. With each stride of the horse, the witch's backside moved against my lap, up and down, rhythmic, until heat suffused my entire body. I glared determinedly at the sky overhead. The situation had grown dire. Soon, she would notice, and soon, I would have to kill her for it.

"Is there a problem, Chass?" she murmured after another moment.

"None," I snapped.

She said nothing for several seconds. Then— "You can tell me if there is." She cleared her throat. It sounded suspiciously like a laugh. "It must be *hard*, riding with me like this."

I would have to kill her.

"Seriously, Reid." Lowering her voice, she turned to look at me in the saddle. I exhaled harshly at the movement. "Do I need to move?" The sudden earnestness in her expression startled me. As did the flush in her cheeks. The dilation of her pupils. "I can sit behind you."

Ahead of us, Beau glanced back at me before winking and whispering in Coco's ear. She laughed. Feverish with rage or—or something else—I shook my head. Their sly behavior chafed. All of it. Though truthfully, one couldn't call them sly at all. Each communicated openly if not clearly, which made it all the more infuriating. They were laughing at my expense.

I just didn't know why.

And I wouldn't be humiliated by a witch.

I jerked my chin behind me. "Move."

She stood in the stirrups without hesitation. Or tried. She couldn't reach both, instead standing on tiptoe atop each of my boots. She nearly lost her balance. I didn't help her. Didn't touch her. Not until she pivoted to face me, her breasts at eye level. I nearly choked. Though she shimmied to maneuver around, they still brushed my cheek, and I lurched backward. She smelled sweet. Too sweet. Swiftly, I wrapped an arm around her waist, propelling her behind me. She clutched my shoulders for balance. Her thighs cradled mine. I held back a groan.

At least her breasts weren't in my face anymore—they were pressed into my back.

God was trying to kill me.

She slid her arms around my torso. "Is this better?"

"How do I restore my memories?" I asked instead. Hideous shame tightened my chest. This physical response—I'd never felt it with such intensity. Worse, the ache didn't ease. It only strengthened with each passing moment. My body felt . . . unfulfilled. Like it knew what came next. Like it craved it. But that was nonsense. It didn't know anything, didn't *crave* anything, and it certainly didn't recognize that sweet smell.

"It'll be painful. I've only done it once."

"And?"

"And I just sort of . . . focused on the holes in the tapestry. I followed the loose threads."

I scoffed. "Riddles."

"No." She squeezed me tighter, her wrist dangerously close to one of my knives. I didn't warn her. "It isn't a riddle at all. Think of a specific gap in your memory. Focus. Remember everything around it—the colors, the scents, the sounds. Logically, your mind will try to fill in the missing pieces, but subconsciously, each explanation will feel wrong." She paused. "That's when you move on to the illogical ones. The magical ones."

Are you sure? Think hard, Reid. Please. Just think. I'm Lou, remember? I'm your wife.

Wanted dead or alive under suspicion of murder, conspiracy, and witchcraft.

I viciously rejected each thought. They simply weren't true. And despite what this creature claimed, they didn't feel *right*. They felt wrong in every way. Unnatural. I gripped the reins tighter, spurring our horse faster. I needed to recenter. To refocus. Plunging a knife in a witch's heart should do the trick. A simple, logical solution.

Even better if she had freckles.

WINTER WONDERLAND

Lou

I wasn't prepared to return to Chateau le Blanc. A chill skittered down my spine at the familiarity of the wind here, the taste of the salt and pine and magic. Beyond the eerie mist of L'Eau Mélancolique, waves crashed and gulls cried. The former had lulled me to sleep every night as a child—and the latter had woken me each morning. My bedroom window had overlooked the sea.

"Stop." Though I said the word quietly, Jean Luc pulled on the reins of his horse, turning to face me. "We should walk from here. My sisters stalk these trees at night."

To my surprise, he nodded and complied without argument or scorn. Reid, however, stiffened and shook his head. "Your *sisters.*"

"Do you have any?" Sliding from the saddle, I voiced the question with casual nonchalance. I knew the answer, of course, but *he* didn't know that. I'd spooked him before with talk of wives and magic. His physical response to me hadn't helped. If I had any chance of rekindling what we'd once had, it would take more than seduction. More than pleas. I'd need to fall in love with him all over again—the person he was now—and he would need to fall in love with me. When he didn't answer, I tried to clarify. "Sisters, I mean."

"I knew what you meant," he said shortly.

Right.

I'd forgotten he was now an ass.

Jean Luc and Coco worked on tying the horses to trees while Célie and Beau approached. Beau rubbed his hands together against the cold. "What's the plan? We charge in, swords drawn, banners flying?"

"Morgane would kill us before we even crossed the bridge." My eyes snagged on Célie's hands. She'd clasped them at her waist, the picture of propriety—except for the needle sticking between them. "What is *that*?"

Slowly, she uncurled her fingers, revealing a crude metal syringe. She didn't cower or flinch beneath my black gaze as she said, matter-of-fact, "An injection. I lost it at the beach, but Elvire returned it to me. I plan to stab it in your mother's throat."

"Ah." Coco and I shared an incredulous glance. "Well, if that's all."

Reid's eyes gleamed as he stepped forward, but Célie snatched it away before he could take it. "Don't even think about it. It belongs to *me*."

Jean Luc and Coco joined us now. "What *is* the plan?" the former asked. "Do we have any strategy at all?"

"How did you sneak in on Modraniht?" I asked Coco.

"Madame Labelle transformed our faces." She shrugged helplessly. Reid, however, frowned at the name, his gaze turning inward, distant, as he found his mother in his memories. When his frown turned to a scowl, I knew he'd remembered her a witch. "Can you do the same? If witches have gathered from all over the kingdom, we could slip inside without suspicion."

"It's possible, but . . ." I shook my head with mounting apprehension. "Morgane might not remember me, but she'll remember how you infiltrated the castle. Others will remember too. I doubt they'll fall for such a trick again—especially after Zenna's attack. Everyone will be on high alert. Every stranger in the castle will be counted."

"How did *you* sneak in?" Coco asked Jean Luc. "You and the Chasseurs?"

"We waited on the beach until Madame Labelle led us through the enchantment. We had no need to disguise ourselves. We wanted the witches to see us approach—to know ours would be the last faces they ever saw."

Célie wrinkled her nose at the gratuitous explanation. "Lovely."

His expression turned solemn. "I'm still a Chasseur, Célie. I still eradicate the occult. What I'm doing now—I'd lose my Balisarda if my brethren caught me here. I'd burn at the stake myself." He gestured between us. "We all would."

"Unless we bring them La Dame des Sorcières's head." Reid looked pointedly at Coco and me. "And those of her *sisters*."

Beau jutted a finger at him. "*You* don't get to talk anymore—"

"Just be sure this is what you want." Jean Luc clutched Célie's hands, ignoring them both. "We can still walk away. You have a choice. You don't have to do this."

Célie's knuckles whitened around the injection. "Yes, I do."

"Célie—"

"And you are not called to eradicate the occult, Jean. You are called to eradicate *evil*." She pulled away from him, stepping backward to stand beside me. "There is evil in this chateau. Truthfully, we have no choice at all."

They stared at each other for several seconds—neither willing to blink—before Jean Luc finally sighed. "If we must enter from the bridge, we need some sort of cover." Reluctantly, he unbuckled his scabbard, retreating briefly to his horse to hide it within his pack. The sapphire of his Balisarda's hilt winked as he withdrew a set of knives instead.

Reid's eyes widened incredulously. "What are you doing?"

"Think, Reid." He tucked one knife into each boot. "The only viable cover available to us is magic." He waved a hand in my direction, refusing to look at me. "Magic will not work if I carry my Balisarda."

Together, they all turned to stare at me. As if I knew the answers. As if I held each of their fates in the palm of my hand. Stomach rolling, I forced myself to return their gaze—because in a way, they were right. This was my ancestral home. These were my kin. If I couldn't protect them here, if I couldn't *hide* them from my sisters, they would indeed die.

"Perhaps I should . . ." I cleared my throat. "Perhaps I should go in alone."

The thought met instantaneous and decisive objection, each of them speaking over the other. Coco and Beau refused to leave me. Célie demanded a chance to prove herself, and Jean Luc insisted I would need his expertise. Even Reid shook his head in stoic silence, his eyes communicating what his mouth did not.

Nothing would stand between him and his conquest.

At the moment, that conquest was Morgane le Blanc. Soon, he would realize his target had shifted, and the fleeting impulse to kill me would solidify into something very real and very dangerous. When he learned I'd become La Dame des Sorcières, I would no longer be safe with him. Not until he remembered. Not until I recaptured his heart.

"We go where you go," he said with dark resolve.

My heart twisted with the words, and I turned away, closing my eyes. A web of golden patterns rose up to meet me. Studying them carefully—my lids fluttering in concentration—I discarded one after another, unsatisfied with each. This sort of magic, the sort to hide six people, would exact a heavy cost. Perhaps I could transform their bodies instead of their faces. They could become birds or squirrels or foxes. A rock in a badger's mouth.

Expelling a sigh of frustration, I shook my head. Such transfiguration would probably kill me. Beau would have to live the rest of his life as a rock—or, more likely, live as a rock forever because rocks didn't die. After another moment or two of my own fruitless searching, Coco said softly, "Could you make us invisible?"

I didn't open my eyes, instead widening my inner sight for such a pattern. My skin tingled at the effort. My chest ached, an uncomfortable pressure building there. These cords—they felt simplistic somehow. Inadequate. Almost weak. Had something happened to my magic? Had Nicholina . . . altered me somehow? I frowned and pushed harder, stamping a metaphorical foot at the injustice of it all. Heat fanned across my face in humiliation.

Here I was, La Dame des Sorcières—famed and all-powerful, Mother, Maiden, and Crone—yet I couldn't even cast an enchantment to protect my friends.

My sister chose wrong.

I could feel their expectant eyes on me now, waiting for a miracle.

I stomped my foot again, this time in desperation, and the web beneath me bowed and rippled outward. Startled, I instinctively stomped once more.

This time, the web broke.

A web of pure, blinding white lay below it, and the tingle in my skin exploded in a wave of raw power. No. *Awareness.* Every blade of grass, every flake of snow, every *needle* of *pine* I felt with such an intensity that I stumbled backward, breathless. Célie caught my arm. "Lou?" she asked in alarm.

I didn't dare open my eyes. Not when the web below offered so much more. I tracked each pattern eagerly, feverish with possibility. I'd thought my magic infinite before. I'd thought it limited only to my imagination.

I'd been wrong.

My magic had flowed through the land, but this magic—it *was* the land. *This* land. The Triple Goddess hadn't merely bestowed her form. She'd bestowed the heart of our entire people. My finger twitched, and the web rippled outward, connected to my every thought, every emotion, every memory. My ancestors' too. I didn't just feel the grass. I *was* the grass. I'd become the snow and pine.

"Lou, you're scaring me." Coco's sharp voice cut through my wonder, and unbidden, my eyes snapped open. She stood directly in front of me. In the brown of her irises, my skin reflected back at me, bright and burnished. Luminous. "What happened?"

"I—" The ache in my chest towed me forward through the trees. I couldn't resist its pull. "I'm fine," I called over my shoulder, chuckling at their wide eyes and parted mouths. Reid had drawn a knife from his bandolier. He regarded me with open suspicion. I couldn't bring myself to care. "I can hide everyone. Follow me."

Coco rushed after me. "*How?*"

I grinned at her. "White patterns."

"Like the one at the blood camp?" Her hopeful expression fell. "The one that led you to Etienne?"

My smile slipped, and I shuddered to a halt, suddenly unsure. "Do you think it's Morgane?"

"I think we should consider the possibility. Your patterns have never been white before, have they?"

"You've never been La Dame des Sorcières before either," Beau pointed out. Though Coco and I both glared at him, it was too late. The damage had been done, and Reid's menacing presence loomed behind me.

"*You're* La Dame des Sorcières?"

With my newfound awareness, I could feel the weight of his footsteps. I could feel the snow and moss tamp beneath his boots. His presence was heavier than the others', harder and stronger. Darker. I scoffed. "Barely." Turning to Coco, trusting Beau and Célie and even Jean Luc to protect my back, I said, "It doesn't feel like Morgane. It feels familiar, yes—almost familial—but it also feels like me. I . . . I think I trust it."

She nodded once in understanding. But how could she? I hardly understood myself. Though I implicitly trusted the wholeness of this magic, the purity, I felt much like a rowboat at sea. The ache in my chest kept building, pulling me adrift. Dragging me beneath the current. "Then do it," she said firmly. "Do it quickly."

Closing my eyes, ignoring Reid's vehement protest, I spread my awareness outward, farther and faster than before. There. A mile north, beneath the infamous bridge, a river crashed into the ocean. With the wave of my hand, the water solidified to ice, changing state of matter. The white pattern burst, and my friends and I dissolved into shadow.

With our first steps on the bridge, my body attempted to rematerialize, limbs accumulating and dispersing with violent shudders. Except it wasn't my body at all. Gritting my teeth in concentration, I glanced down at my unfamiliar, disembodied hand. The Maiden's hand.

"Shit."

My whisper floated in the darkness as said hand dispersed to shadow once more. "What is it?" Coco asked sharply. I could just see her shadowed form beside Beau's, though the finer details of their appearance—such as the expressions on their faces, the gleam in their eyes—had been lost to the enchantment. Now they simply appeared pieces of night darker than the rest. Human-shaped shadows. None would notice us unless they looked, and even then, the smoke obscured all traces of moonlight. We were near invisible.

"Nothing. I just—feel weird." Though incorporeal, my head still swam at the magnitude of power before me. At the sheer breadth of it. How had my mother withstood this? How had it not crushed her? "It's too much. It's like I can't breathe."

"So don't," Reid offered.

If I'd had hands, I might've strangled him. Perhaps I still would've tried if I hadn't looked up, past the gatehouse, to the empty expanse of mountain all around the Chateau. I blinked slowly, unable to believe my eyes. Where before a mighty forest had prospered, now only rocks and dirt greeted me. "Where are the trees?"

Someone bumped into me from behind. Jean Luc. "What do you mean?"

"The trees." I gestured to the rocky incline above us, forgetting he couldn't see me. "There used to be trees here. Trees *everywhere*. They covered this entire mountain face."

"It's true." Reid's heavy footsteps stopped beside me. "I remember."

We all crept forward, slower and warier now. "Perhaps they chopped them down," Beau said. "And recently. Look—no snow."

I instantly disagreed. "They didn't."

"How do you know?"

"I just *do*."

"There are no stumps," Coco said, leaning forward. "See? The ground does look disturbed, though."

"Perhaps Zenna scorched them all, then." Beau pointed to the charred markings on the bridge, on the gatehouse ahead. Evidence of Zenna's wrath. Still, the hair on my neck lifted. These trees hadn't been burned. Of that, I was certain.

"They look like they just . . . uprooted and walked away."

Reid made a low, disparaging sound at the back of his throat. I ignored him. Instead, I started for the gatehouse once more, focusing on the sound of my feet on the wood.

Whatever damage Zenna had caused with her attack, little evidence remained. The structural integrity of the Chateau remained intact, and even the facade bore little sign of fire. Magic was helpful that way. I supposed Morgane wouldn't have liked the soot underfoot. We paused inside the crumbling entrance to listen. Though the air in the courtyard could chill bone, the temperature within felt warm and balmy, despite the overgrown ruins of the hall. And the castle—it came alive at night. Voices echoed from all around: beyond the grand stairwell, through the corridors, within the great hall. Two lovers swept past hand in hand, and soon after, a manservant bustled through with a tray of what smelled like custard tarts. A handful of witchlings passed us a moment later to make shapes in the snow outside. Though I recognized none of them, the familiarity of it all made me smile. Nothing had changed.

Reid unsheathed another knife beside me, and my smile faded.

Everything had changed.

At least Morgane hadn't deployed forces to Cesarine. Not *yet*, anyway.

"Keep close," I murmured, starting toward the staircase. Though my body remained like shadow, I kept to the edges of the room. Smoke had obscured the moonlight outside, yes, but inside, lit candles dripped from their candelabra and cast flickering light. I would take no chances. "Morgane and Josephine are here somewhere. Perhaps Nicholina too."

"And the treasury?" Reid murmured.

"Follow me."

I led them through a narrow door beneath the staircase, into the winding passage beyond. Though it would take longer to reach the treasury's tower this way, few others traveled it, and I... I couldn't explain the creeping dread in my chest. The longer I concealed my friends in shadow, the more agitated I became. Like the magic itself was—was rebelling against me. Against *them*. It made little sense, yet wasn't the purpose of La Dame des Sorcières to protect her home?

We were trespassers here, all of us, intent on thieving a sacred treasure.

My magic didn't trust us, I realized in a burst of clarity.

The air in the passage tasted stale, damp, and the moss on the stones muted our footsteps. A good thing too—for at that exact moment, a door cracked open ahead, and three figures spilled out into the semidarkness. I froze mid-step, my heart pounding in my ears. I heard their voices before I saw their faces.

Morgane, Josephine, and Nicholina.

They strode forward, deep in harried conversation, and I seized Reid before they could see us, pushing him into the nearest alcove. Célie and Jean Luc barreled in behind as Coco and Beau did the same across the hall. The space was too small, however. My cheek smashed against Reid's chest, and behind me, Jean Luc's knee stabbed my thigh. Célie trembled visibly. Contorting my arm, I wrapped it around her to hide the movement and comfort her in equal measure. No one dared breathe.

"I do not *care* what you say," Morgane hissed at Josephine, visibly agitated. She'd swept her white hair into a tangled braid, and her eyes remained shot through with blood. Fatigue lent a grayish hue to her skin. "The time is now. I tire of these incessant games. The trees have mobilized, and we shall follow, striking hard and true while the conclave deliberates."

Josephine shook her head curtly. "I do not think this wise. We must proceed with the plan as scheduled. Your daughter, the king's children, they will—"

Morgane wheeled to face her, nostrils flaring with sudden rage. "For the last time, Josephine, I do not *have* a daughter, and if I must repeat myself again, I shall rend your tongue from your miserable throat."

I do not have *a daughter.*

Ah. My heart twisted unexpectedly. Though I'd suspected she'd forgotten me, suspecting the truth versus knowing it—versus *hearing* it—were two entirely different things. It shouldn't have hurt as much as it did, but here, in my childhood home—surrounded by sisters who'd cheered as my blood had spilled—it . . . pinched. Just a bit. I searched Reid's shadowed face. This close, I could see the shape of his eyes, the set of his mouth. He glared back at me.

I looked away.

Cackling, Nicholina sang, "The dead should not remember. Beware the night the dream. For in their chest is memory—"

Morgane struck her across the face without warning. The angry *crack* resounded through the passage.

"You do not speak"—a vein pulsed in my mother's forehead—"you do not *breathe* unless I will it. How many times must I punish you before you understand?" When she lifted her hand once more, Nicholina flinched. She actually *flinched*. Instead of striking her, however, Morgane rapped her knuckles across Nicholina's forehead. "Well? How many? Or are your ears as addled as your brain, you worthless imp?"

Nicholina withdrew visibly at the insult, her expression emptying. She stared past Morgane as a red handprint bloomed on her cheek.

"As I thought." With a sneer, Morgane proceeded toward us up the corridor, her own mottled cheeks visible even in the candlelight. "I should've killed you when I had the chance."

Josephine only arched a brow at her ward and followed.

Célie wasn't the only one trembling now. My own hands shook as Nicholina drifted after them—as vacant and lifeless as the wraiths outside—and even Reid's heart beat an uneven tattoo against my ear. He stood rigid as she passed, but I felt his hand creep slowly up my back. I felt his knife. Whether he meant to kill me or Nicholina, I never discovered. Because before she disappeared around the corner, Nicholina turned toward our alcove.

Her eyes met mine.

And I knew—as instinctively as I'd known the trees had walked and my magic wanted to protect Chateau le Blanc—I *knew* that she'd seen me.

Reid's knife stilled with her footsteps. "Hello, mouse," she whispered, her fingers wrapping around the bend. Pure, unadulterated fear snaked through me at the words. I could do nothing but stare. Paralyzed. A single shout from her could kill us all.

We waited, breaths bated, as Nicholina tilted her head.

As she slipped around the corner without a sound.

"What are we doing?" Reid's voice sounded in my ear, low and furious. "We can still catch her. Move."

I stared at the spot from which she'd vanished, my mind reeling. She didn't reappear, however, and no sounds of alarm rent the silence. No sounds of pursuit. "She let us go."

"To kill us later."

"She could've killed us just then, but she didn't." I scowled now, thoroughly disenchanted with his single-minded intensity. It bordered on pigheaded. Had he been this stupid when I'd first met him? Was *his* mind the addled one? "I don't know why, but I *do* know I won't be looking a gift horse in the mouth. She's with Morgane and La Voisin," I added when he tried to move around me. I planted my feet. "Now isn't the time for this confrontation. We made a deal with Isla—we get in, we get out, and we give her the ring."

"Unacceptable." That knife finally pressed between my shoulder blades. "I am not here for a magic ring, Louise. If you don't move out of my way, I will find another witch to kill."

I poked him in the chest. Hard. "Listen to me, jackass." My voice rose at the word, and I hastened to lower it once more. "Isla needs that ring. *We* need the melusines. The sooner we finish here, the sooner we can unite our allies, the sooner we can formulate a plan of attack—"

"I have a plan—attack. Morgane is here, not in Cesarine."

"Your *mother* is in Cesarine."

"I don't care about my mother," he snarled, shouldering past me at last. I stumbled into Jean Luc, who overcorrected, knocking Célie into Reid and plunging me into the corridor alone.

I whirled to face him, swearing loudly—then froze.

Manon stared back at me.

"Hello?" Her eyes narrowed suspiciously, flitting over my dark shape, and she lifted a hand as if to touch me. I scuttered backward. I had no choice. If she touched me, she'd realize without a doubt that I was human. When her frown deepened, I winced, realizing too late that shadows didn't *scutter*. "Who's there?" She flicked a thin blade from her sleeve. "Show yourself, or I'll summon the sentries."

Why did every plan I ever made go to complete and total shit?

Lips flattening, I cracked open that door of power in my chest, beneath which the white web shimmered. It would be a risk to change forms, but Morgane was clever. Though she'd undoubtedly realized the Triple Goddess had revoked her blessing, perhaps she hadn't yet told our kin. Either way, I couldn't simply stand here with a knife in front and a knife behind, and I couldn't reveal my true form either. This newfound power would make it easier, surely.

I sought to remember my childhood classroom, wracked my mind for everything I knew of the Triple Goddess and her forms.

Her final counterpart is the Crone, who embodies aging and ending, death and rebirth, past lives and transformations, visions and prophecies. She is our guide. She is dusk and night, autumn and winter.

Fitting, as we'd probably all die here anyway.

I focused on those traits, tried to center myself around them, as other memories consumed—my life in this castle, my blood in the basin, my farewell to Ansel. That feeling of bone-deep acceptance. My transformation into the Maiden had happened easily, without intent, but this transformation came easier still. Perhaps once I would've empathized most with the Maiden—and I still did, to an extent—but that joyous season of light had passed. I'd lived in winter for too long. To my surprise, I didn't regret the change. I relished it.

My hands withered and cracked as the shadows around them dissipated, and my spine bowed beneath years of fatigue. My vision clouded. My flesh sagged. Triumphant—exorbitantly pleased with myself—I lifted a gnarled finger to Manon's startled face. I'd done it.

I'd transformed.

"Out for a moonlit stroll, dearie?" My voice warbled, unfamiliar and deep and unpleasant. I cackled at the sound, and Manon retreated a step. "Not much moonlight tonight, I'm afraid." My tongue flicked past the gap in my eyeteeth as I leered at her. "Shall I join you?"

She sank into a hasty curtsy. "My lady. I am sorry. I—I didn't recognize you."

"Some nights I must pass unseen, Manon."

"Of course." She ducked her head. Too late, I realized she'd been crying. The kohl around her eyes had tracked down her cheeks, and her nose still ran. She sniffed as quietly as possible. "I understand."

"Is something wrong, child?"

"No." She spoke the word too quickly, still backing away. "No, my lady. I am sorry to have bothered you."

I didn't need the Crone's Vision to see her lie. Truthfully, I needn't have asked at all. She still grieved her dead lover, Gilles, the man she'd killed with her own hands. All because he'd been a son of the king. "A cup of chamomile tea, my dear." When she blinked, confused, I clarified, "In the kitchens. Brew and steep a cup. It will settle your nerves and send you to sleep."

With another curtsy and word of thanks, she departed, and I sagged against the nearest wall.

"Holy shit," Beau breathed.

"That was *incredible*," Coco added.

"Release me." Reid broke Jean Luc's hold swiftly, efficiently, his throat corded with strain. He whirled on him in a storm of fury. "She was isolated. The situation controlled. We should've *struck*—"

"And then what?" Flinging my hands in the air, I hobbled toward him. "Really, what's the next step in this master plan of yours, Chass? We hide her body for someone to stumble across? We stuff her in the closet? We can't risk anyone knowing we're here!"

"You're jeopardizing the mission, Reid," Jean Luc agreed darkly, "and you're endangering everyone here. Follow her orders, or I'll incapacitate you."

Reid stepped toe to toe with him. "I'd like to see that, Jean."

"Oh, shut it, or I'll stuff *your* body in the goddamn closet." Losing patience completely, I whirled—though in reality, it looked more like a shuffle—and doddered up the passage once more. "We've wasted enough time here."

Reid followed in mutinous silence.

DEADLY AND BEAUTIFUL THINGS

Reid

Chateau le Blanc was a labyrinth. I hadn't ventured beyond the Great Hall on Modraniht, so I could do nothing but follow Lou. *Lou.* She hadn't told me who she was. Of course she hadn't. She hadn't told me she'd inherited her mother's power—that *she* had become La Dame des Sorcières.

She struggled to climb a set of rickety stairs now. Coco and Beau supported her on either side. Their shapes remained dark. Unnatural. Like shadows. "You could always change back," the latter muttered, catching her stout frame as she stumbled.

"This is better. If we meet anyone else, they won't look too close."

The stairs wound up a narrow tower. Here, however, the ceiling had collapsed in places. As in the Great Hall, the elements had overcome most rooms. Snow fell gently in the solar, where an ornately carved fireplace crackled. Its light danced on tapestries of magical beasts and beautiful women—each of their eyes seemed to follow us as we passed. I swore one even craned her elegant neck.

"This room is for Morgane's personal use." Lou pointed to the wooden desk in the corner. A peacock-feather quill scratched at parchment of its own volition. The falling snow didn't mar the paper, nor the carpets or tapestries. It didn't stain the decorative woodwork. It simply melted into nothing in the warm, balmy air. In the corner, a harp plucked itself gently.

The entire scene was eerie.

"Her bedchamber is also in this tower." She gestured to a room beyond the harp. "And her oratory. She forbade me from entering this part of the castle, but I snuck in anyway."

"And the treasury?" Jean Luc asked.

"Directly above us." Shuffling to the bookcase beside the desk, she studied the tomes there. Her silver brows furrowed in concentration. "The door is somewhere . . ." Her fingers stilled on an ancient book bound in black cloth. On its spine, letters had been stamped in gold: *L'argent n'a pas d'odeur.* She tapped it with a wicked grin. "Here."

When she pulled the book toward her, the entire wall groaned. Gears clanked. And the bookcase—it swung open. Beyond it, a steep, narrow staircase disappeared into the dark. She bowed slightly, still grinning, and snapped her fingers. The scent of magic burst around us—fresher than before—and a torch on the wall in the stairwell sprang to life. "After you."

Beau removed the torch warily. A shadow bearing light. The unnatural sight of it lifted the hair on my arms. My neck. "You didn't tell us the treasury was in her personal chambers."

"I didn't want to scare you."

"Oh, yes." Tentative, Beau stepped onto the first plank. It creaked under his weight. "The shadows, wraiths, and murderous witches would've paled in comparison to Morgane's bed." He hesitated and glanced back. "Unless—do you think she'll be returning soon?"

Coco followed before the coward could reconsider. "I think she's busy plotting the end of the world."

"This place . . ." Célie stared longingly over her shoulder as she too ascended. Her eyes lingered on the peacock quill before settling on the harp. Its golden strings. Her body swayed slightly to the haunting melody. "It's so beautiful."

I rolled my eyes. "You almost died outside, Célie."

"I haven't forgotten," she snapped, suddenly defensive. I bristled at her tone. "Believe me, I remember what magic is. It's just—" Tearing her gaze from the room, she turned instead to Jean Luc, to me. Her hand rose to catch a snowflake between us, and we all watched it melt on her fingertip, transfixed. No. *Not* transfixed—revolted. "You never told me it could be beautiful too," she finished, softer now.

"It's dangerous, Célie," Jean Luc said.

She lifted her chin. "Why can't it be both?"

We both heard what she really meant. *Why can't I be both?*

Jean Luc stared at her for several seconds, tilting his head in contemplation. When at last he nodded, affirming her unspoken question, she kissed his cheek and ascended the stairs with the others. He followed behind like a devoted, lovesick puppy, and my stomach plunged as if I'd missed a step. His response shouldn't have surprised me. Nor hers. Célie had clearly suffered from the witches' influence, and Jean Luc would never utter a word against her.

Still, I felt . . . off, somehow—disjointed—as I jerked my chin toward Lou. She alone remained. The others had left in more than the literal sense. "Go."

Her gap-toothed smile slipped. "Forgive me, but I'd rather not end the night with a knife in my back. You understand, I'm sure." She wiggled her fingers in silent threat, motioning me forward.

Scowling, I followed Jean Luc. Though she'd been right in her suspicions—I *did* want to end her depraved existence—I had no choice but to obey. I'd lost my Balisarda. "I thought the door was guarded by a powerful enchantment."

Her footsteps fell heavy and clumsy behind me, her breath growing louder with each tread. Labored. I didn't offer assistance. If she insisted on this foul magic, she would reap the reward. "That was *a* door," she panted. "It wasn't *the* door. Did you really think my mother would protect her most treasured possessions with only a bookshelf?"

Her most treasured possessions. The words sent a thrill of anticipation through me. Surely, something beyond this door would be useful in eliminating her—in eliminating *all* of them. Perhaps if I liberated it, delivered it to the new Archbishop, I could renew my vows and rejoin my brotherhood. It was where I belonged.

As quickly as the thought materialized, however, I cast it aside. If this new Archbishop accepted me so readily—me, a man guilty of murder and conspiracy—he would be no leader at all. I could not follow him. No, from this point onward, I could seek only atonement. I would kill these witches, yes, but I expected no reward. If the wanted posters had been true, I deserved none.

I would kill them nonetheless.

At the top of the staircase, the others halted before a simple, nondescript door. Lou pushed past me, still wheezing. She clutched her chest with one hand and the door handle with another. "My god. I think my knees might've actually cracked."

"My *māmā rūʻau* can predict the weather with hers," Beau offered.

"She sounds like a fascinating woman, and I mean that genuinely." Straightening as much as possible, Lou twisted the golden handle experimentally. It didn't move. At my derisive snort, she muttered, "No harm in checking."

A beat of silence passed as she stared at the door, and we stared at her.

Impatience sharpened my tone. "Well?"

Flattening her palm on the handle, she cast me a cutting glance. "I was right. A nasty enchantment has been cast on this door, and it'll take time to break—if I can break it at all." She closed her eyes. "I can . . . feel it there. Like a sixth sense. The magic—it pulls at my chest even now." She shook her head, opening her eyes once more. "But I don't know if I can trust it."

Coco's voice turned grim. "I don't think we have a choice."

"It wants to protect this place, even from me."

"You control the magic, Lou. It doesn't control you."

"But what if—"

"Shift your perspective." The response startled even me, and it'd come from my own mouth. Beneath their startled gazes, I immediately regretted I'd spoken. Heat crept into my cheeks. Why *had* I spoken? I needed to get into this room, of course, but—no. That was the only explanation. I needed to get into this room. Looking each one of them directly in the eye, I continued, "This new magic, it wants to protect the Chateau. Why?"

Lou frowned. "Because it's my home. My sisters' home. It's been ours for all of living memory."

"That isn't quite true," Coco whispered.

Lou blinked at her. "What?"

"My aunt remembers differently." Coco shifted in obvious discomfort. "She speaks of a time when Dames Rouges walked these halls instead of Dames Blanches." At Lou's bewildered expression, she hastened to add, "It doesn't matter. Forget I said anything."

"But—"

"She's right," I interrupted, my voice hard. "What matters now is whether you—La Dame des Sorcières—still consider this place your home." When she didn't speak, only stared at me intently, I shrugged. Shoulders rigid. "If not, it stands to reason your magic won't protect it anymore. It'll shift to your new home. Wherever that is."

She continued to stare at me. "Right."

I crossed my arms and looked away, distinctly uncomfortable. "So? Is it?"

"No." After another long, uncomfortable moment, she finally did the same, murmuring, "No, it isn't."

Then she closed her eyes and exhaled. Her entire body

relaxed into the movement, shedding its withered skin until she no longer resembled the Crone but a young woman once more. A vibrant young woman. *A witch*, my mind chastised. A vibrant young *witch*. Still, with her eyes closed, I couldn't help but study her. Long brown hair and elfin features. Sharp-cut eyes. Sunkissed freckles. At her throat, a ring of thorns circled her golden skin. Roses too.

Why can't I be both?

The inexplicable urge to touch her nearly overpowered me. To trace the delicate curve of her nose. The bold arch of brow. I resisted the mad impulse. Only fools coveted beautiful and deadly things. I wasn't a fool. I didn't covet. And I certainly didn't want to touch a witch, regardless of how she looked at me.

She looked at me like I belonged to her and she belonged to me.

"It's a lock," she breathed eventually, her face contorting with strain. Sweat glistened on her brow. "The magic. I'm the key. La Dame des Sorcières cast the enchantment, and only she can break it. But I"—her eyes screwed tighter—"the webs, they're all fixed—I can't move them. They're like iron."

"You believe it a lock?" Célie approached the door hesitantly. "Pin and tumbler or warded?"

Eyes still closed, Lou pursed her lips. I tore my gaze away. "I'm not sure. It's like—it's like I'm inside it, if that makes sense—"

"Description, please!"

"I can't describe the inside of a lock, Célie! I've never seen one!"

"Well, I have, and—"

"You have?" Jean Luc asked incredulously. "When?"

"Everyone needs a hobby." Resolute now, she shouldered past him to face Lou, grasping her hands. "I picked the lock on my father's vault, and I can help you pick this one too. Now, tell me, do the patterns have notches and slots, or do they more resemble a counting frame? Are there three or more parallel rows?"

Lou grimaced. So did Jean Luc. "No rows," she said, her knuckles white around Célie's. "They might be notches. I—I can't tell." She inhaled sharply as if in pain. "I don't know if I have the control for this. The magic—it's stronger than me. I . . ." Her voice trailed off, growing faint, and she swayed on her feet.

"Nonsense." Célie steadied her with a firm hand. "In my sister's coffin—when I felt like I might float away—I counted the knots in the wood to ground myself. There were thirty-seven that I could see. I would count them, over and over, and I would take a breath with each one." She squeezed Lou's hands. "Listen to my voice and breathe." Then— "You need a skeleton key."

I couldn't help it. I stepped forward, eyes rapt on Lou's face.

"A skeleton key?" she asked.

"It's a warded lock. Those notches you see are meant for false protrusions, which prevent the mechanism from opening. A skeleton key has none. Form the key in your mind—long and narrow, with none but two true protrusions on the end. Shape them to fit the last notches, and push."

Coco shifted from foot to foot, her expression bewildered. "I don't understand. Why would Morgane have created simple keys and locks when she has magic?"

"Who the hell cares?" Beau hovered anxiously by the stairs, keeping watch. "It's an enchanted lock for an enchanted door in an enchanted fucking castle. None of this makes sense. Just hurry up, will you? I think I heard something."

Lou gritted her teeth, pale and trembling now. "If one of you had tried to open this door, you wouldn't have seen a lock. It's meant for La Dame des Sorcières alone, but it's also—it's the previous matriarchs' magic testing mine. I can feel their challenge. Their treasures lie within, and I must—earn—entry." Her head twitched abruptly with each word, and her eyes flew open, snapping to the doorknob. It responded with a simple click. Heavy silence descended as we stared at it.

Lifting a single finger to the wood, Lou pushed tentatively.

The door swung inward.

We stepped into a room of gold—or at least, it appeared so at first glance. In reality, the vaulted ceiling and octagonal walls had been erected from plates of mercury glass. They reflected the golden *couronnes*. Hundreds of them. Thousands of them. The coins spilled forth from every corner, stacked precariously into piles, forming towers of their own. Narrow footpaths wove between them as roads and alleys in a colossal, glittering city.

"This . . ." Beau craned his neck to study the highest crest in the ceiling. Built at the top of a tower, the room stretched taller than wide—cylindrical—like we'd walked into a music box. A basin of fire sat atop a pedestal in the center of the chamber. No logs fed the flames. They emitted no smoke. I inhaled deeply. Though magic coated everything, it tasted almost stale here.

Like a thick blanket of dust. "Is not what I expected," he finished at last.

Lou examined a set of rusted chains near the door, the links thicker than her fists. A dried substance flaked from the metal. Brown, almost black. Blood. "What did you expect?"

He picked up what looked like an ancient human skull. "A dusty cupboard full of creepy dolls and old furniture?"

"It's a treasury, Beau, not an attic." She pointed to a heap of gold across the path. A wooden figurine sat atop a stained settee. Beside it lay a golden comb and a rose-handled mirror. "Though there is a doll there. Morgane once said it was cursed."

Beau blanched. "Cursed *how?*"

"Just don't look it in the eye." Replacing the chains, she seemed to choose another path at random and strode forward. "Right. We should split up. Give a shout if you find something that resembles a golden ring, but *don't* touch anything else." She arched a brow over her shoulder at us. "Here there are many deadly and beautiful things."

I slipped behind her as the others scattered to search. At the sound of my footsteps, she turned with a small smile. Here, in this dark room with its cursed gold and magic fire, she looked more a witch than I'd seen her. Strange and mysterious. Almost surreal. "Just couldn't stay away, could you?"

I didn't know why I'd followed her. I didn't respond.

When she slipped behind a wardrobe—its black cabinets painted with tiny flowers—I drew a knife from my bandolier. Her ghostly chuckle echoed through the thickly scented air. It seemed to shimmer where she'd disappeared, firelight illuminating the dust motes gold. A fingertip brushed my nape. Whirling, I found her standing directly behind me. Her eyes gleamed unnaturally bright. Blue. No, green. "I won't let you kill me, you know," she said. "You wouldn't be able to live with yourself later."

My fingers ached on the hilt of my knife. My throat tightened. I couldn't breathe. "I just want my memories back, witch."

Those haunting eyes fell to my blade, and she stepped forward. Once. Twice. Three times. She walked until her chest met its tip, and then she leaned farther still, drawing a bead of blood. Only then did her eyes return to mine. Only then did she whisper against my lips, "I want that too."

I stared at my knife. At her blood. A quick thrust would do it. One simple movement, and La Dame des Sorcières would be dead. Incapacitated, at the very least. She'd be helpless to stop me from pitching her body in the fire—the *magic* fire. It'd be almost poetic to watch her burn upon it. She'd be ash before the others could save her.

A quick thrust. One simple movement.

She would drive me mad unless I did it.

We stayed that way for another second, another hundred seconds—tense, poised—but a shout sounded from across the treasury, breaking our standoff. "It's here!" Célie's laughter swelled between us. "I found it!" With a smirk, Lou stepped backward. Away from me. In her absence, I could breathe again. I could *hate*.

The woman would drive me mad *until* I did it.

"You're lucky," I said darkly, sheathing my knife.

"Funny. I don't feel lucky at all."

Her smirk seemed brittle as she turned to follow Célie's voice, gifting me her back. Every fiber in my being longed to lunge. To attack. I even bent my knees, stopping only when a sapphire glinted in my periphery. I froze. From within a drawer of the wardrobe peeked the silver hilt of a Balisarda. It looked as if it'd been stuffed there haphazardly. Stowed away and forgotten. A jolt seared through my body. A lightning strike.

Carefully, quietly, I slipped the Balisarda into my bandolier.

We found Célie, Jean Luc, and Beau congregated beside the fire. Coco converged on them the same moment we did. Immediately, Célie thrust the unexceptional ring into her palm. "I found it," she repeated, breathless with excitement. With something else. When her eyes flicked to Coco's collar near imperceptibly, I followed the movement. A locket glittered there. "Here. Take it."

Coco examined the ring for a long moment before she smiled. "You *would* be the one to find it." With an appreciative nod to Célie, she handed it to Lou, who slipped it on her finger like it belonged there. I frowned. "Thank you, Célie."

"We should go," Beau urged. "Before Morgane comes back."

In agreement, we retreated down the stairs, but it wasn't Morgane who met us at the door.

It was Manon.

ASK ME NO QUESTIONS

Reid

Feet planted wide—arms gripping each side of the threshold—
she met us with a frighteningly blank expression. Trapping us
here. All traces of her tears had been scrubbed away since the
corridor below. "Chamomile tea, Louise?"

Lou edged to the front of our group, her hand brushing mine
as she passed. The touch tingled. I jerked away. "You looked like
you needed it," she said, gesturing to Manon's general dishevel-
ment. Her airy tone felt forced, as did her smile. "I'm assuming
you didn't heed my advice and drink it. When have you last
slept?" Manon didn't answer. Shouts below wiped the smile from
Lou's face all the same. Her eyes flew wide. "You—did you tell
my mother—?"

"Not yet. I had to be sure of the intruder. But I told others.
They will inform Our Lady soon."

"Shit, shit, shit. *Shit.*" Exhaling a harsh, incredulous breath,
Lou clenched her fists before seizing Manon's collar and yanking
her into the stairwell. Beau slammed the door behind them. "This

is fine. They don't know *I'm* here specifically. We can still—"

"You will not escape again, Louise," Manon said, her eyes still flat and unexpressive.

"Just—just—" Lou wrung a fist in the witch's face, and Manon stiffened like a board, unable to move. "Just shut up for a second, Manon. I need to think." To Coco, Jean Luc, and me, she said hastily, "We can't go out the way we came in. Any brilliant ideas?"

"We fight our way out," I said instantly.

Jean Luc's brow furrowed as he considered strategy. "There are six of us. Enemy numbers unknown. We've claimed the higher ground, but we'd need to form a choke point—"

I pounded my fist against the door. "We have one. They can't break the enchantment—"

"You're both idiots." Lou turned imploring eyes on Coco. "Was there anything in the treasury we could use?"

"Can't you just *show* them the Goddess has revoked Morgane's blessing?" Beau waved his hands wildly. "You *are* their queen now, correct?"

"Again, why didn't *I* think of that? I'll tell you what, Your Highness, why don't *you* command your people to stop burning witches, so all of our problems go away?" She turned back to Coco before he could answer. "There was magic fire."

Clenching her own eyes shut, Coco rubbed her temples. "And plated glass. I also saw chains and swords and—" Her gaze snapped to Lou's once more, and realization passed between them like a bolt of lightning.

"The window," they said together.

Lou nodded frenetically. "We'll need to climb."

Coco was already dragging Beau and Célie back up the steps. "It'll be risky—"

"No riskier than a choke point—"

The implication of their words finally settled in. My stomach churned. "*No.*"

"You'll be fine." Patting my arm in a distracted way, Lou raced toward the stairs. "I won't let you fall." When I made no move to follow—when the shouts behind grew louder—she lost patience, doubling back and yanking at my hand. I yielded one step. Not another. She spoke with frantic cajolement, still tugging. "*Please*, Reid. We have to climb, or we're never getting out of here. They won't just kill me. They'll kill you too. Horribly. Slowly. You want a *choke point*? You don't have a Balisarda, so you'll feel every single moment."

I bared my teeth in a grin. "I'll risk it."

Frustration flared in her eyes, and she lifted her hand once more. "If you don't move, I'll *make* you move."

"Please"—triumphant, I swept my coat aside, revealing the Balisarda and pivoting between her and the stairs—"do."

When her mouth fell open, astonished, I relished it. Relished her surprise, her fear, her—

The hilt of another knife smashed into my crown, and I staggered forward, into her. She tried to catch me. We both nearly broke our necks. Behind, Beau stood panting, knife still raised. "I don't need magic to knock your ass out. I'll *drag* you onto the roof if necessary. You aren't dying like this."

Jean Luc appeared beside him. They stood shoulder to shoulder, towering over me. As if they could intimidate. As if they could *threaten*—

"We can't defeat an entire castle of witches by ourselves," Jean Luc said, treacherous and cowardly in equal measure. Judas incarnate. "This is our best option. Get up the stairs, or I'll help him drag you."

Footsteps pounded louder now. Biting back a curse—because they were *right*—I seized Manon and sprinted past them. The scent of magic burst behind me as Lou relocked the door. Upstairs, she swung her arms in frantic movements. The treasure complied, settees and wardrobes shifting, stacking, to form a precarious ladder. "It's fine." Beau bent double, hands braced against his knees. "They can't get through the door. We have time—"

I flung Manon into an empty chair. "We don't."

Still rigid, she slid sideways to the floor. "They'll surround the castle soon." To Lou, she whispered, "I told you that you won't escape again."

"Oh, for fuck's sake." Lou stomped over as Jean Luc boosted Célie on top of the wardrobe. Beau and Coco scrambled up behind her. Crouching beside the witch's prostrate body, Lou flipped her over with another wave. Manon relaxed instantly, and Lou—I stared incredulously—she helped the witch sit up with gentle hands. "Morgane ordered you to kill your lover, Manon. Gilles is *dead* because of *her*. How can you still serve such a woman? How can you stand idly by as she tortures and kills *children*?"

Her words acted as a spark to kindling. Manon lurched forward with a feral snarl, snatching Lou's shoulders. "My *sister* is one of those dead children, and Morgane did not kill her. *I* did. Gilles died at no other's hands but my own. I made a *choice* in that ally— a choice I cannot undo. I have gone too far now to turn back." Tears spilled freely down her cheeks at the confession. When she spoke again, her voice broke. "Even if I wanted to."

I watched, stricken, as Lou hastily wiped her tears. "Listen to me, Manon. No, *listen*. Look around you"—she motioned to the others, to herself and to me—"and tell me what you see."

"I see *traitors*—"

"*Exactly*." Lou reached up to clutch Manon's wrists, eyes wide and imploring. "I betrayed my coven. Reid and Jean Luc have betrayed their Church, and Beau and Célie have betrayed their Crown. All of us—we're fighting for a better world, just like you are. We want the same thing, Manon. We want *peace*."

Manon's entire body trembled with emotion as her tears continued to fall. They stained Lou's lap. Stained the dirty floor between them, glittering bright in the firelight. At last, Manon dropped her hands. "You'll never have it."

Lou studied Manon's face wistfully for a moment— regretfully—before rising to her feet. "You're wrong. There are very few choices in life that can't be unmade, and the time has come for you to make another one. I won't restrain or otherwise harm you. Go. Tell Morgane you saw me if you must, but don't try to stop us. We're leaving."

Manon didn't move.

Lou stalked to the furniture without another word—then

hesitated. She glanced over her shoulder. Instead of Manon, however, her eyes found mine, and she spoke in a murmur. "You've stalled long enough, Reid. Climb up. I promise you won't fall."

I swallowed hard. Somehow, she knew my chest had tightened and my vision had narrowed. She knew my palms had started to sweat. She knew I'd hesitated beside Manon not to protect the group from her wrath, but to prolong the inevitable. To think of some way—*any* way—out of this room except the window. And that meant she knew my weakness, my vulnerability. Anger blazed through the thick paralysis of my thoughts, spurring me toward the furniture.

"Why did you get to keep yours?" Manon whispered behind us.

Sadness clouded Lou's face as she gazed back at me. "I didn't."

One by one, we squeezed through the window onto the roof. My head pounded. My heart raced. Twice on the furniture, my foot had slipped, and I'd nearly crashed to the floor. Though Lou had maintained a steady stream of encouragement, I longed to wring her neck. This rooftop could've been a steeple, a needle, so pitched was its slope.

"I *will* kill you for this," I promised her.

Crouching low, she peered over the eave to where the others scaled rock with their knives. Their limbs trembled with effort. With strain. "I look forward to it, believe me." She slipped her own knives from her boots. "Until then, do you think you can reach that turret?"

I followed the direction of her knife. Directly below us, at the base of the tower, a spire jutted from the side of the castle. It looked likely to collapse at any moment. "This is madness."

"You go first. I'll follow."

Peeling each finger from the shingles—they'd become my lifelines—I scooted down the slope. Lou crab walked beside me. "That's it." She nodded with excessive cheer, her eyes too bright. Her smile too wide. She either worried more than she said, or she enjoyed this more than she should. Both were unacceptable.

When I inched over the eave, my foot slipped a third time.

A rush of wind.

A sickening, weightless sensation.

And a hand.

Her hand.

It caught mine as it slipped from the edge, and her second followed, wrapping around my wrist. My vision swam with black spots as I dangled midair. As the wind roared past my ears. My heart thrashed wildly. I couldn't see her properly, couldn't hear her panicked instructions. There was only the ground looming beneath me, my body suspended midair. Helplessly, I clawed at her. Her arms shook beneath my weight.

"Lift me up!" My shouts sounded delirious to even my ears. "Lift me up *now*!"

A shadow shifted in her eyes at the command. She flashed a feline grin. "Tell me I'm pretty."

"I—*what?*"

"Tell me," she repeated in a hard voice, "that I'm pretty."

I stared at her for one heart-stopping moment. She couldn't be serious, yet she was. From her weak arms to her spiteful eyes to her sharp smile, she was *serious*. She could drop me—she *would* drop me—if I didn't appease her soon. She couldn't support my weight indefinitely. But what was she asking? For me to lie? To flatter her? No. She wanted something else. Something I couldn't give her. Through gritted teeth, I spat, "You said you wouldn't let me fall."

"You've said a lot of things."

I'd told her the truth. I wanted to kill her. To kill all of them. I couldn't concede to this heresy—this *grand romance* she'd dreamed up between us. As if it were possible. As if a witch and witch hunter could be more than enemies. I remembered none of it. I wanted to remember even less. In that second, however, the wind swept past with terrifying glee, and I glanced down. A mistake. Black edged my vision. My hand slipped a millimeter within hers. "Fine," I said quickly, loathing myself. Loathing her more. "You're . . . you are very pretty, Lou."

"The prettiest you've ever seen?"

I nearly wept in frustration. "Prettier, even. I can't think when I look at you."

She beamed, and the tension melted from her face as quickly as it'd come. Her arms stopped shaking. Too late, I realized her game: her magic couldn't work on *me* because of the Balisarda, but she'd used it to strengthen her own body instead. She'd been pretending to struggle this entire time. Stoking my fear. She probably could've lifted me with a single finger. Fresh anger burned white-hot in my chest. "Now," she said, immensely pleased with herself, "tell me that I'm an excellent singer."

"You—you—"

"I'm waiting," she trilled.

"You're an excellent singer. You sing like a bird. An angel. And if you don't lift me up this *second*, I'm going to snap your pretty neck."

She waited another second just to spite me. Then another. And another. "Well, now that we've sorted *that*." With a mighty heave, she pulled me over the eave once more. I collapsed beside her in a pool of shaking limbs, nearly retching at her feet.

"Don't you *ever* lie to me again."

She poked my cheek. "I wouldn't have dropped you."

"Lies!"

"Well"—she lifted an easy shoulder—"maybe I would've, but I wouldn't have let you splatter." Her smile turned almost self-deprecating. "Come on, Chass. I would've moved the entire castle before I let you die."

"*Why?*" The word burst from me, sudden and unbidden. This wasn't the time for such a question. This wasn't the place, either—not with witches crawling within and without. They probably gathered below even now, waiting to devour us. Manon would've told them. She would've pressed their advantage. No shouts sounded from the ground, however, and no magic ensnared us. "Why did you save me? Why did you let the witch go? You—you comforted her. You wiped her *tears*. We both want to *kill* you."

The realization shocked me into silence. Manon had wanted to kill her. I didn't know *how* I knew, but I did. Manon and La

Voisin and even Morgane, her own mother, wanted her dead. But—my thoughts congealed like mud—that wasn't quite right either. *I do not have a daughter*, Morgane had claimed. Could she too have forgotten her daughter, as I had forgotten my wife? Or had Lou lied about both? I regarded her suspiciously as she rose. "Why?" I repeated firmly.

Patting my cheek, she slipped over the eave without me. Her voice drifted upward with the wind. "Ask me no questions, *mon amour*, and I shall tell you no lies."

I frowned at the simple words. Then winced. These felt different than others, biting and snapping like insects. I shook my head to dislodge them, but they remained. They burrowed deeper. Familiar and painful and jarring. *Ask me no questions.* Though I remained on the rooftop, my vision pitched abruptly, and instead of shingles and smoke, I saw trees, gnarled roots, a bottle of wine. Blue-green eyes. Sickening déjà vu. *And I'll tell you no lies.*

No. I shook my head, wrenching free of the imagery, and stabbed my knife into stone. This was here. Another stab. This was real. I swung myself lower. This was now. *Stab, stab.* I didn't remember her. *Stab.* It hadn't happened. *Stab, stab, stab.*

I repeated the mantra the entire way down. I repeated it until those blue-green eyes faded with the trees and the wind and the Hollow. Fresh pain cleaved my head at the last. I ignored it, focusing on the world below me. The others waited for me in silence. No witches hid in the shadows. Manon, it seemed, had not betrayed us. I didn't understand it. Without looking at anyone, I jumped, landing heavy on my feet.

"Are you all right?" Lou steadied me instinctively. When I cringed away without answering, she sighed and motioned us toward the rocks behind the tower, slipping through the shadows like she'd been born there. I watched her go with a pang in my chest.

Ask me no questions, mon amour, *and I'll tell you no lies.* Another half-formed memory. Useless. Broken.

Like a witch hunter who couldn't kill a witch.

TRUTH OR DARE

Lou

Halfway through our return to L'Eau Mélancolique, Célie fell asleep on her horse. Jean Luc—who'd succumbed to a stupor hours ago—hadn't been able to catch her in time, and she'd plummeted face-first into the mud, bloodying her nose in the process. We'd quickly agreed a rest stop was necessary. Jean Luc had procured two rooms at the next inn, sneaking us in a back door under cover of darkness.

"I'll be back with food," he'd promised. Though smoke still obscured the night sky, it must've been between midnight and dawn. We'd made excellent time, all things considered—in and out of Chateau le Blanc in just over an hour. Still, few inns served supper at three in the morning. I suspected the sight of Jean Luc's blue coat, however, might've helped the innkeeper forget the aberrant hour.

Coco, Célie, and I claimed one of the rooms for ourselves while we waited, and Reid and Beau disappeared into the one next door. Almost immediately, Célie collapsed facedown on the hay-filled mattress, her breath deepening and her mouth falling open. The trickle of drool on her pillow painted her the quintessential gentlewoman. Coco and I each tugged a boot from her foot.

"I don't think I can make it to supper," Coco said, hiding a yawn behind her hand.

My stomach growled audibly. "I can."

"Save me some food, will you?"

I grinned as she flopped onto the bed beside Célie. It was a tight fit. Neither of them seemed to notice. "Will do."

Jean Luc edged the door open a few moments later, carrying a tray of dried figs, brioche, and comté. From the silver tureen at its center, the heavenly scent of beef stew drifted outward, curling around my nose. I immediately began to salivate, but he stopped short when he saw Coco and Célie. Lifting a finger to my lips, I plucked the fruit, bread, and cheese from the tray and left it on the table beside the bed. I motioned him back into the hallway, hesitating for only a second before breaking off a piece of cheese.

I loved cheese.

"They're exhausted." Closing the door behind me, I popped the morsel into my mouth and nearly moaned. "They can eat when they wake."

Though clearly irritated at the prospect of dining with me and not Célie, Jean Luc nodded and led me into the men's room. Beau had lit a candelabra on the dressing table, and it cast soft, ambient light over the sparse furnishings: a single bed, as in our room, and a porcelain bowl for washing. The entire place had a worn yet welcoming atmosphere, probably aided by the colorful quilt on the bed and warm wooden floors.

"The girls are asleep," Jean Luc grunted, kicking the door shut.

"Should I be insulted?" I pirouetted onto the bed, landing dramatically across Beau's lap. He sat with his back against the headboard and his legs stretched out in front of him, taking up more than his fair share of space. Snorting, he shoved me off the bed.

"Yes."

Unperturbed, I crossed the room to investigate the contents of the tureen, but Jean Luc knocked my hand aside. Ladling it into cracked wooden bowls, he jerked his chin behind him. "Go wash, for the love of God. Your hands are filthy."

Unfortunately, Reid stood beside the washbowl. He scowled as I approached, shifting subtly so as not to touch me. When I *accidentally* splashed him with water, he stalked to the other side of the room. "If we leave after breakfast, we'll reach L'Eau Mélancolique this afternoon," I said to no one in particular. Jittery energy coursed through me as I accepted my stew, and I inhaled it greedily—standing over the basin like a rat—to stop from filling the dead air between us. If this was the inner sanctum of masculinity, I wanted no part of it.

My eyes slid to Reid.

Well. I wanted *little* part of it.

We ate in silence until none of the stew remained. Then a light knock sounded on the door.

"Captain Toussaint?" a thin, unfamiliar voice asked. Jean

Luc's eyes flew wide, and he wheeled to face us, mouthing, *The innkeeper.* "My humblest apologies, but might I enter for just a moment? My wife scolded me for my appalling lack of manners below, and she's quite right. I have a bottle of whiskey as recompense—we distill it here with my brother's own wheat"— his voice rose with pride—"and I'd be delighted to pour you a drink personally."

"Er—" Jean Luc cleared his throat. "Just—just leave it at the door."

It sounded like a question.

"Oh." It was a gift of this innkeeper, surely, to pack so much disappointment into one small word. "Oh, well, yes. Quite right. How rude of me. It is very late, of course, and I'm sure you need your rest. My humblest apologies," he said again. The bottle plunked against the door. "Good night, then, Captain."

His footsteps didn't recede. I could almost picture him hovering in the corridor beyond, perhaps leaning an ear against the wood, hoping the great captain would pity him and change his mind. Reid and I exchanged an anxious glance.

As if on cue, Jean Luc groaned quietly. "Er—Monsieur Laurent?" He shot us an apologetic look before hastily stacking our bowls and chucking them behind the washbasin. My eyes narrowed in disbelief. Surely he couldn't mean to—? "I'd love a drink. Please, come in."

Reid, Beau, and I could do nothing but scramble for hiding places, except the room held very little. As the smallest of the three, I dove beneath the bed. As the stupidest, Beau crouched behind the dressing table in plain sight. And Reid, unable to find another spot—not at all small but perhaps stupider than even Beau—rolled under the bed after me, snaking an arm around my waist to prevent me from spilling out the other side. The movement squashed my face against his chest, and I reared back, clutching his collar furiously. *What the hell is wrong with you?*

He rolled to his back, glaring at me, as Monsieur Laurent strode into the room.

"Oh, you can't imagine how pleased Madame Laurent will be, Captain, to know you're tasting our whiskey. She'll be ever so pleased. Thank you, thank you."

Reid's enormous body blocked my view of the room, so slowly, carefully, I leaned over his chest, peering out from across his shoulder. He held very still. He might've even stopped breathing.

Monsieur Laurent was a tall, reedy fellow in his nightclothes and slippers, and he fussed with two tumblers at the dressing table. Jean Luc shifted covertly to hide Beau. "I am honored to taste it, *monsieur.* Thank you again for providing us lodging at such an untimely hour. My companion sleeps in the next room," he added, accepting the proffered glass of amber liquid. He sipped it quickly.

"I must say"—Monsieur Laurent sampled his own glass, leaning against the table with the air of a man getting comfortable—"I was quite shocked to see you on my doorstep, Captain." He chuckled. "Well, I don't have to tell you, do I? Apologies again for the less than warm welcome. One can never be too safe these days. The witches are getting bolder, and they're thick in these parts. You should hear the ghastly sounds of the forest at night." Shuddering, he readjusted his nightcap, revealing a high, balding forehead. Despite his casual tone, beads of nervous sweat gleamed there. He feared Jean Luc. No—my eyes narrowed shrewdly— he feared Jean's blue coat. "Anyway, I assumed most Chasseurs would be in Cesarine with the conclave." He took another hearty drink of whiskey. "I assume you heard news of the trials?"

Jean Luc—who, to my knowledge, hadn't heard news of any such thing—nodded and emptied his glass. "I'm forbidden to speak on such matters."

"Ah, of course, of course. Very good of you, sir." When Monsieur Laurent moved to refill his glass, Jean Luc shook his head, and the innkeeper's expression fell. He recovered from his disappointment almost immediately, however, perhaps a touch relieved, and downed the rest of his whiskey in a single swallow. "I shall leave you to it, then. Please accept the bottle as a mark of our thanks—it isn't every day one houses a hero. We are honored, sir, just *honored*, to have you here."

Reid lay so still and so tense he might've grown roots beneath this bed. Jaw clenched, he glared at the slats overhead without blinking as Monsieur Laurent showed himself from the room, and Jean Luc closed the door once more. The key clicked in the lock.

Reid didn't move for a second, clearly grappling with his desire to flee from me and his desire to hide from Jean Luc forever. I studied his rigid profile in the backlight. I supposed it . . . hurt. To hear Monsieur Laurent's reverence for the person he used to be, the person he could never be again. Jean Luc held that honor now, though truthfully, if he kept hiding witches under his bed, that privilege wouldn't be his for much longer either. Unable to help it, I brushed a lock of copper hair from Reid's forehead. "He doesn't know."

"Who doesn't know what?" he snapped.

"The innkeeper. He doesn't know who he has here." When he shook his head, disgusted—at me, at himself, at the entire situation—I said firmly, "He doesn't know what heroism means."

"And you do?" He turned to sneer at me. "Are you a hero, Louise le Blanc?"

"No. But you are."

Though he pushed my hand away, he still didn't move to leave. "I used to be. Now I'm hiding under a bed with a witch. Did you know I was found in the garbage?" When I said nothing, he scoffed, shaking his head again. "Of course you did. You know everything about me, don't you?" His eyes blazed with emotion in this small, shadowed sanctuary—and a sanctuary it was. Here, cramped and hidden from the rest of the world, we could've been the only two people alive. "Then you know I grew up lost. I grew up alone. They called me trash boy, and I fought tooth and nail for respect—I bloodied noses and broke bones to get it—and I killed the one person who called me family. Does that sound like a hero to you?"

A lump rose in my throat at his expression. He could've been that lost, lonely little boy all over again. "Reid—"

Beau's head popped under the bed. "What are you two whispering about under here?"

As if I'd lit a match in his trousers, Reid surged away from me, up and out of sight. Beau watched him go with a startled expression before extending a hand to me. In his other, he held the neck of the whiskey bottle. "Any luck with the seduction?"

"None, thanks to you."

"I have to protect my investment. But his memories . . . ?"

I frowned. "Coco thinks—"

"I know what Coco thinks." He hooked an arm around my neck, pulling me closer. Reid watched us sullenly from the farthest corner of the room. "I want to know what *you* think. Wager aside, would you rather we focus on restoring his memories? I know we can't force him to reverse the pattern, but perhaps we could help him along."

The weight of his words settled heavy in my chest. A choice. He'd offered me a choice. Free of judgment or disapproval, free of guidance, he'd led me to a fork in the road, and he now waited patiently for me to step left or right. He would follow whatever direction I chose. Except . . . I glanced at Reid. He'd already made a choice—a *stupid* choice, but a choice nonetheless. He'd stepped without consulting me, but he'd obviously thought it necessary. *Had* it been necessary? Morgane had forgotten me, yes, but she hadn't forgotten her wrath against the Church and Crown. The kingdom was in more danger now than ever.

I'll find you, Lou. I promise.

I feigned a smile and flicked Beau's nose. "Don't think you're getting out of our wager."

"I'd never dream of it, sister mine." Still speaking low, he released me with a wink and a grin of his own—our understanding implicit—and wagged the bottle of whiskey in my face. "Perhaps an olive branch, just for tonight? I don't much feel like sleeping."

Snatching the bottle, I downed a gulp. The whiskey burned all those unspoken words from my tongue. All the fear and doubt and restlessness. I swallowed another. "Nor I."

"Now who's whispering," Reid grumbled.

We both looked to Jean Luc, who'd thrown his coat on the dressing table. I lifted my voice and the bottle simultaneously. "What about you, dear captain? Can we tempt you?"

"I'm going to bed. Poison yourselves all you'd like."

I lifted a hand to my mouth, addressing Beau in a mock whisper. "He doesn't want to play."

Jean Luc paused in pulling back the quilt. "Play what?"

"Truth or dare." Batting my lashes, I took another long pull before handing the bottle to Beau. "Just a couple of questions to pass the time until we fall asleep."

"Until you pass out, you mean." He flicked the quilt back and began to climb beneath it. "No, thank you."

"That's probably for the best." I leaned into Beau conspiratorially, my limbs already pleasantly warm. He chuckled in response, a sturdy and familiar presence at my side. An anchor against my riotous thoughts. *You know everything about me, don't you? They called me trash boy.* "I've been spending *lots* of time with Célie lately, so I have all sorts of juicy secrets I might've let slip."

He lurched up instantly—then narrowed his eyes. Slowly, he sank back onto the bed. "I know what you're doing."

"What do you mean?"

"I know what you're *doing*," he repeated, voice emphatic, "and it isn't the reason why I've decided to humor you. Give me the bottle." Beau slapped it in his outstretched hand, and his throat worked on an enormous swallow. Wiping his mouth, he handed it to Reid next. "You start."

Reid examined the bottle in distaste. "I'm not playing."

"Oh, come on, Chass." I rose to my tiptoes, clasping my hands together at my chest and swaying. "Please? I *promise* I won't make you measure your dick against Jean Luc's."

Jean Luc smirked. "Now that *is* for the best. I wouldn't want to embarrass anyone."

Spluttering, Reid's knuckles whitened on the bottle. "You—you can't—" He grimaced. "What are the rules?"

"Rules are simple." Beau plucked the bottle from his hand before draping himself across the end of the bed. I sank to the floor, still cackling with triumph, and curled my legs beneath me. "You choose a truth, or you a choose a dare. If you choose neither"—he lifted the whiskey meaningfully—"you drink. Sound fair?"

Reid remained standing, crossing his arms and glaring down at us like some sort of pink-cheeked, vengeful god.

I sort of liked it.

"I'll go first." Jean Luc cleared his throat and rested his elbows on his knees. His light eyes found mine. "Lou: Truth or dare?"

"Dare."

His shoulders slumped. Clearly, I hadn't given the answer he'd wanted, and clearly, he hadn't prepared a dare in advance. He waved a flippant hand. "I dare you to cut your hair with one of my knives."

I laughed and took a shot of whiskey without a word.

"My turn." Rubbing my hands together, I turned to Reid—then hesitated. This was my first real chance to woo him outside of our usual circumstances, outside of L'Eau Mélancolique, the heist, the rooftop. Outside of danger. I needed to make it count, yet every thought fled my mind as I stared at him. That suspicious gleam in his eyes—the clench of his jaw and the flex of his arms—he might as well have been impenetrable. Like Jean Luc, he knew my game, and he didn't want to play.

How *had* I wooed him in Cesarine?

I wracked my brain, trying and failing to remember. Trapped in Chasseur Tower, surrounded by my enemies, I'd been jagged and sharp and guarded most days, lashing out at the slightest provocation. I'd tried to embarrass him, demean him. I'd mostly succeeded in that endeavor, yet still he'd softened toward me. Still I'd softened toward *him*. How? When? Already, the whiskey slurred my thoughts if not my words, eddying them into a single memory of warmth and nostalgia. There'd been a bathtub and a shared bed in Chasseur Tower, and there'd been books and plays and gowns—

I fought a frustrated groan. Through the thin walls, Coco's snores echoed. She hadn't yet trained me in the subtle art of seduction—if such a thing existed. I hadn't needed it before. He'd simply . . . loved me—despite everything—and that love had led him to this heinous choice, to forget me, to save me.

I would honor it.

It wasn't as if I could reverse the pattern anyway. Even as La Dame des Sorcières. If he couldn't remember our past, I would forge a new future, and I sealed the promise with another swig. "Truth or dare, Reid."

He didn't miss a beat. "Dare."

Shrugging, I pointed the bottle at him. "I dare you to strip naked and dance the *bourrée*. While we watch," I added swiftly when he moved toward the door. I couldn't help my grin. He'd always been unexpectedly quick. "Not out in the hallway."

He scowled and halted mid-step. "Truth."

"Tell me how you're feeling in this exact moment."

"Give me the bottle." He seized it before I could protest, and I smothered my disappointment. Perhaps this was better. Alcohol was its own sort of truth. With a few more shots, he'd become a plethora of information.

"Well, this is going to get ugly early," Beau mused. "I should like to go next. Louise, darling"—he flashed me a charming smile—"truth or dare? And please pick truth."

I rolled my eyes. "Truth."

He gave a feline grin. "Who is the most attractive person here? Be honest, mind you, or it's two drinks."

Winking lewdly, I extended my entire arm toward Reid, condemning him with a finger. "That man there. The copper-haired fellow. He's the one."

Reid scowled and interrupted immediately. "My turn. Lou, what is your deepest fear?"

"You didn't ask truth or dare," I pointed out.

His scowl deepened. "Truth or dare."

"Dare."

"I *dare* you to answer my question."

I chuckled and sat back, crossing my feet at the ankles. *Unexpectedly quick.* Still, his question itself left much to be desired. Of course he'd try to weaponize a game. Of course he'd press every advantage to weaken me. *Well, tough shit, buddy.* "It used to be death," I said conversationally, "but a quick chat with our dear friend Ansel changed that. He's thriving, by the way." All three of the men stared at me with slack jaws. Beau in particular seemed to blanch. "He spoke with me in L'Eau Mélancolique. He'd been following us the entire time, you know—"

"What?" Beau asked incredulously. "*How?*"

"He was a white dog."

"Oh, good Lord." Beau fell back against the quilt, pinching the bridge of his nose. "You mean *the* white dog? I thought he was an *ill omen.*" At my snort, he exclaimed, "He was always there when calamity struck!"

"Probably to *warn* you."

"I didn't realize that he'd—I haven't seen him since—" He swallowed hard. "What happened to him?"

"He found peace." The room fell silent at my gentle words, and I stared intently at my hands, knitting them together in my lap. "But he also made me realize I don't fear death at all. Or at least, it isn't the dying itself that I fear. It isn't the pain. It's the parting with my loved ones forever." I looked up. "But I'll see him again. We all will."

Reid looked as though I'd struck him across the face. He remembered Ansel too, then, if only as an initiate. He remembered his death. Perhaps he just hadn't expected I would mourn, that I'd be capable of such deep feeling for another person—me, a *witch*. I cleared my throat. "I believe it's your turn, Jean Luc."

He immediately looked to Beau. "Truth or dare."

"Truth."

"Did Célie mention me on your travels?"

"Yes." He turned to Reid without expounding on the answer, despite Jean Luc's vehement protests. "Truth or dare."

"Dare."

Another grin. This one harder. "I dare you to magic that copper hair blue."

Reid's face flushed puce. "I can't—how dare you—"

"Compartmentalization isn't healthy, brother. You saw your face on that wanted poster with the naughty W-word, yet I don't think you've acknowledged it." He arched a brow in challenge. "Denial is the first stage of grief."

"Truth," Reid said through gritted teeth.

"Yes, it is." Beau leaned forward earnestly. "Why can't you stop looking at our lovely Louise?"

If possible, Reid's face flushed deeper. It looked physically uncomfortable now, the amount of blood in his cheeks. I started giggling. "Because I want to *kill* her—"

"Ah, ah, ah." Beau wagged a reproving finger before tapping the bottle in Reid's hand. "A lie means two."

When Reid furiously swallowed two shots—without hesitation, without denying his falsehood—an entirely different kind of warmth cracked open in my chest, flowing through my limbs. I sat up on my knees, bouncing with exhilaration. The room swirled with a lovely, rosy hue. "Truth or dare, Jean Luc."

He didn't even pretend to be interested. "Truth."

"Do you regret what happened on Modraniht?"

A beat of silence passed.

Reluctantly, his eyes flicked to Reid, who looked downright murderous now. Or downright nauseous. Still, he didn't interrupt the game, and the sudden sharpness in his own eyes betrayed his interest. He wanted to know this truth. He wanted to know it very much. After a moment, Jean Luc scrubbed a hand down his face and muttered, "Yes and no. I don't regret following orders. The rules exist for a reason. Without them, we have chaos. Anarchy." He heaved a sigh, not looking at anyone now. "But I do regret the rules themselves." Dropping his hand, he asked Reid, "Truth or dare?"

"Truth."

"Is your heart still with the Chasseurs?"

They stared at each other for another long moment. I leaned forward eagerly, holding my breath, while Beau pretended not to listen and hung on every word. Reid tore his gaze away first, breaking the silence. "Is yours?"

Jean Luc leaned over and plucked the whiskey from his hand. After swallowing, he climbed to his feet and handed me the bottle on his way out. "I think I'm done for the night."

The door clicked shut behind him.

"And then there were three," Beau murmured, still toying

with the edge of the quilt. He winked at me abruptly. "I dare you to lick the bottom of my shoe."

Another half hour of antics ensued. The dares from Beau and me grew more and more ridiculous—*serenade us, do four cartwheels, curse like a sailor for twenty seconds straight*—while the questions grew more personal—*What's the grossest thing you've ever had in your mouth? To come out of your body?*—until Reid was good and thoroughly drunk. He staggered over to me at his next turn, crouching down and dropping a heavy hand on my shoulder. Grayish light tinged the window.

His voice slurred. "What's the biggest lie you've ever told?"

I might've snorted whiskey from my nose. "I never told you I was a witch. In Chasseur Tower. You never knew."

"That's stupid. How could I not have known?"

"An *excellent* question—"

"Lou, my darling sister"—Beau flung an arm over his face in a truly dramatic fashion, still lounging on the bed—"you must tell me: Do Coco and I stand a chance?"

"Of course you do! She's head over heels for you. Anyone can see that."

"Does *she* see that?" He peered at me through bleary eyes. The bottle in his hand held an alarming amount of whiskey now—which was to say, not much at all. "She called me Ansel, you know. The other day. She didn't mean it, of course, but it just sort of slipped"—he began to tip the bottle over the quilt, but I crossed the room and snatched it from him just in time—"out. She'd been laughing at a joke I'd made." He looked up at me suddenly, his gaze sharper and clearer. Calmer. "She has a lovely laugh, doesn't she? I love her laugh."

Gently, I pressed him back against the pillow. "You love more than her laugh, Beau."

His lashes fluttered. "We're all going to die, aren't we?"

"No." I pulled the blanket to his chin, tucking it around him. "But I dare you to tell her anyway."

"Tell her . . ." His voice drifted on an enormous yawn. ". . . what?"

"That you love her."

He laughed again as his eyes finally closed, and his body succumbed to sleep.

And then there were two.

I turned to face Reid, startled to find him directly behind me. His eyes fixed on mine with a deep, unsettling intensity that hadn't been there before. "Truth or dare."

Butterflies erupted in my belly as he stepped closer still. Heat washed across every inch of my skin. "Truth."

He shook his head slowly.

I swallowed hard. "Dare."

"Kiss me."

My mouth parted without volition as I looked up at him—as I saw that primal fascination in his eyes—but even through the fugue of alcohol, of keen, desperate *want*, I forced myself back a step. He followed intently. His hand lifted to cradle the nape of my neck. "Reid. You don't—you're drunk—"

The tips of his boots met my bare toes. "What is this between us?"

"A lot of alcohol—"

"I feel like I know you."

"You did know me once." I shrugged helplessly, struggling to breathe at his proximity. At his heat. This glint in his eyes—he hadn't looked at me like this since before the beach. Not on the horse, not on the bridge or in the treasury, not even beneath this very bed. My gaze darted to the whiskey in my hand, and that heat in my belly felt more like nausea now. *Alcohol is its own form of truth.* "But now you don't."

His hand edged to the side of my throat, and his thumb brushed my jaw. "We were . . . romantic."

"Yes."

"Then why are you frightened?"

I clutched his wrist to prevent his thumb from moving to my lips. Every instinct in my body raged against me. Every instinct craved his touch. *Not like this.* "Because this isn't real. You'll wake up with a throbbing headache in a couple of hours, and you'll want to kill me all over again."

"Why?"

"Because I'm a witch."

"You're a witch." He repeated the words slowly, languidly, and I couldn't help it—I leaned into his palm. "And I know you." When he swayed on his feet, my own hands shot to his waist, steadying him. He leaned down to bury his nose in my hair and inhaled deeply. "I've never been drunk before."

"I know."

"You know me."

"I do."

"Truth or dare."

"Truth."

His fingertips traced my scar, and he leaned lower, brushing his nose along the curve of my neck and shoulder. "Why do you have roses on your throat?"

I clung to him helplessly. "My mother disfigured me with hate. Coco transformed me with hope."

He paused then, drawing back slightly to look at me. A nameless emotion shadowed his gaze as it flicked from my scar to my lips. "Why do you smell so sweet?"

Though pressure built behind my eyes, I ignored it, hoisting one of his arms over my shoulders. He would collapse soon. Clumsy with alcohol, his movements lacked their typical grace—lacked even basic coordination—and he continued to sway on his feet. Fervently, I prayed he wouldn't remember any of this tomorrow. I shouldn't have let him drink so much. Pain spiked through my right temple. *I* shouldn't have drunk so much. With slow, heavy footsteps, I lugged him across the room toward the bed. "What do I smell like, Reid?"

His head fell upon my shoulder. "Like a dream." When I deposited him carefully beside Beau—his entire leg spilling free from the mattress—his hand caught my own and lingered there, even after his eyes had fluttered shut. "You smell like a dream."

THE HANGOVER

Reid

I felt as if I'd been hit by a runaway horse.

Our own horses shifted nervously in the alley behind the inn, snorting and stamping their feet. I gripped their reins tighter. Dull pain throbbed behind my eyes. When my stomach rose suddenly, I turned away from them, clenching my eyes against the weak morning light. "Never again," I promised them bitterly.

I would never imbibe another ounce of liquor for as long as I lived.

The horse nearest me lifted his tail and defecated in response.

The smell nearly undid me. Pressing a fist to my mouth, I struggled to tether their reins to the post and fled to our rooms once more. Inside, the others packed the last of their belongings with slow, sluggish movements. Except for Coco and Célie. Smirking, Coco watched from the bed, while Célie flitted to and fro in an effort to help. But she didn't help. Instead, she talked. Loudly.

"Why didn't you wake me?" She swatted Jean Luc's arm before bending to search under the bed for his missing boot. "You know

I have *always* wanted to try whiskey, and you all drank an entire bottle without me! And played truth or dare too! How could you leave me to sleep in the next room while you had all the fun?"

"It wasn't fun," Beau muttered, accepting his shirt from Lou. Sometime in the course of the night, it'd ended up in the wash-bowl. He wrung it out now with a miserable expression. "Fun is the last word I'd use to describe it, actually. Can you stop talking now, darling?"

"Oh, nonsense!" Abandoning her search beneath the bed, Célie rose and planted her hands on her hips. "I want to know every single detail. What questions did you ask? What dares did you undertake? Is that"—her eyes fell to a dark smear on the corner of the dressing table—"is that blood?"

I strode to wipe it away, cheeks hot, mumbling, "Fell doing a cartwheel."

"Oh my goodness! Are you all right? Actually—never mind. Forget I asked. Clearly, you all had a *grand* time without me, so a little blood can be your penance. You *do* have to tell me every-thing that transpired, however, since you couldn't be bothered to invite me. Fortunately, we have plenty of time to recount every detail on our way to L'Eau Mélancolique—"

Jean Luc seized her shoulders then, his eyes bloodshot and pleading. "I love you, Célie, but please—shut up."

"Hear, hear," Beau said, lifting his shoe.

Though she narrowed her eyes at each of them, it was Coco who interrupted, her voice rising to a shout. "What's that?" She grinned wider at our collective wince. Each word was a spike through my eyes. "You can't hear us? Célie, darling, we must speak up for them."

Célie grinned now too. "Of *course*, Cosette. How abominably rude of us! Shall I repeat everything I've just said?"

"I think that would be the courteous thing to do."

"You're right. It would be. What I *said* was—"

"Please—" Beau turned helplessly to Lou, who sat on the floor at the foot of the bed, folding her soiled clothes and replacing them in her pack. My stomach twisted anew at the sight of her. Fresh bile rose in my throat. She hadn't acknowledged anyone this morning. Including me. I could've been sick from shame alone—from the memory of her skin, soft and sweet. Its scent haunted me still.

I'd dared her to *kiss* me.

Stalking to the washbowl to splash my face, I swallowed acid.

When she didn't answer, Beau tapped her shoulder, and she looked up with a vacant expression. Her face wan. Her freckles stark. "Can you force them to shut up somehow?" he asked her. "Perhaps solder their vocal cords?"

Lou lifted a hand to her ears, pulling a small piece of fabric from each of them. "What's that?"

We all stared at her.

Earplugs. She'd made *earplugs* from a piece of the innkeeper's quilt. Beau snatched them from her with an air of reverence, stuffing them into his own ears. "You're an evil genius."

But Lou didn't laugh. She only blinked. Her eyes focused on the room slowly, as if she'd been lost in thought. She still held an undergarment in one hand when she asked, "Should we send word to Claud somehow? About Morgane?" The hateful woman's words echoed between us: *The time is now. The trees have mobilized, and we shall follow, striking hard and true while the conclave deliberates.* "We should really warn Blaise too, and both should know about Isla. We can coordinate some sort of defense—"

I couldn't prevent a scoff. "You think mermaids and were-wolves can coordinate anything?"

Her gaze sharpened abruptly. "I think every plan we've ever *coordinated* has been complete and utter shit and ended in total disaster."

"We need them," Coco agreed firmly, cinching her bag and standing. "I'll send word to them from the beach." She paused. "After Isla agrees to help us."

As one, we all looked to the ring on Lou's finger. She twisted it nervously. "Do you think we can trust her?" Her eyes met Coco's across the room. "Can we trust your mother?"

"We held up our end of the agreement." Coco shrugged. "And the waters prevent falsehood."

"Right." Lou continued twisting the ring. Twisting and twist-ing and twisting. "And—what's the conclave? What are they *deliberating*?"

It was Jean Luc who answered. "Religious leaders from throughout the kingdom have gathered in Cesarine to elect a new Archbishop. They're also"—he cleared his throat, abruptly busy with his satchel—"they're *eliciting* information from Madame Labelle."

The word fell heavy with meaning.

"Eliciting," Lou repeated.

Jean Luc still wouldn't look at her. "Hellfire continues to ravage the city."

"What does *eliciting* mean?" Coco asked him, undeterred.

"You know what it means."

They all stared at me in the ensuing silence. Heat prickled my neck. My face. "I don't care."

Lou pushed to her feet. "She's your mother."

"I *said* I don't care." With a snarl, I pivoted to return to the horses—regretting my decision to rejoin the group, to rejoin *her*—but Célie pointed to my bag with a frown.

"Erm . . . Reid? Your satchel is moving."

My satchel is . . . Her words pierced my thoughts a second too late. I glanced down.

Then I threw my bag across the room.

Something within it shrieked as it hit the wall. Seeds and clothing and weapons spilled forth, along with what looked like a pastry and a—and a *rat*. Célie screamed and leapt atop the bed. Beau joined her. Lou, however, swooped to seize the pastry as the rat bolted through a crack in the wall. She held it up between two fingers. "Is this what I think it is?"

"How should I know?" Furious, I swept the seeds back into their pouch. Jean Luc handed me my shirt. My pants. I stuffed them away without ceremony. Then I snatched the pastry from her. "Whatever it is, it's mine."

"This is a sticky bun." She didn't let go. "Have you had this

x

425

with you the entire time?"

The bun tore between our fingers. "I don't remember."

"Do you remember buying it?"

"No."

"Clearly you bought it for me, then. It's *mine*."

"It isn't yours—"

Célie cleared her throat as we continued to grapple over the admittedly stale pastry. "A rat *was* just eating that, correct?"

"Not all of it." Eyes blazing, Lou tugged hard, and the bun tore in two. She moved to take a mighty bite.

Fire lit in my own chest, and I swiped at it. "Give that back—"

Coco slapped the bun from her hand before I could. "No," she said, matter-of-fact. "We won't be doing that." Dropping the pouch of seeds into my bag, she turned to resume her own packing. "Get along, children."

Lou and I glared at each other.

THE RIFT

Lou

The mist enveloped us later that afternoon.

We dismounted into it at the edge of the path, glancing around for signs of life. Constantin had died; did that mean the waters held no guardian? Could we simply . . . walk to shore? *Should* we?

"Beau, Célie, and Jean Luc, you should all stay here, just in case," I whispered. "Isla's magic protected you before, but we don't know if she'll extend the same courtesy this time. I'll take the ring to her." I looked to Coco. "Will you come too?"

Without a word, she looped her arm through mine in an admirable effort of normalcy. But there was nothing normal about this place. Nothing normal about how we simultaneously bent to draw knives from our boots. Despite the daylight hour, smoke still clouded the sun, and mist darkened the land to perpetual twilight. The latter clung to us as we stepped forward, dense as water, and limited our visibility—which was why we both shrieked when Reid's hand snaked out and caught my elbow. "Don't even think about it."

I shook him off with an indignant cry. "Don't *do* that! If you want to tag along, fine, but *announce* yourself next time. I could've chopped off your hand!"

Coco's eyes narrowed. "He might plan worse."

He glared at her, the fog undulating around his towering frame. "I don't trust either of you. You aren't leaving my sight."

"You aren't exactly endearing yourself to us," Coco said, poisonously sweet.

"I have a Balisarda. There could be witches here."

"Oh, there *are* witches here."

He gritted his teeth. "Manon could've told them what we stole. They could be waiting."

She pretended to consider this for a moment before shrugging. "Fine. As long as you don't stick that Balisarda into *me* instead." It was a mark of how far they'd both come that she turned her back on him, pulling me forward. He followed without comment.

We walked the path as quietly as possible, listening for any sound, but there were none. Not the rustle of leaves or the crash of waves or the cries of gulls. No, this silence was a living creature all its own, unnatural and thick and oppressive. When we stepped onto the beach, we hesitated, blinking into the abrupt sunlight and standing closer together than we normally would've.

"Do we just throw the ring in, or—?"

As if my whisper had broken some sort of spell, Angelica materialized from the water like a specter, silent and ethereal, water streaming from her gown of pure silver. When her eyes landed on Coco, her tranquil face broke into a breathtaking smile. "Cosette. You've returned."

"I told you I would."

Tugging the golden ring from my hand, I hastily extended it to her. "Here. It's yours."

"Thank you, Louise." Her smile faded as she examined the simple band in her palm. Though it sparkled innocently in the sun, we both knew better. Its history had been forged in death and magic until the two had become one. "It has been a long time since I've seen this ring." Regretfully, her eyes lifted to Coco. "Almost twenty years, in fact."

"Does this mean Isla agrees to help us?" I asked.

She ignored me, instead moving to clasp Coco's hands. "Daughter. Events have been set in motion. I fear this is the last opportunity we shall have to speak."

Coco pulled away halfheartedly. "I told you I don't want to talk."

"You must."

"No—"

Angelica dropped her voice to a fervent whisper, drawing closer, but in the silence, her voice still carried. We heard every word. "Please understand. I *never* wanted to leave you, but the thought of you trapped underwater for your entire life—like a fish in a bowl, examined and admired and wooed—I couldn't bear it. You deserved so much more. Believe me. I have watched you always, desperate to join you on the surface."

Now Coco did tear her hands away. "So why didn't you?"

"You know that answer."

"I know you're *afraid*."

"You're right," Angelica continued to whisper, "I abandoned

you to a cruel woman in hopes that she would love you, that she would give you the tools to chart your own path—and she did. You outgrew her. You've outgrown us both."

"Talk to me, Chass," I hissed, wishing desperately that Beau hadn't thieved my earplugs.

He regarded me with open suspicion. "About what?"

"Anything. Whatever comes to—"

"You can try to justify it all you'd like." Coco didn't bother to lower her voice. "How many times did I visit this beach, crying for you? How many times did you ignore me?"

"You would've lived a half life with me, Cosette. I wanted more for you."

Unable to help myself, I glanced behind to see Coco staring at her mother incredulously. "What about what *I* wanted, *maman*? You and *tante*—all either of you have ever cared about is this stupid feud. I'm the collateral damage, aren't I? I'm the one who suffers."

"We *all* have suffered," Angelica said sharply. "Do not mistake me, Cosette. Your aunt and I were among the very first of witchkind. Yes"—she nodded at Coco's dumbfound expression—"I have lived a hundred lives. Perhaps more, even. Time passed differently then." To me, she lifted an impatient hand. "Come, Louise le Blanc. You should hear this too. A battle brews on the horizon more catastrophic than this world has ever seen, and we must all play our parts. This is mine."

I crept closer tentatively. "We really don't have time for this. Morgane has already started for Cesarine—"

"If you wish to defeat your mother—and my sister—you will make time."

Her tone brooked no argument, and in the next second, she'd drawn a thin blade from her sleeve, slicing it across the palm of each hand. Her blood spilled thick upon the sand, and from it, black vines curled upward into the shape of chairs. She pointed to them, blood still trickling down her wrists. Tiny blooms of purple aconite sprouted where it dripped to the beach. "Sit. Now. I will not ask again."

Aconite meant *caution*.

I grabbed Reid's sleeve and forced him to sit, sinking into my own chair without further argument. Opposite me, Coco did the same, and Angelica stood in the center of our macabre little circle. She pivoted slowly to look each of us directly in the eyes. "This is your story—all of yours—so listen now and listen well. In the beginning, magic lived within all witches. Yes, you heard me correctly, Louise," she added when I tried to interrupt. "Though you call us Dames Rouges now, your ancestors' magic was closer to ours than to yours. It coursed through their blood, hummed in their veins. They lived in harmony with nature, never taking more than they gave and never defying the natural way. They lived. They died. They thrived." She bowed her head. "I was one of these original witches, as was my twin sister, Josephine."

"What happened?" Coco whispered.

Angelica sighed. "What always happens? In time, some among us desired more—more power, more freedom, more *life*. When a sect of my kin began experimenting with death, a great rift rose between us." Angelica knelt before Coco now, clasping her hands once more. "Your aunt was among them. I pleaded with Josephine to turn back, to forget this obsession with immortality, but when I caught her eating an infant's heart, I could ignore her sickness no longer. I had to act." A new vine crept up Coco's chair from Angelica's tears. Like the aconite, its petals bloomed purple, but this wasn't aconite at all. It was deadly nightshade. "I forbade my sister from returning to Chateau le Blanc."

"You lived there?" I asked in astonishment.

"We all did. That is what I'm trying to tell you, Louise— this is the great rift between Dame Blanche and Dame Rouge. Though I forbade Josephine from returning, she did not heed my warning, instead gathering the like-minded and organizing a rebellion." Shuddering, she pushed to her feet, and the bella-donna vine slithered higher, curling around the back of Coco's chair. "I've never seen such blood."

I stared at her, heart pounding, as another memory resur-faced: blood running as a river from the temple, soaking the hair and hems of fallen witches in its path. *The Rift.* And suddenly, it made sense—I hadn't seen Coco within this memory at all. I'd seen Angelica. *Angelica* had been the faceless woman.

She closed her eyes now. "They killed them. Our kin. Our mothers and sisters and aunts and nieces—all gone within a sin-gle night, butchered like animals. Despite everything, however, Josephine couldn't kill me. Not after our blood oath."

"She couldn't torture you," I said in dawning realization.

"No, but she *could* banish me, and she did so without hesitation. We would not meet again for many years." Her hands shifted to her elbows, and she seemed to bow into herself. "I watched from afar as her Dames Rouges reaped their just rewards, as they realized the steep cost of their victory—all witchlings born after the massacre held no magic within them. Whether their slain sisters or the Goddess herself had cursed them, I do not know. Forced to draw their magic from the land—and follow the natural order—their daughters, the first Dames Blanches, soon outnumbered their foremothers. My sister's influence dwindled as her experiments continued, growing darker and darker in nature. The Dames Blanches grew suspicious of her, and when the time was right, I capitalized on their hatred, on their fear, returning to the Chateau and driving Josephine from the throne."

Shooting to my feet, I began to pace, my thoughts sporadic and incomplete. "But I didn't know you *were* a blood witch."

"No one ever knew. I guarded the secret jealously for fear of persecution, concealing the truth of my magic with painstaking effort. I was a coward—I always have been—but in the end, it mattered not. When I leapt to my doom in L'Eau Mélancolique, Isla saved me—or rather, she saved my ring." She rubbed her thumb along the band. "My magic. Without it, I am not whole, and without me, neither is L'Eau Mélancolique. For this reason, Isla wishes me to avoid involvement in your war. She does not understand that it is *my* war as well."

Voice raw with unshed emotion, Coco whispered, "If Josephine dies, you will too."

Her words sank like bricks in my stomach.

Abruptly, Angelica turned, her knife a blur as she slashed the nightshade from coiling around Coco's neck. I gasped, Reid startled, and Coco leapt to her feet with a small shriek. None of us had noticed its creeping tendrils, the fruits of Angelica's grief and anger. When she spoke, her voice was soft. "We must all play our parts."

Coco stared at her.

I crossed the circle to squeeze Coco's hand. "Does this mean Isla *won't* join us?"

Angelica's hand closed around her ring. "Isla is many things." Brushing past us, she glided toward the waters. Her chairs of vine withered as Reid joined us, and her aconite flowers blackened to wisps of ash. "But she is not a liar. You returned my ring, and you bested Morgane. You have proven yourself a worthy ally, Louise. Though she cannot directly intervene in the events to come, she allows her melusines to choose for themselves whether to walk by your side in Cesarine. She allows *me* to choose."

"Will they?" I asked.

"Will *you*?" Coco asked at the same time.

She inclined her head. "I will lead the willing to Cesarine myself in three days' time."

"What's in three days?" Reid said, his voice strained.

Angelica merely continued toward the waters, which remained calm and still. At their edge, she drew to a graceful halt, clasping her hands at her waist. "The Oracle offers a final gift." When three iron chalices materialized before us, dread bloomed in my belly. Reid's brows dipped low, and he knelt swiftly to examine one. "Drink of the waters," Angelica said, "and you shall see."

HOLY MEN

Reid

The iron chalice felt familiar in my hand as I lifted it to my lips. *Too* familiar. Like I'd descended a flight of stairs but missed the bottom step. The second the ice water touched my tongue, an invisible force sucked me forward, and I tipped straight over the horizon.

The next second, I resurfaced in the cathedral's formal courtroom. The hard benches and wood-paneled walls I recognized immediately. The honeyed notes in the air. Beeswax candles. They cast the room in flickering light, as curtains had been drawn over its pointed stained-glass windows. I'd guarded those vaulted doors—behind the podium, behind the Archbishop— at least a dozen times while the guilty had awaited verdict. We hadn't committed many inside these halls. King Auguste and his guard had dealt with common criminals, while witches themselves hadn't been afforded trial at all. No, those who testified here had been charged with the crimes in between: conspiracy, aiding and abetting the occult, even attempted witchcraft. In my years with the Chasseurs, only a rare few had openly sympathized with witches. Some had been tempted by power. Others beguiled by beauty. Still others had sought magic for themselves.

To the last man and woman, all had burned.

I swallowed hard as Lou and Coco landed beside me.

Stumbling slightly, Coco knocked into the silver-haired man beside us. He didn't acknowledge her. Indeed, when her shoulder passed through his arm, incorporeal, I frowned. They couldn't see us, then. "Pardon her, sir," I murmured, testing another theory. He didn't respond.

"They can't hear us either." Contrary to her words, Lou spoke in a whisper. Her eyes fixed on something in the center of the chamber. I turned. Blanched. Scowling and fierce, Philippe— once a comrade in arms—dragged my mother to the podium. She'd been gagged and bound. Blood, both crusted black and fresh scarlet, stained the entirety of her gown, and her body hung limp. Drugged. Her eyes fluttered between sleep and wakefulness.

"Oh my god." Coco lifted a hand to her mouth in horror. "Oh my *god*."

Philippe didn't bother to unbind her hands. He simply nailed her ear to the podium. Shrieking, she lurched awake, but the movement only exacerbated her position, tearing the cartilage. Her screams soon morphed to sobs at Philippe's laughter. Under the drug's influence, she couldn't support herself, and when she sank to the floor, her ear tore free completely.

Red washed over my vision. I started forward before I

could stop myself, halting only when another man rose across the chamber. As with the iron chalice, I recognized his face—grizzled beard, gaunt cheeks, stormy eyes—though it took me several seconds to place him.

"Was that necessary, huntsman?" His hard voice cut sharp through the din of the room. At once, every other voice fell silent. Every eye turned to him. His attention didn't waver from Philippe, however. "If I'm not mistaken, this woman has been incapacitated with hemlock, per healers' guidance. She poses no threat in her current condition. Surely such additional measures are cruel and unusual?" Though he posed the last as a question, no one mistook it as such. The censure in his tone rang clear.

And that was when I placed him—standing between pews, holding a pot of stew in his gnarled hands. *Most in the Church wouldn't welcome their own mother if she was a sinner.*

Achille Altier.

Gone was the stooped, cantankerous old man from the graveyard parish, however. He'd combed and oiled his beard. Trimmed it neatly. His robes, too, shone resplendent even in the semidarkness. More so, he held himself differently—straighter, taller—and commanded the room with an ease I envied.

Philippe bristled, squaring his shoulders. Glancing around at the conclave's hard, impassive faces. "It's a witch, Father. Surely no precaution is too great."

"Are you saying you know better than the priests in our infirmary?"

Philippe's face paled. "I—"

"Now, now." The man beside us rose to his feet as well, standing nearly as tall and broad as me. Despite his silver hair—thick and shining as a younger man's—he radiated youth and vitality. Golden skin. Classic features. Some might've even considered him handsome. In his pale blue eyes, however, malice glittered. God had created him as Achille's opposite in every way. "Let us not rush to condemn Chasseur Brisbois for protecting us against the Devil's mistress, whose very power lay within her deceit." He arched a thick brow. "Though I must rebuke the blood he spilled upon our podium."

Philippe hastily bent his head. "My apologies, Father Gaspard."

Father Gaspard. My mind quickly filled the gap. Father Gaspard *Fosse*. I recognized the name from my time spent north in Amandine. There, he'd cultivated the largest parish in the kingdom outside of Cesarine, creating a name for himself in the process. The Archbishop hadn't cared for his ambition, his guile. His clever tongue. I'd adopted the Archbishop's opinion at the time. I'd disliked Father Gaspard on principle. But now—having met the man myself—I realized the Archbishop had spoken truth. At least in this instance.

Father Gaspard wasn't a holy man.

I frowned at my own abrupt conclusion. What had I seen to form such an assumption? He'd defended a Chasseur from open criticism. He'd grown his parish. Both should've been admirable behaviors, biblical ones, but they weren't. They *weren't*, and I didn't understand—not him, not the Church, not this growing heat in my chest or this pricking sensation along my skin. Like it'd grown several sizes too small.

"You are forgiven, child," he said, despite Philippe's gray-streaked beard. "*All* is forgiven in pursuit of our noble cause. The Father knows your heart. In violence against these creatures, he compels your hand."

Gaspard ambled down the steps toward Philippe. Slowly. Almost leisurely. Sleek and proud and superior. Father Achille might've rolled his eyes. Regardless, he hobbled down his own stairs, following Gaspard's lead across the chamber. The two met on either side of the podium. Of my mother.

Achille stepped in front of her. His robes shielded her comatose body. "He never compels our hands to violence."

"Stand down, old man." Though murmured, Gaspard's voice still reverberated through the quiet room. One could've heard a pin drop. "We are here to burn the witch, not coddle it."

My cheeks flushed with anger, with inexplicable hurt. But I *shouldn't* have been agitated, I shouldn't have been *hurt*, and I definitely shouldn't have felt concern for the witch below. As with Célie and Gaspard, however, I couldn't explain my own decisions.

I didn't love her anymore.

I didn't like Father Gaspard.

And I didn't want my mother—a witch—to suffer. I didn't want her to burn.

Sick shame washed through me at the last, and I sank onto the nearest bench. Desperate to regain my composure. When Lou followed, touching a hand to my back, I forced myself to count to three, to five, to ten. Anything to focus my turbulent thoughts. I knew what I should do. I pictured it clearly—unsheathing my knife to lop off her hand. To plunge it into her heart.

Equally clear, I pulled her close and buried my nose in her neck. I tasted her scar. I spread her legs across my lap, and I touched her gently, touched her not gently, touched her any way she wanted. When her lips parted, I stole my name from them, and I kept it forever—not a scream of pain, but a cry of longing.

This is how you touch a woman. This is how you touch me.

Pain cleaved my skull in two at the stark imagery, and I pitched forward, seizing my head. Expelling the hateful words. The hateful voice. As they scattered and drifted, the pain receded, but my shame fanned hotter than before. Intolerable. I moved to fling her hand away from me. I stopped at the last moment.

When she leaned over my shoulder, her hair tickled my cheek. "Reid?"

"No decision has been made," Achille growled.

Gaspard smiled. A cat with a juicy secret. "Of course it has. I cannot blame you for this ignorance, of course, as your idealism has hardened many against you. They dare not speak freely in your presence for fear of censure." When Achille didn't give him the satisfaction of a reply—not a frown, not even a blink—he continued, "By all means, however, let us wait for His Majesty to tally the vote. He arrives at any moment." He leaned forward to whisper something in Achille's ear then. A real whisper, this time. Not a feigned one. Stiffening, Achille muttered something back. As if given permission, the conclave broke into low conversation of their own, all waiting for my father to arrive.

Lou sat beside me. "They won't *really* burn her. Don't worry."

Her thigh pressed into my own. I forced myself to scoot away. "They will."

Coco grimaced and slid beside Lou, bouncing her own leg in agitation. "Unfortunately, I think he's right. Auguste will probably burn her with the Hellfire out of spite."

Lou glanced at me in alarm, eyes wide. "What do we do?"

"Nothing." When she arched a brow, unimpressed, I scowled and added, "There's nothing we *can* do. Even if I wanted to help her—which I don't—there isn't time. My mother is a witch, and she'll burn for her sins."

"*You* are a witch," Lou snapped. "And even if you weren't, you've conspired with us plenty." She ticked off my crimes on her fingers, each a knife coated in poison. "You've married a witch"—I didn't remember—"slept with a witch"—I wished I did—"hidden and protected a witch, multiple times"—I closed my eyes, innards clenching—"and best yet: you've *murdered* for a witch. Four of us, to be precise." My eyes snapped open as she rotated a finger between the three of us. Then jabbed it toward the chamber floor. "And the most important of those is bleeding out on the carpet right now. Because of you, might I add. She sacrificed herself for *you*. Her *son*. Whom she *loves*."

Most in the Church wouldn't welcome their own mother if she was a sinner.

But I wasn't a holy man either.

I clenched my fists and looked away. "I can't do magic."

"You can." Voice conversational, Coco examined a scar on her wrist. "And many times, you practiced when Lou wasn't directly involved, which means you're *choosing* to forget." When I opened my mouth to answer, to snarl, she merely flicked a finger at me. "Shut up. I'm not interested in excuses. Isla gifted us this vision, so we need to pay attention. We're here for a reason."

I glared at her as she glared at me. Crossing her arms, Lou exhaled hard through her nose. Still angry. We had that in common too, apparently. After a moment, she asked, "What does Madame Labelle have to do with electing a new Archbishop?"

"They're using her indictment as their own sort of tribunal." I shouldn't have explained anything to her. I couldn't stop. Jerking my chin toward Achille and Gaspard, I added, "Those two are positioning themselves for the title."

Coco grimaced and scanned the chamber. Presumably for whatever Isla had wanted us to find. "Achille had better win."

Lou glanced between us. "Do you know him?"

"He was the priest in Fée Tombe. He recognized us from the wanted posters, yet he still sheltered us for the night, even fed us his breakfast. He didn't like Beau much," Coco added, as if this were another mark in the man's favor. "He'll make the first decent Archbishop that Belterra has ever seen."

"He won't." To prove my point, I gestured to the men clustered directly below us. They'd pressed their heads together to whisper. Necks tense. Voices strained. Lou and Coco exchanged a glance before leaning toward them to listen.

"... not doing himself any favors," the balding one hissed. "Not with his history."

"What history?" his younger, equally bald companion asked.

The third—also bald, but with a long beard—shook his head. "I suppose you wouldn't know, would you, Emile? It happened before you were born."

"This isn't his first campaign." The balding one sneered down at Achille with unaccountable hostility. "Achille lobbied alongside Florin for support during the last conclave, but he rescinded his candidacy at the last moment."

"Never gave an explanation," the bearded one added. "Just relegated himself to that dismal little parish up north."

"Old Florin took the title, and no one heard from Achille for nearly thirty years—until now."

A knock sounded on the vaulted doors, and the men paused, watching as Philippe slipped into the hall, closing them behind. The balding man snorted and resumed his malicious gossip. "I heard his brother fell in with a witch. I can't remember his name."

"Audric," the bearded one supplied, his expression thoughtful. Unlike his peer, he seemed less inclined to loathe Achille. He peered down at the man in question almost curiously. "My father said Achille helped the whole family slip past the border."

The younger's lip curled. "I didn't know he sympathized with witches."

"How could you not?" The balding man pointed to where Achille still shielded my mother. "He stands no chance of procuring the vote. Not with the way he carries on—all this talk of peace and civility with the *creatures* of this kingdom. The conclave will never appoint him. Clearly, his seclusion has altered his senses."

Lou scoffed with unexpected vehemence. "Do you think he'd feel it if I cut out his tongue?"

Unable to remain still, I stalked down the steps toward my mother. "You will not touch them."

"Why?" She hurried to trail after me. "He's clearly a *bastard*—"

The vaulted doors burst open before she could finish.

Clad in a cape made of lion's fur—the mane draped across his shoulders—my father strode inside the courtroom. Philippe and three huntsmen I didn't recognize accompanied him. As one, the entire congregation rose and bowed at his arrival. Every man. Even Achille. My stomach turned as I lurched to a halt by the podium.

He'd threatened torture the last time I saw him. Threatened rats. Immediately, my gaze dropped to my mother, who lay very still. Though her dress had once been emerald green, I couldn't now place its color—an unpleasant shade of brown, perhaps. I knelt to examine her stomach. When her eyes fluttered at the movement, I froze.

"Yes, yes, *bonjour.*" Auguste waved an agitated hand. He offered no smiles today. No empty platitudes. I surveyed him with mounting hatred. His hair remained immaculate, of course, but shadows deepened his eyes. His fingers trembled inexplicably. He hid them in his cape. "I cannot stay long. Though this damned fire has abated slightly"—several around the room stared at the expletive, but Auguste didn't apologize—"the healers at last believe they've discovered the solution: a rare plant in La Fôret des Yeux." Sweeping forward, he motioned for Achille to move away from my mother. "Let us be done with this."

Coco snorted and muttered, "There is no *solution*, fruit or otherwise."

I frowned. "How do you know?"

"Because the fire stemmed from my grief." Expression solemn, she met my eyes directly. "And there is no solution for grief. Only time. The fire might abate, yes, but it will never truly die."

Lou nodded in agreement, staring at my mother, and my mother—I swore she stared back. Crouching beside her, Lou laid a hand on her arm as Auguste continued his tirade.

"We all know the crimes of the creature." Pointing, he sneered at her soiled form. "From its own lips, it admitted its guilt. It is a witch. A powerful one. It promised to douse this lake of black fire in exchange for its life, but *God* has found our cure. The healers have already begun testing. By the end of the week, they promise an extinguishant to the Hellfire, and at such time, this witch shall burn for her sins."

This witch. The words shouldn't have chafed. She *was* a witch. But she was also my mother and *his* former lover. He'd laid with her. He'd even loved her once, if she were to be believed. She'd certainly loved him. Now her stomach bled from rat bites, and she lifted a ruined hand to Lou's cheek. Lou tried and failed to hold it, her own hand passing through without purchase.

Only then did I grasp the rest of his words: *by the end of the week.*

My heart sank like a stone. She would burn by the end of the week. Too soon for us to reach her. Much too soon.

Several in the audience applauded the king's outburst—including the balding man—but only Achille made a noise of protest. "Your Majesty, there are protocols in place. Without an Archbishop elect, the conclave must cast an official vote—"

"Ah." Auguste's nose crinkled as he turned. "You again, Father . . . ?"

"Achille, Your Majesty. Achille Altier."

"Achille Altier, you do realize the support of the Crown is necessary to obtain bishopric?"

"Preferable. Not necessary."

Auguste arched a brow, scrutinizing him with new eyes. "Is that so?"

"Please, Achille," Gaspard interrupted smoothly. "His Majesty's word is divine. If he proclaims the witch shall burn, the witch shall burn."

"If his word is divine," Achille grumbled, "he should have no qualms putting the matter to vote. The outcome will comply."

"*Something* ought to." Auguste glared at him before lifting his arms to address the room at large, his voice curt and impatient. Out of bounds. "You heard the man. Your Father Achille would like a vote, and a vote he shall have. All those in favor of burning the witch, raise your hand."

"Wait!" Achille lifted his own arms, eyes widening in panic. "The witch could still prove valuable! The healers have not yet perfected their extinguishant—if it fails, if we burn this woman, what hope have we of dousing the fire?" He spoke to Auguste alone now. "Her knowledge has proved valuable to the healers. I can bring in another to testify."

Auguste spoke through his teeth. "That will not be necessary. This conclave has heard enough of your ludicrous ramblings."

"With all due respect, Your Majesty, the pursuit of knowledge isn't ludicrous. Not when a woman's life is in jeopardy—"

"Careful, Father, lest I deem it heretical instead."

Achille's mouth snapped shut in response, disappearing into his beard, and Auguste addressed the congregation once more. "Let us try this again, shall we? All those in favor of burning the witch?"

Every hand in the courtroom rose. Every hand but one. Though Achille watched his peers decide my mother's fate with an inscrutable expression, he kept both hands fixed at his sides. Firm. Implacable. Even under the king's baleful gaze. "It seems you have been outvoted," Auguste sneered. "My word *is* divine."

"We'll rescue you," Lou whispered furiously to Madame Labelle. "I don't know how, but we will. I promise."

Madame Labelle might've shaken her head.

"Why wait until week's end?" Achille's voice shook with restraint. "You've made our decision. Why not burn the witch now?"

Auguste chuckled and clapped a threatening hand on Achille's shoulder. "Because she is only the bait, you foolish man. We have much bigger fish to catch." To Philippe, he said, "Spread word far and wide throughout the kingdom, Captain. Madame Helene

Labelle *will* burn"—he cast a pointed look at Achille now—"and any who object will meet the same fate."

Achille bowed stiffly. "You must follow your conscience, Your Majesty. I must follow mine."

"See that your *conscience* leads you outside the cathedral in three days' time. At sunset, you shall light her pyre." With that, he strode through the vaulted doors once more, and the courtroom vanished into smoke.

PART IV

Qui sème le vent, récolte la tempête.
He who sows the wind shall reap the tempest.
—French proverb

WHAT HAPPINESS LOOKS LIKE

Lou

Though Angelica and her iron chalices had gone when we resurfaced, Beau, Célie, and Jean Luc floated atop the inlet in a fishing boat. A *fishing boat.* Célie grinned with palpable excitement from the flybridge, gripping the helm with both hands. Her smile quickly fell at our grim expressions, however, and she called out, "What's wrong?"

I waited until we'd climbed aboard to answer. "Isla's gift was shit."

We wouldn't be able to reach Cesarine before Madame Labelle burned to ash. When Coco said as much—explaining the conclave's decision, Father Achille's involvement, and Auguste's last words—Beau patted the stern. "*This* is her gift. Or at least, this is Angelica's. It'll get us there in time." He shrugged and added, "I wouldn't worry about my father. He has a flair for dramatics, but he knows what he's doing even less than we do."

"You didn't see him." I wrung out my hair, cursing at the cold. The strands had already started to freeze, and gooseflesh steepled my entire body. "He wasn't acting. He knows we'll come to rescue Madame Labelle. He plans to trap us, like he did before." I glanced around the ramshackle boat. "And *this* won't get us to Cesarine anytime soon."

"It will." Nudging Célie aside, Beau nodded as Jean Luc dropped the sail, and we slipped through the waters with speed. "I learned to sail when I was three." He arched a smug brow at Coco, adding, "The admiral of the Royal Navy taught me himself."

Beside me, Coco rubbed her arms, and Reid clenched every muscle, refusing to shiver despite his lips turning blue. Célie hurried to fetch us blankets in the cabin belowdecks. But blankets wouldn't help. Not really. Reluctantly, I reached for the white patterns, bracing as they shimmered into existence. I frowned at the sensation—the breadth of possibility still startled, but after a second or two of adjustment, it felt . . . good. Like stretching after sitting too long in one position. More curious still, instead of pulling me toward Chateau le Blanc, the magic seemed to be pulling me toward—

What matters now is whether you—La Dame des Sorcières—still consider this place your home. If not, it stands to reason your magic won't protect it anymore. It'll shift to your new home. Wherever that is.

It was too easy to pluck a cord now. A burst of hot air enveloped Reid and Coco—then me—and I watched, bemused, as the snow along the path melted. Warmth for warmth. The white pattern dissipated with it.

"How did you do that?" Coco asked suspiciously.

"I melted the snow."

"I thought nature demanded sacrifice?" Her eyes narrowed, skimming my face and body for signs of damage. "How is melting snow a sacrifice?"

I shrugged helplessly, struggling to articulate this strange new power even to myself. Morgane had seemed limitless as La Dame des Sorcières, and—at least in this natural way—perhaps she had been. "I *am* the snow."

She blinked at me in response. They all did. Even Célie, as she returned with slightly moldy blankets. I wrapped mine around my shoulders, burrowing into its warmth. The pattern had dried us, yes, but the bitter wind still remained. I tried and probably failed to clarify. "It's like . . . before, my magic felt like a *connection* to my ancestors. I gained my patterns through them. Now, as La Dame des Sorcières, I *am* them. I'm their ashes, their land, their magic. I'm the snow and the leaves and the wind. I'm . . . boundless." It was my turn to blink, to stare. I probably sounded like a raving lunatic, but I didn't know how else to describe it. Perhaps words *couldn't* describe it.

"But"—Coco cleared her throat, visibly uncomfortable—"you heard what happened to my aunt without checks and balances. She and her followers pushed too far. They slaughtered their coven as a result, and the Goddess punished them. She—she punished your mother too."

"The Goddess gave my mother a chance to redeem herself at La Mascarade des Crânes. She gave her a warning. When Morgane didn't heed it, Aurore revoked her blessing. See? There *are* checks and balances. And I can't"—I turned my sight inward, examining the patterns there—"I can't do anything *unnatural* with it. At least, I don't think I can. I can't kill anyone, or—"

"Death is natural." Reid stared determinedly over the gunwale. As we hadn't yet cleared L'Eau Mélancolique, the waters below didn't ripple. He clutched his blanket tighter and swallowed hard. "Everyone dies eventually."

"Yes," I said slowly, recalling Ansel's previous words. His had somehow felt comforting, like a benediction. Reid's, however, did not. They felt more like a threat—no, like a promise. I frowned again, eyes narrowing on his heavy brow, his downcast expression. For the first time since he'd lost his memories—aside from our drunken encounter—he didn't project malevolence. He didn't keep one hand on his bandolier. "Death is natural, but murder is not."

Shrugging, he said nothing.

I fought the urge to move closer. "Are you okay, Chass? Beau is right. We *will* reach your mother in time—"

He turned on his heel and stalked belowdecks before I could finish. The door slammed behind him.

Awkward silence descended in his wake, and heat crept up my cheeks.

Coco rummaged in her pack, turning her back to the frigid wind. "You shouldn't need a lesson to know he wants you to go after him." She withdrew a scrap of parchment, a pot of ink, and a quill before sinking to the boat's floor. Without ceremony, she used her knee as a table and began to pen a message. To Claud, probably. To Blaise. "Unless you *do* need a lesson? I could teach you an excellent way to relieve stress—"

"I know *plenty* of ways to relieve stress, thank you." When the wind made it impossible to keep the parchment steady, I waved a hand. It stilled for just a moment, stilling the boat as well. We'd just reached the broader expanse of sea, and waves finally broke against the helm. "He wouldn't be interested in any of them."

"Oh, I think he's *very* interested." Her smirk faded as she looked up, and she tapped her quill upon the paper pointedly. "What am I telling Claud?"

Resigned, I plopped down next to her, spreading my blanket over her as well. Across the small deck, Beau manned the helm while Célie perched atop the boat's single bench. Jean Luc joined her. "My father might plan to trap us," Beau conceded, "but we still have one thing in our favor." He pointed to Célie and Jean Luc in turn. "We have these two this time. He doesn't know about them."

"He knows I abandoned my post," Jean Luc muttered.

Coco shook her head. "But he doesn't know *why*. If he's learned of Célie's absence—which I doubt, knowing Tremblay—he might suspect you followed her, but no one would ever believe she'd seek us out, let alone ally with us. Not after everything that's happened."

"We do have the element of surprise." At the edge of my thoughts, the beginning of a plan began to take shape. I didn't look at it too closely, instead worrying a loose thread in the blanket. Allowing it to form. It wouldn't solve the Morgane problem— though in truth, *problem* seemed too mild a word for the picture Angelica had painted. *A battle brews on the horizon more catastrophic than this world has ever seen.*

We couldn't focus on that now. The plan had changed. Madame Labelle would come first, and then—*then* came catastrophic battles. I tugged at the thread viciously, unraveling part of the blanket. "We won't be able to slip into the city undetected. We couldn't manage it before, even when no one knew we were coming. Now they'll be expecting us."

"Do I hear a *but?*" Beau asked.

I looked up at him then. Looked up at them all. "Maybe we don't *need* to slip in undetected. Maybe we announce our arrival." I grinned slightly, though I didn't particularly feel like grinning. "Maybe we let them arrest us."

"*What?*" Beau exclaimed.

"No, listen." I leaned forward, pointing again at Célie and Jean Luc. "We have an aristocrat with a death wish and a huntsman madly in love with her. A *captain*. He's deadly skilled and highly trained, and—more importantly—he has the respect of the Crown and Church. If Célie struck out on a quest for vengeance—against me, against Reid, against all witches—*of course* he would catch up with her. *Of course* he would incapacitate us, and of course he would bring us back to Cesarine to burn. He would even arrest the lawless crown prince in the process."

"They'll throw you all in prison." The wind ruffled Coco's wild curls as she considered. "The same prison where they hold Madame Labelle."

"Exactly. Jean Luc can relieve the guard, and I'll magic us all out."

"They'll inject you with hemlock," Jean Luc said.

"Not if you've already done it." I slumped as if incapacitated to demonstrate, my head lolling on Coco's shoulder. "You forget I'm an accomplished liar, and your brethren trust you."

"If you escape under my watch, they'll know I've helped you. They'll strip my captaincy."

Coco, who'd been penning our plan—scratching out and writing anew as it formed—looked up with a dark expression. "They'll do a lot worse than that." Slipping a knife from her cloak, she cut a fine line on her forearm, positioning the cut over the paper. With each drop, the paper sizzled and vanished. To me, she said, "I asked Claud—and I assume Zenna and Seraphine—to find Blaise and meet us at Léviathan afterward. If they managed to heal Toulouse, Liana, and Terrance, they'll be able to heal Madame Labelle."

When Jean Luc said nothing, Célie scooted closer, threading her fingers through his. "It's the right thing to do, Jean. Chasseurs are meant to protect the innocent. Madame Labelle has done nothing but love her son. If not for her sacrifice, the king would've tortured Reid instead."

"Also," Beau said, pursing his lips, "not to be *that* person, but your captaincy won't matter after Morgane kills everyone."

"He has a point," Coco said.

Jean Luc closed his eyes, his face tight and strained. Overhead, gulls cried in the filtered sunlight, and to starboard, waves crashed upon the distant shore. Though I didn't know Jean Luc, he still wore his emotions like he wore his coat—a coat he'd worked hard to receive. Harder than most. And all that hard work—all that pain, all that envy, all that spite—it'd be for nothing if he helped us now. In doing the *right thing*, he'd lose everything.

No, I didn't know Jean Luc, but I understood him better than most.

After another moment, he dipped his chin in assent. In sorrow. "Of course. Just tell me what to do."

"Thank you, Jean," Célie said, pressing a kiss upon his cheek.

The last of the parchment vanished with Coco's blood, and the message was sent.

Instead of relief, however, fresh dread crept through me. Fresh dread and stale anger. The latter simmered just beneath my skin as I stared at the cabin door. Jean Luc would help us, yes, and Claud and Blaise would too. We had a dragon on our side, as well as an original witch. Melusines and loup garou. A *goddess* had gifted me the magic of La Dame des Sorcières, so I could change shape—could alter the very fabric of nature—with the wave of my hand. Morgane didn't know I existed, and Auguste didn't know of our plan. Never before had we enjoyed such elements of surprise—indeed, never before had we been quite so prepared for what was to come. Our plan was an excellent one. The best we'd ever concocted.

Except for one very tall, very *obnoxious* problem.

My eyes could've bored holes in the door now.

Following my gaze, Coco nudged my shoulder. "Go talk to him."

"He'll never agree."

"You won't know until you try."

I scoffed. "You're right. He'll probably *love* this plan. It'll give him a chance to act out his martyr fantasies. Hell, he'll probably

want to be lashed to the stake out of self-loathing or shame or—
or some sense of misplaced *duty*."

She cast me a sideways grin. "That isn't what I said."

"It's what you meant."

"It really wasn't." Wrapping an arm around me now, she
leaned close and lowered her voice. "Here's your first lesson in
seduction: honesty is sexy as hell. No, not like you're thinking,"
she added when I scoffed again. "Honesty goes beyond telling
him who you used to be, who *he* used to be, who you used to be
together. You've tried that, and it hasn't worked. You need to *show*
him. Allow yourself to be vulnerable, so he can be vulnerable too.
That kind of honesty—*that* kind of honesty is intimate. It's raw."

I plunked my head against the hull, sighing deeply. "You forget I'm a liar. I don't *do* honesty."

Her smile spread. "You do with him."

"He's fucking infuriating."

"That he is."

"I want to gouge his eyes out."

"I completely agree."

"I might steal his Balisarda and shave his eyebrows with it."

"I wish you would."

"I'll be honest if you will."

Her face snapped toward mine then, confused, and I met her
gaze steadily. "What do you mean?" she asked suspiciously. From
the way her eyes flicked to Beau, however—so quick I might've
missed it—she knew *exactly* what I meant. I pretended to ponder
my words, tapping my chin with a finger.

"Well . . . Célie told me about a certain kiss."

Those eyes narrowed in warning. "Célie needs to mind her business."

"It sounds like *you* need to mind your business too." I fought a grin at her abruptly murderous expression. "Come now. I thought you said honesty was sexy as hell?"

She yanked her arm from my shoulders, crossing it with her other. Huddling deeper within the blankets. "Don't project what you and Reid have onto Beau and me. Ours isn't a grand, sweeping romance. We aren't star-crossed lovers. *We* were a casual hookup, and that's all."

"Coco, Coco, Coco." I bumped *her* shoulder this time. "Who's the liar now?"

"I'm not lying."

"I thought you said honesty was *raw*? I thought you said it was *intimate*?"

She grimaced and looked away, clutching the locket at her chest. "Too raw. Too intimate."

My grin slowly faded at the hurt in her words. "When was the last time you were vulnerable with anyone?"

"I'm vulnerable with you."

But I didn't count, and she knew it. I wracked my memory for each of Coco's serious relationships—a witch named Flore, Babette, and Beau himself. I didn't know if I should count Ansel. Those emotions had been serious, yes, but unrequited on both sides. "Is this . . . is this about Ansel?" I asked tentatively.

She shot me a sharp look. "No." Then— "Well, not anymore."

Her shoulder slumped, and her arms fell loose at her sides. She stared at her palms in her lap. "It was, at first. But he—he visited me in the Wistful Waters, Lou."

Moisture gathered in my eyes. "I know."

She didn't seem shocked by the revelation, her gaze instead turning inward. As if she hadn't heard me at all. "He told me he wanted me to be happy. He said if Beau could do that, I shouldn't hesitate." She shook her head sadly. "But I don't even know what happiness looks like."

"Of course you do—"

"What I *know*," she continued determinedly, speaking over me, "is that it isn't Beau's job to show me. It isn't anyone's job but mine. If I can't make myself happy, how can he? How can my mother or my aunt or my kin?"

Ah. A beat of silence pulsed between us as the pieces clicked into place. I stared, longing to wrap my arms around her tense shoulders. Whether intentionally or unintentionally, Coco had been abandoned by everyone she'd dared to love. Except me. It was no coincidence she allowed herself to be vulnerable with just one person. Still . . . my heart ached when I looked to Beau, who cast covert looks in our direction every few seconds. "He isn't them," I whispered.

She sniffed in response. "He's a *prince*."

"You're a princess."

"We lead two different peoples. His will need him, and mine will need me. Look around, Lou." She splayed her arms wide, as if Morgane and Josephine and Auguste stood here with us now.

"Regardless of how this plays out in Cesarine, our kingdoms are not aligned. They never will be. We can have no future together."

I arched a brow, parroting her own words. "You won't know unless you try." When she glared at me, saying nothing, I took her hands. "No, listen to me, Coco. If you don't want Beau, fine. I promise I won't say another word. But if you *do* want him—and if he wants you—the two of you will find a way. You'll make it work." Unbidden, I glanced back at the cabin door. "Only you can decide what your happiness looks like."

She squeezed my hands tighter, tears sparkling. "I told you, Lou. I don't *know* what my happiness looks like."

"It's fine not to know." Abruptly, I pulled her to her feet, throwing my arms around her at last. Beau, Célie, and Jean Luc ceased their murmured conversation to watch us, startled. I ignored them. I didn't care. "It isn't fine to stop trying. We have to *try*, Coco, or we'll never find it."

Coco nodded against my cheek, and her words echoed in my ears.

Honesty goes beyond telling him who you used to be, who he used to be, who you used to be together. You need to show *him.*

Again, I looked to the cabin door. The anger remained, of course—ever stale—but the dread had been replaced with steely resolve. With newfound purpose. My happiness included Reid, and I would never stop fighting for him. Never stop trying. Coco followed my gaze with a small smile. Pushing me forward gently, she whispered, "Here's to finding our happiness."

TAKE ME TO CHURCH

Reid

I stooped to enter the cabin, nearly cracking my skull in the process, before straightening to inspect my sanctuary. A cluttered galley full of pots and pans to the right. A threadbare sofa straight ahead. A circular table. I crossed the cabin in two strides. A bed had been tucked behind tartan curtains at the bow of the ship. Two more strides. A second set of curtains hid another bed in the stern. The linens smelled faintly of mildew. Of salt and fish.

When my stomach gave an audible growl, I rummaged through the cabinets in search of food. It gave my hands purpose. My mind focus. Hunger had a solution. A clear, tangible solution. That pain could be cured with a loaf of hard bread, a jar of pickled vegetables. I stacked them both on the counter now. I cut the loaf with my knife. I uncorked the carrots and radishes. I searched for a plate, for a fork, without truly seeing. When I found them, I ate swiftly, determinedly, every movement efficient. Focused.

The pain in my stomach didn't ease.

Guilt continued to churn until I shoved the plate away,

disgusted with the carrots. With the boat. With myself.

I couldn't stop thinking about her.

We'll rescue you. I don't know how, but we will. I promise.

I'd thought myself convicted. I'd never heard conviction until this day.

You *are a witch, and even if you weren't, you've conspired with us plenty. You've married a witch, slept with a witch, hidden and protected a witch—multiple times—and best yet: you've* murdered *for a witch. Four of us, to be precise. The most important of those is bleeding out on the carpet right now.*

I'd never heard such vehemence. Such passion.

I hated it.

I hated *her.*

I hated that I didn't hate her at all.

My thoughts spun circles as I washed my plate. The empty jar. As I replaced them in the cupboard, along with the bread. Sinking onto the couch, I stared endlessly at the cabin door. I couldn't kill her. I couldn't touch her in that way. In *any* way. When I thought of it now—thought of giving in to temptation, of trailing my lips down her ribs, or perhaps sliding my knife between them—bile rose in my throat. Maybe I could leave her instead, leave *all* of them, as originally planned.

The thought brought physical pain.

No, I couldn't leave her, couldn't kill her, couldn't *have* her, which left only one solution. One clear, tangible solution. If I were honest with myself, I should've done it already. I should've done it as soon as I saw my face on that wanted poster. It should've been easy.

The right thing rarely was.

The door crashed open before I could finish the thought, and Lou burst into the cabin. Hair wild. Chin determined. She still wore those *filthy* leather pants, and the top lace of her blouse had loosened. Her neckline had slipped over her shoulder. It revealed a single collarbone. Long and delicate. My gaze lingered there for a second too long before I tore it away, furious at myself. At her. I glared at the floor.

"That's *quite* enough sulking, I think." Her boots came into view. They stopped an inch from my own. Too close. Trapped on the couch, I couldn't move away without standing, without brushing my body past hers. This cabin was too small. Too hot. Her sweet scent engulfed it. "Come on, Chass," she needled, bending at the waist to catch my eyes. Her hair fell long and thick between us. I clenched my hands on my knees. I wouldn't touch it. I *wouldn't*. "I know things got a bit—well, *bad* in the courtroom, but we have a plan to save her now. We're going to trick Auguste."

"I still don't care."

"And I still don't believe you." When I didn't look at her, she straightened, and my treacherous eyes followed the movement. She planted her hands on her hips. "We're going to trick Auguste," she continued, determined to tell me whether or not I wanted to hear, "by pretending Jean Luc has arrested us."

Abruptly, my attention sharpened on her face. On her words. "We're going to turn ourselves in?"

"*Pretend* to turn ourselves in." Her brows flattened at whatever she saw in my expression. "We're just pretending, Chass. After we free your mother, we too will be getting the hell out of there.

Coco will round up Claud and Blaise and hopefully even Angelica, and we'll meet them all at Léviathan."

Claud and Blaise and Angelica. Gods and werewolves and witches and mermaids.

I shook my head.

"Stop it." Lou snapped her fingers to reclaim my attention. Her eyes narrowed in suspicion. "I know what you're thinking—I can see it all over your stupid face—and the answer is *no*."

I scowled at her finger. "Yeah? What am I thinking?"

"You want to *ruin* this brilliant plan of mine—"

"It *is* a brilliant plan."

The praise should've placated her. Instead, it stoked her ire. She jabbed her finger in my chest. "No. No, no, no. I *knew* you would try this martyrdom bullshit, as if you rotting in prison or burning at the stake will somehow solve everything. Let me clue you in, Chass—it won't. It won't solve anything at all. In fact, it'll complicate an already complex situation because on top of saving your mother and battling Morgane—and La Voisin, Nicholina, and a whole slew of other fucking unpleasantness—I'll also have to rescue *you*."

My skin flamed hotter at her profanity. At her *mouth*. "Language," I snarled.

She ignored me, prodding my chest again. Harder this time. "I know you're experiencing some *big feelings* right now, but you aren't going to do anything stupid with them. Do you understand? You aren't going to *prison* because you love your mother. You aren't going to *die* because you want to fuck a witch. Get—over—your—self."

Each pause she enunciated with a poke.

My blood nearly boiled now. Ears ringing, I shoved past her toward the door. If she insisted on staying belowdecks, I would return above. I could endure the others, but she—*she* spoke to me as if I were a child. An errant, *petulant* child in need of scolding. Of discipline. It was too much. Wheeling to face her at the last moment, I snapped, "What I do or don't do is none of your concern." A brief pause. "And I don't want to *fuck* a witch."

"No?" Like lightning, she closed the small distance between us. In her eyes, anger glinted brutal and bright and beautiful. And something else—something like resolve. When her chest brushed my stomach, my muscles contracted near violently. "What *do* you want, then?" She leaned closer still, her face tipping toward mine. A hard edge crept into her voice. "Make up your mind. You can't string me along forever, blowing hot one minute and cold the next. Do you want to love me, or do you want to kill me?"

I stared down at her, heat creeping up my neck. Flushing my cheeks.

"It's a fine line, isn't it?" Rising to her tiptoes now, she practically whispered the words against my lips. "Or . . . perhaps you don't want either. Perhaps you want to worship me instead. Is that it, Chass? Do you want to worship my body like you used to?"

I couldn't move.

"I can show you how if you've forgotten," she breathed. "*I* remember how to worship *you*."

Red swept across my vision at the image. Whether rage or lust or sheer *madness*, I didn't know. I didn't *care*. I was damned either way. My hands seized her shoulders, her jaw, her hair, and my lips crashed against hers. She responded instantaneously. Flinging her arms around my neck, she surged upward. I caught her leg as she did, hoisting her higher, wrapping her body around mine. My back collided with the door. We rolled. I couldn't slow my hips, my tongue. Pressure built at the base of my spine as I ground into her. As she tore away on a ragged breath. As she clenched her eyes shut and threaded her fingers through my hair.

I didn't stop.

My knee slid between her legs, pinning her against the door. I caught her hands above her head. Trapped them there. Worshiped her neck with my tongue. And her collarbone—her *fucking* collarbone. I bit it gently, relishing how her body responded beneath me. I'd known it would. I didn't know *how*, but I'd known she'd make that exact sound. Like my body knew hers in a way my mind didn't. Oh, and it knew her. It knew her intimately.

I can show you how if you've forgotten. I *remember how to worship* you.

The words incited me to a fever pitch. Instinct guided me, and I tasted her throat, her shoulder, her ear. I couldn't touch enough of her. The wood groaned beneath my knee, the skin there already chafed and abraded from the pressure, the friction. Instinctively, I transferred her wrists to one hand, using the other to yank her closer, away from the door. I trailed that hand down her back, soothing it, as she rolled her hips along my thigh. Along the hard ridge there.

"Is this how I did it?" I traced her collarbone with my nose, near delirious at the scent of her. My own hips bucked involuntarily. The pressure built. Though a voice at the back of my mind warned me to go no further, I ignored it. We would burn for our sins, the two of us, here and now. I tugged at the laces of her pants. The laces of mine. "Is this how I *worshiped* you?"

Her eyes remained closed as she arched against me, as her entire body shuddered. I savored the sight. I craved it. When her mouth parted on a gasp, I caught the sound hungrily, plunging my hand lower. Fingers curling. Thrusting. Seeking. In this moment, I could have her—I could *worship* her—and pretend she was mine.

Just this once.

My throat constricted inexplicably at the thought, and my chest tightened. I moved my fingers faster now, chasing that empty promise. Pressing her into the door once more. "Show me," I whispered on a ragged breath. "Please. Show me how we used to be."

Her own eyes snapped open, and she stopped moving abruptly. "What's wrong?"

I didn't answer. I *couldn't* answer. Shaking my head, I kissed her again, desperate to try. Desperate to relieve this *ache* between us—this yearning I'd once known and almost remembered. I wanted it. I feared it. I kissed her until I couldn't tell the difference.

"Reid." Her fingers curled around my wrist. With a start, I realized she'd pulled free. She eased my hand from her pants now, her eyes fixed steadily upon mine. They shone with keen emotion. Though I wanted to name the feeling I saw there, to acknowledge it, I wouldn't. I *couldn't*. "Not . . . not like this. You aren't ready."

"I'm *fine*—"

"I don't think you are." Leaning forward, she pressed a kiss upon my forehead, featherlight. The tenderness in the movement nearly broke me. The intimacy. "Slow down, Reid. We have time."

Slow down, Reid. We have time.

We have time.

Defeated, I withdrew at the words, my forehead falling to the crook of her neck. My hands bracing against the door. She sank slowly to the floor as silence descended. When I didn't break it, only clenched my fists against the wood, she nuzzled her cheek against my hair. She actually *nuzzled* me. I closed my eyes. "Talk to me," she whispered.

"I can't." The words fell thick from my tongue. Clumsy. "I'm sorry."

"Never apologize for being uncomfortable."

"I'm not *uncomfortable*. I'm—I'm—" *Adrift.* Though I wrenched my face up to stare at her then, I immediately regretted the decision. Her eyebrows, her nose, her *freckles.* And those eyes— I could drown in those eyes. Light from the windows sparkled within their turquoise depths. This close, I could see the ring of icy blue around her pupils. The sea-green flecks of her irises. She couldn't keep *looking* at me like this. She couldn't keep *touching* me like she—like she— "Why don't I remember you?" I demanded.

Those beautiful eyes blinked. "You chose to forget."

"*Why?*"

"Because you loved me."

Because you loved me.

Throwing my hands in the air, I stalked across the cabin. It made no sense. If I'd loved her, why had I left her? If I'd embraced her as a witch—if I'd embraced *myself*—why had I given it up? Had I been happy? Had *she*? The way she said my name . . . it spoke of more than a fleeting moment of lust.

It spoke of more.

Like a moth to a flame, I faced her once more. "Show me."

She furrowed her brows in response, her hair wilder than when she'd first entered. Her collar lower. Her lips swollen and her pants undone. Through the laces, an inch or two of taut golden skin teased me. When I moved to close the distance between us—again—she tilted her head to one side, catlike. "What are you saying?"

Swallowing hard, I forced myself to stop. To repeat the words. "Show me how we used to be."

"Are you asking me . . . do you *want* to remember?" When I only stared at her, she shook her head slowly, drifting closer. Still studying me. She seemed to be holding her breath. "Silence isn't an answer."

"I don't know."

The words came in a rush, as honest as I could give. Just speaking them aloud stripped me bare. I could hardly look at her. But I did. I looked at her, forced to acknowledge my own indecision. My despair and my hope.

A pause as she considered. A small, wicked smile. "All right."

"What?"

"Sit"—she pointed a finger behind me—"on the couch."

I sank onto the cushions without another word, eyes

wide—heart pounding—as she followed, leaning against the table to face me. As she hoisted herself up on its edge. Close enough to touch. Something in her expression stilled my hand, however, even as she flicked her wrist, locking the cabin door. The scent of magic erupted around us. "There. No one can see us. No one can hear us, either."

"Is that supposed to frighten me?"

"Does it?"

I leveled her with a dark look. Whether intended or not, I'd involved myself with a witch—a witch I wanted in every sense of the word. A witch I wanted to taste and feel and *know*. All of it should've frightened me. The last most of all. But— "It doesn't."

"Tell me where you'd like to touch me, Reid. Tell me, and I'll do it for you. I'll show you how we used to be."

I stared at her hungrily, hardly daring to believe it. She stared back at me. After another moment, she arched a brow, slipping each foot from her boots. Her stockings came next. "If you'd rather not, of course, I understand. There are two beds. We could rest for a while instead."

"No." The word tore from me instinctively. Quick and thoughtless. Cursing my own eagerness, I exhaled an uneven breath. *Slow down, Reid. We have time.* She'd given me this opportunity to master myself. To regain some semblance of control. Obviously she'd underestimated her appeal. My thumbs itched to rub along her bare soles, to slip over her toes and up her ankles. I glanced at the door.

She feigned a yawn.

My eyes locked on hers, searching, and in them, I saw the truth. She wanted my thoughts clear, yes, but not just for my sake. For hers as well. *Make up your mind, Reid,* she'd said before. *You can't string me along forever, blowing hot one minute and cold the next.*

Scooting to the edge of the couch, careful not to touch her, I said, "I want—I want you to—" But the words wouldn't come. Honesty choked me. Honesty and fear. For how far I'd go, how far she'd go, how far we'd gone already.

She cocked her head, her gaze alight with fire. It threatened to devour us both. "Whatever you want, Reid." Softer, she said, "Tell me."

My fear melted at the depth in her voice. The pure, unbridled emotion.

Love.

I quickly shook away the thought. "Take off your pants."

If my request surprised her, she didn't show it. She didn't hesitate. Slowly, torturously, she peeled her pants down her legs. Her eyes never left mine. Not until she'd stripped the leather fabric away completely.

My mouth went dry at the sight.

I'd been captivated by her collarbone. Now the whole of her bare legs stretched out before me. Still perched atop the table, the tips of her toes barely reached the floor. Her shirt billowed around her, however. It hid her from me. Resisting the urge to lean forward, I curled my fingers into the cushion and watched, silent, as she leaned back on her hands, swinging her feet as if bored.

She wasn't bored.

"Now what?" she asked. The hitch in her voice revealed the lie. The breathlessness.

"Your shirt."

"You're supposed to tell me where you'd like to touch me."

"I want to see you first."

And I did. I wanted—no, *needed*—to see her like a starving man needed sustenance. Her eyes narrowed, but she gradually lifted the hem of her top, revealing more of that golden skin. Inch by torturous inch. After sliding it overhead, she tossed it in a pool at my feet. "And now?"

And now she was naked. Gloriously so. Though I longed to touch her, to reach out and trace the curve of her waist, I kept my hands fisted in the cushions. She wanted me to dictate each touch. She wanted to hear every word for what it was—a decision. Small decisions, yes, but decisions nonetheless. Honest ones. There could be no lies between us here. Not like this.

Not like this.

"Your thigh," I said, unable to tear my gaze away from her ankles, her calves, her knees. Unable to think coherently, to speak more than a handful of syllables. Too enthralled to be embarrassed. "Touch it."

Her belly undulated with laughter at the command. Her shoulders shook with it. I feasted on the sound, on the *sight*—each intake of breath, each exhalation. Though each bout rang high and clear, delighted, she had no business sounding so innocent. Not when her body burned as sin incarnate.

"I need more than that, Chass. Be specific." Leaning forward, she swept her hand casually to the middle of her thigh. "Here?" When I shook my head, swallowing hard, she trailed a single finger higher. Higher still. "Or . . . here?"

"What does it feel like?" Unable to help myself, I pitched upright, swift and unsteady. My hands trembled with the need to replace hers, but I resisted. I couldn't touch her now. I'd never stop. "Imagine it's my hand, and tell me exactly how your skin feels."

With a wink, she closed her eyes. "It feels . . . warm."

"Just warm?"

"Feverish." Her other hand drifted to her throat, her neck, as she continued to caress her thigh. Her smile faded. "I feel feverish. Hot."

Feverish. Hot. "Your finger. Move it higher." When she complied, sliding it between her legs, I nearly tore through the cushions. My heart beat rapidly. "What does it feel like there?"

Her breath left in a whoosh as that finger moved. Her legs trembled. I ached to grab them. To pin her to the table and finish what we'd started. But this—this wasn't like before. This was different. This was *everything*. "Tell me, Lou. Tell me how hot you feel."

"It feels"—her hips rocked in slow rhythm with her finger, and her head fell back, her spine arching—"good. It feels so good, Reid. I feel so good."

"Be specific," I said through gritted teeth.

When she told me what it felt like—slick and sensitive, aching and *empty*—I fell to my knees before her. She'd spoken of worship. I understood now. I still didn't touch her, however, not even when she added a second finger, a third, and said on a sigh, "I wish it was you."

I wish it was too. "Part your legs." Her legs fell open. "Show me how you touch yourself."

And she did.

Her thumb made delicate circles first. Then indelicate ones. More and more, her movements growing faster, graceless, as her legs tensed and spasmed. I felt each press of her thumb myself— the building pressure, the sharp ache. The need for release. I managed one breath. Two. Then—

"Stop."

The curt word startled her, and she stilled, her chest heaving. A fine sheen of sweat glistened there. I longed to taste it. Rising on my knees, I gripped the table on either side of her. "Open your eyes." When she did so—still panting softly—I said, "Look at me. Don't hide. I said I want to see you."

Those eyes locked on mine with unerring focus then. She didn't so much as blink as her fingers resumed between us. Slow at first, building faster. And on her lips . . . I leaned closer still, almost touching her now. Never touching her. When she breathed my name—a condemnation, a plea, a *prayer*—the sound virtually undid me. My hand plunged into my own pants. At the first touch, I nearly broke.

"Do I—" Lou rested her forehead against mine, near frantic now. A bead of sweat trickled between her breasts as she moved. I tracked its path mindlessly. "Do I make you feel *wanton*, husband? Does this—make you feel *ashamed*?"

No. *God*, no. Nothing about this felt shameful. My chest constricted tighter at the word—too tight, too small to contain the emotions rioting there. I couldn't describe them, except that they felt—*she* felt— "You make me feel right. Whole."

A shiver swept my spine at the confession. At the truth. My skin tingled in anticipation. Her voice might've broken on a sob, on my name, and the moment she came undone, I did too. One hand rose to clutch my shoulder. Mine seized her knee. Our eyes remained open as we shuddered together, and when I sagged into her—gutted—she brushed her lips against mine. Gentle, this time. Tentative. Hopeful. Her chin quivered. Without a word, I engulfed her in my arms, holding her tight.

She'd seemed so strong since the beach. So tough and unyielding. Impervious to hurt or harm. But here—after breaking, shattering beneath my gaze—she seemed fragile as glass. No, not glass.

My *wife*.

I couldn't remember. Those memories had disappeared, leaving great cracks of emptiness in my identity. In my mind. In my heart.

No, I couldn't remember.

But now I wanted to.

THE BELLY OF THE BEAST

Lou

As the sun crested the horizon on the third morning, we slipped into Cesarine's waters.

Jean Luc gripped the helm tighter than necessary, fingers twisting the wood in an agitated gesture. "This is going to get very ugly, very quickly." His eyes flicked to me and Reid, who stood behind me at the rail. He'd hovered since that first day in the cabin, speaking little and frowning often. I'd expected as much. Reid wasn't the type for casual flings. Our time on the table had meant something to him.

He just didn't know *what*.

Still, when he thought no one could see, I'd catch him furrowing his brows and shaking his head, as if in silent conversation with himself. At times, his face would even contort with pain. I didn't dare speculate at the cause—didn't dare *hope*—instead focusing on what he'd freely given me. Though his words had been few, they'd been precious.

You make me feel right. Whole.

Despite the bitter cold, warmth suffused my body at the memory.

It hadn't been the final decision—not by any means—but it had been *a* decision. In that moment, he'd chosen me. In all the moments since, he'd chosen to stand near me, to sleep beside me, to listen when I spoke. When he'd offered me the last of his food yesterday, scowling and confused, Beau had even offered to pay Célie what he owed her.

It felt too good to be true.

I held on to it for dear life.

"When we dock at port, the harbormaster will call for His Majesty's Guard," Jean Luc said, "who will in turn alert the Chasseurs. I'll order an escort to the castle to request an audience with the king. He'll grant it once he discovers who I've captured."

Célie lifted her injection. "Lou and Reid will feign incapacitation whilst in the city."

"They'll still need to be bound." To Beau, Jean Luc added, "As will you, Your Highness."

"When Célie's parents come to collect her at port, I'll slip beneath their carriage." Coco stared at the skyline of the city as we approached. Though still small and indistinct, it grew larger every moment. "I'll wait with Claud and the others at Léviathan for the signal."

Reid towered behind me, his presence warm and steady. An uncanny sort of calm overtook his features whenever we discussed strategy. Like he'd slipped into another state of consciousness, separate from the chaos and turmoil of his emotions.

I chuckled quietly, hiding the sound behind my palm. The compartmentalization was strong in this one. "After they deposit us in our cells, Coco will create a distraction large enough to merit Chasseur attention," he said. "Jean will insist our guards intervene, and he'll take up their post temporarily."

"I'll magic us all out of our cells," I continued, "including Madame Labelle. Beau and Jean Luc will slip us from the castle undetected via the tunnels."

Jean Luc seemed agitated. "Auguste knows of the tunnels."

"He doesn't know them like me," Beau said grimly. "I can get us out."

Jean Luc's gaze flicked to Reid and me now. His fingers kept twisting. "There will be quite a bit more between the *escort you to the castle* and *deposit you in your cell* parts of the plan. You know that, correct?"

This is going to get very ugly, very quickly.

"Yes." Not for the first time, Estelle's anguished face skipped through my mind's eye. Her limp body. A boot on her cheek and a fist in her hair. Other faces quickly followed, other whispers. *Viera Beauchêne escaped after they tried to burn her and her wife—acid this time instead of flame. An experiment.* And— "I believe His Majesty has an affinity for rats."

"I'll do what I can to protect you, but . . ."

"If this is to work, your performance must be believable," Reid finished for him, voice hard. "All of ours must."

Jean Luc nodded. "It's going to hurt."

"Pain is fleeting." I didn't know where the words came from, but they held true. "And if we slip up—even for a moment—the pain will be much worse. The *stake* will be much worse." Heavy silence descended as I remembered the torment of flames licking up my limbs, of blisters rupturing my skin, of heat peeling muscle from bone. I shuddered slightly. "Trust me."

When we grew close enough to see individual buildings—to see people bustling like ants between them—Jean Luc tossed us the rope. He didn't look at any of us. "It's time."

"Do it tightly," I told Reid, who wrapped it around my ankles a moment later. Crouched before me, he kept his touch gentle, *too* gentle, and seemed loath to tighten the binds. His thumb traced a small vein in my foot up to my ankle, where it disappeared. His thumb kept traveling, however. He stared at it in concentration.

"You'll be feigning incapacitation," he muttered at last. "I don't need to cripple you."

"It needs to be convincing."

"No one will be looking at your ankles."

"Reid." When I sat forward to cup his cheek, he reluctantly met my gaze, and his composure slipped. Just a little. He leaned into my palm, unable to help himself, as emotion finally stirred in his eyes. It looked like dread. "If this goes poorly, I won't be the only one to burn. Your mother will. *You* will too. And that—that is unacceptable."

His throat bobbed. "It won't happen."

"You're right. It won't. Now"—I offered a halfhearted smirk—"can you bind me like a Chasseur binds a witch, or shall I have Coco do it?"

Reid stared at me for a single heartbeat before glancing over his shoulder. Behind us, Coco helped Beau with his own binds while Célie fluttered around them, trying and failing to help. He lowered his voice. "Tell me how to remember."

A pulse of silence—of *shock*—both mine and his.

"What?" I asked dubiously, sure I'd misheard him amidst the commotion. The wind swept past in a gale as we approached shore, and voices rose from the docks. Seagulls cried overhead in the bright morning sunshine. And my heart—it nearly pounded from my chest. "Did you say you want to—?"

"Remember, yes." Again, he looked to Coco and the others, shifting himself slightly to block their view. "You said—earlier, you said only magic could help me. *My* magic. You said I could reverse the pattern. What does that mean?"

"It means"—I forced a deep breath, nodding to him, to myself, to God or the Goddess or anyone who might've been playing such a heinous joke on me—"it means that you—"

"It means nothing for now," Coco said, dropping beside us abruptly. She squeezed my hand before turning to Reid. "Please, think about this. We don't need Morgane to remember Lou while we're all in the city. We have enough working against us without adding vengeful mother to the list."

"But—" I said desperately.

"When you remembered Bas, it almost killed you both." Coco grasped both of my hands now, her expression earnest. Perhaps just as desperate as I was. "We're mere *moments* away from Cesarine's shore, and we have a plan in place to rescue Madame

Labelle. Afterward, if this is what you both choose, I'll help him remember any way I can. You know I will. Right *now*, however, we need to get you both bound, or all seven of us will see the stake before nightfall."

All seven of us.

Shit.

Swallowing hard, I kept nodding even as Reid scowled and began tying his own ankles. This was bigger than us now. It'd always been bigger than us. "There *will* be an after, Lou," Coco whispered fiercely, turning to bind my hands behind my back. She did the same for Reid. "We'll get through this together—*all* of us—and we'll start anew. We'll carve out that piece of paradise. Together," she repeated firmly. "I promise."

Together.

I let my body go limp against the floorboards as she slipped belowdecks, as voices called out to Jean Luc in recognition, as our small boat slipped into port and men leapt aboard to help him tie it down. Reid pressed his head atop mine. The only show of comfort he could give me. Heightened sensation rose like needles along my skin as my magic fought to rise, to protect him, to protect my *home*, but I tamped it down. It was too late to turn back now. We'd entered the belly of the beast.

ALL SEVEN OF US

Lou

Mostly everything went according to plan.

It took a moment for anyone to notice us there, lifeless and forgotten on the floor, but when a hook-nosed gentleman nearly trod on Reid's foot, he yelped in surprise—then yelped louder in fear, recognition dawning over his swarthy features. "Is that—that isn't—?"

"Reid Diggory, yes," Jean Luc said with a sneer, materializing beside us. He nudged my ribs with his boot, and I slipped sideways into Reid. He stiffened subtly. "And his wife, the heiress of La Dame des Sorcières. I apprehended them in a small village north of Amandine."

The sailor's eyes boggled. "All by yourself?"

"I disabled Morgane le Blanc by myself, did I not?" Jean raised an arrogant brow at the man's spluttering. "I think you'll find anything is possible with the proper motivation." He jerked his chin toward Célie, who cowered in proper fashion near the helm, and added, "They had something that belonged to me."

Others had gathered around us now, wide-eyed and curious. Fear hadn't yet taken root. These men lived predominantly on the seas, where witches were little more than fairy stories compared to the very real danger of Isla and her melusines. "Who is that, then?" another asked, staring at Célie.

"Mademoiselle Célie Tremblay, daughter of the viscount. Her father is personal advisor to His Majesty." Jean Luc's jaw hardened. "You might've heard of him in connection to his eldest daughter, Filippa, who was murdered by witches last year. Célie fancied herself a vigilante and went after these two herself." At the sailors' derisive snorts, Célie straightened her shoulders defensively—just for a second—before remembering her role. Casting her eyes downward, she heeded Jean Luc's command when he called her over, tucking her under his arm. His hand on her shoulder clenched tighter than necessary, the only visible sign of his strain. Still, his voice oozed conceit as he added, "She's a foolish girl, but what can we expect from one so pretty?" When the men laughed—like brainless *sheep*—he snapped his fingers at one on the edge of the group. "Send word to her father. He shall collect and discipline her as he sees fit."

The messenger glanced at Beau with a frown. "Hers ain't the only father who'll be administerin' discipline." Then he leapt from the boat and disappeared, replaced almost instantly by the harbormaster. A short, portly man with a spectacular handlebar mustache, he held himself with the ferociousness of a badger as he seized my face to examine it. He wasn't gentle. Reid's muscles tensed beneath me.

"I didn't believe it," the harbormaster growled, jerking my chin this way and that, hard enough to bruise. "But it's her, after all. The bitch witch's daughter in the flesh." He grinned and straightened once more, turning to address Jean Luc. "We'll alert your brethren straightaway, of course, if they're not already on their way. Word like this travels quickly." With the jerk of his hand, another sailor departed. "I'll expect some sort of commendation for allowing you to port. A dual capture, if you will."

Jean Luc glared at him. "You dare to extort a captain of the Chasseurs?"

"Not a captain, no." Undaunted by Jean Luc's ire, the man crossed his arms, still grinning. "Auguste is an old friend of mine, did you know? Rumor has it you've been missed, *Captain*."

Jean Luc's eyes narrowed as my own stomach plunged. "What are you saying?"

The man simply shrugged and glanced behind at the commotion up the street. "I expect you'll find out soon enough."

A virtual battalion of Chasseurs thundered toward us on horseback, eliciting shrieks from pedestrians in their path. More and more people—sailors, fishermen, peddlers—collected around our boat now. All craned their necks from the dock to see what the fuss was about, some clapping hands over their mouths when they spotted us, others hissing through their teeth. One woman even threw a fish with unerring aim. It struck Reid's cheek before falling, dead, to the floor. Beau pretended to struggle in his binds. "That's enough," he snarled.

The harbormaster clicked his tongue. "Well, well, well, Your

Highness." He squatted before him, examining Beau's face from every angle. "The last time I saw you, you were in nappies—" Before he could finish the rest of his humiliating diatribe, however, the first of the huntsmen reached us. I recognized him from La Mascarade des Crânes.

"Philippe." Jean Luc scowled as the man in question—a rather large, frightening man, though not nearly so large and frightening as Reid—shouldered past him with a pointed lack of respect. Indeed, he knocked into Jean Luc like he was a piece of furniture, sending him back two steps. "Have you lost your mind?"

"Secure the area." Philippe snapped and pointed as his brethren fell into place around the boat, around *us*. He ignored Jean Luc completely. To the harbormaster, he said, "His Majesty arrives posthaste."

"He's coming *here*?" Jean Luc lifted his voice above the tumult, determined to be heard. Boots jostled as the King's Guard arrived—the constabulary too—heedless of my fingers. When Philippe stepped on Reid's intentionally, I heard the cruel *crack* of bone. Reid didn't so much as flinch. "*Why?*"

"To secure the prisoners, of course," the harbormaster said.

"No." Jean Luc shook his head wildly. "No, he shouldn't travel out in the open like this. Morgane is here. She's in the city—"

Philippe's smile chilled my very bones. "It isn't up to you, Jean. Not anymore."

The king arrived the next moment—at precisely the same time as Monsieur and Madame Tremblay. Absolute pandemonium ensued. The Tremblays' carriage screeched to a halt beyond the dock, and Madame Tremblay barreled straight into the barricade of soldiers, shouting for her daughter without decorum. "Célie! Célie!" She hardly noticed the guards chasing after her. Jean Luc stepped in front of them, blocking their advance, as she enveloped her daughter in her arms. "Oh, thank *God*—"

"*Control* yourself, woman!" Monsieur Tremblay snarled as he too bolted on deck, skirting around Reid, me, and the barricade of Chasseurs encircling us. "Have you no *shame*? You will *apologize* this *instant*—" I would've laughed at the spectacle they'd created if the king hadn't followed. If his eyes hadn't locked on Reid's. If he hadn't reached into his velvet pocket to extract two metal syringes.

Oh, shit.

"*Rebonjour, fils.*" His eyes moved from Reid to me, and something predatory sparked in them. Something poisonous. A broad, brilliant smile transformed his face from attractive to breathtaking. Quite literally, my breath caught in my throat. That smile belonged to Reid. To Beau. I knew it like the back of my own hand. "*Fille.*"

Chasseur, soldier, and constable alike parted at his approach, and even Madame Tremblay quieted, finally realizing the precariousness of the situation. People didn't smile like that for no reason. Especially kings. I hardly dared breathe as he crouched before me. As he too gripped my chin between thumb and forefinger. His touch was lighter than the harbormaster's. Indeed, he handled me like fine china, his thumb sweeping over the welts as if to soothe them. "Shh, shhh. Fret not, Louise. You cannot know how I have longed for this moment."

Jean Luc hurried to intercede. "Your Majesty, please allow me to—"

"I will allow you nothing." Auguste's coldly spoken words stopped Jean in his tracks. The former's gaze didn't stray from mine, however. He studied my lips as he continued. "You are henceforth stripped of your captaincy, Chasseur Toussaint. All future duties will be handled by your new captain, Philippe Brisbois."

"*Philippe?*" Jean Luc's face twisted, and he glanced between the two, his chest swelling with rage. "I have apprehended and incapacitated two of the most notorious witches in the kingdom. I have returned your *son*—"

"What you have *done*," Auguste snapped, "is disobey my direct command. Your presence at the conclave was not requested. It was required. In forfeiting your responsibilities, you have forfeited your title. I do hope she was worth it." His lip curled as he glanced to Célie. "She *is* very pretty."

Jean Luc opened and closed his mouth, near apoplectic now. Even amidst the dire circumstances, I felt a twinge of sorrow for him. In the breadth of a single moment, he thought he'd lost everything. When Auguste dropped his hand from my chin, however, flicking the first syringe, fear surpassed all other emotions. I cast a panicked glance at Jean Luc, willing him to pull himself together.

"I met your mother once, Louise," Auguste said, still *tap, tap, tapping* the syringe. "Now she—*she* is exquisite. A diamond of the first water. It's too bad, really, that she's a soul-sucking demoness. Just like *your* mother," he added to Reid, tilting his head to examine the quill. A bead of hemlock trickled from its tip. My magic reared its head at the sight, white patterns unfurling all around me. They hummed with the need to protect Reid. To protect all of them. I nearly trembled with restraint. Oblivious, Auguste stroked my hair and pulled my limp body to his lap. "You look nothing like her, of course, poor thing. All your father, aren't you?" He leaned so close that I could smell the mint on his breath. "I loathed that man. Makes this easier, I suppose—a bit *too* easy. When I announced Helene's execution, I knew you'd come, but I never expected this sort of weakness."

He pressed the syringe to my throat.

"Your Majesty." Though Jean Luc didn't dare step closer, his voice rose urgently. "I re-injected the prisoners only moments before docking. If you dose them again so quickly, I fear they'll die before the stake."

Auguste lifted a golden brow. "You *fear* their death?"

"A poor choice of words." Jean Luc ducked his head. "Please forgive me."

But Auguste's gaze had already sharpened with suspicion. "There is only one way to kill a witch, huntsman, and it is not poison. You have nothing to *fear*. Still, however, I am benevolent. I will not dose the prisoners again."

I breathed a long, slow sigh of relief.

Perhaps Auguste felt the movement. Perhaps he didn't. Either way, he gestured Jean Luc toward us, pressing the injection into his palm before rising to his feet. He brought me with him, cradling me within his arms. My limbs dangled helplessly. "*You* will."

Shit, shit, *shit*.

Jean Luc blinked, his expression flattening. "Me, Your Majesty?"

"Yes, huntsman. You. A great honor, is it not? To apprehend *and* incapacitate two of the most notorious witches in the kingdom?"

The implication rang clear in the ensuing silence. Even the wind had fallen silent to listen. As if hoping to prove his suspicions, Auguste pinched the flesh of my thigh and twisted—hard. I clenched my teeth against the pain. He would not break us with a pinch, nor a bruised chin or broken finger. The white patterns still writhed in fury, however. They demanded retribution. I wouldn't use them. Not yet. If I did, all would know Jean Luc had been lying. They would know he'd betrayed them, and he really *would* lose everything—his coat, his Balisarda, his *life*. Célie would be implicated too.

All seven of us.

No, our plan could still work. Jean Luc could fake the injection somehow, and we—

"I am waiting," Auguste said darkly.

Though Jean Luc fought to keep his face impassive, panic flickered within his eyes' pale depths—panic and remorse. They met mine for only a second before dropping to the syringe. In that second, I knew. He would fake nothing. He *could* fake nothing—not with so many eyes on us now. Not under the king's very nose.

Which left me with two options.

I could attack the king now, and we could *likely* fight our way out, condemning Jean Luc, Célie, and Madame Labelle in the process. *Or* I could allow the injection and trust the others to rescue us. Neither option was foolproof. Neither option guaranteed escape. With the latter, at least, we'd be in a centralized location with Madame Labelle. If they rescued one, they could rescue us all. And though Claud claimed he couldn't intervene, he wouldn't truly leave us to die, would he?

I had a split second to decide before Jean plunged the quill into my throat.

Sharp pain flared on impact, and the hemlock—as cold and viscous as I remembered it—spread like mire through my veins. I could just feel the warm trickle of blood before numbness crept in, before my vision faded, before Coco slipped unnoticed from the water to the Tremblays' carriage.

The white patterns resisted the darkness, blazing brighter and hotter as I dimmed.

Auguste held one of my eyes open, even as it rolled back into my head. "Do not fret, *fille*. This pain shall pass. At sunset, you shall burn with my son and his mother in a lake of black fire." When he stroked my cheek—almost tenderly—the white patterns finally softened, finally succumbed, finally dissolved into nothing.

We'd gone from the belly of the beast straight into the shitter.

OUR STORY

Lou

My body awoke in increments. First a twitch of my hand, a tingle in my feet, before lights danced on my eyelids and cotton grew on my tongue. Both felt thick and heavy as my stomach pitched and rolled. My consciousness followed shortly after that—or perhaps not shortly at all—and I felt cold stones beneath my back, hard ridges, dull pain blossoming across my ribs, my temple. Sharper pain at my throat.

Realization trickled in slowly.

Jean Luc had poisoned us. We'd been thrown in prison. We would burn at sunset.

My eyes snapped open at the last.

What time was it?

Staring at the ceiling overhead, I tried to move my fingers, to breathe around the suffocating nausea. I needed to find Reid and Beau. I needed to make sure they were all right—

Only then did I realize two things, like cards flipped over in a game of tarot: warm skin pressed against mine on the right, and wooden bars intersected the ceiling in a cross pattern overhead. Swallowing hard, I turned my head with enormous difficulty. *Thank God.* Reid lay beside me, his face pale but his chest rising and falling deeply.

Wooden bars.

A muffled cough sounded from nearby, and I slammed my eyes shut, listening intently. Footsteps shuffled closer, and what sounded like a door creaked open. After a few more seconds, it clicked shut once more. I opened my eyes carefully this time, peering out through my lashes. The same wooden bars across the ceiling and floor ran perpendicular as well. Smooth and hand planed, they bisected the room and formed a sort of cage around us.

A cage.

Oh god.

Once more, I forced myself to breathe. Though the room beyond remained dark, lit only by a single torch, it didn't look like a dungeon. A colossal table dominated the center of the room—circular and covered in what looked like a map, scraps of parchment, and—and—

Realization didn't trickle now. It rushed in a great flood, and I rolled to my left, away from Reid. We weren't in the castle dungeon at all, but the council room of Chasseur Tower. I would've recognized that table anywhere, except now—instead of charcoal drawings of my mother—portraits of my own face stared back at me. Portraits of Reid. Clearing my throat of bile, I tentatively sat up on my elbows, glancing around the cage. No cots or even chamber pots filled the space. "Beau?" A hoarse whisper, my voice still reverberated too loud in the darkness. "Are you here?"

No one answered.

Cursing quietly, I crawled back to Reid, feeling steadier with each moment. I didn't know why. By all accounts, I too should've been unconscious on the floor, not moving and thinking with relative ease. It made little sense, except . . . I took another deep breath, summoning my magic, both gold and white. Though the golden patterns curled sluggish and confused across the cage, the white ones burst into existence with a vengeance. Their presence soothed the sickness in my body like a balm. My vision cleared, and my stomach settled. The stabbing pain in my temples eased. Of course. *Of course.* These patterns had been gifted by a goddess. They were greater than me, eternal, stronger than my own human flesh and bone.

They'd saved me.

We were going to be fine.

With a triumphant smile, I checked Reid's pupils, his heartbeat, and his breathing. I could sense the poison polluting his blood, could almost *see* it beneath his skin like a black, noxious cloud. Gently, a white pattern coiled around him, illuminating his wan features in a subtle glow. At the brush of my hand, it pulsed and began to sieve the hemlock from his body. The stone around him absorbed the sap like a sponge, returning it to the earth where it belonged. When the last of the poison had gone, the pattern dissolved into white dust, and Reid's eyes fluttered open. I sat back on my heels as he oriented himself with the room. With me.

He reached up to touch a strand of my hair. "You're glowing."

I shrugged, grinning impishly now. "Goddess Divine, you know."

"Such arrogance."

"Such beauty and grace."

He scoffed, sitting up and rubbing his neck. It might've been my imagination, but I thought a rueful grin played on his lips. "Why don't I feel sick?"

I grinned wider. "I *healed* you."

Groaning, he shook his head, and I didn't imagine it now—he definitely smiled. "You really don't know the meaning of humility, do you?"

"And *you* really don't know the meaning of gratitude—"

Footsteps again, quicker this time. We flung ourselves down, feigning unconsciousness, just as the door burst open. "What is it?" a voice asked, unfamiliar and deep.

"I thought I heard someone."

Discomfort seeped into the first's voice. "Should we dose them again?"

The other cleared their throat. "They still *look* incapacitated."

"Philippe will skin us if they die on our watch."

"The hemlock is merely a precaution. The bars will keep them in here." A pause. "Philippe said the wood is . . . special. They harvested it from La Fôret des Yeux."

After another few seconds of anxious silence, they closed the door once more. "Keep your voice down next time," I hissed, poking Reid in the ribs.

His face snapped toward mine in outrage. "I wasn't—"

"I'm joking, Chass."

"Oh." He frowned when I snorted. "Is this really the time to joke?"

"It's *never* the time to joke with us. If we waited until we were out of life-or-death situations, we could only laugh in our graves." Hoisting myself to my feet, I inspected the bars closer. Though clearly wooden, they still felt . . . unnatural. Both made and unmade. The torchlight caught veins of silver in the wood. *The hemlock is merely a precaution. The bars will keep them in here.* I leaned in to sniff them as Reid rose behind.

"What are they?" he asked.

"I don't know. The tree smells like alder, but the timber is . . . metallic? I can't recall any metallic trees in La Fôret des Yeux. Can you?"

"A metallic tree," he echoed slowly.

Our eyes snapped together in dawning horror. "It couldn't be—?"

"It's not—?"

"Oh my god," I breathed, recoiling. The bars felt abruptly cold beneath my touch. Oppressive. "They cut it down. Your Balisarda."

Beside me, Reid closed his eyes in acknowledgment, in defeat, pressing his forehead against the wood. Voice strained, he asked, "How did they even find it?"

"It was along the road. Bas and his cronies called for the Chasseurs when they found us." On a hunch, I pressed a finger to one of the bars. The white patterns dimmed almost instantly in response. No. No, no, *no*. "They would've seen it straightaway—a great tree with silver bark and black fruit and lethal thorns."

"Can you magic us out?"

I released the bar again, returning to the middle of the cage, equal distance from all sides. Though the white patterns flared once more, they floated untethered when they reached the bars, unable to touch them or move past them. Not a promising sign. Closing my eyes, focusing my energy, I sought the lock on the bars—simpler than the one on the treasury door of Chateau le Blanc, made of iron, yet strategically placed outside the magic wood. The harder I tried to reach it, the more the pattern frayed until it disintegrated completely. "Fuck."

To his credit, Reid didn't even flinch. Instead he gripped the bars in earnest, testing their weight. "I can break them."

"You have a broken finger."

That didn't stop him from trying to snap the wood for the next ten minutes. Knuckles bloody, arms shaking, he finally punched the bar with all his might, succeeding in only breaking another finger. When he cocked his fist to strike again, furious, I rolled my eyes and dragged him back to the center of the cage. "Yes, *thank* you. That was helpful."

"What are we going to *do*?" He tore a frustrated hand through his hair. I caught it before he could damage it further. His broken fingers had swelled to twice their normal size, and blood welled dark and purple beneath the skin. He turned away. "This *brilliant* plan of yours has a few holes."

I repressed a scowl, wrapping another pattern around his hand. "I can't control every variable, Reid. At least *this* one didn't involve mustaches and crutches. Now shut it, or I'll give you a real hole to complain about." An empty threat. The Chasseurs had disarmed both of us before throwing us in here.

"Is that supposed to be innuendo? I can never tell with you."

I jerked at the pattern, and it snapped his fingers back into place, shattering my irritation in the process. He winced and wrenched his hand—now completely healed—out of mine. "Thank you," he muttered after another moment. "And . . . sorry." The word sounded pained.

I almost chuckled. Almost. Unfortunately, without irritation to distract me, panic crept back in. I couldn't magic us out of here, and Reid couldn't break the bars physically. Perhaps I could shield us within the cage somehow, like I'd done on the bridge. If they couldn't see us, they couldn't march us to the stake. Even as the thought formed, I knew it was no real solution. We couldn't hide here indefinitely, invisible. Perhaps if they opened the cage to investigate, however . . . "The others will come for us." Whether I spoke to him or myself, I didn't know.

"Philippe won't let Jean Luc within fifty feet of this room."

"It's fortunate, then, that Jean Luc isn't our only ally. Coco will know where we are. She'll bring Claud or Zenna or Blaise, and they'll break us out."

He leveled me with a frank stare. "I don't think you grasp the number of huntsmen living in this tower, Lou."

Leaning forward, I rested my elbows on my knees. "I don't

think *you* grasp that I lived here too."

"You did?" Surprise colored his tone. "How?"

"I was your *wife*. The Archbishop couldn't have separated us, even if he wanted to—which he didn't. He arranged the whole marriage."

"Why?" Now he leaned forward too, his eyes trained on mine. Hungry for information. His earlier words echoed back to me: *Tell me how to remember.* If we were going to die at sunset, Coco's argument hardly applied anymore, did it? Another mad idea formed on the heels of that realization. If Reid remembered, Morgane would too. If the others didn't come for me, *she* would. She'd tear this tower apart brick by brick if she learned the Chasseurs intended to burn me.

Of course, Reid still had a point. She'd never been able to tear it apart before. Stripped of her title, she'd hardly be able to do it now.

"You know why." I shrugged, the thoughts tangling into a helpless knot of confusion. My foot tapped restlessly. "I'm his daughter. He wanted you to protect me."

He scoffed again, an angry sound, and gestured around us. "I've done an excellent job."

"Our friends will come for us, Reid. We have to trust them."

"Where are they, then? Why aren't they here?"

"Hopefully they're out rescuing your mother and brother. That *was* the whole point of the endeavor, if you remember."

His face flushed, and he looked away. "Of course I remember."

The guards flung the door open unexpectedly this time.

In the split second it took for the knob to unlatch, a third idea formed, and impulsively, I transformed into the Maiden as two Chasseurs stepped through. Their eyes flew wide when they saw me. "Oh, please, *messieurs*!" I wrung my hands with a cry, pacing before the bars without touching them. "The witch—she tricked me. I'm a scullery maid upstairs, but while I was washing the linens, I heard a voice singing the most beautiful song." I spoke quicker now, disliking the calculated gleam in the older one's eyes. "I just *had* to follow it, *messieurs*—like some outside force compelled me to do it, like I was in a *trance*—and I didn't wake until I'd unlocked the door and let her go. Please, *please*, let me out while the other still sleeps." Gesturing to Reid on the floor, I allowed my lip to quiver and tears to spill down my cheeks. It was easier to feign distress than I'd anticipated. "I'm so sorry. You can dock my pay, you can relieve me of service, you can *lash* me, but please don't let him hurt me."

Though the younger looked likely to leap to my rescue, the older stilled him with a smile. It wasn't a compassionate one. "Are you finished?"

I sniffed loudly. "Will you not help me?"

In two strides, he crossed the room to the circular table, rifling through the papers there. He pulled one from beneath a crucifix paperweight and held it to the light. Though sketched with rudimentary lines, the drawing portrayed my face—the *Maiden's* face—well enough. My distraught expression fell flat as I leaned against the bars. My form reverted once more. "Good for you."

"Yes," he mused, examining me curiously. "It rather is. It

seems you've inherited your mother's gifts. His Majesty will be pleased to know it."

"That—that's La Dame des Sorcières's daughter?"

"It appears *she* is La Dame des Sorcières now."

The younger's concern vanished instantly, replaced by what looked like awe. Perhaps a touch of fear. Of hunger. "We caught her?"

"You didn't catch anyone." My own fear sharpened my voice. I pushed it down. The others would come. They *would*. "May I inquire as to the time?"

The older replaced the picture before approaching the cage. Though he kept his posture casual, sweat had collected along his upper lip. I made him nervous. *Good.* "You can ask. I won't answer, though. Better to watch you squirm." When I thrust my face at the bars, swift and sudden, he stumbled backward. To his credit, he didn't curse, instead clutching his chest with a low chuckle.

"Shall we inject it?" The younger drew fresh syringes from his coat. "Teach it a lesson?"

"No." The older shook his head and backed from the room. "No, I think we're inflicting just the right amount of torment, don't you?"

The two closed the door behind them with a resounding *click*.

Now Reid pulled *me* away from the bars. "The others will come," he said.

Some time later, a scuffle broke out in the corridor to prove his words. Voices rose to shouts, and the sound of steel against steel rang out in the sweetest harmony. We both launched to our feet, staring at the door and waiting. "This is it." My fingers wrapped around the bars in anticipation. "They're here."

Reid frowned at the high-pitched, feminine voices. Unfamiliar, they didn't belong to Coco or Célie or Zenna or even Seraphine. They sounded like the voices of . . . *children*. "Leave us alone!" one cried, indignant. "Let us go!"

"I don't think so," a Chasseur snarled. "Not this time."

"Your father won't be pleased, Victoire."

"My father can swallow an egg!"

"This isn't *right*," another child cried. "Remove your hands at *once*. That's our *brother* in there, and he hasn't done anything wrong—"

Their voices faded as the Chasseurs dragged them away.

"Violette and Victoire." Reid stared at the door as if sheer will alone might open it. At the intensity of his gaze, I might've believed it too. "They sprang us from the dungeon before La Mascarade les Crânes."

"Follow the memory," I said desperately. If even the king's daughters couldn't enter Chasseur Tower unimpeded, the chances of others doing so had just vanished in a puff of smoke.

"What?"

"You want to remember. This is how." Unable to escape this *hideous* prison, ignorant of the time, of our friends, of our very lives, this suddenly became the most important thing in the world. The most urgent one. He had to remember. If we were going to die at sunset, he had to remember me. The wager, the seduction, the plan—it all fell away in light of this one critical moment. "Follow it forward or backward until you hit a wall. Then *push*."

His mouth twisted grimly. "I—I've *tried*. These past few days—I've done nothing but try to piece it back together."

"Try again. Try harder."

"Lou—"

I crushed his hands in my own. "What if they don't come?"

He clutched mine with equal fervor, his voice low and ferocious as he pulled me closer. "They *will*."

"What if they can't? What if they fail to sneak inside undetected? What if they have to fight? What if Claud can't intervene, or they were captured at the castle, or—" My eyes widened in alarm. "What if they're already dead?"

"Stop, *stop*." He seized my face, bending low to look me directly in the eye. "Breathe. Tell me what to do."

It took a moment to collect myself, to calm my racing heart. He waited patiently, his thumbs kneading my temples. The intimacy of the gesture both agitated and soothed me. At last, I pulled away and said, "After Violette and Victoire rescued you from the dungeons, you returned to Léviathan. Do you remember that?"

He shadowed my footsteps. "Yes. I took a bath."

"And then?"

"And then I"—his face contorted—"I spoke with Claud. I told him about my mother's capture."

Lacing my fingers through his, I shook my head. "You didn't. 'They took her, Lou. They took my mother, and she's not coming back.' That's what you told me."

He stared at me, nonplussed. "What happened next?"

"You tell me." When he said nothing, only stared, I reached up to kiss his cheek. His arms wrapped around my waist. "After I took Bas's memories," I whispered against his skin, "I didn't realize what I'd done until I saw him again. There were these— these gaps in my thoughts. I didn't scrub him away completely, only the romantic moments, but he didn't recognize me at all. I had to find a trigger to help me remember—one memory to spark the rest."

He pulled back to look at me. "But that could be anything."

"For me, it was the moment I met Bas in Soleil et Lune."

"Where did I meet you?"

"Outside of Pan's patisserie." I spun him toward the lock hastily. "Imagine a door. You were blocking the whole thing like a giant asshole, watching Beau's homecoming parade in the street." He turned to scowl at me over his shoulder. "What? You *were*. It was completely discourteous. I tried to move past you"—I imitated the movement—"but there wasn't room for both of us. You ended up turning and nearly breaking my nose with your elbow." When he pivoted to face me in real time, I lifted his elbow and snapped my head back, pantomiming the injury. "Does any of this ring a bell?"

He looked thoroughly miserable. "No."

Fuck. "Maybe this isn't your trigger." I fought to keep my voice even. "It could be something else—like when you chased me in Soleil et Lune, or when we married on the bank of the Doleur, or—or when we had sex for the first time on the rooftop."

His eyes narrowed. "We consummated our relationship on a rooftop?"

I nodded swiftly. Too swiftly. "Soleil et Lune again. It was so cold—try to imagine it. The wind on your bare skin."

When fresh guards popped in to check on us, we ignored them, and after a taunt or two, they left. The clock ticked onward. Every second, it brought us closer to sunset. No other shouts rose from the corridor. No second rescue attempt. Where *were* they? Reid shook his head, scrubbing a hand over his face as he paced. "I don't remember any of this."

"But you—I've seen you as you've started to remember. I've seen the pain in your expression. It *hurts*."

He threw his arms in the air, growing more and more frustrated. Or perhaps flustered. Perhaps both. "Those times have been few and far between, and even then, when I try to push through—to follow the memory—it's like I'm jumping into a void. There's nothing *there*. No wall to break. No door to open or lock to pick or window to smash. The memories are just *gone*."

Wretched tears gathered in my eyes. "The pattern can be reversed."

"What *pattern*?" His voice rose to almost a shout as he whirled to face me, jaw clenched and cheeks flushed. "The entire *world* seems to think I'm a witch—and I'm about to burn at the stake, so it must be true—but I can't—I don't—I've never *seen* a pattern, Lou. Not a single speck of gold or white or fucking indigo. It's like this person you know—he doesn't *exist*. I'm not him. I don't know if I'll ever be him again."

When the tears fell freely down my cheeks, he groaned and wiped them away, moisture glistening in his own eyes. "Please, don't cry. I can't stand your tears. They make me—they make me want to rend the world apart to stop them, and I can't—" He kissed me again, fierce with abandon. "Tell me again. Tell me all of it. I'll remember this time."

Within the hard shield of his arms, I repeated everything. I told him the story of us: the slashed arm and spattered sheet, the book called *La Vie Éphémère*, the trip to the theater and the market, the temple, the troupe, the shop of curiosities. I told him of Modraniht and La Mascarade des Crânes and every moment spent together in between. Every momentous shift in our relationship. The bathtub. The attic. The funeral.

I told him of magic.

He remembered nothing.

Yes, his face twisted occasionally, but upon embracing the pain, chasing the memories, he'd find only smoke and mirrors.

We gradually realized the guards rotated in two-hour shifts— Reid *could* remember that—checking in every half hour. When the last set appeared, I wept openly as Reid cradled me in his lap. "Not long now," one of them had jeered. The other hadn't wanted to linger, however, pulling his companion from the room with a discomfited expression.

Still no one came for us.

I hoped they'd survived. I hoped they'd rescued Madame Labelle and Beau, and I hoped they'd fled the city. I couldn't bear the thought of them watching us burn. Though it wouldn't be their fault, they'd never forgive themselves, and Coco—she'd suffered enough. She'd *lost* enough, as had Madame Labelle and Beau and Célie and even Jean Luc. Perhaps we'd been stupid to dream of something more. Something better. I still hoped they'd found it.

If anyone deserved peace, it was them.

Reid rested his cheek against my hair. "I'm so sorry, Lou." Silence stretched between us, tautly strung like a bow. I waited for it to snap. "I wish—"

"Don't." Slowly, I lifted my head to look at him. My heart contracted at the anguish on his familiar face. I traced the shape of his brows, his nose, his lips, staring at each feature in turn. Deep down, I'd known how this would end all along. I'd sensed it from the moment we'd first met, from the time I'd first glimpsed the Balisarda in his bandolier—two star-crossed lovers brought together by fate or providence. By life and by death. By gods, or perhaps monsters.

We would end with a stake and a match.

Waving my hand, I shielded us from any huntsman's gaze. Magic erupted around us. "Kiss me, Reid."

CONFESSIONAL

Reid

I stared at her tearstained face, chest aching. She didn't need to convince me. I'd do anything she asked. If kissing her would stop another tear from falling, I'd kiss her a thousand times. If we survived the night, I'd kiss away every tear for the rest of her life.

Where you go, I will go. Where you stay, I will stay.

She'd whispered the words to me like a prayer. And I still felt them. I felt each one.

How could I have ever thought this emotion between us wasn't sacred? This connection. What I felt for Lou was visceral and raw and *pure*. It would consume me, if I let it. Consume us both.

But I stared for too long. With fresh tears, she flung her arms around my neck and buried her head in my shoulder. Cursing my mistake, I cradled her face in both hands. Gently. So gently. I tipped her face up to look at me. And then—with deliberate care—I pressed my lips to hers.

I couldn't soothe this ache. I couldn't right this wrong. In all likelihood, we'd both burn at sunset.

But I could hold her.

"I love you," she breathed, lashes fluttering as I brushed soft kisses along her cheeks. Her nose. Her eyelids. "I loved you then, I love you now, and I'll love you after." My lips trailed down her throat. Toward her scar. Her head fell back in response, baring it to me. Completely vulnerable. "Before my mother slit my throat on Modraniht"—the words sounded like a confession—"I thought I'd never see you again. A witch and a witch hunter can't have each other in the afterlife."

I lifted my head then. "I'll find you again, Lou." The words came readily, as if they'd been waiting on the tip of my tongue. A confession of my own. Perhaps I'd said them before. I couldn't remember. It didn't matter. Though I'd lost our past, I refused to lose our future too. Even death wouldn't take it from me. "I promise."

She met my eyes with languorous heat. "I know."

Despite the urgency of our situation—the huntsmen patrolling outside, the sun setting over the city—Lou didn't rush as she slipped her palms into my collar, as she slid them down my back. My own hands moved leisurely to the hem of her shirt. Peeling the fabric from her belly inch by inch, I lowered her to the floor. She stripped my own shirt overhead. Heat pooled between us as she traced the scar on my torso, as I eased down her body. As I tasted each curve. With every breath, every touch—sultry and slow, as if searching—the intensity built. The quiet desperation.

Her fingers curled in my hair.

My tongue stroked her hip.

"You called me your heathen," she said on a sigh, arching and shifting my mouth lower. Lower still.

I would find her again, yes, but we still had this moment. This last breathless hour. "You still are." Sliding her pants down her legs, I flipped her over. Trapping her. Her nails raked against the bars on the floor as I lifted her hips to kiss her. As I stroked her there instead. Her trembling built and built until at last she fractured—biting her hand to stifle the sound—and I hauled her flush against my chest. Pressed her against the bars. Waited with ragged breaths.

Her head fell back on my shoulder, and she snaked an arm around my head. Her lips slanted up to meet mine. "Don't you dare stop."

I plunged into her without another word—unable to speak if I'd tried—snaking one arm around her waist. Heat ripped through my entire body. Overcome, my other arm wrenched her backward, wrapping around her shoulders. Holding her to me. When her fingers braced against my forearm, I couldn't look away from them. Smooth and golden atop my own paler, rougher skin. The simple sight of it tightened my chest to the point of pain. So similar. So different. I couldn't take it. I couldn't *breathe*. She felt—she felt like heaven, but I forced myself to move slowly. Deeply. To savor her. At her moan, I clapped a hand to her mouth. "Shh. They'll hear."

She had other ideas.

Twisting in my arms, she bore me back to the floor and pinned my hands above my head. Leaning low, she bit my lower lip. "Let them."

The last of my breath left in a rush. I fought to remain still as she moved atop me, pressure building until I clenched my eyes shut. Until I couldn't help it. Until my hands descended on her hips, and I coaxed her to move faster, adjusting her angle. Watching as her lips parted, her breath quickened. Though the pressure at my core swelled to physical pain, I gritted my teeth against it. *Not yet.* Her body moved in perfect unison with mine. *She* was perfect. I'd been so foolish to not realize before. So blind.

When she shuddered in release a moment later, I let go too— and in that moment, gold winked in my periphery. Just a flash. There and gone before I could fully register it. A figment of my imagination.

A fragment of memory remained, however. A handful of words. *My* words.

It heeds those who summon it.

Pain wracked my senses at the realization, and I bowed over with it, nearly toppling sideways. Lou's eyes shot open in alarm. "Reid?" She shook me weakly. "What is it? What's wrong?"

"Nothing." The pain passed just as quickly as it'd come. Just as inexplicably. When she remained unconvinced, I shook my head. "I'm fine. Truly."

"A memory?"

"It's gone now."

With a weary sigh, she wrapped her arms around me. I crushed her in my own. We sat like that for several minutes, simply holding each other. Breathing. Her cheek fell heavy upon my shoulder. "You should dress," I murmured at last. "The huntsmen . . ."

"I don't think I can move."

"I can help."

Her arms constricted briefly, but she didn't protest as I slipped first her shirt overhead, then mine. I tugged her pants into place next. She didn't bother lacing them. Instead, she collapsed back against my chest. Her eyelids fluttered. Swallowing hard, I stroked her hair. "Sleep. I'll wake you if anything changes."

"They could still come, you know." She smothered a yawn, her eyes drifting shut. "The others. They could still rescue us."

"They could."

I held her tighter than necessary as she slipped under. The silence seemed to grow and stretch in her wake. The torchlight flickered. "They could," I repeated firmly. To her. To myself. To anyone who would listen.

They could still rescue us.

But they didn't.

A SINGLE SPARK

Reid

When the door opened an hour later, I knew immediately the time had come.

Two huntsmen followed the first, shoulders rigid and Balisardas drawn. Two more filed in after that. Another set. Another. They kept coming until they filled the council room completely. Others waited in the corridor beyond. Dozens of them. Though I scanned their faces in search of Jean Luc, he wasn't there.

Lou startled awake at the footsteps, her eyes still heavy with sleep. "What is—?"

She inhaled sharply as she took in the room, jerking upright. The Chasseur nearest us dropped his eyes to the laces of her trousers. He barked a laugh. Swiftly, I twisted to block her from sight—pulling her to her feet—but she merely leaned around me and flashed a catlike smile. "See something you like?"

Despite her bravado, her eyes remained red-rimmed and puffy. Overly bright. Her hand trembled against my arm.

The huntsman's lip curled. "Hardly."

Sniggering, she surveyed his trousers pointedly. Stepped around me to lace up her own with casual nonchalance. "I doubt that very much."

"You little—" He lunged for the bars, but when Lou met him there, moving with lethal speed, he changed his mind mid-step. Pointing his Balisarda at her face instead, he said, "You'll sing a different tune soon, witch. Your last word will be a scream."

She beckoned him closer. "Why don't you come in here and show me?"

"Lou." Voice low in warning, I pulled at the back of her shirt. She yielded only a step. Around us, the Chasseurs shadowed the movement, pressing closer. "Don't provoke them."

"It's a bit late for that, I think."

"That it is." Philippe's deep rumble preceded him into the chamber. At his appearance, the Chasseurs separated in two waves on either side. Lou's grin turned feral. Dressed in an impeccable suit of royal blue and gold—captain's medal shining on his lapel—he regarded her as a bug beneath his boot. Then he smiled coldly. Bowed. "The sun has set, *ma Dame*. Your funeral pyre awaits."

Lou retreated another step. Her arm brushed mine. Though her smirk remained fixed in place, her gaze darted from the room to the corridor. From Philippe to his Chasseurs. My heart pounded violently as I counted. A score of them in all. An entire squadron. "There are too many."

Lou gestured to the cage's door with a brittle laugh. "Good thing we have a choke point."

I glanced down at her. Her chest rose and fell in shallow breaths. My own limbs shook with adrenaline.

A Chasseur behind us sneered, "You have to come out eventually."

She whipped around to glare at him. "We really don't."

"You'll *starve*."

"Come now. His Majesty won't exhibit such patience. He decreed we would burn this evening." Her grin widened. "It won't reflect well on him if this execution doesn't go to plan, will it? I imagine his denizens are already rather restless about the Hellfire. Rather frightened." She addressed Philippe directly now. "It won't reflect well on *you* either."

On sudden impulse, I added, "Especially after my mother escaped."

Low murmurs broke out across the room at the allegation, and Philippe's face hardened. His expression said everything. Short-lived relief swept through me. They'd saved her. Coco and Jean Luc and Célie—somehow, they'd saved my mother. She was safe. Lou practically cackled now, casting me an appreciative look from the corner of her eye. "She will be apprehended," Philippe said tersely. "Make no mistake."

"You need a win, Phil. You can't afford to wait." Lou waggled her fingers at him. "I think you'll be coming in sooner rather than later."

A different Chasseur—this one younger than the others, practically an initiate—wielded his Balisarda like a crucifix. "You think your magic can harm us, witch?"

"I *think*," she said slowly, "that it won't be terribly difficult to disarm you, *mon petit chou*. I believe you've all met my husband." She hooked her thumb at me. "Youngest Chasseur in the brotherhood. Youngest captain too."

"He is no captain," Philippe said darkly.

Lou arched a brow. "Well. He did kick *your* ass."

I placed a hand on her shoulder, distinctly uncomfortable. Cold sweat trickled down my spine. When she glanced up at me, I shook my head. Near indiscernible. *What are you doing?* I tried to ask.

When she lifted said shoulder—so slight no one else could see—I had my answer. She didn't know. The bluster, the jeers, the threats—all desperate bids for time. For help. For *anything*.

We'd run out of ideas.

"Come on, Phil," she coaxed, and at her words, the faint scent of magic enveloped me. The others smelled it too. Some snarled and stiffened, knuckles tightening on their Balisardas, and looked to Philippe for instruction. Others shifted uneasily. A few, however, studied Lou in fascination as her skin began to glow. "Open the door. Play with me."

Different words resounded in my head. Still her voice, but soft and scared. *Reid.*

I stared at her.

When they open the door, she said, still watching Philippe, *stay close to me. I can't harm them directly with magic, but I can bring this tower down on their heads. It's the best chance we have. Then— Do you think Beau escaped too?*

I didn't know, and I couldn't answer. Not as Philippe accepted a bow from the Chasseur next to him. A quiver of blue-tipped arrows. "Not today," he growled, notching one with expert precision. When he pointed it directly at Lou's face, her eyes narrowed. She no longer smiled. "As you've pointed out, I have little time for games. The kingdom awaits."

He loosed the arrow without warning. Before I could vault forward—before I could even shout—it shot toward her with unerring aim. She whirled at the last second, however, faster still, and dropped into a crouch as the shaft lodged into the wall behind us. The Chasseurs there had already moved. They formed ranks on the front and sides of the cage, forming a sort of corral. A bull's-eye.

More bows emerged around us. More arrows.

I hurtled toward her, seizing her hand and dragging her to the back of the cage. I had to do something. *Now.* Lou had spoken of magic, of willing golden cords into being. I focused on them now—on a shield, on a weapon, on a fucking *key*. Anything to escape this cage. No patterns answered. Of course they didn't. I rolled sideways as Philippe launched a second arrow.

"Why bother with the stake?" Snarling, Lou lifted her hand, and the bolt fractured midair. When it fell to our feet, I seized it, spearing a foolish Chasseur who'd tried to creep behind. He fell like a stone. Eyes rolling. Limbs twitching. Lou stared at him in horror. "What the—?"

Philippe notched another arrow. "Hemlock."

This one nearly clipped my shoulder. So close it split the sleeve of my shirt. Lou's eyes blazed at the torn fabric. Her skin pulsed with unnatural light. When she stepped in front of me, her voice rang with deadly calm. *Ethereal* calm. Not a single voice, but many. They reverberated together in a chilling timbre. "You will not touch him."

Immune to the enchantment, Philippe motioned for the others to raise their bows. All twenty of them.

Lou bared her teeth.

At his sharp command, arrows hurtled from two sides. More than twenty. More than *forty*. They cut through the air with lethal precision, but each turned to dust in a three-foot radius around us. They simply—disintegrated. I sensed the barrier in the air rather than saw it. A thin film, like the soap of a bubble. A shield. Lou's fists shook with the effort to maintain it as more arrows flew. "How do I help? Tell me, Lou!"

"A pattern," she said through gritted teeth. "You can strengthen—my magic."

"How?"

"Focus." The air rained thick with arrows now, each Chasseur notching and firing at different times. A constant onslaught. Lou winced at the strike—as if she could *feel* each poisoned tip—and the shield rippled in turn. "You *are* a witch. Accept it. Focus on the outcome, and—the patterns will appear."

But they didn't—they *weren't*—no matter how hard I focused. No gold sparked. I focused harder. On her. On her shield. On the arrow tips tearing it apart. A strange thrumming started in my ears. Voices. Whispers. Not mine or Lou's but *others'*. Still no gold surfaced, however, and I let out a roar of frustration, of *rage*.

"You can do it, Reid," Lou said urgently. "You've done it

before. You can do it again. You just have to—"

She didn't finish her words. Unnoticed, two Chasseurs had succeeded where their fallen brother had not. Hands snaking between the bars—using her shield to their advantage—they seized Lou's shirt and wrenched her backward against the wood.

Her shield vanished instantly.

Shouting her name, I dove forward, prying one's arm from her neck, but sharp pain pierced my thigh. I didn't look. I *couldn't*—not as they plunged a syringe, two syringes, *three*, into Lou's throat simultaneously. Not as her back bowed, her body thrashed, her hands reached for me. "Reid! *Reid!*" Her voice sounded as if from a tunnel. At last, she tore free, catching me as my knees gave out. The Tower shook around us. Her body jolted from impact as she shielded me from arrow after arrow. More than one protruded from her back now. Her arms. Her legs. Still she dragged me toward the cage's door, which Philippe had flung wide.

Hands pulled at our clothing, our hair, flinging us to the council room floor. My vision faded as they descended on Lou like ants. As she collapsed, unmoving, under their syringes. They would kill her before she reached the stake. *Lou.* Clenching my teeth, delirious with pain—with fear—I focused on her dimming skin harder than I'd focused on anything in my life. Hard knees pressed into my back.

She'll die she'll die she'll die

Gold exploded in my vision—and I to my feet—but it was too late.

A quill stabbed into my neck, and the world went dark once more.

I woke to shouts.

To smoke. The scratch of hay at my feet and hard wood at my back. Tight binds on my wrists. Stomach lurching, I pried my eyes open. It took a moment for them to focus. My vision swam.

Torches.

They flickered in the darkness, casting an orange haze over the scene. Over the faces. So many faces. The entire city pressed together in the street below. With a start, I realized I stood above them. *No.* I closed my eyes, pitching forward with a heave. The ropes kept me upright. They held me in place. I didn't stand at all. My eyes snapped open again at the realization.

The stake.

They'd tied me to the stake.

Details rushed in quickly after that, disorienting my senses— the steps of the cathedral, the wooden platform, the warm presence at my back. "Lou." The word slurred on my tongue from the hemlock. My head pounded. I struggled to crane my neck. "*Lou.*" Her hair spilled over my shoulder, and her head lolled. She didn't respond. Unconscious. I strained in earnest now, trying to see her, but my body refused to obey. Someone had removed the blue-tipped arrows, at least. They'd clothed her in a clean chemise. Anger fanned as quickly as the drug at that fresh injustice. A Chasseur had undressed her. *Why?*

I glanced down at my own simple shirt and woolen trousers. They'd removed my boots.

Leather doesn't burn.

Blue coats lined the streets, forming a barricade. They kept the crowd at bay. My eyes narrowed, and I blinked slowly, waiting for the scene to sharpen. Philippe stood among them. Jean Luc too. I recognized his black hair. His broad neck and bronze skin. He didn't look at me, his attention focused on Célie, who stood at the front of the crowd with her parents. No Coco. No Beau. No Claud or Blaise or Zenna.

No one.

"Lou." Careful not to move my lips—to keep my voice quiet— I tried to nudge her with my elbow. My arms wouldn't move. "Can you . . . hear me?"

She might've stirred. Just a little.

More shouts sounded as a child broke free of the line. A little girl. She chased a . . . ball. She chased a ball. It rolled to a stop at the base of the platform. "You aren't as tall as I thought you'd be," she mused, peering up at me beneath auburn fringe. Familiar. My eyes fluttered. There were two of her now. No—another child had joined her. A pale boy with shadows in his eyes. He held her hand with a solemn expression. Though I'd never seen it before, I almost recognized his face.

"Do not lose hope, *monsieur*," he whispered.

Another shout. A Chasseur strode forward to shoo them away.

My mouth couldn't properly form the words. "Do I . . . know you?"

"*Le visage de beaucoup,*" he said with an unnerving smile. It pitched and rolled with my vision. Garish in the firelight. "*Le visage d'aucun.*" His voice faded as he trailed away.

The face always seen, the face never remembered.

Meaningless words. Nonsensical ones. "Lou," I pleaded, louder now. Desperate. "Wake up. You have to wake up."

She didn't wake.

Imperious laughter beside me. Golden patterns. No—hair. Auguste stepped into my line of vision, a torch in one hand. The flames burned not orange, but black as pitch. Hellfire. Eternal fire. "You're awake. Good."

Behind him, Gaspard Fosse and Achille Altier climbed the platform, the former with an eager smile and the latter with a sickened expression. Achille glanced at me for only a second before murmuring something to Auguste, who scowled and muttered, "It matters not." To me, Auguste added, "Your Balisarda's fruit may not have curbed this wretched fire—not yet—but its wood certainly carried this momentous day." He lifted his hand to catch a strand of Lou's hair. "We had the cage crafted just for the two of you. A bittersweet end, is it not? To be killed by your own blade?"

When I said nothing—only stared at him—he shrugged and examined the torch. "Though I suppose it will not be the Balisarda to deliver the final blow. Perhaps I should be grateful the priests have failed. Now you shall burn eternal."

"As will your . . . city," I managed.

The words cost me. Achille flinched and looked away as I choked on bile, coughed on smoke. He didn't intervene this time. He didn't say a word. How could he? The pyre had been built. He would burn next.

With one last sneer, Auguste turned to address his kingdom.

"My loving people!" He spread his arms wide. His smile wider. The crowd quieted instantly, rapt with attention. "Tonight, at last we eradicate a great evil plaguing our kingdom. Behold—Louise le Blanc, the new and nefarious La Dame des Sorcières, and its *husband*, the man you once knew as Captain Reid Diggory."

Boos and hisses reverberated from the street.

Though I tried to summon my patterns, they shimmered in and out of focus in a golden blur. The hemlock had served its purpose. My stomach rolled. My hands refused to move, to even twitch. They'd coated the ropes. *Concentrate.*

"Yes, behold," Auguste continued, quieter now. He lifted the torch to our faces. "A witch and a witch hunter, fallen in love." Another chuckle. Some in the crowd echoed it. Others did not. "I ask you this, dear subjects—" The torch moved to Achille now, illuminating his dark eyes. They simmered with revulsion as he stared at his king. With rebellion. "Did it save the kingdom? Their *sweeping romance?* Did it unite us, at last?" Now he gestured to the smoke overhead, the charred stone of the church, the blackened and broken buildings that littered the street. Chasseurs stood at every ruin, containing the flames. "No," Auguste whispered, his gaze lingering on their blue coats. "I think not."

When he spoke again, his voice lifted to a shout. "Do not think I haven't heard your whispers! Do not think I haven't seen your doubt! Do not fear that the Peters and Judases among you, the forsakers and betrayers, will continue to roam free! They will not. Ours is a nation divided—we stand at the very precipice—but allow me to elucidate the truth, here and now: we shall not fall."

He seized Lou's chin. "This witch, this *she-devil*, may resemble a woman—your mother, perhaps. Your sister or daughter. It is not them, dear ones. It is not human at all, and it is certainly not capable of *love*. No, this demoness has cursed our kingdom with death and destruction. It has stolen your children and livelihoods, corrupted our once great and noble protector." Dropping her chin, he turned to me, lip curling. I fought for sensation in my hands. *Any* sensation. The golden patterns flickered.

"Reid Diggory." He shook his head. "Traitor. Murderer. *Witch*. You are this kingdom's greatest disappointment."

Behind him, Achille rolled his eyes.

I frowned at the incongruent gesture. The first needle of awareness pierced my palm as Lou's head lifted.

"Lou," I whispered desperately.

It fell once more.

"Hear me and hear me well!" Auguste raised his arms, the torch, with wild passion in his gaze. The people watched with bated breath, following the torch's trajectory hungrily. "I shall not be deceived again, loving people! I have captured this great foe, and with their deaths, we shall alight on a path of victory and salvation. *I* shall lead you through it. The Lyon legacy shall endure!"

Great cries rose from the crowd at the last, evoked by Father Gaspard. They stomped their feet, clapped their hands, even as Philippe and his Chasseurs exchanged cautious glances. Moonbeam hair flashed. Thrusting the torch toward Achille, Auguste said, "Do it, Father. Kill them—kill these creatures you so pity—or you shall join them in Hell."

Though Achille hesitated, he had no choice. His fingers curled slowly around the torch. My frown deepened. They looked . . . straighter than I remembered. The skin younger. Tawny and smooth. When my gaze snapped to his face, his cheeks seemed to broaden, to *move*, the bones inching higher. His eyes lengthened. His nose too. His grizzled beard fell out in pieces, his hair deepened, and his skin—the wrinkles faded as he winked at me.

Then he turned to the king. "You know, *père*," he drawled, the last of Father Achille's features melting with the words, "it's rich of *you* to speak of great disappointments."

Disgusted, Beau shook his head.

I gaped at him.

Beau.

"But you—you were—" Mouth slack, Auguste raked his eyes over his son before his teeth snapped together audibly. A vein bulged in his forehead. "*Magic.*"

The real Father Achille emerged from an alley behind the cathedral. Expression hard, he held the hand of the auburn-haired girl from earlier. With a cheery wave, Claud Deveraux stepped from behind, and—and Coco. She grinned at me in triumph, blowing a kiss. The cut on her palm still bled.

They'd come.

Relief so keen I nearly laughed swept through me.

Lou expelled a ragged breath. "Reid . . ."

The tingling in my palm spread to my fingers. The patterns began to sharpen. "I'm here, Lou. They're all here."

"Sorry we're late, sister mine." Beau darted to her—careful of his torch—as the Chasseurs surged forward, their shouts lost amidst the sudden mayhem. Philippe gestured wildly as those in the crowd fled. As they screamed. As they pulled children away or pressed closer to watch, shoving past the King's Guard, the constabulary. One man even vaulted to the platform with a fierce "Burn the king!" before Philippe caught his collar and threw him back to the ground.

"Maintain the line!" he roared.

When Chasseurs charged the platform, Blaise materialized from beneath it—and Liana and Terrance, Toulouse and Thierry. The werewolves had half-changed, their eyes glowing and their canines lengthening. Dozens more spilled forth from the crowd to join them. Snapping. Snarling. Fully transformed wolves hurtled from every alley. They met the Chasseurs' steel with claws and teeth.

Beau tugged at Lou's ropes with one hand. Hasty. Clumsy. "Turns out Chasseur Tower is a bit of a fortress. Who knew? We couldn't reach you there, but *here*—" His rapid explanation broke off at Lou's moan, and his gaze dropped to the blood on her chemise. The punctures in her arms, her chest. His voice dripped with quiet menace. "What the hell happened to her?"

Though my hands twitched and spasmed, I couldn't readily move them. Couldn't *help*. I strained to regain control. "Poisoned arrows. Hurry—"

"You dare to choose them?" Auguste hissed. Another vein throbbed in his throat. He looked less handsome now. More deranged. "Over your own *father*?"

Before Beau could answer, Philippe finally breached the platform, and Auguste lunged.

It happened in slow motion.

Beau whirled to drive him back, sweeping the torch wide, and a single spark snapped into the air. It hung motionless for a second—for a thousand seconds—before drifting almost lazily to the platform. To the hay.

I could do nothing but watch, horrified, as we went up in flames.

A SHOWER OF LIGHT

Reid

The fire spread quicker than natural, licking up the haystack, our feet, within seconds.

The Hellfire. The eternal flame.

There is no solution, Coco had told me, *fruit or otherwise.*

How do you know?

Because the fire stemmed from my grief. And there is no solution for grief. Only time.

Despite the sweltering heat, cold dread seized me. Shouting Lou's name, I twisted toward her, determined to shield her. To protect her from the inevitable. I would not give up. I would not cede. If we could free ourselves, we could jump to safety—

Panicked, Philippe crashed into Auguste, knocking him from the platform. A flame caught the king's sleeve. It engulfed him instantaneously, and he fell to the ground—writhing, shrieking—as Philippe swiftly stripped the king of his lion's cloak, attempted to strip him of his burning shirt. But the fabric had already melted into his skin. Philippe recoiled instantly, recognizing the battle lost. "Oliana!" Auguste flung a hand toward his wife, who stood beside the platform. Without a word, she turned and entered the church. Blanching at the havoc on the street, Father Gaspard followed quickly behind.

Philippe crushed Auguste's hand underfoot as he too fled.

"Get . . . out of here." Barely audible, Lou jerked her head toward Beau. He still grappled with the rope, grimacing against the flames. They curled up his boots. His leather boots. "*Leave.*"

"No," he snarled.

The heat was all-consuming now. The pain. Below us, Auguste's shrieks stopped abruptly. His limbs stilled. Skin and flesh melting into bone. With empty eyes, he stared at his burning city forevermore.

The flames danced on his corpse.

"I can't—I can't extinguish them." Adrenaline roared through my ears, deadening Lou's voice. Though her face contorted with concentration, I could scarcely see through the smoke, could scarcely *breathe*. The fire raged on. It crept from the alleys, the hidden doors, the cracks and the crannies as Chasseurs left their posts. It snaked up drainpipes. It slithered through windows. Devouring the city inch by inch. Homes. Shops. People.

A keen cry sounded from the street.

Coco.

She fought to reach us, knives flashing, plunging into anyone foolish enough to block her path. The crowd compounded to a mob around her. Bodies collided. Women pulled their children from the street, shrieking and pounding on the nearest doors, while foolish men attempted to enter the fray.

"The magic—it's too—" Lou shuddered on a cough, still immersed in her patterns, as Coco finally broke through the crowd. "It isn't *mine*."

Coco circled the platform frantically, seeking a gap in the flames. Her cries were lost amidst the tumult.

"I've almost"—Beau's fingers scrabbled at the ropes—"got them."

Lou's voice rose to a scream now. It tore from her throat, raw and vicious. Terrified. "It's too late—"

"Just *leave*, brother!" My own voice joined hers. "GO!"

The fire climbed up our legs now. Up his. It consumed all in its path: rope, clothing, *skin*. Without the stake to support him, Beau fell against us. "I'm *not* leaving you." But his knees gave out with the words, and he crumpled. His face contorted as he bellowed in pain, as blisters ruptured his throat, his face.

"Yes, you are," Lou said through gritted teeth. She looked to Coco with tears in her eyes. "Take care of each other."

The ropes at her ankles had disintegrated, and she lifted a leg, kicking him squarely in the chest. He stumbled backward from the platform—a pillar of flame—and fell straight into Coco's arms.

Coco stared at him in horror.

"No." She shook her head frantically, dropping to the snow. Packing it over his skin. He thrashed helplessly. "Beau. Beau, look at me—" Tendrils curled up her arms now, but she ignored them. My own muscles jerked and twitched as I watched, helpless. The snow did nothing to suppress the flame. There was no escape from this, no extinguishant, no magic to help us now. Not even Lou's. "No, no, *no*. Please, Beau. *Beau*."

"I'm so sorry, Reid," Lou gasped. "I can't stop it, but I can—I can help—" She twisted to look in my eyes. "I love you. Find peace."

Find peace.

The words snapped and cracked between us, out of place. Surely I'd misheard her. They couldn't be right. Because here— burning in a lake of black fire—there could be no peace. Not for her. Not for me. Not as our bones melted and our skin peeled.

She flexed her hand.

The ropes on my wrists snapped in response, and I flew from the platform in a rush of hot air. Landing hard on the street, I twisted to look at her. But I could no longer see, no longer *hear*. Pain stole my senses, and my golden patterns scattered into dust, settling as a veil over the scene.

Except it wasn't *this* scene any longer.

The mob dimmed amidst the gold, replaced by another crowd. The black fire vanished. A different stake pierced the sky, and a different witch writhed against it. Her cornsilk hair burned first. I stood before the platform, hands clasped, with the Archbishop beside me. A Balisarda gleamed at my chest.

Witch killer witch killer witch killer

The memory dissipated before I could fully grasp it.

But the pain—the excruciating *heat*—it vanished abruptly as new magic burst around us. Its scent overpowered the smoke.

The cooked flesh. Though flames still devoured my clothing, blistered my skin, I felt only cold snow. Beside me, Beau's eyes snapped open. He settled in Coco's arms.

Then Lou began to scream.

She screamed, and she screamed until her throat should've torn open at the sound. Until her heart should've stopped. The agony on her face shone clear as she writhed. Like her pain had tripled. Quadrupled.

Understanding dawned.

I struggled to my feet.

She'd taken our pain from us. It was all she could do.

"*Lou.*" Coco sobbed her name, rocking Beau as they burned. Pleading. When her tears fell, they hissed against his face. Instead of stoking the fire, however, the drops quenched it. His skin sizzled. *Healed.* Thunder rumbled overhead. "Don't do this, Lou, *please*—"

Another memory resurfaced without warning. Stronger than the first. I fell to my knees once more.

When? When did you know?

During the witch burning. When—when Lou had her fit. Everyone thought Lou was seizing, but I saw her. I smelled the magic.

A deeper pain than fire erupted at the memory, even as Coco's tears thickened. As the first drops of rain fell—Coco's rain. She'd said all along her grief had sparked this fire. Now it seemed her love would soothe it. Wherever the drops touched, the ground sputtered and steamed. The flames quelled. But Lou's screams— they continued. They cleaved me in two. Clutching my head, I pitched forward. The rain soaked my shirt. My skin.

My blisters closed.

She was burning, Reid. I don't know how, but she took away that witch's pain. She gave it to herself.

But I'd already known. In the deepest part of me, I'd drawn the connection. I'd recognized Lou's selflessness, even then. Her sacrifice. I'd been unable to admit it at the time. Unable to confront the truth, even as I'd nursed my dying wife back to health. Because she *had* almost died to save another.

In that moment, I'd fallen in love with her.

The pain in my head built to a crescendo at the realization. I couldn't bear it. Incoherent—aching, roaring—I clawed at my hair. Tore at my face. Vaguely, I heard the platform collapse, felt urgent hands on my shoulders. "Reid! *Reid!*" But Beau's and Coco's shouts couldn't pierce the turmoil of my mind. Darkness edged my vision. Unconsciousness loomed. The ground rose up to meet me.

A pattern shimmered into existence.

At first look, it appeared gold, winding from my chest to the wreckage of the platform. To where wood and smoke and fire had engulfed Lou. When I lifted a trembling hand, however, I realized I'd been wrong. The cord glimmered with dimension.

The blue of my coat. The white of snowflakes. The red of blood in a blacksmith's shop.

A hundred more colors—*memories*—all twining together, pressed into a single strand.

I pulled it.

Energy pulsed outward in a wave, and I collapsed beneath its weight, ears ringing with silence. *Bleeding* with it.

A high-pitched, primal scream shattered the street.

Not from Lou. Not from Coco. Struggling to lift my head—to see through the hysterical crowd, the pouring rain—I recognized the pale features and moonbeam hair of Morgane le Blanc. She too had crumpled. Those nearest her bolted when they saw her, slipping in the melted snow. The mud. Weeping and crying out for loved ones. Their faces smeared with soot.

Josephine crouched beside Morgane, her brow furrowed in confusion.

Behind them, Nicholina smiled.

I hurtled toward the platform without a backward glance. My voice broke on Lou's name. I remembered her. I *remembered*. The Doleur, the attic, the rooftop—the entire story she'd woven in the wooden cage. It'd all been true. It'd all been *real*.

I'll find you again, I'd told her.

She'd taken the promise to heart. She hadn't given up on me. Not when I'd insulted her, threatened her, envisioned a thousand different ways to kill her. I'd think of a thousand others to atone. I'd never leave her again. My voice gained strength. It gained hope. "Lou! LOU!"

She still didn't answer. With the fire at last extinguished by Coco's rain, the wreckage smoked gently. Diving into it, I tore through the charred boards, the ash, the remnants of the stake. Beau and Coco followed hot on my heels. "Where are you?" I asked under my breath, wresting aside plank after plank. "Come on. Where *are* you?"

Pale hands joined mine as I searched. Célie. Darker ones. Jean Luc. They met my gaze with determined expressions and terse nods. They didn't falter, even as my own body shook. *Please, please, please—*

When a board to my right shifted, untouched, I wrenched it free. She had to be here. She *had* to be—

Lou exploded upward in a shower of light.

THE FINAL BATTLE

Lou

Power flooded my limbs and lungs, and I burned not with fire, but light. It shone through my bloody chemise, through the wounds across my body, bursting outward in blinding rays of magic. Though Coco's rain still fell thick and heavy around us, the drops didn't soak me as the others—no, my skin and hair absorbed each one, and they healed me, strengthened me, soothed my aching heart. They tasted of hope. Of *love*.

I found her tearstained face amidst the wreckage, grinning and descending gently beside her.

She'd done it. Though the city still smoked around us, undulating softly—though she would *always* grieve for Ansel—the black fire had gone. She'd conquered it. She'd conquered *herself*.

Returning my grin, she clasped Beau's hand and nodded.

"Lou." Still crouched with a board in his hand, Reid looked up at me, his eyes brimming with tears. With love and relief and—and *recognition*. Awareness. It sparked between us like a living thing, as shining and bright as a pattern. He rose slowly to his feet. We stared at each other for a long moment.

"You found me," I whispered.

"I promised."

We moved at the same time, each staggering toward the other, our limbs tangling until I couldn't tell where his ended and mine began. Breathless, laughing, he swept me into the air, and we whirled round and round again. I couldn't stop kissing his smile. His cheeks. His nose. He didn't protest, instead laughing louder, tipping his face toward the sky. The smoke cleared as Coco watched us—the rain clouds too—until only a crystal winter night remained. For the first time in weeks, the stars glittered overhead. The waning moon reigned supreme.

The beginning of the end.

When at last Reid placed me on my feet, I punched his shoulder. "You absolute *ass*. How *could* you?" I seized his face between my hands, near feverish with laughter. "Why didn't you give me that sticky bun?"

His own cheeks remained flushed, his smile wide. "Because it wasn't *yours*."

A fresh wave of screams sounded behind us, and we turned simultaneously, our giddiness puncturing slightly. The scene returned in degrees. Chasseurs and loup garou still battled in the street—soaked to the skin, bleeding—while pedestrians fled or fought. Some sobbed and clung to fallen loved ones in the mud. Others pounded relentlessly on shop doors, seeking shelter for the injured. For themselves.

On either side of the street, witches had risen, barring all exits.

I recognized some of them from the Chateau, others from the blood camp. More of them than I'd ever believed existed. They must've crawled forth from every inch of the kingdom—perhaps the world. My skin dimmed as gooseflesh rose.

Worse still—across the street, Morgane climbed to her feet.

"Here." Célie slung her bag from her shoulder and upended it. Reid's bandolier spilled across the ground. His knives and seeds. Her own injection. Coco and Beau swooped to retrieve their daggers, and I followed suit, my magic pulsing with eagerness. It sensed the danger here. It yearned to attack, to *protect*, as Morgane squared her shoulders. As she lifted her chin and met my gaze.

Though the sounds of clanging steel and snapping teeth should've muted her voice, I still heard it crystal clear. Like she stood right beside me. "Hello, Daughter."

My own words rose calmly. "Hello, Mother."

I glanced at Reid's bare feet. His sodden chest. My own pitiful chemise. Even the others wore only woolen garments—and Célie a *gown*, at that—leaving them woefully vulnerable to attack. Perhaps not from magic, but steel could cut just as deep. I took a deep breath. We couldn't fight like this. Not yet.

Waving my hand, I scanned the white web of patterns for something more suitable, something defensive, something like—something like a *web*. I grinned anew as the idea took hold. Nicholina had spoken of a spider deep within La Fôret des Yeux. L'Enchanteresse, a cannibalistic creature with silk among the lightest and strongest materials in the natural world.

I searched for the spiders now, spreading my awareness north, east, toward the ancient trees around the city. Their homes. The patterns didn't follow, however, instead plunging directly into the street. I hesitated. Trees didn't live below. Perhaps—perhaps the spiders had burrowed underground for winter. I didn't have time to speculate, however. Not with Morgane across the street, flanked on either side by Josephine and Nicholina. Not with witches closing in.

With another deep breath, I pulled six identical cords. The patterns stretched width-wise until myriad fibers appeared—as thin as webs—and knit themselves tightly into armor.

Dark and fitted, light and flexible, it replaced our clothing in a burst of glittering dust.

Somewhere below, six spiders withered.

Morgane clapped her hands in applause. "How clever you are, darling. How prettily you wear my magic. At last, you suit the company you keep—thieves, all."

"I've stolen nothing from you, *maman.*"

"You have stolen *everything.*" Her emerald eyes glittered like broken glass. Jagged and sharp. The emotion within them transcended malice into raw, unadulterated hatred. "But do not question—I am here to reclaim what is mine, and I will butcher every last man, woman, and child who attempts to keep it from me." She jerked her chin, and the witches advanced in earnest. "Kill them all."

A mighty roar shook the city in response, and a dark wing shadowed the moon.

Zenna landed beside me a second later. The cobblestones cracked beneath the sheer weight of her. When she snorted derisively, flame spewed forth. Witch, werewolf, and huntsman alike leapt from its path. From atop Zenna's back—dressed in armor of her own—Seraphine drew an ancient longsword.

I couldn't help it. I laughed in delight.

Coco had told me of Toulouse's and Thierry's torture. She'd told me of Zenna's promise to *eat* my mother. Leaning around Zenna's haunch now, I asked her, "What about dragons?"

Zenna punctuated the challenge with a fresh bout of flame.

Snarling with rage, Morgane scrambled backward as Chasseurs and witches charged. Balisardas flashed. Magic erupted. Zenna snorted again, launching into the air, plucking them from the street one by one and—

And eating them.

"Oh, that is *disgusting*," Beau said, grimacing. "The indigestion alone—"

Before he could finish, Morgane brought her palms together one last time. The sharp scent of magic flared.

The ground trembled in answer.

All across the fray, people fought to keep their footing. Even Philippe paused, staggering slightly, with his Balisarda an inch from Terrance's lupine throat. Reid tensed. His eyes narrowed. Then—

"Get down!" He tackled me from the platform, and we landed hard, whirling as branches shot forth from the very earth, splintering the church steps. They didn't stop there. Dozens more surfaced rapidly, larger than life, growing trunks and roots, shattering the beautiful stained-glass windows. Growing *through* them. Stone rained down on our heads, forcing us to scatter into the crowd. I immediately lost sight of Coco and Beau, Célie and Jean Luc. Too short, too slight, I couldn't navigate the tide of people. I couldn't tell friend from foe.

Only Reid's hand in mine kept a loup garou from knocking me back to the ground.

The trees kept growing. They crushed spires and mangled arches until Cathédral Saint-Cécile d'Cesarine crumbled in ruin. Until the forest reclaimed it.

That explained the spiders.

But it didn't make *sense*. The forest belonged to *Claud*, not Morgane. How had she——?

The trees have mobilized, and we shall follow, striking hard and true.

The trees around the Chateau. My stomach twisted. She'd brought her own soldiers.

They didn't stop there, however, fracturing the street now, their branches catching hair and cloaks as they stretched toward the sky. The woman next to me screamed as one hooked her skirt. As it lifted her higher and higher until the fabric tore. The branch snapped.

She plummeted toward the street.

My magic darted wildly. Panicked, I fought to calm it, to concentrate, but the woman fell too quickly——

Scant seconds before she hit the ground, the tree seemed to shudder. I stared incredulously as Claud Deveraux strolled into view. As he whistled a merry tune. As the tree itself *bent*—creaking and groaning—and its branches curled to catch the woman midair. To cradle her in a macabre embrace.

Claud winked at me. "Fancy meeting you here, poppet. How did you like my sister?"

I choked on a laugh while the woman shrieked, contorting her limbs to escape the tree. It had ceased moving. "I thought—I thought you couldn't intervene?" And if not— "Where have you *been* all this time?"

He clicked his tongue playfully. His mere presence seemed to act as a shield; the crush of bodies waned around us, parted, as if all instinctively knew to change direction. "Tut, tut, Louise," he said, "or I shall think you self-absorbed. Though it pains me to admit, you and your friends manage quite well without me, and I have an entire realm of the natural world to govern."

"Like *hell* we can." Bemused, I helped Reid untangle the woman from the tree. Self-absorbed. *Pfft*. "But *again*, I thought you couldn't—"

"Oh, you thought correctly, peach." Though Claud still smiled, the air around us thickened with the scent of rot. Of decay. Poisonous toadstools split open at his feet. The loup garou nearest us swelled with rage, snarling as if possessed, and attacked with newfound savagery. "I am not intervening. Indeed, I am governing said realm as we speak." His smile darkened at the last, and he turned to search the street. His eyes flashed catlike. "And defending it from trespass."

I knew without asking for whom he searched.

And Morgane had called *me* a thief.

"How does she control them?" Reid yielded a step as the woman shoved him and fled up the street, still screaming hysterically. "The trees?"

"They loved her once too."

With those forbidding words, Claud's frame nearly doubled in size, and he transformed in full: enormous stag antlers burst from his head. Cloven hooves shredded his shoes. And the trees—they bowed to him as he advanced up the street as the Woodwose.

Their king.

Their god.

"Wait!"

He paused at my shout, arching a brow over his shoulder. The gesture seemed too human on his animalistic features now. "My mother," I continued with both anticipation and dread. "What will you do to her?"

Those yellow eyes blinked. His voice rumbled deep, like that of a bear's roar. "She has invaded my realm. My being. I will punish her."

Punish her.

He turned and disappeared in the trees without another word. Too late, I realized I should follow. He'd left little doubt of his intention—he was a god, and she had exploited him. Though he'd warned her—though the Triple Goddess herself had stripped her of power—she hadn't listened. She hadn't surrendered. My battle had become their battle. Claud would lead me straight to Morgane, and together, we could—

Reid pulled me in the opposite direction, where the crowd flowed thickest. "We need to evacuate these people."

"What? No!" I shook my head, but without Claud to protect us, the crush resumed. "No, we need to find Morgane—"

"Look around, Lou." He didn't dare let go of my hand, even as those nearest us fled a Dame Rouge who'd torn the beating heart from a man's chest. Though they hammered against shop windows—pleading for entry—the merchants barred their doors. On both ends of the street, blood witches had cut open their arms. Where their blood spilled, black vines twisted skyward, forming a thick hedge. A barricade. "These people—they have nowhere to run. They're *innocent*. You heard Morgane. She won't stop until all of them are dead."

"But I—"

"Claud is a *god*. If he intends to kill Morgane, he'll kill her. We have to mitigate the casualties."

My magic pulsed beneath my skin, urging me to listen. To go with him. He was right. Yes. Of course, he was right.

With one last anxious glance at Claud's back, I nodded, and we sprinted toward Father Achille and Gabrielle, Etienne's sister, who'd been trapped in a circle of vines. A blood witch coaxed the thorns tighter around them. Behind, Célie rushed Violette and Victoire to safety in the nearest shop—a patisserie manned by none other than Johannes Pan.

At Gabrielle's cry, he burst into the street with a rolling pin, shouting and swinging it wildly. It struck the blood witch's head with a sickening crunch. When she crumpled, her thorns shriveled, and Father Achille and Gaby leapt free.

"Come, come!" Pan ushered Gaby toward him while Reid, Jean Luc, and Father Achille converged.

Other witches did too, their eyes intent on the three little girls.

It seemed they still planned to exterminate the Lyon line, regardless of Auguste.

Drawing a deep breath, I plucked a pattern, and it shimmered and expanded like a film over the patisserie. The same protection existed over Chateau le Blanc, over the door to the castle's treasury. It was a piece of my magic itself—a piece of all Dames des Sorcières who'd come before me. As it left my body, the white patterns dimmed. Just a bit. My connection to them weakened. A worthy sacrifice.

None would enter the patisserie but those I permitted. I caught Gaby's hand as she passed, squeezing fiercely. "Stay inside," I told her. My eyes met those of Violette and Victoire. Beau's sisters. Reid's half sisters. "All of you."

Though Gaby and Violette nodded fervently, I didn't like the stubborn set of Victoire's chin. Célie pushed all three into the shop before ushering a hysterical couple in after them.

"Cut down the barricades!" Father Achille pointed to the thorn hedges. A handful of Chasseurs fought to drive the witches back. "Anyone with a blade!"

"We *have* no blades," a panicked man said, pushing forward.

Reid thrust his Balisarda at him in answer. "You do now. *Go.*" When more men clambered forward, hands outstretched, Reid tore another knife from his bandolier. Another and another until none remained.

"What are you doing?" I asked in alarm.

Voice grim, he lifted his hands. "I am a weapon."

Each man turned and fled toward the vines, hacking at the thorns with all their might.

Without pause, Reid pointed at the neighboring shops. To Jean Luc, he said, "Break down the doors. Get these people inside every building. Lou and I will follow behind to enchant them locked—"

He broke off as Philippe and a score of huntsmen blasted through the witches' line, slaughtering them with brutal efficiency. Bite wounds bled freely on his leg. Leveling his Balisarda at Reid and me, he snarled, "Kill them."

I lifted my own knife and stepped in front of Reid. We *were* weapons, yes—our magic sharper than any blade—but only as last resorts. If he'd taught me anything, it was not to cut myself. He wouldn't either. Before I could strike at Philippe, however, Jean Luc planted his feet before both of us. To my surprise, his handful of Chasseurs did too. "Don't be stupid, Philippe. These people are not our enemies."

Philippe's eyes bulged. "They're *witches.*"

"They're *helping* us," another Chasseur snapped. I didn't recognize him. I didn't care. "Open your eyes before you kill us all. Do your duty."

"Protect the kingdom," the one beside him added.

"Children." Achille pushed roughly between them. "We don't

have time for this, nor the forces to stand divided. Those with Balisardas *must* strike against our attackers."

"He's right." Reid nodded, already scanning the street beyond. Huntsmen fought witch, fought werewolf, while both sides fought each other. Pandemonium reigned. "Chasseurs, if you cannot kill, aim for their hands. Dames Blanches cannot cast accurately without dexterity—cut them off at the wrist, but do not draw blood from a Dame Rouge under any circumstance. Unless dead, their blood will maim you."

"How do we tell the difference?" the first Chasseur asked.

"Dames Rouges are heavily scarred. Strike quickly, and strike true. Leave the werewolves, and leave the trees."

"*Leave* the—?" Philippe's face flushed puce. He jerked his head back and forth. "We will not. Chasseurs—to me. Do not listen to these heretics. I am your captain, and we *will* strike fast and true." To prove his point, he stabbed his Balisarda into the heart of the nearest tree. Claud's roar reverberated from somewhere beyond the cathedral. Face twisting in delight, Philippe thrust deeper. "Cut them down! All of them! Tree, werewolf, and witch alike!"

"*No.*" I pushed past Jean Luc as Philippe's huntsmen obeyed, goring the trees with brutal efficiency. Roots snapped upward like the crack of the whip to ensnare them. "No, *stop*—"

But agonized shouts soon sounded from the hedges, and I turned to see witches impaling men on the thorns. *Shit.*

Reid tore after them without hesitation. His hands moved in the air, searching, pulling, as fresh magic burst around us. Three of the witches screamed in response, and fresh burns licked up

Reid's arms. But he couldn't save the men. Without Balisardas, each person here stood vulnerable—including Reid.

The fourth witch clenched her fist, and Reid stumbled, clutching his chest.

Shit, shit, *shit*.

My feet moved instinctively. Seizing the Balisarda from a trapped Chasseur, I sprinted toward him. Veins bulged in his neck, his face. His hands moved instinctively to his bandolier for a knife. They came away with only seeds. Tossing them aside, he collapsed on his hands and knees.

I hurled the Balisarda straight through the witch's forehead.

Zenna took care of the rest. Her jaws snapped viciously as she swooped low, incinerating witch and thorn alike. When the flame abated, I wrenched the Balisarda from the witch's skull and shoved it at Reid. "*I* am a weapon." Panting, I imitated his stupid voice. Breathless laughter rose. I didn't fight it, despite the gruesome circumstances. Despite the charred witches at our feet. I'd never fight laughter again. Not for their sake. "The world shall *tremble* and *fear me*—"

"Shut"—his own voice broke on a gasp of laughter—"up."

I dragged him to his feet. "My enemies shall *rue* the day they ever dared to challenge—"

"I'm fine." He shook his head as if to clear it. "Go help the others."

"I am." Pressing a hard kiss to his lips, I shoved him back toward the patisserie. "I'm helping them by helping *you*, you great selfless prick. If you give that Balisarda away again, I'll make you swallow it. Consider chivalry dead."

He huffed another laugh as we rejoined the fray.

The next moments passed in a blur of magic and blood. Following Reid's instruction, free huntsmen hacked at witches' hands, while those trapped in Claud's trees hacked at roots. Father Achille led a party of able-bodied men and women to the nearest smithy for weapons. Those unable to fight followed Célie into boucheries and confiseries, any shop that would open its doors. Jean Luc and Reid kicked down the rest. I followed behind, feeding my magic into each lock.

The witches were undaunted. I felt them attack each door, each window, their patterns hissing and striking like snakes against my magic. They taunted those within—taunted *me*—whispering the ways they would kill them. Reid and Jean Luc hacked their way through them, leaving a trail of bodies behind.

Halfway down the street, Reid noticed my pale face, and his brows furrowed. I only shrugged and continued. It didn't matter. Fewer allies littered the ground than foes. Though Zenna couldn't breathe fire freely—not without roasting us in the process—she snatched witch after witch from the street. When they backed Coco and Toulouse into a corner, she plucked the two free. When they pursued Beau and Thierry—the former shouting for Coco at the top of his lungs—Seraphine cut them down from above. We'd prepared for this. Blaise and his pack, Troupe de Fortune, even Jean Luc and his Chasseurs— all around, they exacted their vengeance. Liana and Terrance gnawed hands from wrists while Toulouse and Thierry injected a trio of witches with hemlock.

Still, overwhelming unease crept down my spine. It near paralyzed me.

Morgane had vanished without a trace.

As the battle spread down the streets, I searched for her. For Claud. Any sign of horn or moonbeam hair. He could've disposed of her already, but for some strange reason, I didn't think so. The air in the city remained foul with the stench of magic and rot. Where Balisardas had pierced the trees, dark sap wept like blood. Fungi crept up the front of homes. Of the castle itself. The entire atmosphere felt charged—*angry*—and continued to build.

More than once, I swore I heard Morgane's laughter. My unease deepened to dread.

For his part, Reid had procured three more Balisardas—from where, I didn't know—for Gaby, Violette, and Victoire, who cropped up every few minutes, hissing and spitting and bloody in their pursuit of those who pursued them. He and Beau had exploded, near apoplectic with rage, on the third time.

"They are trying to *kill* you!" Beau had torn open the door of Soleil et Lune and thrust them inside. "I swear to God, I will tie you to those seats—"

"They're trying to kill *you* too," Victoire had snarled as Reid slammed the door behind. She'd pounded on the door. "Let us out! Let us fight!"

Another bout of laughter drifted on the wind, and I whirled, searching. The hair rose on my neck. I hadn't imagined it that time. She'd sounded close enough to touch. In proof of my point, Reid frowned at the theater door. "What was that?"

"Lock them in."

"What?" His gaze snapped to mine. Sensing my intent, he stepped forward, but Victoire flung the door open once more. He hesitated. "Lou, what are you—where are you *going*?"

I didn't answer, already racing down the street, ignoring his shouts. It didn't matter how many times Beau interceded, how many people Reid led to safety. No one was safe here, not truly—not with Morgane still pulling the strings. Every move she'd ever made had been calculated. Tonight was no different. She'd *known* Claud and Zenna would join us—she'd known about the loup garou too—and she would've taken offensive action. The witches would keep coming. They wouldn't stop until they'd finished this, destroying the Crown, the Church, their persecutors at last. But witches alone couldn't down a dragon. They couldn't kill a *god*.

No, these witches were the defense, not the offense.

And this was undoubtedly a trap.

"Where are you?" I slid down a side street, following a flash of moonbeam hair ahead. Reid's voice faded behind. "I thought you didn't want to play anymore? Come out. Come out and face me, *maman*. That's what you want, isn't it? Just the two of us?"

Another street. Another. I gripped my dagger in one hand, white patterns coiling and twisting through cobblestones, trash bins, wooden doors and broken windows and herb gardens. She laughed again. When I darted after the sound—bursting into Brindelle Park—a hand snaked out to catch mine.

I nearly stabbed Manon straight in the eye.

"She isn't here, Louise." Voice quiet, she didn't meet my gaze, hers darting all around us. Twin gashes slashed each cheek.

Though one bled freely—fresh—the other looked older. It'd started to scab. She backed away, pulling her clammy hand from mine and melting into the shadows. "You must turn back."

"What are you doing here? Shouldn't you be with our *sisters?*"

She hesitated at the bitter note in my voice. Quieter still, she said, "You speak as if we have a choice."

"Where is she? Tell me, Manon."

"She'll kill us." When she brushed the healing wound with her fingertips, I understood. Though Manon hadn't revealed our identities to Morgane, she *had* let thieves escape. Backing away once more, Manon touched her other cheek now. The one with fresh blood. "Or your huntsmen will."

My stomach sank. Conscious of every step, every sound, I followed after her, extending a hand. A lifeline. "Come with me. I won't let anyone hurt you."

She only shook her head. "The dragon will fall, but still we're outmatched. Morgane knows this. Don't allow her to manipulate the—"

A branch snapped behind us. I jumped, slashing my knife backward, but Coco's voice rose in a shout. She lifted her hands wildly. "It's me! It's only me! What's going on? I saw you tearing past earlier. Is it Reid? Is it *Beau?* I lost track of him, and—"

"They're both fine." I clutched my chest with insidious relief. "It's Manon. She said—she said that—"

But when I turned to face her once more, she wasn't there. She'd vanished.

In her place stood Josephine and Nicholina.

WHEN A GOD INTERVENES

Lou

It happened too quickly to stop. Snarling, Coco pulled me behind a tree, slashing open her arm in the same movement. The instant my back touched the trunk, I registered two things: first, a warm, wet substance coated the bark—mixed with stinging nettles—and second, it melted my armor instantly.

Then came pain. *Violent* pain.

It ripped through my limbs as serrated branches pierced my hands and my feet, lifting me in the air like Jesus to the cross. Though I tried to scream for Claud, for Zenna, for *anyone*, thorns shot forth across my mouth. They lacerated my lips, my cheeks, gagging me with poisoned tips. Helplessly, I thrashed, but the spikes and thorns bit deeper.

Though Coco reached for me in horror, Nicholina pounced, giggling when Coco sprayed blood across her face—then punching her fist into Coco's rib cage. No. *Through* it. Straight toward her heart. Choking on a gasp, Coco clawed at Nicholina's wrist, her eyes wide and unseeing.

When Nicholina squeezed, she fell frighteningly still.

"Nicholina." Josephine's deep voice cut through the night. "Enough."

Nicholina glanced back at her mistress, laughter fading. They held gazes for a second too long before—reluctantly—Nicholina withdrew her hand from Coco's chest cavity. The latter's eyes rolled, and she collapsed, unconscious, to the ground. "Nasty," Nicholina muttered.

Josephine didn't react. She only stared at me. No longer impassive, she lifted her chin with the chilling words, "Bring me her heart."

If Nicholina hesitated—if a shadow crossed her expression— the movement was near indiscernible. I could do nothing but watch, delirious with pain, as she took a single step in my direction. Two. Three. My heart pounded savagely, pumping more of Josephine's blood through my veins. More poison. I wouldn't close my eyes. She would see her reflection in their depths. She would *see* this monster she'd become, this perversion of the person she'd once been: her own features, her *son's* features, twisted into something sick and wrong. Four steps now. Coco's blood still dripped from her hand. It scorched the skin there.

She ignored it.

On the fifth step, however, her eyes flicked to the Doleur. It wound behind us though the city, the river where the Archbishop had almost drowned me, where Reid and I had spoken our vows. Josephine followed her gaze, snarling at something I couldn't see. I strained to hear, but the dull roar of the water revealed nothing.

"Do it," Josephine said quickly. "Do it *now*."

Though Nicholina moved with renewed urgency, her entire body shuddered with the next step. Her foot lurched. Slipping, she crashed to her knees in a graceless movement. Confusion warped her ghastly face. Confusion and—and *panic*. Gritting her teeth, she struggled to stand as her muscles spasmed. As they rioted against her.

I stared at her now, hardly daring to hope.

"Naughty, nasty." Each word burst from her in a sharp exhale, as if she suffered terrible pain. Her entire body bowed. Still she crawled forward, her nails tearing through earth. "Tricky— little—*mice*—"

"Useless." Lip curling with disgust, Josephine strode toward me, kicking Nicholina's ribs as she went. Hard. "I will do it myself."

Nicholina's head lifted with a frighteningly blank expression.

On my first day in Cesarine, a stray dog had meandered into the garbage where I'd hidden. Shivering and alone, his only possession had been a bone. I'd watched as a cruel child had stolen it from him, as she'd beaten him with it until the dog had snapped, lunging forward to bite her hand. Later that day—after the girl had scampered away, crying and bleeding—a man had patted the dog's head as he passed, feeding him a bit of calisson. The dog had followed him home.

Like a stray dog in the garbage, Nicholina snapped, plunging her nails into her mistress's calf.

Josephine jerked as if startled, her eyes narrowing with incredulity—then widening with rage. With a feral snarl, she swooped to seize Nicholina's hair, wrenching her attendant upward and sinking her teeth deep into her throat. Bile rose in my own as those teeth crunched and snapped—feasting hungrily—while Nicholina kicked helplessly. Her screams ended in a gurgle.

Josephine had torn out her vocal cords.

Even then, she didn't stop. She drank and drank until Nicholina's hands slackened and her feet fell limp. She drank until splashes sounded behind us, accompanied by piercing undulations. Battle cries. When the first naked woman sprinted past—silver hair rippling and trident flashing—I never thought I'd be so grateful to see Elvire's backside.

Dropping Nicholina's body, Josephine whirled with wild eyes. Blood poured from her mouth, but she caught Elvire's trident before it connected with her skull. Aurélien felled my tree with the single stroke of his club. He caught me with surprising tenderness, while Lasimonne dropped to his knees beside us. "My lady sends her regards," he rumbled. "Forgive me. This is going to hurt."

He peeled the thorns from my mouth, drew the spikes from my hands and feet, as Olympienne, Leopoldine, and Sabatay fell upon Josephine. Dozens of others streaked past, finding prey within the trees—the blood witches who'd gathered to watch my execution.

As I coughed and spluttered, Aurélien and Lasimonne dragged me from harm's way. "What can we do?" the former asked. "How may we heal you?"

"You can't do anything unless you're hiding an antidote to poison in your . . . not pocket." I coughed on a laugh, cradling my hands in my lap. They'd rested me against another tree. This one thankfully free of blood. "Go. My body will heal."

Just slowly.

They didn't need to be convinced. With two impeccable bows, they charged into the fray once more. I tried to breathe, to anchor myself in my magic. It had purged the hemlock from my body. It would cleanse Josephine's blood too. Though the patterns shone dimmer than before—stretched too far and too thin across the city—the Brindelle trees helped. Even now, the power of this sacred grove flowed through me, deepening my connections. Restoring my balance.

I just needed time.

With a jolt of panic, I remembered Coco.

Trying and failing to stand, I searched for her amidst the chaos—blood witches and melusines weaving through the shadows of the trees—and found her sitting up amidst the roots of another sapling. At her back, Angelica helped her stand.

I heaved a shaky sigh of relief—until the two turned to face Josephine.

She fought with blood and blade, slicing and swiping at the melusines with preternatural strength and speed. If their blood didn't spill, hers did, and she spattered it in their eyes, ears, noses, and groins. Every vulnerable spot in their human bodies. When Elvire fell backward, tangling in another witch's black thorns, Angelica cut her free with equal skill.

Josephine snarled.

With the shake of her head, Angelica cleaned the thorn's sap from her blade, wiping it on her gown. She'd worn a gown. "You've chosen the wrong side, sister."

"At least I've chosen a side." Josephine didn't cower as Angelica approached. Coco crept behind, her eyes wide and anxious. I tried again to stand. "For too long, you have spoken of right and wrong, of good and evil, of facile concepts that do not exist. Not truly." She prowled around Angelica, who waved her hand to still Elvire's approach. "There is only pursuit, dear sister. Of knowledge. Of power. Of *life*. But you have always been afraid to live, haven't you? You craved power, yet you betrayed your own people. You sought love and affection, yet you abandoned your child. Even now, you yearn for freedom, yet you remain trapped beneath the sea. You are a *coward*." She spat the word and continued circling.

Angelica turned with her, keeping Coco at her back. "You're such a fool," she whispered.

"*I* am the fool? How do you envision this ends, sister?" Josephine's mouth twisted as she gestured between the two of them. "Shall we carry on the pretense? Will you cut yourself to cut me? We both know it cannot go beyond that. One cannot live without the other. I cannot kill you, and you cannot kill me."

"You're wrong."

Josephine's eyes narrowed at the words. "I think not."

"We must all play our parts." Lacing her fingers through Coco's, Angelica glanced back and squeezed. "For a new regime."

Josephine stared between them. Perhaps it was the way Coco shook her head, the tears in her eyes, or perhaps it was the profound acceptance in Angelica's smile. The way she touched Coco's locket and whispered, "Wear it always."

Whatever the reason, she yielded a step. Then another. Indeed, when Angelica faced her once more, advancing slowly—knife in hand—Josephine abandoned all pretense. She turned and fled.

Nicholina caught her ankle.

Unseen by all, she'd dragged herself forward, throat mangled, each breath a wet, hollow sound. Her skin had grayed beyond pale. Corpselike. Even now, she struggled to keep her eyes open as her lifeblood poured freely.

She didn't let go.

Appalled, Josephine tried to kick free, but she slipped in Nicholina's blood, falling hard to the ground. The movement cost her. Mustering the last of her strength, Nicholina crawled up her legs as Angelica advanced. "Get *off* of me, you disgusting little—" Though Josephine scrambled backward, kicking harder, she couldn't dislodge her attendant.

"Miss . . . tress . . ." Nicholina gurgled.

Josephine's eyes widened in true panic now. Turning, she attempted to push to her feet, but Nicholina held on, trapping her legs. Angelica loomed behind. When Josephine crashed back to the ground—twisting, snarling—Angelica knelt beside her, sliding her blade neatly through her sister's neck.

Right at the base of the skull.

The three of them died together.

It wasn't poetic. It wasn't grand or heroic or momentous, like one might've expected. The heavens didn't part, and the earth didn't swallow them whole. These three women—the oldest and most powerful in the world—died just like anyone would: with their eyes open and their limbs cold.

Coco pulled her mother apart from the rest, fighting tears. Heedless of the fighting around her.

I staggered to her side. When she saw me, she gasped my name, flinging her arms around me. "Are you all right?" She pulled back to look at me, frantic, wiping her tears. Her fingers touched my face. "Oh my god. Here—let me—let me heal you—"

"Save your strength. I'm already healing."

Her eyes dropped back to her mother. "We need to finish this, Lou."

Slowly, I knelt to the ground, closing each of their eyes in turn. Even Nicholina's. Even Josephine's. "And we will."

She supported my shoulders as we hobbled through the trees to the street. To Coco's surprise—and less to mine—a handful of blood witches ceased fighting when they recognized Josephine's corpse on the ground. Some knelt beside her. Others fled. Still more looked to Coco as if lost, mirroring her own unnerved expression. At the blood witches' abrupt withdrawal, the melusines moved on, following the sounds of shouts and steel.

Claud—still shaped as the Woodwose—thundered around the corner at the far end of the street. When he saw us, he moved faster, raising his voice to shout, "What is it? What happened? I heard your call—"

Something moved too quickly behind us.

A flash of white. Of moonbeam hair.

"LOOK OUT!" Célie's unexpected shriek nearly rent the sky, but it was too late. We couldn't stop it. Paralyzed with fear, we stood rooted as Morgane rose up to meet us. As she lifted her hand to thrust a dagger in my heart. As Claud blasted us backward, and her lips curled into a macabre smile.

"Oh no." Her ghostly laughter reverberated through the grove. "Oh no, no, no."

The ground beneath us began to quake.

"It seems you've broken the rules, darling." Tutting, she shook her head. "Old ones."

Sickening realization dawned. "He's intervened," I repeated on a whisper.

As one, Coco and I turned to Claud, who stood alone in the street, his face a mask of calm. The cobblestones cracked and fissured around him. The earth trembled. He looked us squarely in the eyes. "Run."

THE CHASM

Reid

"Would you *run?*" Incredulous, I glanced over my shoulder at Beau, who lagged behind. He clutched his ribs with one hand. With each stride, he nearly impaled himself with his Balisarda.

He'd stolen it from Philippe.

We hadn't bothered to free him.

"*You* run." Panting, he gestured around the empty street with his other hand. It held another knife. "I can't fucking *breathe*, and if you haven't noticed—there's no one here!"

I scowled and pushed onward.

He had a point.

This street—that street, every street we'd passed for the last quarter hour—had been virtually empty. We'd succeeded in sequestering most pedestrians inside their homes, inside shops. Inside any buildings we could fortify. Father Achille and Johannes Pan had converted the boucherie next door into an infirmary. They treated the injured there. They gathered the dead.

The witches had . . . withdrawn.

It'd happened slowly. Almost imperceptibly. One moment, we'd fought scores of them. Too many to count. Werewolves and huntsmen, men and women—even melusines, rising up from the Doleur like sea serpents—had fought tooth and nail to contain them. As the hour had passed, however, each had slipped from the fray one by one. Slipped through our fingers. As if answering some unspoken call.

My own breath quickened with each step. They couldn't have simply *vanished*.

My voice hardened with resolution. "We need to find them."

"We *need* to find our wretched little sisters." Waving his knife for me to stop, Beau clutched his knees. I scowled, doubling back, and pulled him onward. We would find them. If not, we'd regroup with Lou and Coco, with Father Achille and Jean Luc and Célie, and we'd determine another strategy.

When we rounded the corner, however, all plans of *planning* fled.

At the end of the street, a horde of witches collected in the shadows.

Beau hissed as I shoved him behind a garbage can, but it mattered not—dozens of heads snapped in our direction. I exhaled a heavy breath. A resigned one. Slowly, I rose to my feet. Beau followed with a curse, muttering, "Have you ever heard of manifestation?"

"Shut up."

"*You* shut up." He lifted his Balisarda and knife with white knuckles as three witches broke apart from the rest. The others refocused their attention on something at the center of the group. Something that . . . rattled. Eyes narrowing, I stepped closer. "Actually, don't. I'd love to hear the next step in your *let's find the bloodthirsty witches* plan—"

The clink of metal. Thick rings.

A chain.

My brow furrowed as the three witches moved shoulder to shoulder, blocking my view. It was a chain. An ancient, crusted *chain*. From the glimpse I'd gotten, it'd looked long enough to encircle half of Cesarine. Wide enough too. A memory harried my subconscious, half-realized. I'd seen this chain in Chateau le Blanc's treasury. "Hello, princelings," the middle witch crooned.

With a jolt of shock, I recognized her amber face from Modraniht. It felt like years ago. "Elaina."

"No." Beau winced as they drew to a halt before us. Identical black hair and narrow noses. Full lips. They twisted with identical menace. "That one is Elinor. I'd recognize her aura of disdain anywhere." He pointed a finger to his teeth, flashing a charming smile. "Do you remember me now, sweetheart? Do you *see* the opportunity you missed?"

"Oh, I remember you, *Burke*. You made me look a *fool* in front of the entire coven."

"It doesn't matter now," her sister said, either Elaina or Elodie.

"We've been looking for you both all night," the other finished. "Thank you for making this easy."

Though all three crooked their fingers at once, nothing happened. No patterns reared to strike. Beau waggled his Balisarda at them, grinning anew. "Something wrong?"

Elinor bared her teeth. "Ask your sister."

"What does that—"

They attacked before he could finish, slipping knives from their sleeves and launching toward us. Elaina and Elodie at me. Elinor at him. Though quick—though furious—the sisters clearly hadn't trained for physical combat sans magic. With a sense of dread at those chilling last words, I dispatched the first of them swiftly while Beau battled Elinor strike for strike. Her sister's blood still dripped from my blade when I turned to face Elodie.

The earth beneath us rolled.

I staggered at the movement, glancing down incredulously. Cobblestones broke to pieces. All around, foundations cracked. Tiles littered the street. And Zenna—from somewhere above, she let out a mighty roar. The witches ahead tensed, renewing their efforts with haste. Half had climbed the drainpipes, stringing the chain taut between rooftops, like a wire. Magic coated everything.

I couldn't make sense of it. Couldn't think. The ground kept shaking. Sensing my distraction, the sister slashed her blade down in a mighty strike. Though I recoiled, though I lifted my own blade to parry, another knife whizzed past my face—close enough to feel its heat on my cheek—and lodged in the sister's chest.

With a squeak of surprise, she sank to her knees, slipped sideways, and moved no more.

Behind us, Beau stood triumphant. Elinor stilled at his feet. "Did you *see* that?" Though he waved his Balisarda at the vengeful witch's body, he glanced away quickly. He swallowed hard. "I saved your life."

I blocked his view of their corpses. Knocked his shoulder with my own. Forced him to turn. "You also set me on fire."

"Perhaps you could conjure some up for the rest of these—"

With another thunderous roar, Zenna swept into view. The sight of her wings against the sky, of her white-hot flame, stole the breath from my throat. And I remembered. A torch-lit stage. A starry cloak. And Zenna—Zenna weaving a heart-wrenching tale of dragon and maiden.

A magic chain, her kin doth wield to stay him on an even keel.

And when Tarasque did spiral down, her father felled him to the ground.

With Seraphine atop her back, Zenna dove low—too low— scouring the streets for persons unknown. When she saw us, she swooped even lower. She didn't see the chain until it was too late.

"Wait! No, STOP!"

At the desperate wave of my arms, she banked, but her foot still caught the links. The chain moved of its own volition, slinging rapidly around her leg, up her haunch. With a bellow of rage, she began to fall, and as she did, her leg—it transformed into that of a human. Gruesomely. The witches descended like ants when she crashed to the ground. The impact threw Seraphine through the air with frightening speed. She collided with the trash cans nearest us.

"Oh my god," Beau said. "Oh my god, oh my god, oh my *god*."

Zenna's roars transitioned to screams as Seraphine struggled to move. I bolted toward her, kicking the trash cans aside. "Seraphine—"

She pushed my hands away with surprising strength. "*Go.*" Though Beau attempted to drag her upright, she shook him off too, unsheathing another sword from down her back. She swung both equally with surprising dexterity. "Find Claud and the others. Find Lou. He *intervened.*"

"What?" Beau asked, perplexed.

My gaze darted toward Zenna, who the witches had lashed and beaten with the chain. She'd fully transformed now. Human once more. Vulnerable. "Let us help—"

"I am no damsel." Springing to her feet, she knocked us aside and streaked toward her mate. "Find Claud. Leave Zenna to me."

The ground gave a mighty lurch in response, and we had no choice.

We sprinted up the street.

"Where are we *going?*" Though Beau's shout tore through my senses, I ignored him, pressing harder. Faster. Blood roared in my ears as we followed the fissure, tracking its path through West End, past the Tremblays' townhouse, and skidding to a halt outside Brindelle Park. Buildings crumbled now. Witches and melusines alike scattered.

Claud stood in the middle of the street, completely and carefully still. He faced the spindly Brindelle trees.

He faced Coco and Lou.

The fissure ran directly between them, cracking wide, forcing them to leap apart. "LOU!" Her name shredded my throat, but I shouted it louder. I shouted it crazed. When her face jerked up— her eyes meeting mine—a cold fist of fear gripped my heart. Though I cast for a golden pattern, none could've prevented this. None could've stopped it. She tried anyway, flinging both hands toward the ground. Her entire body strained. Trembled. The sharp scent of magic exploded over the grass, the rocks, the trees—stronger than ever before—but this fissure was stronger, deeper, *older*, than even La Dame des Sorcières.

Together, helpless, we watched as the earth broke open completely.

As Claud plummeted into its depths without a word.

As the fissure kept growing, kept *spreading*, until Brindelle Park—until half of the entire *city*—fractured from the rest, separated by a yawning chasm. Still it grew. Coco's voice rose to join mine, and she backpedaled, preparing to take an impossible leap—

Beau caught her shirt at the last second. He ripped her toward him. "Are you *crazy*?"

"Let me *go*!" She pounded his chest, stomped on his feet, twisted to elbow him viciously. Only then did he release her with a gasp.

"Please, Coco, *don't*—!"

But she didn't leap this time. Instead she dove to the chasm's edge, hands latching onto a blood witch's wrist. Another. Screaming, they dangled hopelessly. Their nails clawed at rock, at Coco's skin. Realizing her intent, Beau dashed to help, and together, they pulled the witches to safety, collapsing together in a heap.

When the dust settled, Beau, Coco, and I stood on one side of the chasm.

Lou and Célie clutched each on the other.

Behind them loomed Morgane le Blanc.

AS WE STARTED

Lou

The horror on Reid's face, the absolute *terror*, was an image I'd never forget. Though he charged up and down the chasm's edge, searching for the narrowest lip, for a pattern, for a *miracle*—it was better this way. Truly. Whatever happened now, it would be between my mother and me.

Just as we'd started.

In line with my thoughts, Morgane swept her hand in a burst of magic, and Célie soared through the air, crashing into a Brindelle tree. Two blood witches who'd been trapped here dropped to seize her, to—no. Hope burned savage and bright in my heart. To *help* her. They were helping her. In that split second, I thought of Manon, of Ismay, or Dame Blanche and Dame Rouge alike who'd been harmed by Morgane's hatred. Who'd felt trapped between Church and coven. Who'd lived in fear as debilitating as mine.

Hope isn't the sickness. It's the cure.

Of all people, of course it had been Célie to find Morgane.

To stalk her unseen as she slipped through the city. My mother never would've suspected it. She never would've believed such a pretty porcelain doll could grow teeth. If she thought Célie would shatter, however—if she thought *I* would—it would be the last mistake of her life.

This time, I wouldn't hesitate.

"Lou! LOU! *Célie!*"

Reid, Coco, Beau, Jean Luc—they called our names in a frenzy, voices blending into one. Resolve hardened to a sharpened point in my chest as I looked at them. We'd already lost so much, each of us. Fathers and mothers and sisters and brothers. Our homes. Our hope. Our very *hearts*.

No more.

I found Reid's gaze last, holding it longer than the others. When I shook my head slowly, determinedly, he drew to a swift halt, chest heaving. We stared at each other for the span of a single heartbeat.

Then he nodded.

I love you, I told him.

As I love you.

Morgane sneered, lowering the hood of Auguste's lion-skin cloak as she advanced. She'd stolen it from his corpse at the cathedral. Though charred black in places, she wore it as a trophy now. Its teeth glinted around her throat in a gruesome smile, and its mane spread proudly across her shoulders. "No more running, Louise. No more hiding." She jabbed a finger across the chasm, where Blaise and the remains of his pack had gathered. Where

Elvire and her melusines still attempted to cross, where Claud had fallen to fate unknown. "Your god has fallen, your dragon has perished, and your precious *allies* cannot reach you here. I must admit . . . you are far cleverer than I ever gave you credit. How cunning it was to hide behind those more powerful than yourself. How *cruel*. We are more alike than you realize, darling, but the time has come at last. You are alone."

But I wasn't alone. Not truly. In life or in death, I'd have someone to meet me. Someone to *love* me. My stomach curdled at Nicholina's congealed throat. At Josephine's empty expression. Though the former might've found peace with her son, could the latter say the same? Could Morgane? She stepped over their corpses without acknowledgment. Already, they meant less to her than the mire beneath her boots. "Your generals are dead," I said quietly. "I think *you* are the one alone."

The blood witches stiffened as Morgane paused, turning to kick Josephine's vacant face. "*Good riddance.*"

With a crippling sense of sorrow, I stared at her as my white patterns undulated weakly. I couldn't kill her with them. Not outright. Death was natural, yes, but murder was not. It hardly mattered now either way. When I'd clasped two sides of the very world, trying to save Claud—a god, a *friend*—from his own magic, I'd nearly rent myself apart. My patterns had distended past the point of reparation. Some had snapped altogether. Those remaining had grown dim with weariness.

Morgane didn't know that.

I searched each carefully now, seeking a distraction, something to allow me near. Something to debilitate her long enough for me to strike. Gently, I fed the patterns outward. "Have you loved anyone in this world, *maman*?"

She scoffed and lifted her hands. "*Love.* I curse the word."

"Has anyone loved you?"

Her eyes narrowed on mine. Her mouth twisted in question. "It's true," I admitted, quieter still. "I did love you once. Part of me still does, despite everything." I twitched my finger, and the water of the Doleur trickled steadily, silently, through the grass beneath our feet. It melted the snow. It cleansed the blood. If Morgane noticed, she didn't react. Though her features remained riddled with spite, she studied me as if enthralled. As if she'd never heard me say it, though I'd told her a thousand times. A single tear slid down my cheek in response, and the pattern dissipated. A tear for a river. Both held endless depths.

"You gave me life," I continued, stronger now, the words spilling faster than I'd intended. Cathartic. "Of course I loved you. Why do you think I allowed them to *chain* me to an *altar*? At sixteen years old, I was willing to *die* for you. My mother." Another tear fell, and the water flowed faster. It touched her hem now. "You never should've asked me. I'm your daughter."

"You were never my daughter."

"You gave me life."

"I gave you *purpose*. What should I have *done*, darling? Cradled you in my arms while others' daughters perished? While they *burned*? Should I have valued your life more than theirs?"

"Yes!" The confession burst from me in a shock of cold regret, and I capitalized on it, clenching my fist. The water around Morgane's feet froze to solid ice. It trapped her. "You *should* have valued me—you should've *protected* me—because I am the *only* person in this world who still loves you!"

"You are a *fool*," she snarled, fire lashing from her fingertips. "And a predictable one at that."

With the slash of her hand, the ice melted, and the ground itself desiccated in a fiery path toward me. It didn't burn my skin, however, instead passing through it—straight to my organs. My body temperature spiked as my blood literally began to boil, as my muscles cramped and my vision spun. Crying out, Célie attempted to leap to my aid, but the blood witches held her back, recoiling from Morgane. In fear. In hatred.

With seconds to react, I seized another pattern, and the Brindelle tree nearest me withered and blackened to ash.

The lion of Auguste's cloak began to reanimate.

I fell to my knees, smoke curling from my mouth, as its teeth sank deep into Morgane's neck. Screaming, she whirled, pulling a knife from her sleeve, but the half-formed lion clung to her back. Tendon and muscle continued to regenerate with gruesome speed. Where sleeves had been, mighty paws rose to grip her shoulders. Its hind legs kicked at her back.

Morgane's fiery hold dissipated as she struggled, and I fought to rise. To *breathe*.

When she buried her blade in the beast's chest, it gave a final snarl before falling limp. She heaved its carcass between us. Blood poured from wounds on her neck, her shoulders, her legs, but she ignored them, clenching another fist. "Is that the best you can do?" Beneath my armor, against my skin, arose an alarming tickle. The skitter of legs. "You may call yourself La Dame des Sorcières—you may kill trees and steal rivers—but you will never know this magic as I have known it. You will never conquer its power as I once did. Just *look* at yourself. Already, it has weakened your feeble spirit." She advanced in earnest now, a lethal gleam in her eyes. "The Goddess has chosen wrong, but I do not need her blessing to conquer *you*."

Scrambling backward—hardly hearing her words—I pulled hastily at my armor.

Hundreds of spiders burst from the woven fabric. From their own silk. They scuttled over my body in a wave of legs, piercing my skin with their fangs. Each bite brought a prick of pain, a tingle of numbness. Shrieking instinctively, heart palpitating, I crushed all within reach, sweeping their wriggling corpses from my arms, legs, chest—

"You were born to be immortal, Louise." Morgane lifted her hands, pouring her rage, her frustration, her *guilt* into another bout of fire. I rolled to avoid it—squashing the last of the spiders—and seized the lion's skin as a shield. "Though destined to die, your name would have lived forever. We could have written history together, the two of us. You may scorn me now, you may hate me always, but I gave everything—I *sacrificed* everything—for you. For *love*."

Feeding strength to the fur through another pattern, I crouched lower. The grass beneath her feet ignited instead. She leapt away from it with a hiss. "You cannot imagine the grief of your birth. Even *you* cannot imagine the bitterness I felt. I should have killed you then. I'd even lifted the knife, prepared to plunge it into your newborn heart, but you—you clasped my finger. With the whole of your fist, you clutched me, blinking those sightless eyes. So peaceful. So content. I couldn't do it. In a single moment, you softened my heart." Her flames subsided abruptly. "I failed our people that day. It took sixteen years to harden myself again. Even then, I would have gifted you everything. I would have gifted you *greatness*."

"I didn't *want* greatness." Casting my shield aside, I pushed to my feet at last. Her heart might've softened for a newborn babe, but she hadn't ever loved me—not *me*, not truly, not the person. She'd loved the idea of me. The idea of greatness, of salvation. I'd mistaken her attention for the genuine thing. I hadn't known what real love looked like then. I glanced across the chasm to Reid, Coco, and Beau, who stood hand in hand at the edge, pale and silent.

I knew what it looked like now—both love *and* grief. Two sides of the same wretched coin. "I only wanted *you*."

When I clenched my fist, exhaling hard, my grief ruptured into a storm wind: grief for the mother she could've been, grief for the good moments, for the bad moments, for all the moments in between. Grief for the mother I had lost, truly, long before this one.

The wind blasted her backward, but she twisted midair, and the momentum carried her closer to Célie. Wicked intent flared in Morgane's eyes. Before I could stop her, she jerked her fingers, and Célie skidded from the blood witches as if pulled by an invisible rope. Morgane caught her. She used her body as a shield, pressing her knife to Célie's breastbone. "Foolish child. How many times must I tell you? You cannot defeat me. You cannot *hope* to triumph. Once upon a time, you could've been immortal, but now, your name will *rot* with your corpse—"

She broke off inexplicably, her mouth falling open in a comical O.

Except it wasn't funny. It wasn't funny at all.

Stumbling backward, she thrust Célie away with a noise of surprise and—and glanced down. I followed her gaze.

A quill lodged deep in her thigh, its syringe quivering from impact.

An injection.

I stared at it in shock. In relief. In horror. Each emotion flickered through me with wild abandon. A hundred others. Each passed too quickly to name. To *feel*. I could only stare, numb, as she slid to her knees in a smooth, fluid motion. As her hair rippled down her shoulders, less silver now than bloody scarlet. Eyes still rapt on the syringe, she slipped sideways. She didn't move.

Cold metal touched my palm, and Célie's voice drifted from afar. "Do you need me to do it?"

I felt myself shake my head. My fingers curled around the hilt of her dagger. Swallowing hard, I approached my mother's limp body. When I brushed her hair from her face, her eyes rolled back to look at me. Pleading. I couldn't help it. I pulled her across my lap. Her throat worked for several seconds before sound came out. "Daugh . . . ter . . ."

I memorized those emerald eyes. "Yes."

Then I drew Célie's blade across my mother's throat.

IT ENDS IN HOPE

Lou

The first time I'd slept beside Reid, I'd dreamed of him.

More specifically, I'd dreamed of his book. *La Vie Éphémère*. He'd gifted it to me that day. His first secret. Later that night, after Madame Labelle had issued her warning—after I'd woken in a fit of tangled sheets and icy panic—I'd crawled next to him on the hard floor. His breathing had lulled me to sleep.

She is coming.

Fear of my mother had literally driven me into his arms.

The dream had crept over me slowly, like the wash of gray before dawn. As in the story, Emilie and Alexandre had lain side by side in her family's tomb. Their cold fingers had touched forevermore. On the final page, their parents had wept for them, mourning the loss of life so young. They'd promised to set aside their blood feud, their prejudice, in the name of their children. It was of this scene I'd dreamed, except it hadn't been Emilie's and Alexandre's bodies, but mine and Reid's.

When I'd woken the next morning, unease had plagued me.

I'd blamed it on the nightmare. On the memory of my mother.

Now, as I held her in my arms, I couldn't help but remember that peaceful image of Emilie and Alexandre.

There was nothing peaceful about this.

Nothing easy.

Yet still Reid's voice drifted back to me as he'd clutched *La Vie Éphémère* in hand . . .

It doesn't end in death. It ends in hope.

PAN'S PATISSERIE

Reid

Lou held her mother for a long time. I waited at the chasm's edge, even after Coco and a handful of blood witches built a bridge of vines. Even after Célie and her newfound friends—two witches named Corinne and Barnabé—crossed on shaky legs. Jean Luc had enveloped Célie in a desperate hug, while Coco had tentatively greeted the witches. She'd remembered them from childhood. They'd remembered her.

They'd even bared their throats before leaving to find their kin. A sign of submission.

Coco had watched them go, visibly shaken.

Not all had been so courteous. One witch—a sobbing Dame Blanche—had attacked my back as I'd waited. Jean Luc had been forced to inject her. To bind her wrists. He hadn't killed her, however, not even when Célie had stepped aside to speak with Elvire. Aurélien had fallen. Others too. As the Oracle's Hand, Elvire had begun to collect their dead, preparing to depart for Le Présage once more.

"We cannot leave our lady waiting," she'd murmured, bowing low. "Please say you will visit us sometime."

Beau and Coco hurried to find Zenna and Seraphine.

Though I started to follow, Coco shook her head. Her gaze drifted to Lou, who hadn't moved from beneath her mother. "She needs you more," Coco murmured. Nodding, I swallowed hard, and after another moment, I took a hesitant step on the bridge.

Someone shouted behind me.

Unsheathing my stolen Balisarda, I whirled, prepared for another witch. Instead, I met two: Babette supporting Madame Labelle as they hobbled into the street. An enormous smile stretched across my mother's face. "Reid!" She waved with her entire body, presumably healed by Babette's blood. The lesions and bruises from the trial had vanished, replaced by vibrant skin, if a touch pale. I exhaled a sharp breath. My knees weakened in a dizzying wave of relief.

She was here.

She was *alive*.

Crossing the street in three great strides, I met her halfway, crushing her in my arms. She choked on a laugh. Patted my arm. "Easy, son. It takes a bit more time for the insides to heal, you know." Though she still beamed, clapping my cheeks, her eyes tightened at the corners. Babette looked unusually grave behind.

I met her gaze over my mother's head. "Thank you."

"Do not thank me." She waved an errant hand. "Your mother supplied my first job in this city. I owed her one."

"And still owe me many more," Madame Labelle added, turning to eye the courtesan waspishly. "Do not think I've forgotten, Babette, the time you dyed my hair blue."

Only then did Babette crack a sheepish grin. After another moment, she glanced around us covertly. "Pray tell, huntsman, have you seen our lovely Cosette?"

"She's with Beau. They headed north."

Her smile fell slightly. "Of course. If you'll excuse me."

She left without delay, and I wrapped a steadying arm around Madame Labelle's waist. "Where have you been? Are you well?"

"I am as well as possible, given the circumstances." She shrugged delicately. "We took a leaf out of your wife's book and hid in Soleil et Lune's attic. No one bothered us there. Perhaps none knew of its importance to Lou. If they had, I suspect Morgane would've razed it out of spite." When I nodded to them across the chasm, her expression crumpled. She shook her head. "Oh, dear. Oh, *dear*. How sickening." Those piercing blue eyes flitted up to mine, filled with regret. "Babette told me that Auguste perished by his own fire. Stupid, *arrogant* man." As if realizing the tactlessness of her words, she patted my arm again. "But he—he was very—"

"He tortured you," I said darkly.

She sighed, crestfallen. "Yes, he did."

"He deserved worse than death."

"Perhaps. We must content ourselves that wherever he is, he is in great pain. Perhaps with *rats*. Still . . ." She wobbled slightly, unsteady on her feet. My arm tightened around her. "He was your father. I am sorry for it, but I am never sorry for you." She touched my cheek once more before glancing at Lou. "You must go. If you could walk me to the nearest bench, however, I'd be most grateful. I should like to watch the sun rise."

I stared at her incredulously. "I can't leave you on a bench."

"Nonsense. Of course you can. No witch with any sense would attack us now, and those that do—well, I believe more than one Chasseur survived, and that Father Achille has *quite* a nice—"

"I'll stop you there." Though I shook my head, one corner of my mouth curled upward. Unbidden. "Father Achille is off-limits."

It wasn't true. She could have whoever she wanted. I would personally introduce them.

After situating her on a bench—beds of winter jasmine blooming on either side—I kissed her forehead. Though night still claimed the sky, dawn would come soon. With it, a new day. I knelt to catch my mother's eyes. "I love you. I don't think I've ever told you."

Scoffing, she busied herself with her skirt. Still, I saw her eyes. They sparkled with sudden tears. "I only expect to hear it every day from this moment onward. You shall visit at least thrice a week, and you and Louise shall name your firstborn child after me. Perhaps your second too. That sounds reasonable, does it not?"

I chuckled and tugged on her hair. "I'll see what I can do."

"Go on, then."

As I walked back to Lou, however, I heard low voices down

a side street. Familiar ones. A keening wail. Frowning, I followed the sound to Gabrielle and Violette. They stood huddled on a stoop between Beau, who'd wrapped one arm around each of them. Coco hovered behind, one hand clapped to her mouth. At their feet, Ismay and Victoire lay sprawled unnaturally, face-down, surrounded by a half-dozen witches. None stirred.

Stricken, unable to move, I watched as Beau's face broke on a sob, and he pulled the two girls into his chest. Their shoulders shuddered as they clutched him. Their tears raw. Anguished. Intimate. The sight of them punched me in the gut. My siblings. Though I hadn't known Victoire as well as Beau, I could have. I *would* have. The pain cut unexpectedly sharp.

It should've been me on those cobblestones. Morgane had wanted *me*, not her. She'd wanted Beau. Not Victoire, a thirteen-year-old child.

Guilt reared its ugly head, and I finally turned. I walked back to Lou. I waited.

This time, she lifted her head to greet me.

I held her gaze.

Nodding, she smoothed Morgane's hair, her touch tender. Full of longing. She closed her mother's eyes. Then she rose heavily to her feet—bent as if bearing the weight of the very sky—and she left her there.

When she crossed the bridge, I extended my arms to her at last, and she fell into them without a sound. Her face pale and drawn. Broken-hearted. I leaned to rest my forehead against hers. "I'm so sorry, Lou."

She held my face between both hands. Closed her eyes. "Me too."

"We'll get through this together."

"I know."

"Where you go—"

"—I will go," she finished softly. Her eyes opened, and she brushed a kiss against my lips. "Who survived?"

"Let's find out."

As I'd suspected, the chasm split the entire city in two. Lou and I walked it hand in hand. Near the cathedral, we found Toulouse and Thierry. They stared into the chasm's depths with Zenna and Seraphine. No one spoke a word.

"What do you think happened to him?" Lou whispered, slowing to a stop. This wake wasn't meant for us. It was meant for them. Troupe de Fortune. Claud's family. "Do you think he . . . died?"

I frowned at the prospect. Pressure built in my chest. Behind my eyes. "I don't think gods *can* die."

When we turned to go, Terrance stepped forward from the shadows. Like us, he, Blaise, and Liana hovered a respectable distance away. Ignoring Lou and me, he caught Toulouse's and Thierry's eyes. "You could come with us." His voice resonated deeper than I'd remembered. Blood dripped down his bare chest. The side of his face. His ear had been torn off completely— whether in battle or before, I couldn't tell. With a start, I realized he must've met Toulouse and Thierry at Chateau le Blanc. When they'd all been . . . tortured together. Liana too.

The thought turned my stomach.

Blaise stepped to his son's side, clasping a hand on his shoulder. "We would be honored." He cleared the emotion from his throat. "My children . . . they have spoken of how you comforted them. How you gave them hope. I can never repay either of you for this kindness."

The twins cast subtle glances at Zenna and Seraphine. The former shrugged. Though link-shaped burns marred her visible skin—she'd somehow donned a sparkling fuchsia gown—the rest of her appeared relatively unscathed. Seraphine too. Blood coated her armor, but it didn't seem to belong to her. I stared at them both incredulously. "How did they escape?"

"Who?" Lou asked. "What happened?"

"The witches—they felled Zenna with a magic chain."

"Ah." A hint of a smile touched her lips. "Tarasque's chain."

"Like in Zenna's story."

"She *did* say that wasn't her real name."

I frowned as she pulled me away in search of the others.

We ended up in Pan's patisserie.

Outside the boarded windows, Father Achille and a score of huntsmen attempted to free their brethren. Philippe still bellowed orders within his cage of roots. None listened. When at last they freed him, he swiped wildly at Achille, who dodged with the speed of a much younger man before knocking Philippe to the ground. It took five huntsmen to subdue him. Another to clap irons around his wrists.

"You can't *do* this!" Veins throbbed in his forehead as he thrashed. "I am a *captain* of the Chasseurs! *Father Gaspard!*" He'd nearly burst blood vessels. "Someone summon him—FATHER GASPARD!"

Father Gaspard hadn't heeded his summons, instead remaining crouched behind a tree in the sanctuary. The Chasseurs had flushed him out while searching for Queen Oliana, who they'd found trapped beneath the pulpit. Though her leg had been fractured, she would face greater pain soon. I didn't envy the Chasseur who would tell her about her child. For the first time in a long time, I didn't envy any Chasseur at all.

Unsure what to do with Philippe, Jean Luc and Célie settled on chaining him to a horse post down the street. Out of hearing distance. Thankfully.

They joined us in the patisserie moments later.

Collapsing in a vacant chair, Jean Luc scrubbed a hand down his face. "We'll need to coordinate shelter as soon as possible. Petition citizens to open their homes to those without."

Célie sat beside him with quiet calm. Soot smeared her white cheeks, and her hair hung lank from Coco's rain. From sweat. A gash still bled from her temple. She gestured next door to the boucherie. "The injured will need treatment. We must summon healers from the nearest metropolises."

"Oh God." Jean Luc groaned and shot to his feet. "Were there priests in the infirmary? Has anyone checked for survivors?" At our blank looks, he shook his head and stalked outside to find

Father Achille. Instead of joining him, Célie looked between us anxiously. She knitted her hands in her lap.

"Er—Lou? Do you think—I'm terribly sorry, but—might you be able to return my gown now?"

Lou blinked in confusion. With a breathy laugh, Célie gestured to her armor.

"*Oh.*" Lou chuckled too and waved her hand. The sharp scent of incense erupted. "Yes, of course."

From her feet, Célie's armor unraveled into a black mourning gown, and she patted her waist anxiously. At whatever she found, tension left her shoulders, and she relaxed. Just a little. "Right. Thank you so much." A bright smile at Lou. A quick glance at me. It seemed . . . inexplicably significant. When Jean Luc shouted for her a moment later, however, she grimaced and strode toward the door. "I shall return in just a moment."

Lou watched her go with a bemused grin, stretching to watch her through the window. "What was *that* about?"

"She must . . . really like dresses?"

Lou rolled her eyes.

Coco and Beau found us next. Though tears still stained my brother's face, he rubbed them away with a weak smile, pulling a chair around to sit beside Lou. Then he wrapped her in a headlock and ruffled her hair. "Did Reid tell you I saved his life?"

She didn't push him away. "He *didn't.*"

"Then he is a *spectacular* ass. I threw a knife with such precision that it would've put Mort Rouge to shame—"

"You also caught me on fire," I said scathingly. "Her too."

"Nonsense. Also—nuance." Sighing dramatically, he held Lou there for another moment. They locked eyes, and both of their grins gradually faded. "How are you, sister mine?" he asked seriously.

Her hands came up to grip his forearm. "I'm . . . better now, I think. The shock is starting to wear off. It's like—like I can finally take a breath." Her fingers squeezed, and she blinked rapidly. "I'm so sorry, Beau." When she looked to Coco, he released her from his grip. "To all of you."

Coco traced a pattern in the tabletop's grain. "I lost my mother a long time ago."

"My father too," Beau added, his voice quiet.

But not Victoire. The guilt resurfaced with a vengeance. I'd survived enough to know it always would. There'd been no sense in that little girl's death. No explanation to make it right. There'd been none when we'd burned the witches' children, either. Victoire had deserved better. They all had.

We did too.

Pushing to my feet, I craned my neck in search of Pan. He'd disappeared into a back room at my arrival, but he couldn't hide from me forever. I strode to the counter and rang the bell. I rang it again. If a small voice in my head chastised me—if it called me rude for harassing a baker after he'd risked life and limb for mine—I ignored it. The witches hadn't doused his hearth. I would bake the pastries myself if he couldn't. Surely I could figure it out.

"What are you doing?" Lou eyed me suspiciously from the

table. "You need to be nice to Pan."

"I'm always nice to—"

"You're ringing his bell."

"Isn't that why it's here?"

"He isn't a *cat*, Reid," Beau said with a smirk.

"It's rude to ring the bell," Coco agreed.

Lou nodded. "Also annoying."

"Very," Beau said.

I grimaced at them all. "I am *trying* to purchase us sticky buns." To Lou, I grumbled, "I think I owe *you* one, in particular."

Her face cleared instantly, and she leaned forward with bright eyes, knitting her fingers together atop the table. "Have I told you today how absolutely and completely attractive I find your ass?"

I snorted just as Pan strode into view. Scowling, he snatched the bell from his counter. "What is it? What do you want? Can you not see I am closed for business?" He gestured a wild hand at the window. "There was a *war*, young man. Wake up!" When he snapped his fingers beneath my nose, I fought the urge to roll my eyes. "We cannot all cower and tremble, forsaking our loved ones. Oh no! Some of us must protect this great kingdom of ours. You treat our fair Lucida like a princess now, yes?"

I cast a scathing look over my shoulder. Both Beau's and Coco's shoulders shook with laughter. Lou gazed back at me with a perfectly placid expression. She batted her lashes. "Like a queen," I said wryly.

Pan frowned at me as if considering. "Very well. I shall make you the sticky buns"—he snapped his fingers again—"but you shall pay full price."

I flashed a hard smile. "Thanks."

Back at the table, Lou pressed her foot over mine. "A truly spectacular ass."

A moment of silence stretched between us. Then another. Outside, Father Achille still coordinated with Jean Luc. With Célie. They'd sent word to neighboring villages for supplies. For healers. Two had survived Morgane's attack on the Tower, but they needed medical treatment themselves. At least, I thought they'd said two. Behind the counter, Pan bustled ostentatiously, banging every pot and slamming every utensil. "Double price," he'd muttered at one point.

At last, Beau heaved a shattered sigh. His smirk had faded. His eyes gleamed anew. "What are we supposed to do now? The cathedral is destroyed. The castle too, by the looks of it. The Archbishop is dead, the king is dead, La Dame des Sorcières is dead—er, the old one, anyway." He shot Lou an apologetic glance.

She shrugged stiffly, tracing the lines on my palm. "The Chateau remains standing. I suppose it's mine now. We can . . . live there." Her eyes flashed to Coco. "All of us."

A wide smile spread across Coco's face. "I don't think Father Achille will give us any trouble."

"*If* he's elected."

"He will be," Beau said. "Father Gaspard nearly pissed down his leg when Morgane showed up. He's a politician." He jerked his head to the window. To Father Achille. "Not a leader."

"Are you a leader, Beau?" Coco asked quietly.

He studied her for a moment, his lips pursed. Undecided. "I don't know yet."

She smirked at him. "We have that in common."

"You can say that again," Lou muttered. "I couldn't manage an attic, let alone a fucking *castle*."

We lapsed into silence until Célie poked her head into the patisserie once more. With a quick wave, she motioned me forward. I kissed Lou's hand before rising to meet her. Jean Luc stood on the other side of the door. Leaning past me, he pushed it closed behind us, and Célie—she actually *bounced* on the balls of her feet. "I have something for you." She spoke over me before I could answer. "When Jean Luc stole your items from the Tower, I chose not to keep it with the rest—your bandolier and knives and such—because it looked too important. I didn't want you to lose it in the heat of the battle."

Jean Luc nodded. "I told her it belonged to your mother."

Realization sparked. Anticipation.

"Of course, when Lou enchanted our clothing, I thought *I'd* lost it." She shook her head, grinning but frazzled. Reaching into the band at her waist, she extracted a familiar ring with a thin golden band and mother-of-pearl stone. It gleamed even in the grayish light. Her smile widened as she placed it in my hand. "Here. Do as you wish with it. It's yours."

I stared down at it in wonder. Warmth radiated through me at the point of contact. My heart pounded. "Thank you, Célie."

"That isn't all." Jean Luc touched the hilt of the Balisarda in my bandolier. Its sapphire winked through the leather. "I spoke with Father Achille. We agreed, both of us—you have a place within our ranks if you want it. That Balisarda is yours."

The happiness in my chest punctured slightly. But—no. I wouldn't let it. Not this time. Unsheathing the Balisarda with one hand, I extended it to Célie. "I think there are others better suited." When her fingers curled around it, her eyes widening in shock, I said, "Two clever little girls once told me they wished to be huntsmen. Not as they are now, but as they should be: proper knights riding forth to vanquish evil. Defending the land and protecting the innocent. One of them even swore she'd wear a dress."

"Oh, I can't"—she shook her head swiftly, attempting to return the Balisarda—"I don't know how to wield a sword. I couldn't possibly use this."

"You don't need to wield a sword to protect the innocent, Célie," Jean Luc said, nodding to me in appreciation. In respect. He glowed with pride as he looked at her. "You've proven that more than anyone."

I nodded too, stepping away from the door. Opening it wide. "The Tower is broken. It's time to rebuild."

She flashed a tentative smile before Jean Luc swept her through it.

I didn't follow. Not right away. Instead I stared at the ring in my hand.

"What are you doing out here?" Lou touched my shoulder,

and I turned, tucking the ring into my pocket. She looked left and right with a pointed smirk. "Having fun with all your friends?"

At her inquisitive gaze, I couldn't help it. A broad smile split my own face, and I kissed her full on the mouth. When I pulled back, she flicked my nose before soothing the spot with her thumb, her hand lingering on my cheek. "Come back inside. Pan says the sticky buns are done."

I brushed my lips across her palm. "That sounds like paradise to me."

EPILOGUE

Ansel

Summer bloomed slow and languorous at Chateau le Blanc. Wild sage and lavender rippled across the mountain in dusky purple and blue; white and yellow marguerites grew rampant between rocks, along creek beds, joined by the blushing pink of thrift and clover. I'd never seen such colors in life. I'd never felt such warmth on my cheeks, like the kiss of a mother, the embrace of a friend. If the voices—no, the *laughter*—of my own friends hadn't called to me, I could've stood within the peace of those wildflowers forever.

Lou wore a spray of each on her wedding day.

Sitting cross-legged atop her childhood bed—the golden thread of her quilt sparkling in the late afternoon sunlight—she waited impatiently for Coco to weave the blooms into a crown. "Stop squirming," Coco chided, grinning and tugging a strand of Lou's hair. "You're shaking the whole bed."

Lou only wriggled her hips more pointedly. "Oh, it'll be shaking tonight."

Célie's cheeks warmed along with my own. When she swept a simple ivory gown from the armoire to cover her embarrassment, I smiled, settling on the chaise beside Madame Labelle. She couldn't see me, of course, but from the way her eyes sparkled, from the way they danced, I thought she might feel me instead.

"You, my friend, are delectably depraved."

"Oh, I'm sorry." With another wide grin, Lou twisted to face Coco. "*Who* was it who lost her virginity atop a—?"

Coughing delicately, Célie asked, "Might I suggest we postpone this conversation for more appropriate company?" Her eyes flicked to Violette and Gabrielle, who flitted about the room, examining anything and everything. The gold leaf across the ceiling. The moondust on the sill. The gilded harp in the corner and the tin soldiers beneath the chaise. Lou had etched mustaches on them as a child. A trunk at the foot of her bed still held toy swords and broken instruments, half-read books and a white rabbit. Stuffed, of course.

The very real cat at my feet hissed at it.

Melisandre, Lou had named her. The cat. Not the rabbit. With her broken tail and crooked teeth, the gray tabby wasn't beautiful, but one wouldn't know it from the way Lou looked at her. She'd found the cat yowling indignantly in a back alley after the battle of Cesarine, and she'd promptly adopted the pitiful creature, much to Reid's chagrin.

Melisandre didn't like Reid.

"Please do not worry yourself, Mademoiselle Célie." With poppy blooms braided into her black hair, Violette giggled and bounced on the balls of her feet as Madame Labelle cackled beside me. "We know all about the birds and the bees. Don't we, Gaby? It's *terribly* romantic."

"*I* think the euphemism is silly." Gabrielle now sat beside me on her knees—wrinkling her olive dress—and attempted to coax Melisandre closer with a piece of string. The cat hissed again before glancing at me with a pained expression. Grinning, I knelt to scratch her ears, and the hiss transformed to a purr. "As if we *need* the imagery of a bird laying eggs to understand ovulation, or a bee depositing pollen to understand fertiliza—"

"Oh, dear." Célie's cheeks washed as pretty a petal pink as her dress, and she draped the ivory gown across the foot of the bed. "That is *quite* enough talk about that, I think. It's almost time for the ceremony. Shall we help you don your gown, Lou?"

When Lou nodded and rose to her feet, Melisandre abandoned me instantly, darting to her mother's side. Lou didn't hesitate to scoop her up and cuddle her against her chest. "And how is my *darling* honeybee? So fetching." She nodded appreciatively to Célie, who'd woven a miniature version of Lou's flower crown for the cat. Melisandre purred under Lou's praise, craning her neck, exorbitantly pleased with herself.

Snorting, Coco helped Célie unlace the wedding gown. "You know Reid is currently plotting her demise."

Madame Labelle rose to join them with a chuckle. "It was his own fault. Vanity, thy name is cat, after all."

Even Manon—who'd hovered silently in the corner, unsure of her place among these people—inched forward tentatively, clutching the handfasting ribbons. When Lou winked at her, she smiled. It was a small, unsure sort of smile, but a smile nonetheless. I recognized it well. I'd worn it many times. Pushing to my own feet, I strode to stand beside her.

She would find her new place here. They all would.

"He'd insulted her!" Lou pressed a kiss to Melisandre's scarred nose, undeterred. "Besides, the piss washed right out of his pillow. No harm done." To Melisandre, she crooned, "He won't mock your singing again, will he, honeybee? No, he won't."

Melisandre yowled in answer, rubbing her head against Lou's chin.

I looked away as they helped her into her gown.

Though heat still suffused my cheeks, it was no longer embarrassment but . . . pride. I nearly burst with it. For too long had Lou deserved this moment—*all* of these moments, the large ones and the small ones and the ones in between. She'd suffered more than most, more than any one person ever should. I could only hope that she'd delight in just as much from this day forward.

Hope.

It wasn't the sickness.

God, she'd done so beautifully. They all had.

Reid would cherish her, I knew. He would do everything in his power to ensure her happiness, and she would return his efforts tenfold. Though I'd known little of life when I'd walked beside them, even then, I'd recognized theirs was a love that would change everything. A love that would break the world. A love that would make it new.

Their love had been the cure.

"What do you think?" Lou's low murmur brought pressure to my eyes. "Will it do?"

I waited to hear Madame Labelle's and Célie's exclamations, Violette's and Gabrielle's laughter, Coco's sniffle, even Manon's soft inhalation before turning to look at my dearest friend.

Reid paced in the early evening sunlight of the old pear grove. It burnished his hair more golden than copper, caught the fine stitching of his jacket and made the threads shimmer. He'd forgone his bandolier for the occasion, instead buckling a single sword at his waist. He steadied it with one hand as he trod a well-worn path in the grass. His other he dragged through his hair.

Beau watched him with unabashed amusement. "Tell me you aren't nervous."

"I'm not nervous." Reid scoffed as if insulted, but his eyes still darted to the opposite end of the grove, where guests had already begun to arrive. It would be an intimate ceremony. They'd invited only those they loved or trusted: Zenna and Seraphine, Toulouse and Thierry, Johannes Pan and his wife. Babette mingled with a handful of other witches, all of whom kept one eye on Jean Luc and Father Achille. Blaise and his children hovered at the edge of the grove, speaking little, until Toulouse beckoned them to come sit. Even Elvire and Lasimonne were in attendance, lounging regally with their diamond gowns and fishhook earrings.

Reid, Beau, and Jean Luc had spent the morning filling the grove with chairs. On the backs of each, they'd painstakingly

looped brightly colored ribbons and flowers—poppies, mari-
golds, peonies, and cornflowers. Scarlets and golds and blushes
and blues, all nestled in beds of deep green. More blooms spilled
from the stumps of pear trees throughout the grove, where lush
moss crept over gnarled wood.

Reid glared at the stumps, the only piece of the scene out of
place. Only yesterday, he'd painstakingly constructed the arbor
of vines and florets overhead. Every detail had been planned.
Every flower plucked to perfection.

Beau followed his gaze with a wistful expression. "If only
Claud were here. He could've grown new trees."

Reid looked at him incredulously. "He could also be *dead*."

"We don't know that. He's a god. Perhaps after he's served his
time—"

"The ground opened up and swallowed him."

"—he will return to us, good as new," Beau finished determinedly, clasping Reid's shoulder. Forcing him to a halt. "Loosen
up, brother mine. It's your wedding day."

"I know." Reid nodded to himself, shaking free to pace again.
"I *know*. I just want it to be perfect."

"And it *is*."

He was right. Lou would love it.

If my heart ached that I too couldn't be part of this moment,
this memory, the pain eased when I caught sight of an empty
chair in the front row. In a burnished oval frame, a picture of my
likeness had been affixed to a bouquet of sunflowers. Warmth
radiated through me as I knelt to study it.

They'd saved me a seat, after all.

When Coco swept forward in her own gown of ivory—with flowers braided into her black curls—the warmth in my chest bloomed tenfold. Exertion flushed her cheeks, and her dark eyes sparkled with excitement as she looked to Reid and Beau, lifting the sunflower bouquet from my seat. "It's time." She dipped her chin to Beau. "She's waiting."

With a smirk, Beau straightened his jacket and smoothed his immaculate waves. "Finally." He clasped Reid's shoulder before turning on his heel. "My moment to shine."

Snorting, Coco rolled her eyes and said, "No one will be looking at you."

He arched a wicked brow. "*You* will be."

She lifted a casual shoulder, speaking over it as she strode back up the aisle. "We'll see."

"*Yes*, we—" He skidded to a halt in his pursuit of her, his eyes falling on Jean Luc. The spray on the latter's chair had loosened, and he was attempting to reattach it. "Honestly, Jean, what did I tell you? We want it to appear *artfully* strewn, as if the daisies sprang up from this very chair. You're tacking them on too neatly." When Jean Luc scowled, unimpressed, Beau elbowed him aside to do it himself. "Like tits on a boar."

"Careful, Your Majesty." With a wry grin, Jean Luc tossed a handful of fallen edelweiss at his head. The King of Belterra lurched away with a violent curse, finger combing his hair frantically. "You'll muss those luscious locks."

"I will *kill* you—"

Coco caught his hand and dragged him up the aisle before they could brawl. Grinning despite myself, I followed them around the bend, where Lou stood out of sight with Madame Labelle, Célie, and Manon. Beau shook his head when he saw her, whistling low and appreciative. "Reid is going to lose his mind."

Lou winked and shimmied her shoulders. "That's the plan."

Madame Labelle fixed one of her soon-to-be daughter's curls, arranging it artfully around Lou's freckled cheek. "You look beautiful, *fille*. I shall see you soon. Come." She motioned for Célie and Manon to join her, leaving Lou, Coco, Beau, and me alone in the shadow of a withered pear tree. The only one that'd survived. When Reid had suggested holding the festivities here, Madame Labelle had protested, explaining again how Morgane had torched these trees in a fit of rage. Reid knew that, of course. He knew how love could twist even the most beautiful of people, of places, into cruel and dark things. He also knew how special this grove had once been to his mother—to all the Dames Blanches.

Lou had agreed, and together, they'd made it beautiful once more.

When Coco extended the sunflower bouquet, Lou's grin dimmed slightly. Her finger traced the curve of the frame. "Do you think he's watching?"

Coco looped an arm through hers. "I think he wouldn't miss it for anything."

"He should've been here. He should've given me away too."

Beau claimed Lou's other arm, tapping my face in the frame. "He still is."

"I still am," I whispered with a smile. In response, a soft breeze rustled the branches overhead, bringing with it a pleasant warmth, a low hum of bees, a faint scent of daffodils. Of new beginnings.

I walked beside them as they led Lou up the aisle.

Though Claud had gone, his empty seat remained next to mine, and Seraphine crooned a lovely ballad of love lost and love found while Reid waited beneath the arbor. Madame Labelle stood beside him, the handfasting ribbons woven between her fingers. She winked at Father Achille in the audience.

Beau cleared his throat, and every person—every human, witch, werewolf, and mermaid—turned as one to look at us. To look at Lou. Her breath caught in her throat, and her hands tightened instinctively on Coco and Beau. "Breathe, sister mine," the latter murmured. "Just breathe."

"Go on, Lou." Though she couldn't see me, couldn't hear me, I spoke the words regardless, pushing her forward gently. "Find peace."

She seemed to relax at the warm touch of wind on her face.

Then her eyes found Reid, and the entire world faded to that blinding, soul-deep connection. Anyone could see it. Everyone could *feel* it. If I reached out a hand now, I sensed I could've touched it. Though I knew not of magic patterns, this thread that connected Lou and Reid—this gravitational pull, this *cosmic* one—it was a magic in itself. It pulled them together. It would keep them there.

He gazed at her with the most brilliant, devastating smile.

She blinked at the sight of it, her own slightly dazed, slightly awed, as Reid took in her ivory gown, her trailing sleeves, the rich flowers atop her long, loose hair. The scarred roses at her throat. Summer sun had gilded her skin once more. It burnished the freckles across her nose. When he stepped forward to take her hand, he brushed his lips across them, trying to kiss each one. "See something you like?" he murmured in her ear.

She eyed him appreciatively. "Let's make this quick."

Their vows were not traditional. Not this time. Nor was their ceremony. It ended just as the sun touched the mountains, its golden light lengthening the shadows of the grove. Fireflies winked into existence. Ever curious, feu follet soon followed, their eerie glow lighting a path through the gnarled trees. Twice, Beau snatched an inquisitive Gabrielle away from them, much to her indignation. "You *rotten* brother! I just want to *see* them!"

Her protests could barely be heard over the music.

Several more witches had trekked from the castle with mandolins, lutes, and lyres underarm. Others had brought wine. Indeed, most who'd remained at Chateau le Blanc gathered in the grove now, curious and wary. Though they gave Jean Luc and Father Achille a wide berth—and Elvire and Blaise too—no one lifted a hand against them. Toulouse even managed to charm a pretty young witch into dancing with him. Another asked Liana for a turn.

It took little for the rest to follow.

Except for Lasimonne, who—with a cry of "It has *four* legs!"—chased after Melisandre with abject fascination. The cat hissed and yowled and streaked toward the safety of the castle. With the roll of her eyes, Elvire continued to examine the flowers, taking a tentative bite of a peony. Pan swatted her hand away in horror. "No," he said sternly, wagging his finger. "Absolutely not, *ma douce.* You come to Cesarine, and I will bake you something sweet, yes?"

Turning away, I watched Coco and Beau dance for one long, bittersweet moment. He said something to make her laugh— *really* laugh, the sort of laugh that transformed her entire face. The sound of it made him giddy. He twirled her closer next time, his attention rapt on her expression. Drinking in the sight. "I could do more than sail at the age of three," he told her imperiously. "Sir D'artagnan Delmore le Devere taught me to dance as soon as I could walk."

Unfortunately, he chose that moment to spin directly into Jean Luc and Célie. Jean Luc compensated seamlessly, twirling Célie outward with one hand while catching Coco's waist with the other. Beau, who'd slipped on impact, reeled into a stump and nearly lost his footing. Jean Luc smirked. "Sir D'artagnan Delmore le Devere is my godfather, Your Majesty."

Coco howled with laughter.

I hoped she never stopped laughing.

At the center of it all, Lou and Reid whirled with flushed cheeks and bright eyes. When she stepped on his toes for the third time—tipsy with drink—he swept her up in his arms and spun wildly, round and round until Lou shrieked with delight, tipping her head and urging him faster. He never lost his footing. He never loosened his grip.

He even joined her when she belted out "Big Titty Liddy."

Though both sang horribly off-key, all applauded their efforts when they'd finished, and Lou swept into a dramatic bow. Cheeks red, Reid chuckled and tried to move away—out of the limelight—but Lou pulled him back. "Wasn't he *marvelous*?" She crowed the words with pride, cackling as his flush deepened. Madame Labelle whistled from Father Achille's arm. "Everyone tell him how marvelous he is. Tell him how *impressive*."

Shaking his head, he tucked her firmly into his side and dragged her toward the nearest stump. "You're embarrassing me, wife."

"Look how red your face is." She cackled and wrapped her arms around his waist. "Just wait until the honeymoon—those few blissful days where I'll have you all to myself."

Reid smirked. "I'll believe it when I see it. Your sisters can't leave you alone for more than an hour."

"That's why we're leaving the Chateau."

He raised a brow. "Oh?"

"*Oh*," she confirmed, matter-of-fact. "There's an old cottage on the beach. It belonged to my grandmother. I've cleaned it out for the two of us." She nuzzled his chest, much like her cat. "Coco can handle the castle without me."

Reid shrugged, the corner of his mouth still quirked. "You're probably right. She's much more diplomatic."

"*Excuse* you." Lou elbowed him in the ribs in feigned outrage, raising her voice for the others to hear. "Should I tell them about your *impressive* foot size? What about those other *marvelous* things you can do with your tongue?"

Reid actually clapped a hand over her mouth.

Shoulders shaking, the two devolved into laughter as a wizened old woman hobbled into the grove.

I didn't recognize her, but the others clearly did: Lou and Reid straightened, Coco and Beau stilled, and even Célie stepped closer to Jean Luc. Though none appeared outright alarmed, a definite current of tension had materialized with the woman. Curiously enough, Zenna smiled.

"Hello, dearies!" Bracelets clinked on the woman's wrist as she waved gaily, heedless of her less-than-warm reception. Her scarlet robes billowed around her. "What a *sublime* evening for a wedding. And truly, you could not have chosen a more fortuitous locale."

"Madame Sauvage." Reid cast a quick, nervous glance toward Coco, Beau, and Célie. His next word sounded a question. "Welcome."

Lou's eyes narrowed. "How did you find this place?"

"Ah." Madame Sauvage clasped Lou's hands in her own, pressing a kiss to them. "Felicitations, my dear, on your recent nuptials. It seems I missed quite a delightful evening, and you, in turn, missed my winsome company." Her clouded eyes lingered on the witch with the mandolin. "I trust you provided the correct designation this time? None of this *Larue* business?"

Lou's frown deepened, but she didn't pull her hands away. "How do you know about that?"

Madame Sauvage ignored the question, instead turning to Reid. She pinched his cheek. "And you, young man? Did you plant those seeds as you promised?"

"I"—he looked again to Lou, more panicked now than before—"I'm sorry, Madame Sauvage, but I—I misplaced them."

"You *lost* them, you mean?" When Reid nodded, she clicked her tongue in disappointment. I inched closer, studying her face. She seemed . . . familiar, somehow. Like I'd met her before. And her disappointment—I glanced around, uncertain—it felt staged. Zenna still smiled behind us, and that smile had spread to Seraphine, Toulouse, and Thierry. Madame Sauvage winked at them. "Well, Monsieur le Blanc, just how should we proceed? We made a *bargain*, you remember."

Reid nodded grimly. "I'll procure another pearl for you, *madame*. I promise."

"You promised"—Madame Sauvage unfurled her fingers slowly, revealing a handful of seeds in her palm—"to plant the seeds."

We all stared at them.

"How did you—?" Reid started.

Her dark eyes gleamed. Pressing the seeds into his hand, she said, "A fortuitous location, indeed. If you plant them—if you *care* for them—they will grow." When Reid didn't move, when he only studied the seeds with open suspicion, Madame Sauvage poked his chest. "Well, what are you waiting for? Do it now! I'm not getting any younger."

"I don't have a *shovel*—"

With an impatient sigh, Lou waved her hand, and the seeds flew outward in a sharp burst of magic, scattering across the grove. In the next second, they burrowed into the ground of their own accord. "There." She thrust her arm through Reid's. "Are we settled? Have we honored this ridiculous bargain?"

Trees burst from the ground as Madame Sauvage's answer.

Pear trees.

They climbed skyward at a rapid pace, white blossoms blooming and falling to reveal hard green fruit. A dozen in all—one tree for each seed planted. Lou gasped as Reid stared, as Beau leapt backward, and Madame Labelle stretched incredulously to touch one of the low-hanging fruit. Shaking her head, she whirled to face the old woman. "Who *are* you?"

Madame Sauvage bowed, looking meaningfully at Lou. "A friend."

She turned without another word, and as suddenly as she'd hobbled into our presence, she hobbled out, leaving only the peculiar scent of . . . of *earth* in her wake. Of fresh grass and pine sap and pears. Still smiling, Zenna, Seraphine, Toulouse, and Thierry followed after her.

Lou watched them go, slack-jawed, until unexpected laughter burst from her. Until she was breathless with it. She turned to Reid, tears of mirth lining her turquoise eyes. "That nosy son of a *bitch*—"

I didn't hear the rest, however. Because at the edge of the grove, Madame Sauvage looked back to meet my gaze. *My* gaze. With a small smile, she inclined her head toward something behind me.

"Ansel."

I turned at that voice, at that presence. I recognized it now as innately as my own.

Two figures stood on the path down the mountain. His hair and his jaw were my own. Her eyes and her skin, as well. "Are you ready, darling?" The woman extended an olive hand to me, and her smile—it was as warm as I'd always dreamed it. As warm as this summer night.

"That boy is asking after you again," the man said, wrapping an arm around her shoulders. "Etienne."

Butterflies erupted at the name.

Unbidden, my feet drifted toward them, my lips lifting in a smile. I couldn't help one last look, however—at Lou, at Reid, at Coco, at Beau. They milled around the pear trees, feeling each trunk, testing the leaves. Laughing at themselves with Terrance and Liana and Manon.

If you plant them—if you care *for them—they will grow.*

My smile widened. Madame Sauvage had vanished, leaving them to life anew.

Taking my mother's hand, I did too.

ACKNOWLEDGMENTS

I owe a great debt to many people for not only the creation of this book, but also for the creation of this entire series. To cut straight to the heart of it, the most important of them is *you*. The reader. *Thank you* seems too commonplace an expression to convey my gratitude, but truly, no words can describe the emotion in my chest when I think of how kind you've all been, how enthusiastic. Though the pandemic struck just months after *Serpent & Dove* was published, each one of you went above and beyond to support these books. The beautiful photos, illustrations, cosplays, lyrics, reels—I have a lump in my throat thinking of them now. The past three years have changed my life, and readers continue to be the heart of that. From Lou and Reid, from Coco, Ansel, Beau, and *me*, thank you, thank you, *thank you*.

Jordan, I've told you a million times, but I'll tell you again—I couldn't have written this book without you. When writers ask me for guidance, I often tell them to find what they love and lean into it unapologetically. You give me permission to follow my own advice. This book—*all* my books—wouldn't contain half the wit, half the kissing, half the *fun* without your input. Are you my muse? Probably. I love you to the moon and to Saturn.

RJ, Beau, James, and Rose, words will never be able to convey the depths of my love for you. This deadline could've been a burden, but it wasn't. Thank you for your patience. Thank you for your understanding. Thank you for your love and respect and support as together, we chase our crazy dreams. Zane and Kelly—and Jake, Brooke, Justin, Chelsy, and Lewie—we don't get to choose our family, but even if we could, I would choose you anyway. Thank you for being my collective rock. I love you all more than you know.

Jordan, Spencer, Meghan, Aaron, Adrianne, Chelsea, Courtney, Austin, Jamie, Josh, Jake, Jillian, Aaron, Jon, and Kendall, you are my favorite people on this earth, and your wholehearted support of both me and my books has been so precious to me. I don't deserve any of you. Katie, Carolyn, Isabel, Kristin, Adrienne, Adalyn, and Rachel, there is something so special about writing friends who become real-life friends, and I couldn't be more honored to call you mine.

Sarah, I feel so incredibly grateful to have such a warm and approachable agent in my corner. Erica, editor extraordinaire, I can't thank you enough for your unending patience and your infallible vision for this series. (And I promise I'll make my next deadline! I promise!) Stephanie Guerdan, it was so wonderful to work with you. Alexandra Rakaczki and Jessica White, I'm so grateful for your sharp eyes, and I similarly promise there will be no Philippe in my next book! Allison Brown, thank you for all the time and energy you poured into this series. Jessie Gang and Alison Donalty, these covers have continued to blow my mind; I attribute so much of this series' success to your and Katt Phatt's skills. Rachel Horowitz, Sheala Howley, and Cassidy Miller, as well as Sophie Kossakowski, Gillian Wise, Sam Howard, Karen Radner, and the entire sales team, thank you for working behind the scenes to make these books successful.

Mitch Thorpe, Michael D'Angelo, Ebony LaDelle, Audrey Diestelkamp, and the entire team at Epic Reads—you are all rock stars. Truly, I can't thank you enough for your enthusiasm and support of this series, as well as the resources and opportunities you provided.

EVIL LURKS IN BELTERRA.
READ ON FOR A SNEAK PEEK AT

The Scarlet Veil.

PROLOGUE

It is a curious thing, the scent of memory. It takes only a little to send us back in time—a trace of my mother's lavender oil, a hint of my father's pipe smoke. Each reminds me of childhood in its own strange way. My mother applied her oil every morning as she stared at her reflection, counting the new lines on her face. My father smoked his pipe when he received guests. They frightened him, I think, with their hollow eyes and quick hands. They certainly frightened me.

But beeswax—beeswax will always remind me of my sister.

Like clockwork, Filippa would reach for her silver brush when our nursemaid, Evangeline, lit the candles each evening. The wicks would fill the nursery with the soft scent of honey as Filippa undid my braid, as she passed the boar bristles through my hair. As Evangeline settled into her favorite rose-velvet chair and watched us warmly, her eyes crinkling in the misty purple light of dusk.

The wind—crisp on that October night—rustled at the eaves,

hesitating, lingering at the promise of a story.

"Mes choux," she murmured, stooping to retrieve her knitting needles from the basket beside her chair. Our family hound, Birdie, curled into an enormous ball at the hearth. "Have I told you the story of Les Éternels?"

As always, Pip spoke first, leaning around my shoulder to frown at Evangeline. She always frowned, my sister. Equal parts suspicious and intrigued. "The Eternal Ones?"

"Yes, dear."

Anticipation fluttered in my belly as I glanced at Pip, our faces mere inches apart. Golden specs still glinted on her cheeks from our portrait lesson that afternoon. They looked like freckles. "Has she?" My voice lacked Evangeline's lyrical grace, Filippa's firm resolve. "I don't think she has."

"She definitely hasn't," Pip confirmed, deadly serious, before turning back to Evangeline. "We should like to hear it, please."

Evangeline arched a brow at her imperious tone. "Is that so?"

"Oh, please tell us, Evangeline!" Forgetting myself entirely, I leapt to my slippered feet and clapped my hands together. Pip—twelve years old to my paltry six—hastily snatched my nightgown, tugging me back to the armoire seat. Her small hands landed on my shoulders.

"Ladies do not shout, Célie. What would Pére say?"

Heat crept into my cheeks as I folded my own hands in my lap, immediately contrite. "*Pretty is as pretty does.*"

"Exactly." She returned her attention to Evangeline, whose lips twitched as she fought a smile. "Please tell us the story,

Evangeline. We promise not to interrupt."

"Very good." With practiced ease, Evangeline slid her lithe fingers along the needles, weaving wool into a lovely scarf of petal pink. My favorite color. Pip's scarf—bright white, like freshly fallen snow—already rested in the basket. "Though you still have paint on your face, darling. Be a lamb and wash for me, will you?" She waited until Pippa finished scrubbing her cheeks before continuing. "Right, then. Les Éternels. They're born in the ground—cold as bone, and just as strong—without heart or soul or mind. Only impulse. Only *lust*." She said the word with unexpected relish. "The first came to our kingdom from a faraway land in the East, living in the shadows, spreading her sickness to the people here. Infecting them with her magic."

Pip resumed brushing my hair. "What kind of magic?"

My nose crinkled as I tilted my head. "What is *lust*?"

Evangeline pretended not to hear me.

"The worst kind of magic, darlings. The absolute *worst* kind." The wind rattled the windows, eager for the story, as Evangeline paused dramatically—except Birdie rolled over with a warbled howl at precisely the same moment, ruining the effect. Evangeline cut the hound an exasperated look. "The kind that requires blood. Requires *death*."

Pippa and I exchanged a covert glance.

"Dames Rouges," I heard her breathe at my ear, near indiscernible. "Red Ladies."

Our father had spoken of them once, the strangest and rarest of the occultists who plagued Belterra. He'd thought we hadn't heard him with the funny man in his study, but we had. "What are you whispering?" Evangeline asked sharply, stabbing her needles in our direction. "Secrets are quite rude, you know."

Pip lifted her chin. She'd forgotten that ladies do not scowl, either. "Nothing, Evangeline."

"Yes," I echoed instantly. "Nothing, Evangeline."

Her gaze narrowed. "Plucky little things, aren't you? Well, I should tell you that Les Éternels *love* plucky little girls like you. They think you're the sweetest."

The exhilaration in my chest twisted slightly at her words, and gooseflesh erupted down my neck at the stroke of my sister's brush. I scooted to the edge of my seat, eyes wide. "Do they really?"

"Of course they don't." Pip dropped her brush on the armoire with more force than necessary. With the sternest of expressions, she turned my chin to face her. "Don't listen to her, Célie. She *lies.*"

"I most certainly do not," Evangeline said emphatically. "I'll tell you the same as my mother told me—Les Éternels stalk the streets by moonlight, preying on the weak and seducing the immoral. That's why we always sleep at nightfall, darlings, and always say our prayers." When she continued, her lyrical voice rose in cadence, familiar as the nursery rhyme she hummed every evening. Her needles *click click click*ed in the silence of the room as even the wind fell still to listen. "Always wear a silver cross, and always walk in pairs. With holy water on your neck and hallowed ground, your feet. When in doubt, strike up a match, and burn them with its heat."

I sat up a little straighter. My hands trembled. "I always say my prayers, Evangeline, but I drank all of Filippa's milk at dinner while she wasn't looking. Do you think that made me sweeter than her? Will the bad people want to eat me?"

"Ridiculous." Scoffing, Pippa threaded her fingers through my hair to replait it. Though clearly exasperated, her touch remained gentle. She tied the raven strands with a pretty pink bow and draped it over my shoulder. "As if I'd ever let anything happen to you, Célie."

At her words, warmth expanded in my chest, a sparkling surety. Because Filippa never lied. She never snuck treats or played tricks or said things she didn't mean. She never stole my milk.

She would never let anything happen to me.

The wind hovered outside for another second—scratching at the panes once more, impatient for the rest of the story—before passing on unsatisfied. The sun fully slipped beneath the skyline as an autumn moon rose overhead. It bathed the nursery in thin silver light. The beeswax candles seemed to gutter in response, lengthening the shadows between us, and I clasped my sister's hand in the sudden gloom. "I'm sorry I stole your milk," I whispered.

She squeezed my fingers. "I never liked milk anyway."

Evangeline studied us for a long moment, her expression inscrutable as she rose, returning her needles and wool to the basket. She patted Birdie on the head before blowing out the tapers on the mantle. "You are good sisters, both of you. Loyal and kind." Striding across the nursery, she kissed our foreheads before helping us into bed, lifting the last candle to our eyes. Hers gleamed with an emotion I didn't understand. "Promise me you'll hold on to each other."

When we nodded, she blew out the candle and made to leave.

Pip wrapped an arm around my shoulders, pulling me close, and I nestled into her pillow. It smelled like her—like summer honey. Like lectures and gentle hands and frowns and snow-white scarves. "I'll never let the witches get you," she said fiercely against my hair. "Never."

"And I'll never let them get *you*."

Evangeline paused at the nursery door and looked back at us with a frown. She tilted her head curiously as the moon slipped behind a cloud, plunging us into total darkness. When a branch clawed at our window, I tensed, but Filippa wrapped her other arm around me firmly.

She didn't know, then.

I didn't know either.

"Silly girls," Evangeline whispered. "Who said anything about witches?"

And then she was gone.

CHAPTER ONE

EMPTY CAGES

Twelve Years Later

I will catch this repugnant little creature if it kills me.

Blowing a limp strand of hair from my forehead, I crouch again and readjust the mechanism on the trap. It took *hours* to fell the willow tree yesterday, to plane the branches and paint the wood and assemble the cages. To collect the wine. It took hours *more* to read every tome in Chasseur Tower about lutins. The goblins prefer willow sap to other varieties—something about its sweet scent—and despite their crude appearance, they appreciate the finer things in life.

Hence the painted cages and bottles of wine.

When I hitched a cart to my horse this morning, loading it full of both, Jean Luc looked at me like I had lost my mind.

Perhaps I *have* lost my mind.

I certainly imagined the life of a huntsman—a hunts*woman*—being somewhat more significant than crouching in a muddy ditch, sweating through an ill-fitting uniform, and luring a crotchety hobgoblin away from a field with alcohol.

Unfortunately, I miscalculated the measurements, and the bottles of wine did not *fit* within the painted cages, forcing me to disassemble each one at the farm. The Chasseurs' laughter still lingers in my ears. They didn't care that I painstakingly learned to use a hammer and nails for this project, *or* that I mutilated my thumb in the process. They didn't care that I bought the gold paint with my own coin, either. No, they saw only my mistake. My brilliant work reduced to kindling at our feet. Though Jean Luc hastily tried to help reassemble the cages as best we could—scowling at our brethren's witty commentary—an irate Farmer Marc arrived soon after. As a captain of the Chasseurs, Jean needed to console him.

And I needed to handle the huntsmen alone.

"Tragic." Looming over me, Frederic rolled his brilliant eyes before smirking. The gold in his chestnut hair glinted in the early sun. "Though they are *very* pretty, Mademoiselle Tremblay. Like little dollhouses."

"Please, Frederic," I said through gritted teeth, scrambling to collect the pieces in my skirt. "How many times must I ask you to call me Célie? We are all equals here."

"At least once more, I'm afraid." His grin sharpened to a knife point. "You are a lady, after all."

I stalked across the field and down the hill, out of sight—away from him, away from *all* of them—without another word. I knew it was pointless to argue with someone like Frederic.

You are a lady, after all.

Mimicking his asinine voice now, I finish the lock on the last cage and stand to admire my handiwork. Mud coats my boots. It stains six inches of my hem, yet a flicker of triumph still steals through my chest. It won't be long now. The lutins in Farmer Marc's barley will soon smell the willow sap and follow its scent. When they spy the wine, they will react impulsively—the books say lutins are impulsive—and enter the cages. The traps will swing shut, and we will transport the pesky creatures back to La Fôret des Yeux, where they belong.

Simple, really. Like stealing candy from a baby. Not that I'd *actually* steal candy from a baby, of course.

Exhaling a shaky sigh, I plant my hands on my hips and nod a bit more enthusiastically than natural. Yes. The mud and menial labor have most definitely been worth it. The stains will lift from my dress, and better yet—I'll have captured and relocated a whole burrow of lutins without harm. Father Achille, the newly instated archbishop, will be proud. Perhaps Jean Luc will be too. Yes, this is *good*. Hope continues to swell as I scramble behind the weeds at the edge of the field, watching and waiting. This will be perfect.

This has to be perfect.

A handful of moments pass without movement.

"Come on." Voice low, I scan the rows of barley, trying not to fidget with the Balisarda at my belt. Though months have passed since I've taken my sacred vow, the sapphire hilt still feels strange and heavy in my hands. Foreign. My foot taps the ground impatiently. The temperatures have grown unreasonably warm for October, and a bead of sweat trickles down my neck. "Come on, come *on*. Where are you?"

The moment stretches onward, followed by another. Or

perhaps three. Ten? Over the hill, my brethren hoot and holler at a joke I cannot hear. I don't know how they intend to catch the lutins—none cared to share their plans with me, the first and only woman in their ranks—but I also don't care. I certainly don't need their help, nor do I need an audience after the cage fiasco.

Frederic's condescending expression fills my mind.

And Jean Luc's embarrassed one.

No. I push them both away with a scowl—along with the weeds—climbing to my feet to check the traps once more. *I should never have used wine. What a stupid idea—*

The thought screeches to a halt as a small, wrinkled foot parts the barley. My own feet grow roots. Rapt, I try not to breathe as the brownish-gray creature—hardly the height of my knee—sets his dark, overlarge eyes on the bottle of wine. Indeed, everything about him appears to be a bit too . . . well . . . *too*. His head too large. His features too sharp. His fingers too long.

To be quite frank, he looks like a potato.

Tiptoeing toward the wine, he doesn't seem to notice me—or anything else, for that matter. His gaze remains locked on the dusty bottle, and he smacks his lips eagerly, reaching for it with those spindly fingers. The moment he steps into the cage, it shuts with a decisive *snap*, but the lutin merely clutches the wine to his chest and grins. Two rows of needle-sharp teeth gleam in the sunlight.

I stare at him for a beat, morbidly fascinated.

And then I can no longer help it. I smile too, tilting my head as I approach, still studying the strange creature. He isn't anything like I thought—not repugnant at all with his knobby knees and round cheeks. When Farmer Marc contacted us yesterday morning, the man raved about *horns* and *claws*.

At last, the lutin's eyes snap to mine, and his smile falters.

"Hello, there." Slowly, I kneel before him, placing my hands flat on my lap, where he can see them. "I'm terribly sorry about this"—I motion my chin toward the ornate cage—"but the man who farms this land has requested that you and your family relocate. Do you have a name?"

He stares at me, unblinking, and heat creeps into my cheeks. I glance over my shoulder for any sign of my brethren. I might be wholly and completely ridiculous—and they would crucify me if they found me chatting with a lutin—but it hardly feels right to trap the poor creature without an introduction. "My name is Célie," I add, feeling stupider by the second. Though the books didn't mention language, lutins must communicate *somehow*. I point to myself and repeat, "Célie. *Say-lee.*"

Still he says nothing. If he's even a *he* at all.

Right. Straightening my shoulders, I seize the cage handle because I *am* ridiculous, and I should go check the other cages. But first—"If you twist the cork at the top," I murmur grudgingly, "the bottle will open. I hope you like elderberries."

"Are you talking to the lutin?"

I whirl at Jean Luc's voice, releasing the cage and blushing. "Jean!" His name comes out a squeak. "I—I didn't hear you."

"Clearly." He stands in the weeds where I hid only moments ago. At my guilty expression, he sighs and crosses his arms over his chest. "What are you doing, Célie?"

"Nothing."

"Why don't I believe you?"

"An excellent question. Why *don't* you believe—" But the lutin snakes out a hand before I can finish, snatching my own. With a shriek, I jerk and topple backward—not because of the lutin's *claws*, but because of his *voice*. The instant his skin touches mine, the strangest vocalization echoes in my mind: *Larmes Comme Étoiles*.

Jean Luc charges instantly, unsheathing his Balisarda between one stride and the next.

"No, wait!" I fling myself between him and the caged lutin. "*Wait!* He didn't hurt me! He meant no harm!"

"Célie," Jean Luc warns, his voice low and frustrated, "he could be rabid—"

"*Frederic* is rabid. Go wave your knife at him." To the lutin, I smile kindly. "I beg your pardon, sir. What did you say?"

"He didn't *say* anything—"

I shush Jean Luc as the lutin beckons me closer, extending his hand through the bars. It takes several seconds for me to realize he wants to touch me again. "Oh." I swallow hard, not quite relishing the idea. "You—yes, well—"

Jean Luc grips my elbow. "Please tell me you aren't going to touch it. You have no idea where it's *been*."

The lutin gestures more impatiently now, and—before I can change my mind—I stretch out my free hand, brushing his fingertips. His skin there feels rough. Dirty. Like an unearthed root.

My name, he repeats in an otherworldly trill. *Larmes Comme Étoiles*.

My mouth falls open. "Tears Like Stars?"

With a swift nod, he withdraws his hand to clutch his wine once more, glaring daggers at Jean Luc, who scoffs and tugs me backward. Near light-headed with giddiness, I twirl into his arms. "Did you hear him?" I ask breathlessly. "He said his name means—"

"They don't have names." His arms tighten around me, and he bends to look directly in my eyes. "Lutins don't speak, Célie."

My gaze narrows. "Do you think I'm a liar, then?"

Sighing again—*always* sighing—he sweeps a kiss across my brow, and I soften slightly. He smells like starch and leather, the linseed oil he uses to polish his Balisarda. Familiar scents. Comforting ones. "I think you have a tender heart," he says, and I know he means it as a compliment. It *should* be a compliment. "I think your cages are brilliant, and I think lutins love elderberries." He pulls back with a smile. "I also think we should go. It's getting late."

"Go?" I blink in confusion, leaning around him to peer up the hill. His biceps tense a little beneath my palms. "But what about the others? The books said a burrow can hold up to twenty lutins. Surely Farmer Marc wants us to take them all." My frown deepens as I realize my brethren's voices have long faded. Indeed, beyond the hill, the entire farm has fallen still and silent, except for a lone rooster's crow. "Where"—something hot like shame cracks open in my belly—"where is everyone, Jean?"

He won't look at me. "I sent them ahead."

"Ahead *where*?"

"To La Fôret des Yeux." He clears his throat and steps backward, sheathing his Balisarda before smiling anew and bending to pick up my cage. After another second, he offers me his free hand. "Are you ready?"

I stare at it as sickening realization dawns. He would have sent them ahead for only one reason. "They've ... already trapped the other lutins, haven't they?" When he doesn't answer, I glance up at his face. He gazes back at me carefully, *warily*, as if I'm splintered glass, one touch away from shattering. And perhaps I am. I can no longer count the spider web cracks in my surface, can no longer *know* which crack will break me. Perhaps it'll be this one.